Mrs Charles B. Mearo 7/4/98

W9-BRP-197

You Have More to Offer a Man Than You Could Ever Imagine

Eyes suddenly hot, hungry, swirled with dark mysteries. His gaze flicked to her lips, lingered there, his thick, dark lashes falling to half-mast. He didn't have to touch her mouth with his. She felt his intensity down to her very toes.

"Hannah . . . I . . ." He reached behind her nape, catching the thick rope of her braid with his hand, winding the shining plait around his palm as if to make himself prisoner to the wild enchantment even now whirling up between them.

She stared into his eyes, wanting . . . wanting . . . yet so very afraid. Afraid of the vulnerable places he could see in her candlelit face, places she couldn't hide when he was touching her. But there was no triumph, no scorn, only astonishment in his handsome features, as if he were as surprised as she was.

Ever so slowly Austen tipped her face up to his. Hannah couldn't breathe, time froze as his sensual mouth hovered over hers for an instant. She was terrified he would pull away.

But he did not. With indescribable tenderness, the warmth of his mouth sought hers. . . .

Critical Acclaim for
the Splendid Romances of

KIMBERLY CATES

STEALING HEAVEN

"Kimberly Cates has the talent to pull you into a story on the first page and keep you there. . . . *Stealing Heaven* is a finely crafted tale . . . a tale you won't soon forget. It can stand proud beside Ms. Cates' other excellent romances."

—*Rendezvous*

"Stunning in its emotional impact, glowing with the luminous beauty of the love between a man and a woman . . . *Stealing Heaven* is another dazzling masterpiece from a truly gifted author."

—Kathe Robin, *Romantic Times*

"[A] beautifully poignant tale. Kimberly Cates can always be counted on for a choice reading occasion, and this time is no exception."

—Harriet Klausner, *Affaire de Coeur*

"A powerful and enduring tale filled with the magic and lore of Ireland. . . . This idyllic romance will capture readers' hearts."

—Elizabeth Hogue, *Gothic Journal*

THE RAIDER'S DAUGHTER

"A wonderful and neatly blended mixture of romance and suspense. . . . Kimberly Cates always provides her readers with a treasure; but in this work, she displays new profound literary depths."

—Harriet Klausner, *Affaire de Coeur*

"A special book for readers looking for an out-of-the ordinary adventure. You will long remember the tenderness, passion, and excitement of this well-written sequel."

—*Rendezvous*

"Spunky Lucy and tormented, sexy Valcour's thrilling adventures, dangerous escapades and sensual encounters engulf the reader in a riveting tale. . . . Another stunning achievement from a master of the genre."

—Kathe Robin, *Romantic Times*

THE RAIDER'S BRIDE

"Kimberly Cates takes the reader to new emotional heights. . . . *The Raider's Bride* is more than just an enthralling reading experience; it's a gateway to a world of mystery, intrigue, and historical insights."

—Harriet Klausner, *Affaire de Coeur*

"High adventure, suspense, and sensuality make *The Raider's Bride* a story you must read."

—*Romantic Times*

"Original . . . endearing characters. . . ."

—*Publishers Weekly*

Books by Kimberly Cates

Morning Song
Angel's Fall
Gather the Stars
Crown of Dreams
Only Forever
The Raider's Bride
The Raider's Daughter
Stealing Heaven
To Catch a Flame
Restless Is the Wind

Published by POCKET BOOKS

For orders other than by individual consumers, Pocket Books grants a discount on the purchase of **10 or more** copies of single titles for special markets or premium use. For further details, please write to the Vice-President of Special Markets, Pocket Books, 1633 Broadway, New York, NY 10019-6785, 8th Floor.

For information on how individual consumers can place orders, please write to Mail Order Department, Simon & Schuster Inc., 200 Old Tappan Road, Old Tappan, NJ 07675.

KIMBERLY CATES

MORNING SONG

POCKET BOOKS

New York   London   Toronto   Sydney   Tokyo   Singapore

The sale of this book without its cover is unauthorized. If you purchased this book without a cover, you should be aware that it was reported to the publisher as "unsold and destroyed." Neither the author nor the publisher has received payment for the sale of this "stripped book."

This book is a work of fiction. Names, characters, places and incidents are products of the author's imagination or are used fictitiously. Any resemblance to actual events or locales or persons, living or dead, is entirely coincidental.

An *Original* Publication of POCKET BOOKS

 POCKET BOOKS, a division of Simon & Schuster Inc.
1230 Avenue of the Americas, New York, NY 10020

Copyright © 1997 by Kim Ostrom Bush

All rights reserved, including the right to reproduce this book or portions thereof in any form whatsoever. For information address Pocket Books, 1230 Avenue of the Americas, New York, NY 10020

ISBN: 0-671-56873-6

First Pocket Books printing July 1997

10 9 8 7 6 5 4 3 2

POCKET and colophon are registered trademarks of Simon & Schuster Inc.

Cover art by Alan Ayers

Printed in the U.S.A.

To Tami Hoag, whose twisted mind never ceases to delight me. Thank you for Good Luck Trolls, sequin tiaras, plastic hula dolls, glow-in-the-dark stars, and for applying steak sauce where necessary. And most of all, bless you for teaching a "straight arrow" to question authority.

MORNING SONG

Chapter

1

Hannah wished the child would cry, add his thin wails to the keening lament of the wind lashing against them. There was something terrible in his silence. Something frightening in the stillness of the tiny hand she held in her own as he trudged along beside her.

Pip had to be exhausted. Her own feet dragged through the sucking mud as if the soles of her shoes were millstones. The sodden layers of her skirts and meager cloak bowed her shoulders and weighted her chest, holding the chill against her skin. The portmanteau she carried in one hand felt as if it was stuffed with iron bars instead of what few clothes she'd managed to fling together for Pip and herself.

At least the rain had finally stopped.

Night bruised the edge of the horizon, devouring what little light managed to pierce the last wisps of storm clouds.

It seemed as if she and Pip had been wandering forever, braving the Irish Sea in a dilapidated fishing boat, battering themselves in countless jolting mail coaches carrying them to no destination in particular, only farther and farther away, deeper into the English countryside.

Worse still, they'd been on foot for two weeks now, ever since the store of coins she'd carried away from the pawnbroker's shop in far-off Ireland had dwindled away.

This was a journey that would never be finished, not until Pip had grown into a man. A man who could fight back, rather than a little boy at the mercy of someone who could batter with fists and words.

Her one hope was that she'd managed to buy them enough precious time to vanish into the mist—but at what price? She'd betrayed those who trusted her, failed those who had depended on her, lied and deceived them in quiet desperation until they would never forgive her.

Her stomach growled and she pressed her hand against it, fighting back waves of sick hunger. It was three days since she had eaten, a handful of green apples that had left her retching in a ditch.

She'd fed the little boy the last crushed bit of pie that she'd snatched from a wooden bowl of chicken feed set out on the doorstep of a cottage a village ago. But his stomach must be devouring itself by now, torn by the talons of hunger.

He was far too small for his five years. Cheeks that should have been rosy and plump were pale hollows; hands that should have been dimpled and busy with mischief were thin and uncertain. His narrow shoulders braced against the wind with the stoic resignation of someone who had weathered far more devastating storms than the one that had pummeled them from the west.

He hadn't murmured a word of complaint, but she knew he couldn't go on much longer. The cough that had plagued him these past weeks was growing worse and worse, hammering at his narrow chest. A raw knot of despair lodged in her throat. Had they traveled so far only to die on some unfamiliar road? Starving? Cold? Alone?

No, she'd promised she would take care of him. She'd guard him with her life. But she was tired. So tired. And grief pressed like a boulder against her battered heart.

"Just a little farther, Pip," she encouraged, more for herself than the boy.

He turned his face up to hers, huge gray-green eyes conveying words he'd never say: *I'm frightened. I'm hungry. Please don't let him hurt me.*

Helplessness and desperation gnawed at Hannah's courage. God in heaven, they needed somewhere to rest, just for a little while. Long enough to get a decent night's sleep. Long enough to untangle the aches from their knotted muscles and dry their clothes beside a heavenly warm fire.

Long enough to mourn . . .

No, she couldn't think about that now. Didn't dare. She had to find some way to go on. She sought strength the way she had throughout their trek.

Though her own arms were throbbing, Hannah shifted the handle of the bag into her left hand, then bent down and scooped Pip up, pressing his small body so close she could feel the beat of his heart. After a moment the boy melted against her, burrowing his face into the hollow of her neck. It was a gesture of trust, all the more precious because it was so hard-won.

It was dangerous to love anyone so much. That was a lesson Hannah had learned with brutal clarity over the past few months. Her heart, ever wary, seldom risked, was in danger of being broken yet again. But she couldn't help it, couldn't stop it. Each time she looked at him, she saw another gentle face with eyes the gray-green of a mist-shrouded glen.

Don't let him suffer as I have done. The plea would haunt her for eternity.

A cough racked Pip's small frame. He stifled it against her shoulder, then glanced up at her with guilt-ridden eyes. How many times in years past had he been made to feel ashamed, thinking he'd committed some dire transgression by succumbing to that cough?

She battled rage and pressed a fierce kiss to his damp temple. "There now, my little man. It's all right," she soothed. "Just cough it out."

But a splinter of alarm twisted deeper into Hannah's frayed nerves. A hale, hearty child's strength would be challenged by the brutal trek the two of them had made these past two months. Pip's lungs were already weakened.

He'd terrified her three times already, stricken by spasms in his breathing that turned his lips blue, his eyes wide with panic. A panic that had magnified itself a hundredfold in Hannah's own breast because she was helpless against the malady that racked him.

She had to find some kind of shelter before it was too late. Find a temporary job where she could earn enough coin to fill Pip's stomach, and to rent the small cottage she'd promised him, hidden like a fairy-tale bower so deep in the Yorkshire moors that no one would ever find them.

But when she'd stopped in the tiny hamlet of Nodding Cross that morning, pleading for some employment, the cluster of villagers lounging near the smithy's had admitted that there was only one place she might hope to find a situation.

Her gaze swept up to the crest of a hill. There out of a wreath of mist rose a shadowy structure, smears of candlelight setting the windows aglow.

It didn't look like the house of an ogre, but the villagers had painted it in tales dark as legend, wrapped in some evil enchantress's spell. Within its confines supposedly dwelt a most capricious dragon.

One so vain he'd swept aside his tenants' cottages so his view of a nearby lake would be unobstructed. A taskmaster so ruthless he'd gobbled up a dozen assistants in the past eight months and spat them out, broken and babbling.

4

The men had stumbled into the village after they'd escaped, with tales so grim they chilled the bone. Tales of their master rousing them in the middle of the night, keeping them at their desk for days at a time, forcing them to choke down whatever food they could manage as they labored.

And his fits of temper when they failed the Herculean tasks he set them rivaled those of any tyrant who'd ever lived.

"You'd be better off to let the wee lad perish in the hedgerow in peace," a stingy goodwife had advised, busily tucking a clean cloth over a basket of bread.

Hannah glanced down at the wet guinea gold curls plastered against Pip's head, her jaw tightening with determination. She'd bargain with the devil himself to get the boy into shelter tonight.

"Is that the mad bastard of Raving-scar's house?" Pip quavered.

"Master of Ravenscar, sweeting. *Master."* Hannah corrected him, but from all accounts the man *was* exactly what Pip had labeled him. "And yes, sweeting. It is his house."

His little arms clasped tighter about her neck. "The lady with the bread said the bastard is mad."

Hannah understood all too well the vibrating terror in Pip's faint voice.

"I hope he *is* in one of his notorious temper fits," she said, tossing a stray strand of auburn hair away from steady gray eyes. "If we're very lucky he'll be angry enough to have thrown out a few more of his servants. If he needs someone to light his fires or clean his clothes, he might just let us inside."

Pip burrowed closer. "Don't want to go inside."

"Hush now. It will only be for a little while. I won't let anyone hurt you." It was a rash promise. One she knew all too well she might not be able to keep.

Worse still, hadn't she been hurting Pip herself? Dragging him from pillar to post without food, without

5

shelter, without any place to call home? A child needed a home.

A wide carriage sweep wound in a silver ribbon to the grand entrance of the mansion. Braces of lanterns blazed on either side of the massive twin doors, spreading puddles of gilt across the Palladian portico with its graceful white pillars. Hannah searched for a path that would lead her to the servants' entrance. As they trudged toward the far side of the house the front door suddenly flew open, spewing out a spindly ink-stained man with wild eyes, a half-open portmanteau tucked under one arm. A trail of clothes spilled out in his wake.

"Get back here before I break your neck, you bloody fool!" A deep voice roared from the cavernous interior of the house. "I haven't even paid you yet!"

Not even the inducement of coin could give the little man pause. He jumped as if a firebrand had just been thrust down the back of his breeches, and he all but bowled Hannah over in his haste to flee.

Pip scrabbled down to the ground in raw terror and shrank back to hide behind a stone pillar, but Hannah couldn't take her eyes from the man charging out the door in pursuit. She knew in a heartbeat that it was Austen Dante, Master of Ravenscar.

Eyes like blue flame glittered in the lantern light, something hard and dangerous in those heart-stoppingly handsome features.

He towered over most men, emanating such fierce intensity it seemed as if charges of lightning flowed through his veins instead of mere blood. Barely controlled energy pulsed from every inch of his frame, making one wonder—or fear?—what might happen if ever he fully unleashed it.

Patrician cheekbones slashed down to a blade-straight nose. His hair was tossed in wild black waves across a noble brow, and a cleft marked a chin of granitelike stubbornness.

"What the devil—" The man slammed to a halt a mere instant before he would have crashed into Hannah. "Get the blazes out of my way so I can drag the incompetent fool back by his infernal collar! I've the devil of a lot of work to do tonight!"

Hannah stood her ground, fighting back the alarm clamoring in her chest. "I suppose you *could* shackle him to a wall, provided you have some chains stashed in a stray dungeon somewhere," she managed to say without so much as a betraying tremor in her voice.

He shot her such a searing glance she was stunned that the moisture soaking her clothes didn't turn into steam. "I'd do it, by damn, if I thought it would do any good! But the authorities get infernally touchy about a little reasonable torture nowadays, no matter how much the blackguard deserves it." A mouth full and sensual curled with the ruthlessness of one unused to being thwarted. "Oh, what the hell, the little weasel is probably halfway to Nodding Cross by now."

He reeked of recklessness, every line of the muscular form beneath the exquisitely tailored claret-colored coat and biscuit-hued breeches proclaiming there would be hell to pay for anyone foolhardy enough to dare cross his will.

Hannah had read countless philosophers in her father's library, dissecting the perilous intoxication of power, and absolute power was more dangerous than any other. This man's authority was far-reaching, absolute in this area where he would control every enterprise from here to Nodding Cross.

At a glance, she could tell that he was everything she loathed—and feared. She'd seen men like him before. Ireland was packed with absentee landlords bleeding their estates dry, petty tyrants in their own miniature kingdoms.

Perhaps she was the one not in her right mind, bringing Pip to such a place, putting him in the power of

7

such a man again. Yet this was only a temporary measure. She and Pip wouldn't be important enough to stir up the notorious Austen Dante's formidable wrath.

Muttering an oath, the man turned back to the house and started up the stairs. Hannah couldn't let him slam the door. She grabbed his arm, stunned at her own rashness.

"Wait, sir! Please!"

He turned to glare at her hand clutching his sleeve. "I prefer to get back under a roof."

But when her fingers only tightened, his scowl carved deeper. His eyes glittered, his voice suddenly terrifyingly soft. "Before you wreak any more destruction on my sleeve, perhaps you might enlighten me on one point. Who the devil are you, and what the blazes are you doing on my doorstep?"

She would have been less alarmed if he'd bellowed at her. Hannah bolstered her courage and forced herself to meet his smoldering gaze. "I've come to save you the inconvenience of—of digging the manacles out of your dungeon, sir."

"You what?" he demanded in deadly quiet.

"I heard about your difficulties while passing through Nodding Cross."

"Is that so?" His lip curled in a sneer. "And just which difficulties are those? As you see, I haven't sprouted three heads and I don't spit fire—at least unless I'm severely provoked. However, if ever I *were* going to roast somebody, now would be the time."

Hannah fought the urge to take a step backward. "I heard that there are few stouthearted enough to be in your service long. And since I never could resist a challenge, I was searching for the servants' entrance to ask for employment."

"Of course you were." He gave a bark of harsh laughter. "After all, I always make it a practice to hire vagrant women wandering past my door, then show them the key to the silver closet."

Outrage and shame seared Hannah's cheeks at his contemptuous dismissal. One would think in the past months she'd have grown accustomed to people regarding her the way they did the dirt beneath their feet— bothersome and vaguely unpleasant, something to be brushed away as hastily as possible so as not to dull their own luster.

But her greatest blessing and most hazardous curse had always been a core of inner pride, one that hadn't allowed her to crumble when the family fortunes had been swept away. One that stung and pinched like a slipper three sizes too small beneath this arrogant cur's contempt.

She wanted to tell him to go to the devil, but the muffled sound of a cough from behind the pillar made her bite her tongue. Steel poured into her spine, defiance bumping her chin up a notch. "Sir—"

His eyes narrowed. "I know I'm reputed to be a few steps shy of a waltz, madam, but even I'm not crazy enough to usher someone of your ilk into my house. Besides, I've got an entire staff of servants who, believe it or not, are able to tolerate my moods well enough. It's just these damned weak-spined assistants who aren't man enough to endure a little bellowing."

"Then maybe you need a woman."

"A woman?"

She'd thought her humiliation couldn't get worse, but the insufferable man eyed her with a new, even more cutting disdain, and Hannah was appalled to realize he thought she was propositioning him in a most improper way. Doubtless the arrogant oaf couldn't conceive of why else he could possibly need a woman. Only the stifled sound of another of Pip's coughs kept her from slapping the master of Ravenscar square on his obnoxious face.

"A tempting offer, but I fear I must decline," he mocked. "My tastes tend to be a trifle more fastidious."

"I was offering nothing of the kind!" she blustered. "I

9

only meant to say that maybe you need a woman to do whatever tasks the weak-spined men can't."

"You mean be my assistant? Don't be ridiculous," he scoffed. "You couldn't possibly take over Willoughby's tasks."

"How can you be so certain unless you tell me what they are?" At this point she wouldn't have been shocked to learn that Willoughby's job was feeding virgins to the monster under the stairs and starching neckcloths in a brew made of babies' teeth.

"Tell me, Miss . . . Miss . . . whatever-your-name-is—"

"Miss Hannah Gray—Graystone," she lied hastily.

"What are your particular talents, Miss Graystone? I mean, besides running about the countryside looking like a drowned cat? I don't suppose your accomplishments include the ability to transcribe music?"

"M–Music?" She echoed dully, gaping at him. Music seemed as incongruous to a man like Mr. Dante as a fetching rose pink bonnet would be tied beneath his intimidatingly masculine chin.

As for her knowledge of the stuff, it ended at singing the Celtic folk songs she'd once heard about her father's estate.

"That's right. *Music,*" he repeated. "Melodies, harmonies, often played upon instruments like the pianoforte—usually so badly it assaults your ears."

"I–I adore music." It was true. She adored it the way she adored the art of Michelangelo, with a good deal of awe and absolutely no aptitude. The statues might as well have been sprung from Zeus's head for all she understood the process of their creation.

"But why—I mean, if you're a composer, why not write it yourself?" What was she trying to do? Convince the man *not* to hire her? Blast her blunt tongue—she never could leave well enough alone.

"Why don't I write the music down myself?" he echoed. Was he mocking her? Mocking himself? He extended beautifully shaped hands, long-fingered and strong and dauntingly masculine, a signet ring glittering in the light spilling from the door. "I'd get ink stains on my fingers. There's nothing so appallingly vulgar."

"I—I can do that," Hannah burst out, totally unsettled as she tried to read his expression.

"Do what? Be appallingly vulgar?" The devastating power of his smile leveled Hannah. A smile brimming with irony.

"I can write music." It was a blatant lie, but the possibility of pleading with this man, asking him for safe haven out of the generosity of his heart would be as futile and humiliating as begging the moon for a cup of sunshine.

He stared at her, obviously stunned. "I'd have to be mad to take you into my house—a total stranger. I doubt you have recommendations from your former employers stashed beneath your shawl."

"What do you have to lose? If I fail to suit, you can fling me out in the morning. But there is a chance I might just answer your need."

He frowned. "There *is* something puzzling about you. You wander the countryside like a beggar woman—yet the cut of your clothes is genteel enough."

"I'm so relieved that you approve of my seamstress, *sir*," Hannah couldn't help snapping.

"Even more intriguing, you speak with the culture of a lady in any drawing room I might name. To be sure, you're muddled up a bit with that Irish accent, but I'd wager you weren't spawned in some thatched hovel despite your appearance."

"Of all the insufferable arrogance! My birth is every bit as respectable as yours, I assure you. A name without stain—with some honor—" Hannah ground her teeth to stop the words.

"No, you're most certainly not a servant. I'd advise you to be careful where you get a job. I know plenty of masters who wouldn't think twice before using a cane to beat your kind of impertinence out of their servants. The question is, what are you doing shaming this illustrious name, wandering about at night in the middle of nowhere begging for some menial job?"

She dared not give him a hint of where she'd come from, lest the hunter tracking her and Pip should somehow catch word of it. "That is my affair. Whether you choose to hire me is yours."

Desperation clawed at Hannah, pride choked her. She'd never begged in her life. But she was excruciatingly aware of the tiny boy even now cowering behind the cold stone pillar. "Please, sir, I . . . I beg you." She forced the words from her throat. "I've traveled so far to find work. You're my last hope."

She half expected the ruthless Mr. Dante to brush her out of his way, stalk into his house and slam the door. But he said nothing, only ground his fingertips against his left temple.

"Do you have family, sir?" she asked.

His gaze flashed to her, eyes piercing, broad shoulders suddenly rigid. "The villagers may claim I hatched from beneath a rock, but believe it or not, I do have family— far away from here." He grimaced, irritation marking his features. "What damnable impertinence! Well, it's no more than I deserve, I suppose. After all, I've been brainless enough to stand out in the carriage sweep babbling to you."

He was going back inside; she saw the intent in every harsh line of his face. She had to take a risk, see if this arrogant Englishman had a heart. She knew from experience that it wasn't a part of the human anatomy necessarily included with the ownership of a vast property. And this man with his hard face and burning eyes seemed more implacable than most.

"I'm not begging a job for myself alone," Hannah began, but a rash of coughing erupted from behind the pillar.

"What in damnation is that infernal racket?" the man blazed.

"Pip."

One brow arched with caustic humor. "Pip? Don't tell me. It's some sort of new plague brought back from the West Indies."

"No. Pip is a little boy. Pip, come here," Hannah called. She prayed that if they could get inside, Pip would at least be fed, get a little warm. Surely once in the house she could manage to stall this man long enough to do the child some good.

Ever so warily, Pip stole out from behind his hiding place, edging toward her as if he were a mouse crossing the gaze of a ravenous hawk. But once he stepped into the light spilling from the door, he stood stiff as a lead soldier, braced for the man's inspection. Hannah was certain the child wanted nothing more than to bury his face in her sodden skirts. His courage broke her heart.

"What the—God's wounds!" Dante swore as a horrible cough racked Pip's delicate frame.

Eyes of lightning storm blue flashed to hers. "Are you out of your senses, dragging a child about in this? You could have at least waited until the storm passed!"

He was glaring at her as if she were an idiot. No other attitude could have scraped more ruthlessly across Hannah's ragged nerves. She would have liked nothing better than to fling an epithet into his arrogant teeth and walk away, but she didn't dare for Pip's sake.

"What a pity you weren't there to consult before we set out!" she said with a preciseness that bespoke her inner fury. "But we're here now."

"Where the devil did you get the child?"

"You don't know where children come from, sir?" She evaded desperately, expecting him to rage. Instead, a spark of hard amusement lit his eyes.

"I own to having some idea, ma'am. Is he yours?"

"Yes."

13

She saw his gaze flick down to her left hand, bare of a wedding ring. Let the man think whatever he wanted of her. She didn't care. If he concocted some explanation in his own mind—however sordid—he'd be less likely to be prying about searching for real answers.

"You came out chasing that poor man, raving that you had work to finish tonight. Take us in and I'll go straight to the task, start right away and stay up all night if you'll just let Pip curl up by the fire." It was a risky gamble. She only hoped she could hide her own abysmal ineptitude until the boy was warm.

Dante shot her a glare, his eyes dark with what must be impatience. "Absolutely not."

Hannah's heart fell like cold stone.

"Wet as you are, you'd ruin the upholstery. Besides," he pulled a sour face, "you smell like a wet dog." That taunting light glinted in his eyes again, daring her to what? Despise him? He was wasting the effort. She already did. "It can wait until morning when you're less likely to offend my sensibilities," he finished.

"Pardon us for being wet and cold," Hannah snapped, about to add that she and Pip would quietly begin to starve on his front step. Then she stopped, the meaning of his words suddenly striking her with such force she all but dropped to her knees with relief. "M—Morning? You mean . . ." She hardly dared give voice to it, she'd known so many crushing disappointments these past months.

"I might as well give the folk of Nodding Cross one more example of my insanity. Simmons!" Dante bellowed. A strapping footman dove from the door, a healthy respect for his master's ill temper showing in his simple face.

"Aye, master. You wish me to sweep 'em off the property?" Simmons asked, casting a glance at the two disreputable forms the storm had blown in.

"I want you to put them in Willoughby's room."

"Willoughby's?" The servant couldn't have appeared

more stunned if his master had commanded him to set fire to his coattails.

"Yes, Simmons. The craven cur has gone the way of all the others. Miss Graystone will be taking his place."

"Will she, sir?" the servant said, but Hannah could tell it translated to *have you lost your mind?* "You want me to—to install the lady and young gentleman in the chamber across the hall from your own." It was a statement, but Simmons was obviously trying to make certain his master was aware of what he'd ordered.

"How the devil else am I going to wake her up in the middle of the night if genius burns?"

"Yes, sir, but—perhaps you would like me to lock them in?"

"Afraid they might murder us all in our sleep, eh, Simmons? Well, if she has a butcher's cleaver stashed in that bundle, I'd just as soon she kill me first. That way I won't have to listen to the maids wailing."

"Aye, sir."

"And Simmons," he cast out. "That meat pie Cook served tonight was definitely inferior to her usual standards. You might as well feed it to them instead of the dogs."

Hannah's mouth was already watering, but it pinched her pride dreadfully to take Mr. High and Mighty's castoffs. She should be grateful, but he was making it difficult with his mockery, his arrogance, his negligent casting out of favors that meant so much to both her and Pip.

Yet what had she expected? That the man would usher them into his own library, draw off her half boots and stockings, and chafe her numb feet until they were warmed by his own exalted hands?

Why was it that the image of those strong fingers on her bare ankle started a trembling deep in her core? And what in the world possessed her—practical, unflappable Hannah Gray, who had never been prey to fluttering pulses and breathless excitement even when confronted with the handsomest of men—even to think such improper thoughts about this arrogant lout in the first place?

"Miss Graystone."

She jumped at the rough satin of his voice, and guilt stung her cheeks as if he could peer past her lowered lashes with those fire blue eyes and read her very mind.

"I'll be in the Music Room at dawn. Be late at your own peril. You've heard tales of my temper. I'd advise you not to court it." With that he turned on the heel of his glossy Hessian and stalked into a chamber three doors down. After a moment a ripple of notes drifted out, oddly discordant, igniting the restlessness, uncertainty, and fears clamoring in Hannah's breast.

But she had no time to linger, to analyze the strange mixture of feelings the notorious master of Ravenscar unleashed in her. Simmons was already herding her and Pip through the magnificent house, back outside, then into the separate building that housed the kitchen. The servant bustled about preparing a tray with the scorned meat pie, oblivious to Pip's gasp of awe as he peered at tables groaning beneath freshly baked bread, baskets of apples ready to be made into tarts or pies or sauces. But Hannah heard him, sensed his delight. And she wished she could let him run wild—pilfer the puddings, munch fistfuls of cake, lick the sugarloaf that glistened at the far end of the table.

But even if Austen Dante had been the kind of man who would allow such antics, Hannah knew with a pang of sadness that Pip would never be the sort of child who would racket about the room squealing and laughing, sticky with mischief and sugar.

She took the child's hand as the footman retraced the path to the main house, then led them up the servants' stairs to a wide corridor painted the soft green of spring's first leaves, iced with moldings of white. Portraits lined the walls, Elizabethan sea hawks in white ruffs, reckless cavaliers with smiles more dashing than the plumes decking their rakish hats, a lady with a secretive smile who must have sent her husband off to fight the War of the Roses.

Hannah wondered if those painted faces had learned how swiftly their fortunes could fall, everything swept away in a heartbeat. How short a journey it could be from ropes of pearls and cloaks of velvet to rain-sodden gowns and nothing but the night sky as a roof overhead.

She stumbled, her half boots making damp squishing sounds, tracking water across the elegant marble floor. At length, Simmons flung open a door, and Hannah entered a bedchamber still reeling from poor Willoughby's flight.

Armoire doors gaped open, everything in disarray. One shoe was still abandoned near the washstand, a man's crudely mended nightshirt straggled out of a clothespress, and the desk was littered with blotted sheaves of paper, an inkstand, penknife, and bouquet of quills.

But the fire was dancing merrily on the grate, and there was a huge bed with its thick coverlets turned back so invitingly that Hannah wanted to fling herself down on it, wet clothes and all. Instead, she drew Pip near the blaze and started stripping off layers of his wet garments.

She glimpsed Simmons setting the tray down atop a delicate gilt table. "Don't even think of trying anything foolish, Miss," the footman warned, casting her a hard glance. "The master might not take exception to being done to death in his bed, but I do."

"I'm far too tired to contemplate murder tonight. Perhaps tomorrow."

Simmons made a harrumphing sound deep in his throat. "You'd best have a care, Miss Graystone. The master is not a patient man."

Hannah grimaced. "I figured that out for myself when I saw that poor Willoughby fleeing for his life."

"Willoughby's not the first who's run away."

"I won't be running anywhere," Hannah promised as

Simmons stalked out. Her mouth twisted wryly. She wouldn't have to run. Doubtless the *master* would be flinging her out by her petticoats tomorrow. Unless she could find a way to deceive him a little longer.

She dug a somewhat dry nightshirt from the center of her bag and dragged it over Pip's head. "Get into bed, little man, under those lovely warm covers, and I'll bring over a plate so you can munch the pie there."

Pip should have felt delight at such pampering, like any other child she'd known. Instead, he nibbled at his lower lip and eyed the bed warily. "But what if–if I spill? The mad bastard might get even madder."

"Master, darling. We're to call him the master, and he wouldn't even know. He's got an army of servants below stairs to clean up after him. Don't worry, sweeting. Come now, hop up before you get even more chilled."

The boy gave her one last look of indecision, then climbed up onto the bed as gingerly as if the coverlets were woven of strands of glass.

Yet as she served him a thick wedge of pie, Hannah couldn't help acknowledge that she would be the one to incite the master of Ravenscar's infamous rage in the morning.

What reaction would a man of Austen Dante's temperament have when he realized she had duped him? Would he bellow? Rage? Chase her halfway to Nodding Cross the way he had his last assistant? Hannah shuddered.

No. The man would not intimidate her, curse his exquisitely tailored hide. He was dictatorial and vain, so arrogant he thought he could blast anyone less exalted with his temper tantrums, trample them beneath his will. She would not buckle under to him.

Her intentions were of the very bravest, and yet . . .

She'd seen the devastation such a powerful man's ire could leave behind. She'd felt the searing helplessness, tasted the fear.

"Nanna," Pip's small voice came to her from the

reaches of the great bed. "Do you think the mad Raven man will come at night and de-bower us? That's what my nurse said Sassenachs did to naughty boys. Ever since debil Cromwell the 'Ninglish got a taste for gobbling Irish boys all up."

Hannah would have given her bit of meat pie for the chance to tell his nurse exactly what she thought of her. "That's just a story, Pip. One that mean-spirited grown-ups use to frighten children into doing what they want. You're the best boy in the whole of England. And as for Mr. Dante, he has far too discerning a palate to be tempted by us, moppet. I'm quite certain we've not been seasoned to his taste."

Pip licked the last flake of crust from his upper lip, then his mouth widened in a rare smile of such piercing sweetness it hurt Hannah's heart. "I think Heaven has warm fires in it and meat pies that you can eat in bed." He caught Hannah's hand and held it tight. "I'm 'fraid of mad mans, Nanna."

"I know. But you won't even have to see him if you don't want to. You can stay up here and practice making your letters, and read from your book the way I taught you. Then whenever I'm done with my work you can show me all you've learned." She took the child's plate and set it aside, then snuggled the coverlets under his soft chin.

"Do you think we'll be getting to stay here very long?"

"No, precious," she answered honestly. "But we're going to enjoy it while we do! Sleep now, *mo chroi.*"

She sang the child the soft Irish songs she'd learned a lifetime ago, when she'd been happy and safe and had never been afraid. When she'd believed that nothing would ever change.

His lashes drifted down and Hannah watched him slip away into sleep. She brushed aside the damp tumble of curls from his brow and kissed it, knowing that she would kiss away the nightmares that haunted him, take them into herself if she could. But that was a hope as futile as learning to transcribe music before the morning came.

She shed her own garments, slipping into a nightgown that was slightly damp about the hem. Then she hung the wet things near the fire to dry. She should feel heartened. Two hours ago she'd been on the road. Now they were both fed and warm, and Pip was tucked in bed. Yet their good fortune tonight only made her realize how bleak their existence had become. The thought of returning to it was intolerable.

Lord, she needed a miracle. A miracle for Pip. At that instant a gust of wind struck the panes of the window, ruffling the papers on the desk. Hannah latched the window more tightly, then turned.

She crossed to the desk, staring down at the litter of papers—papers ruled with grids of lines, marked with dots and sticks and odd-shaped symbols. Music—she'd seen it often enough when her sister Elisabeth was practicing the pianoforte before their father had died.

She grabbed up a sheaf of the papers, her heart thundering in her breast. She might not be able to promise Pip a warm fire and meat pies in bed forever, but the more closely she could approximate what was on these sheets of paper, the longer the child could stay under a sturdy roof, out of the rain and the wind and the relentless night.

Her eyes were gritty with exhaustion, her fingers so tired and cold they trembled, yet she settled her aching body at the desk. She'd never be able to make sense of the blurred jumble of notes by morning she thought bitterly, examining one of the blotted pages.

But she'd tutored herself in Latin and Greek from the few books she'd managed to smuggle out of her father's library years ago. She'd taken charge of her family's meager finances and taught herself to manage an entire household when she'd never so much as buttoned up her own gown before. Maybe she could learn to copy music passably enough to give Pip at least a day of rest. She cast one last longing glance at the warm bed, then resolutely turned away.

Gripping the pen tightly in an effort to still the quivering in her fingers, Hannah scribbled and scratched, blotting ink and muttering curses until the symbols danced before her blurry eyes.

She was never certain exactly when her head drooped down to the sheaf of papers she'd labored over for so many hours.

But her dreams were haunted by a man with eyes of lightning-flash blue, hair like a midnight sea, and the face of an angel exiled from heaven.

A man who could barely contain the emotions racing through him—passion, anger, and something more, something secret and mysterious and unnerving. Dread clung in a hard knot in her heart, questions echoing through her mind.

What would happen when the Master of Ravenscar discovered her deception? Had she and Pip found shelter from the tempest outside these walls? Or had they entered the eye of the storm?

Chapter

Hannah jolted awake as if struck by lightning, blinded by sunlight prying at her gritty eyelids with bright, insistent fingers. Pain shot through every aching joint of her body, panic and confusion making her head swim as she sprang upright, almost tripping over the chair she'd been drowsing in. A piece of paper clung to a damp spot on her right cheek, and she clawed it away, shaking the tumbled mass of her hair out of her face.

Where on earth was she? Her gaze slashed from the dying fire to the remains of last night's dinner, then to the ink-splotched page in her hand.

Her heart slammed to the soles of her bare feet as the events of the past night dawned on her. Mr. Dante—writing music—he'd commanded her to be in the music room at dawn.

"Sweet mercy!" she choked out, racing to don her relatively dry but hopelessly crumpled clothes. "Pip! Pip, I have to go! I'm late." Without so much as glancing in the mirror she raked her brush haphazardly through the tangled mass of her hair, bundling it out of the way into a knot at her nape.

Pip emerged from the cocoon of coverlets, blinking and wide-eyed, a child who understood far too well for his tender years what a calamity this was. "But the Mad Bastard said you had to be there early, or else . . ."

"Pip, you have to stop calling him that!" she pleaded. Hopping on one foot, then the other, she jammed her muddy half boots on, not even bothering with stockings. Regret stole through her as she glimpsed the child's chagrined features. "Don't worry, sweetheart. I suppose he *is* a mad bastard if nothing else." She grimaced. "Everything will be all right. When they bring up your breakfast, eat everything you can."

"Maybe I shouldn't. Maybe I should just eat a little an' tuck the rest in a napkin an' hide it in our bag like you did at the inn."

Hannah cast him a smile. "Don't worry about that. Eat until you can't eat anymore. I love you." She kissed him on the top of his head, swept the sheets of ruled paper into her arms.

"Nanna, wait—you need to—"

"Whatever it is, it can wait till I get back," she said, then bolted down the hall.

After three wrong turns she managed to find the music room. Her spirits plummeted when she heard music issuing from within. Tumultuous, it thundered with frustration, flashed with bright bursts of anger. One thing was certain. Today, Pip's "Bastard" was most definitely *mad*.

Hannah straightened her shoulders, and forced herself to hurry into the chamber. The instant she closed the door the music ceased in a crash of discordant notes. Dante swung around on the chair drawn up to a magnificent instrument.

The sound of his music made her expect him to look like a whirlwind—tousled and a little unkempt.

But every knot and button and fold of clothing the man wore had been fastened and smoothed to perfection. The waves of his hair were tamed except for one stubborn black lock that tumbled across his brow. How was it possible for a man so tempestuous to appear so polished, so elegant? Only his eyes betrayed the fierce passions inside him.

"Miss Graystone," he said with scathing mockery. "Perhaps they have a different definition for dawn in Ireland?"

"Forgive me, sir."

"Under no circumstances. You've left me to struggle alone for the past four hours, and now you shall pay the price for it."

Hannah stopped breathing, stopped moving. No. He couldn't dismiss her before she'd even had a chance to try—to try what? To deceive him? To make a fool of him? "Sir, I . . ."

"Don't worry, girl. I'm not going to fling you into the streets. At least not yet. Believe me, your aching fingers by the time this day is over with will be punishment enough for your tardiness. Now get your ink and pen out before I forget this aria."

Hannah scrambled to prepare herself, taking a seat at the small table near the pianoforte. It was arranged so that she could watch the man's fingers. But how did one transcribe the wind? His hands flew over the keys so fast they blurred before her eyes. His jaw knotted, his brows lowered in concentration. Fast as she was able, she worked the symbols she'd practiced the night before, yet there was no rhyme or reason to them. Instead of appearing like a swift stream, they were garbled and blotted, smeared and tumbled from line to line.

"Have you got that?" Dante demanded, turning to glare at her after he finished the first passage. Something strange flickered in his eyes, and he stared at her with an odd intensity.

She scribbled a trifle longer, then glanced up. "I believe so. Play it once more to be certain."

He began it, then fumbled to a stop, his gaze flicking again to her face. Her cheeks heated at the displeasure that darkened his blue eyes. What was she doing to irritate him still? She couldn't afford to court any more of his wrath.

"I've got it." She lied, hoping to allay the danger in his expression.

He plunged on for a few more moments, but the notes fit together ill. He stopped with an oath. "God's feet, wasn't it bad enough that you were late this morning? Do you have to come here looking like *that?*"

Hannah dropped the pen, running one hand over the wrinkled mess of her gray gown. "I didn't want to waste time on my appearance when I was already late."

"From the look of you, you wouldn't concern yourself about it if you had three days to prepare."

"But if I'm only writing music, what should it matter?"

"It matters to me. Bloody hell, your present state is enough to shatter any creativity I might be able to muster. You're distracting the blazes out of me."

"Then perhaps you should keep your eyes on the keys of your instrument."

"I would, except whenever I look at them all I can see is that infernal mess of a face of yours."

She'd never been considered a beauty by suitors or by herself. Her sisters had been gifted with lovely curls and rose petal cheeks, sweet dimpled smiles and voices lilting as silver bells. Yet there was something in this insufferable man's contempt that slipped like the poison of nettles under her skin.

"I regret not meeting your impeccable standards. Perhaps you could find me a loo mask that I could wear."

"It wouldn't matter a damn. Not now that I've already seen you."

He shoved himself to his feet and stalked to where a decanter of water sat on a wooden stand, two glasses beside it. Grabbing a handkerchief from his pocket and dousing it in water, he stomped over to her, towering above her chair.

"Make use of the mirror," he snapped, thrusting the damp cloth into her hands. Stinging with humiliation and outrage, yet knowing that her tardiness had already jeopardized her position with him far too much to risk angering him further, she squared her shoulders and made her way to the gilt-framed looking glass hanging on a nearby wall. Gazing at her reflection, she wondered if it were possible to perish of embarrassment. No, if it were, she'd be laid out for her own funeral by now.

Her hastily put-up hair was tumbling out of its knot, and her cheeks, still waxen pale from the ordeal of the past weeks, appeared to have caught some horrible contagion. One that left black blotches all over the right side of her face. Not blotches . . . ink blots.

Oh, heavens, when she'd fallen asleep last night, the notes she'd been working on must still have been damp. Somehow, that fact made her feel more vulnerable than ever in Austen Dante's eyes. She hated the sensation.

"Do you have some eradicator?" she asked with as much dignity as she could muster.

"Eradicator?" he echoed with a blank look.

"To dissolve the ink."

He flushed, then scowled. "We're out of the stuff at present. It was among the supplies my steward is to bring back from his journey. Water will just have to do."

Setting her teeth, she wadded up his handkerchief and scrubbed at the marks so fiercely her skin should have peeled away with the force of it. Worst of all, she could glimpse the man reflected in one corner of the mirror. Arms crossed over his chest, the unyielding square of his jaw outlined to perfection by the snowy, impeccably starched folds of his cravat, he scowled at her as if she'd purposely scribbled on her face.

Her cheek was fire red, yet despite her efforts she could still see only marginally faded splotches of ink.

"Thunderation," he growled after a moment. "At this rate we won't get any work done until next Thursday. Give the infernal cloth to me."

She wheeled around to see the Englishman closing in on her like a stalking wolf. He snatched the smudged cloth from her hand. Realizing his intent in that instant, she stumbled back a step, but he was too fast for her.

Grasping her chin between fingers surprisingly calloused, he tipped her face up as if she were a naughty child, angling it into the light.

"You've made even more of a mess, if that's possible," he said, then set to work himself. Doubtless he expected the ink blots to flee for their lives when faced with the wrath of such an exalted personage. But they were Hannah's ink blots, after all. It seemed they weren't so easily intimidated.

At the moment, Hannah would have scraped the offending marks off with a blacksmith's file rather than be subjected to the man's assault.

He was too close, too overwhelming. The energy emanating from his tall frame pressed against her like the aura of a coming storm, squeezing her lungs until she could scarce draw breath, making her heart race.

She expected him to smell like Hungary water, or some other expensive brew of scent, but instead the man smelled of wind across the moors, bay rum, and leather, and a restlessness that stirred up an answering echo in Hannah's own breast, one buried so deep she hadn't even realized it was there.

His dark brows were drawn down in concentration; firm, sensual lips curved in a frown. Only his breath was soft, stirring the fine curls at her temple.

"Blast and damn," he burst out suddenly, flinging the ruined handkerchief away. "It won't come off!" He made it sound like an accusation.

"Then I suppose we'll both have to make do," Hannah answered. "Unless, of course, my ink blots are more important than the aria you were composing."

Dante swore under his breath and released her chin. "There's no help for it. Just—just move the table to the other side of the pianoforte, so at least some of that side of your face will be concealed."

Hannah did as he ordered, then plunked down onto the chair. It was as if the man hoped to blaze the marks off her face by the force of his music. He flung himself into it the way he might a wild ride on a horse, dragging Hannah along with him.

Her fingers cramped, her jaw ached from biting back the sharp retorts she wanted to fling at him. Yet he barely glanced at her, merely hurling out chains of music with the zest of Thor casting thunderbolts.

Before an hour was out, Hannah understood exactly why Willoughby had run away. The question was, how had the man found enough energy even to open the door?

Time sped by, and her stomach knotted with the strain as she attempted to conceal her writings from the man as long as possible. She prayed Pip had gotten breakfast and tea, for she certainly hadn't. A maid had brought in a tray, but the high and mighty Mr. Dante had not so much as glanced at the delicious-smelling concoctions that made Hannah's mouth water. It seemed whirlwinds didn't need to be fed like mere mortals.

She managed to distract him every time he started to lean over to look at her work, either concealing it with her arm or asking him to play the last passage again, whatever ruse she could think of.

And with each scrawled note, her own dread grew; with each staining of twilight at the windows, her sick certainty ground her down. Soon, all too soon, Mr. Dante would discover that she could no more transcribe music than she could make the ink disappear from her face.

And once he did . . .

But still he drove her until she no longer cared if he

saw what she'd written, until she would have rejoiced at a bout of temper, anything so she could pry the pen from her cramping hand, stand and stretch muscles that had grown tight as iron bands. She was sick, tired, so much so she could barely keep her eyes open.

The crash of a chord made her jump in her seat, silence tumbling down about her head as if the ceiling itself had broken loose.

"Well?" The man demanded, turning to face her, a challenging light in his eyes.

"W—Well, what?"

"I am curious to know what you think of my composition."

"M—My opinion can be of no importance to you."

"Neat evasion, madam, but you don't escape so easily. I asked you a question. I expect an answer."

"It is competent enough, I suppose," she said. "But it lacks imagination." The words were out before she realized it. Blast her bluntness! When would she learn to come up with the pretty lies that tripped off the tongues of so many other young women? If the man was so desperate for praise he'd even seek it from an ink-splotched, far from satisfactory assistant, why hadn't she made something up?

You are brilliant . . . the music is breathtaking . . . oh, great and mighty god of the pianoforte, let me worship at your feet. . . .

But no, she had to dash any chance she and Pip had of remaining here another night. Not that it would matter anyway in the end. The instant he saw the gibberish she'd been laboring over all day, he'd be flinging her out the door.

She dragged her gaze up to his face, expecting a reflection of pure disaster. But she froze, stunned. She'd never forget the way he looked at her—vivid blue eyes widening, square jaw dropping in astonishment. And then—testimony to his unstable mind, no doubt—the man started laughing. Rich, deep, roaring gulps of laughter that made tears breach his impossibly thick lashes and trickle down his cheeks.

Hannah took a wary step backward. How far was it from this wild laughter to flinging vases at her head? It seemed as if an eternity passed before he scrubbed away the traces of tears with his knuckles, his voice breathless.

"What you lack in tidiness, Miss Graystone, you make up for in courage. Let me congratulate you. You are the first person who has had the nerve to tell me the truth." He pulled a face. "Bah! As if I don't know I'm composing rot. But it will have to suffice until I can teach myself to do better. And you will have to learn to set your superior taste in music aside and listen to my fumblings."

That dark amusement faded and he paced to the window, staring out across an ocean of green. Restlessness was carved deeply in every cord and sinew of his body, and Hannah sensed that something was wrong, discordant, like the faintly off-kilter tone she heard in his music.

Yet Austen Dante was obsessed with his composing, driven beyond the bounds of reason. He'd attacked it with passion, driving her to exhaustion, even though he still looked as if he could run to London and back without beading a sweat.

Still, his passion wasn't that of a man trying desperately to write down music playing too rapidly, too vividly in his head. Rather, it was the tempestuous passion of a wild stallion caged in a stable too small for him, one he'd rather kick his way out of at any moment. The question was, what invisible bars were holding the Master of Ravenscar inside?

A soft knock sounded at the door. The man turned, calling out. "It's safe to enter."

The footman from the night before came in, a silver tray in his hand, piled high with letters. "Sir, the post has just arrived."

Mr. Dante gave a heedless shrug. "I suppose there's nothing I can do to prevent it."

"Sir, there are letters from your mother, and several from your sisters."

The face that had been filled with such mirth moments ago shifted, changed; his eyes shuttered, his mouth firming into a pale line. Did he fear some bad news?

"Put them with the others," he said, waving a hand toward the desk in the corner. Hannah turned and was surprised to see the footman slide the pile of letters atop a veritable mountain of missives, their wax seals glowing in the candlelight, unopened.

Mr. Dante crossed to a mahogany stand, picking up a decanter of brandy. He poured himself a glass and drained it in one fiery gulp. "I suppose you've suffered enough for the first day, Miss Graystone. Go and rest your poor, abused ears for the rest of the night."

She bobbed a curtsey and went to gather up the pages of her work, scarce able to believe her good fortune. If she could just escape without the man examining the gibberish she'd written, Pip could spend another night in a warm bed. She almost made it out the door.

"Miss Graystone!" He said sharply, and she wasn't certain if he was impatient with her or with himself. "Let me see those pages before you go."

Hannah's knees started to shake. "You were going so fast, some of the passages got quite blotted up," Hannah lied, pressing the pages to her bosom. "I thought I would recopy them before morning."

"You're either very dedicated or you do slipshod work." He stalked across to her and took the pages from her hands. Hannah surrendered them, a sick knot in her stomach. Heat spilled into her cheeks, and she willed herself to stand straight, to weather whatever temper fit the man was about to throw. She wouldn't give him the satisfaction of knowing that she was so desperate.

Those blue eyes flashed over the pages with piercing intelligence, his silence tightening about her throat like a hangman's noose as he examined one sheet of paper after another.

Finally, she couldn't bear the suspense any longer. All she could do was play for time. "Sir, I–I can explain. My skills are a trifle rusty, and you go so fast—"

His gaze sprung up to hers. She expected fury, confusion, censure. She almost fainted when he flashed her a distracted smile. "Tolerable enough, Miss Graystone. You are hired for however long you can endure the pace of work I set. I might suggest, however, that you make certain you collect your salary, unlike that stupid Willoughby."

She stumbled back a step, staggered by this unexpected turn. What was he doing? Luring her into a false sense of security before he lambasted her with accusations? Before he cast the nonsense she had written into the fire? "I . . . are you jesting?" she asked.

"You don't want the position, then?" he asked.

"Yes! I mean, of course I do," she said with a mixture of relief and gnawing guilt. "That is, if . . . if you are . . . satisfied."

"I am. You may go, Miss Graystone. And I trust I will have the honor of your company in the drawing room a trifle earlier tomorrow."

"Yes, sir. Of course, sir." *Have you lost your mind, sir?* she added silently, gathering up the sheaf of music. She must have faked it better than she thought.

Or was he playing some sort of vicious jest on her? Paying her back for her deceit?

But wouldn't she have been able to sense such suppressed emotions in him? Like the danger of a gathering storm?

Or was it that for all his careful examination, he'd been peering at a language he wasn't able to comprehend? Was it possible the man couldn't read music any more than Hannah could?

Absurd. Ridiculous. And yet, that would give a logical explanation of why he had hired her. Better still, if it were true, the possibility of staying in this place, warm and fed, increased a thousandfold. The hope of building up her and Pip's strength, until they were ready again to face the open road, grew. Perhaps this was the miracle she'd been praying for.

Heart in her throat, she made her way out of the room feeling as if she were walking on powder kegs and her shoes were soled with bits of burning kindling.

At the door she turned and looked back at the man standing in the chamber, suddenly seeming so alone, strangely vulnerable.

He crossed back to the pianoforte. Hannah was not sure what held her captive as he sat down at the instrument once again, his fingers flying over the keys.

This time she was stunned. Emotion poured from his fingertips, took flight in his song. It was breathtaking, a wild and soaring ride to the clouds.

In the middle of a phrase he stopped, despair carving deep in his face, his fist slamming down on the keys.

What possessed Hannah, she would never know. She dared to enter the chamber again, crossed into the ring of candlelight. "Mr. Dante, I was wrong about your music," she breathed. "That was . . . exquisite."

He gave a bitter laugh. "It's not mine. My father composed it when he was just six years old. Do you think he would be impressed with what I've composed today?"

Heat stung Hannah's cheeks, and she winced at the raw pain in those fire blue eyes. "I . . . I don't know your father well enough to predict—"

"Oh, I think you can hazard an accurate guess, Miss Graystone. Unless my father has suddenly gone tone deaf."

With that, he bolted to his feet and stalked out of the chamber, bellowing for a footman.

"Tell Withers I want Fire Eater saddled and brought round at once."

"Of course, sir. But . . . your dinner. Cook has prepared your favorite."

"Devil take dinner. I've got more important matters to tend to."

Hannah withdrew to a window alcove, watching as he flung himself on a spirited flame roan stallion. Blast the man, he had more energy after this gruelling day than she'd felt when she'd rushed down to the music room that morning.

Where on earth was he going now, at such an odd time? How could he possibly not be collapsing with exhaustion? He'd pushed himself to the limits of any mortal strength this day, hadn't taken so much as a crumb of food all day.

The footman returned inside. He cast Hannah a grimace. "Don't know why Cook even bothers making him anything. Most times he doesn't eat it. Ah, well. Just makes the table in the servants' hall all the more elegant. You and the boy will find out for yourselves tonight. It'll be a regular feast."

"Where—where is Mr. Dante going?" Hannah couldn't help but ask, although she knew it was none of her business if the man were riding his Fire Eater to the moon.

The footman shrugged. "Who knows. To the quarry or the mill or any one of a dozen places. Might have even gone to tinker with his inventions. He'll be gone till dawn if he's in one of his moods. Otherwise, he might be back in a few hours. After he's run the fever out of him."

"Mr. Dante is ill, then?" she queried, taken aback.

"Aye. But not so any doctor can fix him, bless him." A sadness veiled the man's features, tempered with a very real affection as he peered out after his master.

Affection? It took Hannah completely by surprise. How was it possible to feel such a tender emotion for a man who drove everyone around him mercilessly?

Lord, she'd have thought everyone in the house would have breathed a sigh of relief when the man rode away. All she wanted to do was go upstairs and collapse facedown on the bed.

She frowned. Was it possible that the same man who was such a merciless taskmaster was wasting away from some hidden disease? Was that the demon that drove him so relentlessly? He didn't look pale and wan and feeble.

No, if anything the man seemed *too* stuffed with good health. His muscles were honed to such sinewy splendor that not even the most elegant garments could conceal their strength. Skin burnished honey brown by the sun stretched over the aristocratic planes of his face, while his eyes . . . they fairly crackled with life.

Not that it should matter to her. What was she doing puzzling over him anyway? Whatever was wrong with the man was none of Hannah's concern. She hadn't come to this place to worry about a man she barely knew.

She'd listened as her pretty sisters commiserated with suitors confronting some grave tragedy—a hunter who had refused to jump a fence, a waistcoat not tailored to perfection, a phaeton overturned in a race upon which a month's allowance had been wagered, yet she'd never been any good at it herself.

Hannah had always been far too busy for such nonsense, obsessed instead with finding the cheapest method of remaking one of Mama's old gowns into something pretty for Elisabeth, or how to keep Mama provided with the imported coffee that made her eyes sparkle with rare delight, while trying to figure out how to get through the last week of the month when the allowance had already been spent.

She'd never had the time or the inclination to play compassionate angel to any man, and she wasn't about to begin now.

Especially with a man like Mr. Dante—all quicksilver emotions and dark enigmas.

Heaven forfend, she didn't even *like* the man.

Her only goal in staying here at Austen Dante's estate was to buy a little time to plan what to do next. Her one concern was to keep this roof over Pip's head for as long as possible, to try to remind the child what a full stomach felt like and how cozy it could be to sleep in a bed.

Whatever was troubling the imperious Mr. Dante wasn't her problem. Heaven knew, she had enough problems of her own. Problems she was solving by deceit. It was a dangerous game, one that might have grim consequences.

Hannah caught her lip between her teeth. She'd always hated dishonesty of any kind. But there was nothing else to be done under these circumstances. The only blessing to be found was that the man's music was—what had he called it? *Rot?* It wasn't as if her lack of skills was squandering away any music that would be a gift to the world. But even if it were a tribute worthy of the angels, it wouldn't make any difference.

No, she'd do what she had to do, just as she had from the instant she and Pip had stolen away into the night.

She turned, dragging herself up the stairs to the room she shared with Pip. Outside the door, she paused long enough to paste on a weary smile. The child was far too adept at reading the moods of adults—a lesson in self-preservation he'd learned at his father's knee.

She forced the thought away and opened the door. At first, it seemed as if the child had vanished. The room was lost in silence, neat as if the maid had just left it. A flutter of unease worked through Hannah. Where could Pip have gone? And what would happen if he ran afoul of Mr. Dante? He didn't seem the sort of man to tolerate children well.

"Pip?" she called out. "Pip, where are you?"

The tiniest rustle from a curtained window seat made Hannah jump.

"I'm here," the child said in a small, grateful voice.

She hustled over to draw back the curtain, and what she saw wrenched at her heart. Pip was crowded back in the corner like a frightened mouse. He'd packed up all the clothes she'd hung to dry the night before, and a lumpy bundle tied up in a napkin sat on his lap, a dribble of cherry juice staining one side.

"Whatever are you doing, *mo chroi?*"

"Waiting to have to go away. There's enough food for days and days. The maid brought up breakfast an' then tea, so I packed the best bits of food away for later."

"Oh, Pip! I told you to eat your fill!" Hannah said in dismay.

"I did eat lots and lots," Pip insisted, then looked away, guilt staining his cheeks with hot spots of color. And it touched Hannah to her core that the child had saved the food for her. "It's just that my stomach shrinked."

It was probably all too true, with the meager fare the boy had been eating the past few weeks. The knowledge made Hannah sick with regret.

"Are you . . . mad at me, Nanna?"

"No, angel. Of course not," she stroked his hair with fierce tenderness. "We'll be going down to the servants' hall soon to eat a lovely dinner. As for the food you saved, well, you can just nibble at the treats all tomorrow, and soon you'll be eating enough to feed a horse."

A horse . . . she would have yanked the words back into her mouth if it were possible. But the damage was already done. Pip's mouth pinched, his cheeks paling even more. His eyes grew wide and afraid, guilty and so very, very sad. She could have kicked herself for her carelessness.

Wasn't it bad enough that she had to leave the boy alone all day as she battled with the insufferable Austen Dante? Alone with no one to talk to, no one's hand to reach for when the shadows in his memory grew too long or dark or frightening? Did she have to make it worse by reminding him of the disastrous incident that had led to their flight?

Lifting the bundle from his lap and setting it aside, she gathered Pip into her arms, resolved to distract him. "I missed you so much while I was working. It must have been dreadfully dull up here."

"It wasn't so *very* bad," Pip allowed in a tone that let Hannah know it had been pure torture. "'Cept when I started thinking."

"Thinking what, treasure?"

"What if Papa comes when you aren't here? What if he finds me an' takes me away? I listened an' listened for his clompy boots until my head got all achy."

No wonder the little mite had been hiding! Hatred for the man who still had such power over Pip surged through Hannah, black and thick and overwhelming.

"He will never take you away from me, Pip. I swear it." She pressed him close against her, her heart swelling with a love too great to hold, a fear too deep to banish. "Remember what I told you? I know a secret your papa doesn't want anyone else to know. I left him a note. Told him to stay away or I would tell everyone I knew."

"It must've made him real angry."

"It doesn't matter. We'll be safe here," she said, as much to comfort herself as the little boy. "Remember what the tinker said when he took us to ride in his painted Gypsy cart?"

"He said he had lots of practice to slip the noose. But I didn't know what a noose was."

Hannah's heart warmed at the memory of the grizzled old traveler with eyes bright and cunning as a fox. "That's right. Old Tito said to figure out where everyone will think you're going, and make it look as if you've gone there. Then—"

"Run, run, run in the opposite direck-shun."

"That's right. Run to a place where no one would guess you've gone. A place where no one knows you, where you have no ties."

"So you maked all the people at the dockyard think we were going to 'Merica. Askin' them about how to get on a ship. An' you wrote letters telling Grandmama an' the aunts."

A twinge of guilt bit deep. "Yes, I did. So everyone will be searching in the wrong places, and maybe by the time they figure that out, it will be impossible to find our trail. Then everyone will give up and leave us in peace."

The words should have provided comfort, but the old traveler who had given her such good advice had never looked into the eyes of Mason Booth, seen the cruelness hidden like an image in a sorcerer's trick mirror where only she could see. She wasn't the only one who had witnessed what lay behind that urbane smile. Pip had looked into that ugly mirror as well, and it had left its scars buried deep in his gray-green eyes.

She shuddered. Booth was the kind of man who would run his quarry to the ground even if he had to ride his horse through a wall of flame to do it.

"Papa never will give up." Pip burrowed closer, waving one small hand toward the darkened window. "When he finds out we tricked him, he'll be madder than anything. An' once he's mad, he never, ever stops . . ."

He didn't have to continue. Hannah knew what the child was trying to say. He never stops—stops beating, stops terrorizing, stops making anyone foolhardy enough to incur his wrath pay a terrible price.

"He's out there someplace," Pip said with a shiver.

"Far away from here."

"How do you know for sure?"

"Remember what I told you? Even once he finds out we didn't sail for America, he'll waste a great deal of time searching other places—all my old schoolmates from Miss Adam's academy, cousins, friends, anywhere I might have gone for help."

She didn't add that her mother and sisters would be the first ones racking their brains to provide Mason Booth with a list of her possible destinations. The truth hurt, but it did nothing to change her love for them or cool the stinging burn of homesickness in her heart.

Mason Booth had fooled far wiser people than Mama, with her countless list of ailments, or Hannah's innocent sisters, their heads stuffed with fairy-tale dreams of happily ever after. They still believed in Mason's dashing facade, as blindly as everyone else in County Wicklow.

But one day Booth would exhaust even all of those prospects to search, and then . . . She shivered. What would happen once he'd discovered Hannah had played him for a fool? He would hunt her and Pip with an even more horrific fury.

One thing was certain. She had no delusions about what would happen if the beast did find them and expose the truth.

Mason Booth had unlimited power and wealth, and a genius for hiding a vicious brutality behind his handsome facade. One who had already proven he would do whatever was necessary to get his way. He was exactly the kind of man Austen Dante would understand. Worse still, any court in the land would support his claim to his son.

Hannah closed her eyes against the image of merciless arms dragging Pip out of her embrace, a nightmare that had tortured her countless times during their flight. She tried to beat back the panic that pressed against her ribs. No. The worst would never happen. Booth would never find them, and as for the master of Ravenscar, he had been easy enough to fool about the music. He would never guess what they were fleeing from. She'd certainly never betray it, and Pip was so terrified of men he still trembled whenever one drew near. He'd sooner approach a rabid wolf than the insufferable Austen Dante.

Hannah buried her face in Pip's curls, her mind haunted by the fierce intelligence, the dangerous probing in the man's eyes. She'd known enough men of his kind to predict what he'd do if he learned the truth. The volatile man would deliver them to the authorities himself.

They must be long gone from this estate before Mr. Dante guessed their secret, because Pip was right.

She might have bought them a little time with her desperate gamble, but in the end it wouldn't matter.

The hunter was out there somewhere, stalking them in the night.

He would never rest.

Chapter

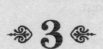

3

He should have been exhausted. Aches screwed deep into every sinew of Austen Dante's body. A half-dozen new bruises throbbed beneath his sweat-soaked clothes and a nasty cut in his right forearm was bound up in strips torn from his cravat. But it seemed that no matter how badly he mistreated his body, his infernal mind would not be beaten into submission. It still raced with a turbulence so wild even the vast night-washed sweeps of moor could not contain it.

What had he done? Riding off into the darkness again, as if he could somehow outstrip all the guilt, all the failures that mocked him.

He should have learned by now that running away didn't change anything. It might have bought him a few hours respite, and yet they only made it worse when he came dragging back to Ravenscar. The house watched for him in the night, glaring balefully out with one candlelit eye. The wind jeered at him as it tangled through gorse and heather, while the music room waited to swallow him yet again, condemning him to his own private hell.

One he now shared with an ink-stained Irish woman whose tongue was sharp enough to flay a man alive, and eyes so passionate, so disturbing that they'd haunted him through this interminable night. The eyes of someone hunted . . . hunted by demons as Austen himself was. He had tasted desperation enough himself to know its bitterness in someone else.

He drew rein near the portico and dismounted, tossing the reins to a sleepy-eyed groom. Blast, hadn't things been bad enough before? Bumbling along with incompetent assistant after incompetent assistant? He'd had to make things downright impossible by dragging this strange woman into his house. Where had she come from? And what was she running away from? Bah! Did it really matter? Obviously the fates had brought her here. The question was—who had sent her? Some guardian angel or a devil with a warped sense of humor?

Austen started to reach for the door handle, but it swept from beneath his hand. The footman looked out at him as if he expected to be staked out for a dragon.

"Mr. Dante, Mr. Atticus has returned from London. He is awaiting you in the library."

Dante frowned. His steward back from London already? "But he wasn't supposed to return for three more weeks. What the devil is he doing at Ravenscar House at this time of night?"

"I don't know, sir."

"Tell him whatever business he has can wait until tomorrow."

"Yes, sir. I will, sir. But—but it seemed rather urgent."

Austen drove his fingers back through his hair in disgust. Of course it was blasted urgent. Just one more disaster on this hell of a day.

His jaw knotting, he strode to the library. It might have been a tomb, so seldom did he enter the room. But Atticus had taken to waiting in it whenever he came to Ravenscar. At present, William Atticus sat in a leather wing chair before the fire, a thick tome in one hand, a glass of brandy in the other.

Dante would sooner have faced a firing squad than those piercing hazel eyes that saw too much and knew him too well. Austen had been six years old when he'd met William Atticus beside their grandfather's sickbed. A cousin twice removed, Atticus was poor as a country parson's pockets, living on charity at Austen Park.

In the years that followed their grandfather's astounding recovery, Atticus had extracted Austen from countless scrapes, listened to his complaints about his too-sober father, and added jibes in his own dry wit. There had been plenty of thinly veiled sneering at Joseph Dante's foreign ways—a man whose cheeks would be wet with tears over the death of his daughter's kitten or the strains of an opera or the lines of a poem. A man who had more interest in books than in fox hunting or breeding hounds.

At times, the scorn of his grandfather and cousin toward Joseph Dante had chafed at Austen, yet it was far easier to mock his father than to face the disappointment so often clouding his serious face.

Years later, on the awful morning when Austen had stumbled out to the coach to leave Austen Park forever, he had found Atticus perched on the coach seat, a box of belongings on his knee, an implacable light in his eyes. Austen would need someone he could trust, since his own father had cast him off, Atticus had insisted, and there had been real outrage in the older man's eyes.

"What the devil are you doing back here already?" Austen groused, trying damned hard not to be glad to see the gray-haired man. "I thought I was to have three more weeks of peace."

"Sorry to disappoint you." Atticus closed the book with a snap and placed it on the table beside him. "It was lovely to see my sister and everyone else in Norfolk, but I couldn't enjoy myself, despite the beauty of the lake country. I had this recurring dream that Enoch Digweed had flooded the western meadow and that Simmons was planting the silver service in the fallow field in an effort to grow more soup spoons. I was forced to return home to satisfy my unease."

"Is this the urgent business that has you haunting my doorstep at such an ungodly hour?"

"No. It's just . . . when I arrived, I was told . . ." Atticus hesitated, clearing his throat. "The servants are all in an uproar about something. I heard them muttering about being murdered in their beds. I fear they weren't making much sense."

"Are they still going on about that? Doubtless they're twitchy because I've hired a replacement for Willoughby."

"Willoughby? Is he ill? Tell me you didn't work him into a state of collapse!"

Dante crossed to where the decanter of brandy sat, and poured a draught into a crystal snifter. "I can assure you Willoughby is in tolerable health. Last I saw of him was heels and elbows as he ran to Nodding Cross at a speed that might have beaten my best hunter."

"He fled his post?"

"Exactly." The fiery liquor burned Austen's throat. "So I took matters into my own hands."

"But it is my duty to employ the servants."

"You weren't supposed to be back for three more weeks. I wasn't about to sit on my hands until you returned."

As if suddenly realizing his impertinence, Atticus flushed. "Forgive me, sir. Of course, you may do whatever you wish. It's just that I feel as if I'd failed in my duty to you. You have so many important matters to attend to, I hate to have you distracted by such mundane affairs. It seems such a waste of your time."

"The one thing Miss Graystone doesn't waste is anyone's time, Atticus." Dante said grimly. "She'd do any lieutenant in the army proud, the way she charges into the fray."

"Then I assume you were fortunate to find her." The words didn't banish the dubious light in the old man's eyes. "May I be so bold as to inquire who recommended this . . . *Miss Graystone* to you?"

"Recommended?" Dante finished the brandy and set the glass on the edge of the table.

"Who was her former employer? I'm certain they sent some kind of testimony to her character. May I have your permission to examine it?"

"There are no such papers."

"But . . . but . . . how . . . where did you find her?"

"Outside the front door, wet as a half-drowned cat."

If he'd said she were one of the undead come back to haunt them, Atticus couldn't have looked more aghast. "Surely you cannot be serious."

"I assure you, I am."

"But—but what do you know about this woman?"

"She can transcribe music, she has a tongue sharp enough to flay the skin off a man at twenty paces, and she's Irish."

"Irish!" Atticus screwed up his face as if he'd stepped on a dead rat. "A more villainous breed never existed! Doubtless she's a thief!"

"If she is, she's not doing a very profitable job of it," Dante snapped. "She looked as if she hadn't eaten in weeks."

"I must beg you to reconsider. It's too dangerous to take such a person under your roof! It's entirely possible she's—she's here for some nefarious reason! Perhaps she works with a housebreaker, and will let her master in the door at night to steal God knows what! Or maybe she's been hired by one of your rivals at the Scientific Society, to steal one of your inventions. Stranger things have happened."

Dante grimaced. "If that's the case, I'd help her load half of them in a wagon and tell her she's welcome to the lot. They sure as thunder haven't been working all that well lately."

"But you are close—so close. Especially with the reaping machine. Why with a little alteration—"

"I almost *altered* poor Enoch Digweed by the weight of his head when we tried my last model out. Broke his leg, but it could've been far worse. Thank God the man was spry enough to leap out of the way. Must be from chasing all those children about."

"Sixteen and another on the way." Atticus shuddered. "It's almost indecent, such lack of self-restraint."

Dante arched a brow. "If he were a stallion, he'd be praised to high heaven for producing such an output."

Atticus flushed; the old bachelor was totally discomfited. And Dante knew a sharp sting as if for an instant he were looking into his own face years from now—a man who had been alone so long, a wife and children were as alarming as creatures from another galaxy.

"Regarding your inventions again, I'm certain with the new supplies I bought in London you'll remedy the defects in them."

Dante sighed, pressing his fingertips to his throbbing forehead. "Sometimes I think you're more enthusiastic about my inventions than I am, Atticus. I doubt I'd be so willing to be sent off on wild-goose chases time after time, searching for God knows what. Worse still, discovering I've changed my mind and need something else altogether by the time you return to Ravenscar."

"You may always depend on me to take care of your needs, sir. That is why . . . forgive me for being tenacious, but if you would allow me to take the liberty, I would be happy to summon this Irishwoman and inform her that her services are no longer required. I'm certain I can find you a suitable assistant given a little time."

"I've wasted too much time already. And anyway, the assistants you've chosen so far haven't displayed particularly sturdy nerves. No. I prefer my own choice this time. Miss Graystone gives the impression she could face down six brigades of artillery and still keep fighting."

"Hardly a characteristic that soothes my misgivings.

Sir, have you stopped to wonder what this woman was doing wandering about alone? Who knows where she's come from? What disagreeable—if not dangerous— habits she might have? It is no small feat to keep a household running smoothly. The balance of servants must be just right. One troublemaker can cause everything to fall into ruin. If this woman is as given to fighting as you imply . . ."

"It was a figure of speech, old man! I hardly think she'll break out in fisticuffs!"

Atticus looked hurt. "I'm merely asking you to consider—"

"I have. The woman stays until she gives me some reason to dismiss her. That's the end of it, Atticus."

Dante had known Atticus long enough to realize how much it cost the man to swallow the rest of his arguments. Likely the poor old martinet would implode. Dante grimaced. Atticus would have made a far better landlord than he did under his grandfather's terms— bellowing at the underlings, ordering everyone about in that voice that seemed forceful enough to crack marble. Austen wondered why his grandfather hadn't taken that into consideration before choosing to adopt an heir.

"Yes. Of course." The steward bowed and walked to the door, his tones dropping so low Dante could barely hear. "Will it be reason enough to fire her if she filches the silver?"

"Only if she wedges them between the wires in the pianoforte," Dante called out. "Makes it dashed hard to play with them rattling around that way."

The steward turned at the door, drawing his tattered dignity about him. "And when will I be allowed to meet Miss Graystone?"

"Soon enough, old man." Dante rubbed at his temple where the tension was beginning to pound.

After a beat, Atticus spoke. "If you'll forgive me for saying so, sir, you look as if you should get some sleep. Surely you must be exhausted."

If only it were that simple!

But Austen had spent most of the night running away. It was time he paid the price. "I do need to change, but then I intend to go back to work. Have Simmons inform Miss Graystone I'll expect her in the music room in a quarter of an hour."

He could see the old curmudgeon's eyes spark with aggravation. "I'll see to it."

He started to walk away, but Dante called out again. "Atticus?"

"Yes?"

Dante hesitated. He shouldn't ask. Shouldn't tear back the fragile flesh over that wound. He couldn't help himself. "Did you—see anyone while you were in Derbyshire? My mother? Sisters?"

"In passing," the steward said carefully. "They looked well enough."

"Is there any news?"

Atticus hesitated, then plucked at one of his buttons with nervous fingers. "Your sister, Miss Leticia, is to be married come April."

Regret and impossible longing thudded into Dante's chest. Letty—she'd still been a bundle of flyaway curls and torn petticoats when he'd left, a skinned mark on her pert little nose from running into a low-lying branch while she'd been walking through the orchard engrossed in a volume of Milton. Eight years . . . it seemed like a lifetime.

"What's he like? The man who is to be her husband?"

"Her future bridegroom is a fine gentleman—a Mr. Fitzherbert. Of course Miss Letty *would* have him, for he's the only man in Norfolk who can quote more Greek poets than she can."

"Father should be pleased." Dante tried to quell the stab of envy that twisted inside him as he remembered how Joseph Dante's eyes had shone with pride when he gazed at his studious daughter.

"Your father is delighted. It's said he's never looked so

invigorated. Fitzherbert is everything your father admires in a man. Elegant manners, well read. It's said he can read eight languages and speak six. He and Letty and your father are forever sitting in the library, debating far into the night. My sister says old Mr. Dante loves Fitzherbert like a son." Atticus choked off the word, his face flooding with color. "I'm sorry. Forgive me."

"Don't regard it. I did ask you for the information."

"There is one thing I almost forgot. A small package sent by your mother. Some handkerchiefs she marked with your initials. I had Simmons place them in your bedchamber."

Handkerchiefs—such a simple, homely gift. It had become a joke between them when he was a grubby-faced boy. Every treasure he'd ever found had been bound up in the squares of soft linen—bird's eggs and shiny rocks, the paws of injured rabbits and a hundred cuts and scraps gathered in hours of running wild across the family estates.

Never once had Anne Austen Dante complained at his use of her gifts—she'd merely delighted in every boyish prize he trundled back to her, from luminescent feathers to sun-warmed blackberries. She could always stitch another handkerchief, she said, but no one else knew the trick for capturing a summer day in his hands the way her Austen could.

But that had been before. Before he had left his parent's home and moved to his grandfather's sprawling manor house. Before confusion had shadowed his mother's lovely eyes whenever she looked at him. Before he'd disappointed her, failed her. Before his deceit had made him hide away from the family he loved so they would never know . . .

Without a word, Dante started up the stairs again.

"I believe it is my duty to inform you that your mother and Miss Leticia are most hopeful that you will attend the wedding. If I may be so bold, it would be unwise to

50

attend. It can only make things uncomfortable for all concerned. You see, your father . . . I am quite certain his anger toward you has grown harder if anything."

"They'll scarce notice I'm missing." Perhaps it was better that way. Especially after the disaster the last time Dante had attended a family function. Dante winced inwardly at the memory of his mother's tear-streaked face, the lace shawl that had been his father's gift drooping off one shoulder like the wing of a storm-battered fairy, her hands trembling as they clutched at her son's sleeve.

"Austen, you don't mean it—tell your papa you don't mean it!"

He'd been all of twenty that horrendous day—would have given his mother the moon if it had been in his power. But this was a disaster as unavoidable as two bulls on a narrow ledge—the clash inevitable, the one certainty that someone had to fall. In the end, Austen hadn't fallen. He'd taken the situation in his hands and leapt off the ledge himself.

He had torn everything he loved to shreds with his own hands because he could see no other way—no choice but the unthinkable. Better to suffer hatred rather than pity. God forbid that Joseph Dante should ever know his only son . . . Even now, Dante couldn't form the words.

He started to awareness. *It's almost as if Mr. Dante has a son again . . .*

Was it possible he'd be too late, that he was on a futile quest? That it would be impossible to heal the breach with the father whose heart he'd broken?

The only thing that was certain was he couldn't hope for his father's forgiveness until he proved—what? That he wasn't a hopeless wastrel? A disgrace?

There was only one way to do that.

Dante closed his eyes, Hannah Graystone's voice echoing in his memory as she judged his music.

It's competent enough, but it lacks imagination.

He'd known the truth, but that hadn't stopped the bitter sting. He'd fought damn hard to hide behind his laughter, but he'd hated her a little for putting the stark reality into words.

I know it's rot, but it will have to suffice until I can do better . . .

But what if he never could convey in the music things he could never say, emotions so raw, so powerful, mere words could never capture them?

No, he'd try again. He'd keep trying until his fingers bled as painfully as his heart. There were countless ways to say he was sorry. But there was only one way he could be certain his father would understand.

Hannah was so tired she could walk into walls and never know what hit her. But if the merciless Mr. Dante commanded her to run through Nodding Cross five times in her nightgown she wouldn't have complained. Not while the image of Pip slumbering soundly upstairs ran through her head. Safe, for this tiny space in time, from the monster that chased him.

Gritting her teeth against waves of exhaustion so numbing she felt sick to her stomach, Hannah scrawled passage after passage of the music, trying to keep her leaden eyelids open with every ounce of energy she possessed.

She bit her lip until it bled, hoping the stinging pain would keep her awake, cramped her toes in her half boots until they screamed in agony, but still the man behind the keys of the instrument plunged on with a wild desperation almost frightening to behold.

She wanted to hate him—this selfish man who didn't give a damn if he drove anyone around him beyond the bounds of their endurance. But she couldn't waste the strength. She had to keep marking the tiny meaningless symbols on the paper with her quivering hand. Had to keep wrestling with the fear that perhaps this was his idea of punishment for her attempt at deceiving him. She just had to keep the pen moving across the page. Perhaps if she leaned on her other hand . . . just for a moment, if she lay her head down beside the page. Surely she could keep scribbling. He couldn't go on forever.

Dawn streaked the windows candy pink when Dante rippled out one last arpeggio, then cast a glance at his assistant. "The next movement is in the key of C minor—" he began, but the directions ended in a low curse. "Bloody hell!"

Instead of seeing a woman industriously scribbling away, what he saw tightened both irritation and regret inside him. Hannah Graystone's stubborn head was cradled in the curve of one arm, wisps of auburn hair straggling down around a face so ashen pale it seemed translucent. The pen trailed a squiggly line down across the page, then dangled from limp fingers.

Perdition, had he killed her? Dante grimaced. No, Hannah Graystone was made of sterner stuff. But she looked as damned wrung out as his sister Madeline when she'd gotten lost in the woods for three days after taking a wrong turn hunting for her precious botanical specimens.

Dante's brows lowered as he glared down at the sleeping woman. It was a face few would call pretty, and yet a damned compelling one nonetheless.

He could picture all too clearly the silvery eyes, sharp with intelligence, now hidden beneath surprisingly delicate lids. The decided curve of her chin was half buried against her sleeve, her mouth a little too full.

From the first moment he'd set eyes on her she'd looked like the very devil—first half-drowned from the rain, then her face spotted with ink. Yet there was something about her that wouldn't be dismissed as he had dozens of blossom-lovely faces.

Hannah Graystone was the kind of girl boys had

Kimberly Cates

delighted in tormenting since the beginning of time, one who refused every social dictate commanding that she bow to their whims, one who dared to tell the truth, masculine pride be damned.

But now in the first whisperings of dawn, the formidable Miss Graystone looked almost, well, fragile. The fine bones of her face were softened by the gentle pink-stained light from the window. The mouth that could cut a man off at the knees was vulnerable, while huge, dark circles bruised the tender skin beneath her eyes.

Dante was stunned to discover even the notoriously ruthless master of Ravenscar wasn't heartless enough to shake her awake and make her transcribe the rest of what he'd composed.

What the blazes was he supposed to do with her? Let her sleep on the table until she woke up?

No. With his luck, she'd tumble off and break her wrist. Then she'd be of no use to him. Better to summon a footman to haul her upstairs. His hand was on the bellpull when he suddenly hesitated. An almost painful sense of kinship stole through him, and he knew that Hannah Graystone would loathe anyone seeing this side of her. She would guard her vulnerabilities with the same fierceness with which Dante hid his own.

Dante chewed at the inside of his lip in indecision. Blast, she'd fallen asleep on the job. Why the devil should he trouble himself about guarding her pride?

Because he'd been the one who had driven her beyond her limits. He'd been the bastard who'd drained the color from her cheeks, put the dark smudges beneath her eyes. He'd been the one responsible for bowing down that proud head. He'd not so much as glanced at her since she'd stumbled in to begin work.

Hell, it never even occurred to him that she would be so exhausted.

There was only one thing to do.

Dante crossed to where Hannah sat and scooped her into his arms with astonishing care. She barely murmured, some sleep blurred words. "Don't be afraid. I'll keep you safe . . ."

Who the devil was she making that promise to? he wondered. But she said no more. Her dark head lolled back onto his shoulder, exposing the pale arch of her throat.

Dante looked down into her face, bemused. Damned if she didn't puzzle him. Intrigue him. He would never understand how a destitute, abandoned, drowned rat of a woman begging for a job could manage to have the aura of an empress—one with an iron hold on her kingdom.

No, she wasn't the soft, delicate kind of woman who made a man feel as if he could slay dragons in her name. Hannah Graystone seemed far more likely to snip the poor beast's scaly belly from stem to stern with her sewing shears, then turn like a fury on any man who dared try to come to her aid.

Any man? At least a man like the master of Ravenscar. He'd seen the contempt in her face when she'd looked at him. Not that he cared. God knew he should be used to such reactions by now. But he couldn't help wondering what had put that distrust in her eyes.

She made him as uncomfortable as the time he'd thrown a rock at a hive of bees and been stung until his eyes swelled shut.

Still, she felt so warm curled against him, her heat seeping into his chest, her breath soft upon his neck. And her hair, it brushed his cheek in wisps soft as silk.

Blast, what was he doing standing here like some moonstruck fool? He wasn't thinking of starting a liaison with her, for God's sake. Maybe he hadn't had a woman in his bed since he'd arrived at Ravenscar a year ago, but he was hardly depraved enough to seduce his servants. Doubtless Miss Graystone would find something more tender and private to snip than an imaginary dragon's belly if Austen dared to try it.

Grimacing, Dante carried her up the stairs, then

elbowed open her bedchamber door. Light from the fire flickered in the room, illuminating the big bed with its tumbled coverlets. And Austen was damned uncomfortable imagining all too clearly Hannah curled up in that nest of warmth, her hair tumbled, the hunted, haunted light gone from her eyes for just a little while.

How long had it been since she'd slept, safe and warm? Since she'd eaten her fill? Her body was too thin, her clothes too large, as if she'd been hungry for longer than Dante cared to imagine.

The insight irritated him, unnerved him. Hell, he'd heard the whispers. The footmen claimed with some pride that the master of Ravenscar could walk over the bones of his servants and not even hear them crunch beneath his boots.

Maybe it was true—not because Austen didn't give a damn, but because his head was stuffed so full of other things. He bloody well resented this irritating woman for making him hear her bones crunch. It made it a hell of a lot harder to keep tramping merrily on his way.

He was just lowering her down onto the coverlets when he suddenly glimpsed a shadowy form on the far side of the bed. Tumbled gold curls rested in the hollow of the pillow, the downy whiteness framing the face of a slumbering child.

What the blazes? Dante's eyes widened in astonishment. Where had it come from? Awareness rocketed through him. Blast, she *had* had a child with her that first night in the carriage circle. What was his name? Pops? Plimpton? Pip—that was it. Dante had forgotten all about him! And she had not mentioned a word.

What the devil had the woman been doing with the boy for the past few days? Locking him in the closet? Austen knew from experience there was nothing more dangerous than an idle lad with no one to mind him. But none of the bed hangings had been set afire, the carved oak tree on the bannister hadn't been hacked down with a hatchet, nor had the white laundry been dyed blue. Dante grimaced, remembering his own boyhood pranks.

He scowled. Damn, this situation was growing more infernally complicated by the minute. He lay Hannah down on the bed and prepared to pull the covers over her and beat a hasty retreat. Hell's bells, he knew she was bound up in her clothes, but he could hardly be expected to undress her, could he?

A smirk played about his lips as he imagined her reaction to waking up, wondering who had dressed her in her nightgown. Tempting as it was to poke at Miss Graystone's dignity, he would forgo the opportunity. She was sleeping like the dead. He doubted a few yards of muslin bunched up around her would keep her from her rest. More than a little irritated, he grasped the coverlets. But before he could pull them up, he glimpsed her worn boots, still caked with dried mud. He could hardly leave her in those infernal things.

Gritting his teeth, he leaned over to take them off.

He'd undressed women before. Removed far more interesting articles of clothing than these cracked, disreputable half boots. But no froth of lace, no silky corset, no sleek, low-cut bodice framing ripe breasts had ever made him feel so blasted uncomfortable in the process. It was as if he were a green boy attempting to peek under the skirts of a sleeping shepherdess.

With more haste than gentleness, he managed to tug the first boot off and cast it to the floor. But as he turned to rid her of the other one he froze, his gaze locked on the delicate arch and small toes. She wore no stockings; her foot was naked and pale and vulnerable.

God in heaven, what had she done to it? He cupped her foot in his hand, turning it into the light. The flickering fire glow mercilessly revealed a half-dozen places where giant blisters had been rubbed, then broken, all in various stages of healing. One wound on her smallest toe seemed to be festering.

Dante drew the remaining boot from her other foot as if it were made of spun glass. The skin beneath was even worse than the first one. How the devil had she managed not to limp? Why the blazes hadn't she said anything?

Pure bloody stubbornness, Austen would wager. If Hannah Graystone had been fed to the lions in a Roman arena, she would have chided the lions on poor table manners rather than give them the satisfaction of hearing her cry out.

The housekeeper had a chest full of remedies—but no, Hannah Graystone hadn't even had the common sense to ask for a handful of bandages.

Dante squirmed inwardly, understanding all too well why she hadn't asked for help. To admit any kind of weakness would raze Hannah Graystone's pride intolerably. Far better to suffer in silence, dignity intact, than to let anyone suspect your weaknesses. It was an impulse he'd surrendered to himself countless times.

What had driven such a woman to come to Ravenscar in the first place? How much had it cost her to ask for aid when he was downright certain she'd rather have starved quietly in the streets? She had done it for the boy.

Please . . . I beg you . . . her words in the rain-gilded carriage circle echoed in his memory. Dante could almost feel the way they had raked at her throat in a thorny lump, impossible to swallow yet far more difficult to endure than the burning pain that must have tormented her feet.

Suddenly the thought of her being even a little uncomfortable disturbed him. With deft fingers, he loosened the fastenings that marched down her ramrod-straight back, the cloth parting to reveal the slight bumps of spine that ridged the hollow between her shoulder blades. He stopped when the bodice gaped, soft and loose, drooping over one shoulder, falling away ever so slightly from her breasts. Velvety shadows dipped their fingers into the valley of her cleavage, accenting the fullness of the ivory globes.

The transformation from stiffly bound adversary to drowsy woman was so astonishing that for an instant, Austen couldn't help wondering what it would be like to loosen the rest of Hannah Graystone—the hair she kept knotted back so tightly it all but pulled her face awry, the tight secrecy in those gray eyes, the firmness in her lips.

But he shoved the thought away. With unaccustomed gentleness, Dante drew the coverlets up over Hannah. The boy whimpered in his sleep. At the tiny sound, Hannah rolled over, instinctively curving one arm about the child's tiny body.

"Hush . . . love. No one . . . ever hurt you . . . again . . ."

Again? What did she mean by that?

Dante glanced at the boy as if for the first time. There was a fragility about Pip—not of the bone, though he was small and thin—rather, there was a fragility of the spirit. One Hannah Graystone was determined to protect.

Words of comfort despite her own exhaustion, stubborn stoicism despite the wreck of her feet. Who was she, this woman who had come to Dante in the night?

He couldn't afford for her courage to squeeze so at his heart. God knew, he could barely carry the weight of his own misery.

Still, he couldn't stop himself from brushing a skein of dark red hair away from her cheek, the faint blotches of ink barely visible in the dim light. He hesitated, his fingertips lingering. He'd been wrong. There *was* something soft about Hannah Graystone—the skin that covered her obstinate chin felt like the petals of a late-summer rose, creamy smooth, sun warmed.

Austen's chest ached. It had been a long time since he'd touched anyone. Since anyone had touched him with more than the brisk necessity of his valet tying his cravat or brushing his hair.

There had been a time when he'd suffered his mother's hugs with gruff boyish indignance, when he'd grimaced in irritation at one of Maddy or Letty's kisses. He'd never suspected how precious they were, or that he would miss them so much.

Was Hannah missing someone, too? The man who had fathered Pip? The man who had shared her bed—

Blast, it was none of his affair. She was his servant, nothing more. He'd see she was well fed and housed, had a warm bed, and was paid for services rendered. That was the extent of his obligation. He was not required to learn the bosom secrets of the staff at Ravenscar House. God knew, he didn't want anyone pawing about in his own.

But he'd be damned if he was going to let the woman perish under his roof from some untended cut turned putrid. It was nothing more than selfish interest that was moving him, Dante assured himself. After all, the woman wouldn't do him any good if she were laid up sick. He'd suffered enough delays.

In the morning he would summon Miss Hannah Graystone to his study and they'd reach a blasted understanding, her pride be damned.

Austen stalked from the bedchamber, resolved to put Hannah Graystone and the boy from his mind until he caught a little sleep. But still he found no rest. The dying moon ghosted across dawn-pinked clouds in the rectangle of his own bedchamber window, wistful, solitary, and refusing to be comforted despite a sky filled with the faint smudges of stars.

He should have shut his eyes, shut out the image and the answering ache it awakened in his belly, but he didn't.

Not bothering to summon his valet, he stripped to his skin, then lay on his back atop the coverlets, sinewy arms folded beneath his head.

As always, his window had been left half open to let the scent of the moors and the keening of the wind creep into the chamber in its primitive lullaby. Yet tonight it only added to the hollow ache in his chest, the loneliness he tried to bury in a devil-may-care aura, and a restless energy that raked him even in sleep.

Only now, that energy was trapped in an odd stillness, like the calm just before the sea cast a storm across the wild lands.

Dante felt the soft brush of the breeze against his skin, felt the bittersweet kiss of the wind, his only lover for so very long.

He stared out at the lonely moon melting into the glow of day, and he wondered—who comforted Hannah Graystone when she cried out in the night?

Chapter

 4

She was late. Mist swirled about her bare feet like silver dust, the distant sound of music drawing her deeper into a labyrinth of lilies and heather. Hannah scooped up the skirts of a gown gossamer as fairy wings and ran, trying to find the source of that music, knowing she should be copying it down—the heavenly cascade of harp sounds mingled with a wild, restless keening that might have been the wind.

She had almost surrendered, sagged down by a druid oak twisted and gnarled from the beginning of time. But at that instant, she glimpsed a door carved in the tree's massive roots.

She stumbled down a curved stair, the music growing louder, sweeter, more passionate. It should have become shadowy, darker within the tree, but she found herself drawn into a chamber fashioned of light.

He was there—the master of Ravenscar. His broad shoulders bent over a pianoforte made of glass. His dark eyes blazed, commanding the wind and the sea and the moors, even Hannah's own heart to sing in a primitive language only he could understand.

And she knew she had to capture his sorcerer's melody, had to let it fill the empty places in her soul. She rushed to her little table in the corner, scooped up pen and ink and scrawled desperately, hopelessly, knowing that if she failed he would never forgive her. She would never forgive herself.

But the music seemed to sift between her fingers like silken bits of rainbow, impossible to hold.

She glanced up at the man sitting in a blaze of candlelight. His dark hair tumbled in a silky mane past his collar, the planes and hollows of his face almost unearthly in their raw masculine beauty, his eyes burning blue coals that seemed to pierce to her very soul. While his hands—they flashed and swept, rippled with strength and power as they coaxed a tempest of music from the heart of the instrument he played.

Yet as Hannah stared at his hands, she imagined them stroking her with the same primal fervor, fierce intensity, his eyes hot and wild with hunger. Her pen split, the nib broke, ink splattering across the page, her hands wet with it.

She tried to scrub the ink away with her other hand, but the stains spread up the cuff of the silvery spencer that molded to her breasts.

"You know I cannot bear spots of ink." Dante's voice, low and rough above the sound of the music, his long, sensitive fingers grasping her wrist. He turned it over to expose the buttons that fastened the cuff across the soft underside where her pulse beat.

His fingers worked the tiny loops over buttons like drops of silver, scattering fairy dust in their wake. Callused, sensitive, hot, his touch sent rivers of fire up her arm as the fabric fell away. He unfastened the other cuff as well, then slowly, ever so slowly, dipped his fingers into the shadowy hollow between her breasts, loosening the buttons that held the spencer together.

The tight-fitting jacket spread as the buttons popped free, her breasts seeming to swell, to strain beneath the skimming of his fingertips. It was as if she were naked beneath that touch despite the fragile bodice of her gown, hidden and creased beneath the silvery fabric.

The music swelled around them, feverish, wild with emotion. He conjured up music from within Hannah's own soul, his hands not even touching the pianoforte's keys. The instrument was alive like the light in Dante's incredible eyes, alive with heat and fire and passion as he stripped the spencer away.

His gaze swept down her wrinkled bodice, and he dipped one long finger into a little puddle of spilled ink on the table. He took that finger and, eyes pulsing with night blue fire, he pressed the ink-dampened tip into the fabric bare inches above her nipple.

"Wh–what are you doing?" Hannah stammered, appalled at the wildness within her that wanted him to touch that finger against her bare skin.

"You've managed to blot your bodice," he murmured.

"No! You did it! I—"

"Shh, I warned you I couldn't be distracted when I am composing."

"No! You don't understand . . . the music, I can't . . . can't write . . ." But her protest melted into a sibilant shimmer of violins summoned up from the very air. He was too close, the smell of heather and wind and leather filling her with his own moor-swept scent. His breath caressed her cheek, warm with promises of things she'd never dared dream of.

The lacings of her gown fell away beneath his big hands.

"Forgive me, Hannah." His breath was hot against her nape. "I have to do this."

The thought of this man needing her, wanting her with such urgency made a hard knot of desire form in her belly.

"Hannah, it's the only way . . . I won't be distracted from my purpose. The ink blots . . ."

The ink blots? Of course, Hannah grimaced with dark

humor. She'd been mad to think a man like Austen Dante would want her. It was the ink blots on her gown he wanted to be rid of. She was one of the few women in the world who would be less distracting to a man of Dante's fierce passion when she was undressed.

Those big hands, so deft at the pianoforte, so long and dark and sensitive, slid her gown down her shoulders. Hannah caught it against her breasts with her hands, fear echoing through her that he might be able to see the treacherous emotions that lay hidden beneath the cloth—a woman's longing, a woman's need, shame in aching for something she knew was impossible.

But Dante's gaze locked on to her spread fingers, where they crushed the cloth against her own breasts. When he raised his eyes, wild heat ignited. She was drowning in eyes like lightning, sizzling with intensity, those sensual male lips parted with hunger. Hunger for her? Hannah Gray? Impossible! She must be insane. Then why was she loosening her hold on the folds of cloth she clutched? Letting the gown float down? Her breasts strained against the constraint of her short corset, then her undergarments evaporated as if burned away by the hunger in Dante's eyes.

"I told you I wouldn't be turned away from my purpose." He moved toward her, hands outstretched. Hannah closed her eyes, breathless, waiting for the first touch, her imagination filled with hot kisses, eager caresses, all the things she'd been certain she'd never have.

Dante's hands closed about the fragile arch of her throat, gentle, so gentle, thumbs pressing against the pulse point.

Hannah's eyes flew open in alarm. He glared down at her from a pool of mist, eyes glittering as if he would strip away every pretense, down to her very skin.

"I know everything," he said with silky menace. "You left me no choice."

At that instant shrieks split the air, the shrieks she'd

heard in a hundred nightmares. Pip! She saw him lost beyond the druid tree, frozen with terror, imprisoned in Mason Booth's arms.

A scream rose in Hannah's throat, a terrible, silent scream stifled by Dante's hands. She kicked, struggled, as the chamber of light melted away, waves of darkness threatening to consume her.

A hammering set off in her head, loud, so insistent it shattered everything. Hannah bolted upright, horror still suffocating her as her eyes flew open. No—she wasn't in some mystical chamber at all! Brilliant sunlight poured through the windows of the bedchamber she and Pip shared.

Yet her gown was gaping, sliding off her shoulders, just like in her dream, and her feet were bare. How had she gotten here? She closed her eyes, trying to remember returning to the room, but in every wisp of memory, the music room still swirled in sleepy circles around her, the scent of ink, the grit of exhaustion filling all her senses, while the man plunged deeper and deeper into the tormented flow of his music.

The hammering came again, and Hannah's heart stopped as she glanced beside her. Pip was gone! Panic engulfed her.

"Miss Graystone? Miss Graystone?" came a tentative voice with a Cornish burr.

Hannah stumbled out of bed. Clutching her gown against her front, she went to open the door a crack.

An apple-cheeked maid peeked in, wisps of red hair escaping from a mobcap that sat slightly askew. Hannah's heart sank when she saw the urgency in the little maid's face.

"Ah, there you are, miss," the girl said with some relief. "I'm sorry to wake you, but you're to be summoned downstairs. The master is in one of his moods, I fear. Been snapping and snarling all morning."

"Morning? It can't be . . ."

"No, miss. It's afternoon, I think. Don't know what

the master is so stirred up about, but I heard him muttering. Said he's going to get to the bottom of something once and for all."

Hannah's blood ran cold.

"If I were you, miss, I'd take a bit of advice. Tell the master whatever it is he wants to know. He gets in a rare temper when anyone crosses him."

"My . . . My Pip, he's gone—"

"Don't be worryin' about him. Scooped him up early, just like the master ordered, so's he wouldn't wake you. He's been stayin' with me while I put some of the chambers to rights. Still in the Red Room, he is. Found an old Noah's ark on one of the shelves."

"You—you took Pip?"

The girl flashed a cheery smile. "Just borrowed him for a little while."

Hannah nibbled at her lower lip, relief warring with the need to scoop the boy up, sneak away from Ravenscar House while there was still time. Before Mr. Dante learned . . .

Learned what? The voice of reason intruded. There was little chance the man could've discovered the truth. It was only the dream that had upset her so much, thrown her off balance. She had to remain logical, sensible, if she were to keep Pip safe. She couldn't be driven to wild flight by nothing more than a nightmare.

"Ah, I understand, miss. You're worrying about the little one. Don't. I know all about 'em. I already helped him get hisself dressed and scrub behind his ears. Had a whole bundle of sisters and brothers—eight of 'em— when I left home. Miss 'em something awful. But I came to work hoping to help my little brother Freddy go to school. Bright as a new button, Freddy is. Too smart by half to break his back in the mines."

Hannah started to fasten up her gown, then glimpsed herself in the mirror. Rumpled and creased, her hair wild. The thought of facing Mr. Dante in such condition made her feel intolerably vulnerable. She went to the armoire and took out a gown of dark green, somewhat worn at the elbows. But it buttoned up to her throat, and at this moment, she wanted to cover as much of herself as possible from Dante's probing gaze.

"Let me help you," the maid offered with an eager grin.

"No, you don't have to—"

"It'll be fun. I can pretend I'm a lady's maid—that's what I always wanted to be. Not that there'll ever be a lady about Ravenscar House. The master is handsome as a devil, but his spirit's too restless to tame."

The girl took over for Hannah's shaking hands. The last subject Hannah wanted to discuss was the insufferable Mr. Dante's restless anything—the adjective called up too many images of those dream-spun hands and the response they'd stirred in some hidden part of her.

She groped to change the subject. "Thank you for offering to look after Pip. He can be shy—"

"They all can, my mum says," the girl observed, bundling her into the fresh gown with almost dizzying speed. "Just have to tease 'em out of it, an' make 'em feel all cozy and safe. There you are." She shook out the hem, and Hannah gaped, astounded.

"Doesn't take me long, that's for certain. All those brothers and sisters wiggling like puppies—learned to dress 'em quick. My name's Becca."

"Thank you, Becca. I'm . . ."

"Hannah. I know. And you're so nervous that if you was a horse you'd be twitchin' your tail. Don't worry about your boy. You just go on down to the master. I think he's had the blue blazes of a night from the look of him."

Hannah flushed, unnerved by the vividness of her dream. The blue blazes of a night? It seemed they had both had one. And this afternoon promised to be worse.

After all, she'd never faced a man who had undressed her before—even in a dream.

Heaven's sake, it wasn't as if he really had! Hannah

brought herself up sternly. The mere idea of *the exaulted master* lowering himself to such a task was ridiculous.

After knotting back her hair, satisfied with her appearance, she went downstairs. Gritting her teeth, she measured her stride, refusing to let herself rush.

Elisabeth had always claimed that if Hannah had been Anne Boleyn she would have run to the block, laid her head down, and demanded that the headsman move his axe. But Austen Dante was not a foe to be underestimated. She would have to be careful, very careful, not to betray her fears. For if she did she'd focus all that keen intelligence on herself, bring down the restless, probing light in those azure eyes.

She hesitated at his study door, then knocked.

She wasn't certain what she expected when he summoned her to enter, but as she swung open the door it wasn't anger or irritation that marked that handsome face. There was something odd in his expression, almost a trifle sheepish for just a heartbeat. Then it was gone, in its place a terrifyingly fierce resolve.

Hannah braced herself. "You said you wanted me." Such innocent words. Yet hot embarrassment surged into her cheeks as she remembered her ridiculous dream, those moments when hunger had changed his eyes to midnight.

Dante's gaze locked with hers, relentless, implacable as a wall of granite. His voice was terrifyingly soft. "What the devil are you doing with that child?"

Hannah's heart plunged like a cold stone. Her head spun and she gripped the back of a carved gilt chair to keep her knees from buckling. "I . . . don't know what you mean." Her voice sounded like a stranger's—thin and thrumming with fear she prayed Dante would not detect.

"The question is clear enough. I've been working with you for two days now—days, and long into the night. And in all that time, I haven't seen a glimpse of the boy. I haven't heard so much as a whisper. I asked my servants, and they claim they haven't seen him either. It's like living with an accursed ghost. He disappears, vanishes, almost as if he's hiding."

Panic pulsed thick and hot in Hannah's throat. "Pip . . . is not accustomed to strangers."

A bark of grim laughter breached the abominable man's lips. "That, Miss Graystone, is an understatement. I didn't even remember the boy existed until this morning. Surprised the living hell out of me when I went to lay you down in your bed and found him there."

"You--you were the one who . . ." She couldn't even put it into words, it was too preposterous. The arrogant, thoughtless, selfish master of Ravenscar carrying her up the stairs, tucking her into bed?

Alarm jolted through her with even more power as she remembered her drooping gown, unfastened, spilling away from the vulnerable curve of her breast.

Was it possible that *he* had unfastened it?

"Miss Graystone, from the look of you, you weren't merely strolling along looking for a job when you turned up on my doorstep. You were damned desperate. It's a miracle you could walk with your feet torn up so badly."

Humiliation pierced through her as she remembered the ugliness of countless blisters and all that they revealed. What lie would he believe? Better to tell a small piece of the truth.

"We hadn't had shelter in weeks. Little food."

"It doesn't surprise me. There is no creature so thin and worn as one who is running away."

Hannah reeled inwardly, trying to keep her expression from betraying her terror. "Why would you think I was running away?"

There was something unreadable in those storm blue eyes. "I know the signs all too well. Besides, you spoke in your sleep before I put you to bed."

God in heaven, what had she said? A montage of scenes spilled into her head—vivid splashes capturing her most terrible fears. Had she betrayed any part of the truth?

"What did I . . . say?"

"You told the boy not to be afraid." There was something surprisingly gentle in the timbre of Austen Dante's voice. "That no one would hurt him. Hannah." It was her name, just her name. The sound of it shouldn't have made her heart leap. "Who are you afraid of?"

"No one! I . . . I must have been babbling in my sleep. I do it all the time."

"For as long as you stay at Ravenscar House you are safe."

Her pulses fluttered and for an instant she wondered what it would be like to feel safe again, to share her fears and her burdens and secrets for just a little while.

She wondered what it would be like to be sheltered under the protection of this man. The thought pierced her. Thunder in heaven, had she lost her reason? Hadn't she learned the grimmest of lessons about how perilous it was to trust anyone stronger, more powerful than she was? Lord, he was dangerous to her, to Pip . . . with his recklessness, wildness, temper. She must never forget it.

"Thank you for your offer, sir, but Pip and I are well used to taking care of ourselves."

"If that is the case, you were doing a damn rotten job of it."

Hannah recoiled as if he had slapped her.

"The boy was all but stricken with lung fever when you arrived here," Dante snapped. "You were both half starved. You wouldn't have lasted three more days if I hadn't been fool enough to take you in."

It was the truth, scathing, infuriating. Hannah struggled for inner balance. "I would have come up with some solution," she insisted.

"Is that so? I'm not accustomed to being defied, Miss Graystone. I asked you a question. Who are you afraid of? The boy's father?"

She couldn't stop her gaze from leaping to his in utter panic. His eyes narrowed. "Tell me the truth, for God's sake. I can't help you unless you do."

Heavens, the temptation—it tormented her. But she didn't dare spin out her story. Still, Austen Dante would not be denied. She could see it in the stubborn set of his chin, the grim cast to his mouth. There was only one way to evade him—tell him part of the truth, just enough to satisfy him for a little while.

"You ask why Pip is afraid. That much I can tell you. His father was . . . the cruellest man I've ever known. He enjoyed tormenting . . . anyone weaker." Her voice quavered with hatred and despair and loss.

"He hurt the boy?"

"All I can say is that Pip has reason to be wary, to be afraid. It was bred in his bones, the one lesson he learned from the time he was yet a babe."

Dante was watching her, his eyes seething with outrage, all the more unnerving because it was so quiet, so restrained. A muscle ticked in his jaw. "And you, Hannah. Did that sadistic bastard hurt you as well?"

"More than I ever believed possible." The words tumbled out before she knew it, ripping away pretense, dragging her through jagged waves of grief. Humiliation stung her cheeks as she saw Dante's eyes narrow with intensity, that odd way he had of stripping her down to her very soul with just a glance.

Hating herself for revealing even a glimpse of her own vulnerability, Hannah turned away, fighting against the sensation the only way she knew how—with fire and temper, crushing softer, more tender emotions.

"What happened between me and Pip's father is none of your concern. I did not ask for your interference. It seems to me you should be attending to your own problems."

"What problems are those?"

"I'd hardly call you an expert in family relations. Your own can't be too exemplary at the moment."

In a heartbeat the light in his eyes shifted, something shadowy, wary, unnerving flickering in his gaze. "Miss Graystone, you know nothing about my family."

"I know that you have a mountain of letters on that desk from your mother and sisters. I know that you haven't even bothered to open them."

Those aristocratic cheekbones stained dull red, his jaw knotting. "I've been rather preoccupied of late. They hardly expect me to answer."

"I'm certain that will be a great comfort to them. Do you have any idea how fortunate you are? It's obvious that they love you, miss you."

"Madam, you forget yourself."

"No. You've forgotten them. They must want to hear from you desperately to write so often, especially since you're far too busy to bother dashing off a reply. They must run to get the post every day, hoping to receive some sort of letter from you."

She could see him stiffen for an instant, then his shoulders rolled in an indolent shrug. "If they do they're the most singularly optimistic people in Norfolk. Of course, hope springs eternal—especially in Letty. The girl never did have much sense."

A smile, iron hard yet devilish, curved that sensual mouth. "Ah, Miss Graystone, I can hear your teeth grinding over there. Best let out whatever you have to say before you explode."

"I have nothing to say. It's not my place."

"It might not be your place, but I'd wager you have plenty to say. You don't think much of me, do you? A woman of intuition."

"I don't think about you at all."

Hannah tensed, her memory filling with the images her dream had conjured. Disturbing images of a man of flame and passion, muscular shoulders, and callused hands, fingertips dipping between her breasts to unfasten tiny buttons, smooth the cloth out of the way, unveiling her to his gaze.

"Come, Miss Graystone," Dante goaded as if he'd seen the shameful scenes in her mind. "Be honest. I didn't take you for a coward."

She raised her chin, refusing to be shaken. "I learned early not to value the gift with the prettiest wrapping above all others. It's what is inside that really matters."

Dante gave a predatory laugh. "And just what do you think is inside me, Miss Graystone?"

"It's not my place to say."

"I command you to. The truth."

Thunderation if he didn't deserve to have her tell him! "You are arrogant, lazy about tending to other people's feelings, and you're vain. I see occasional flashes of brilliance in you, but it doesn't matter. You have no more value than a bright stone at the bottom of a stream, useful for nothing."

"You cast out a hard judgment, madam."

"You commanded that I tell the truth. You're selfish when you have had everything poured into your hands—wealth, position, power. You won't even bother reading letters written by your family."

"Ah, so it's back to that again, is it?"

Pain and loss raked Hannah, images of her sisters' faces swimming before her—little Theophania with her wooden sword and her tangled hair, Harriet forever carting about her art supplies, dreaming of studying with a French drawing master, and Elisabeth, beautiful and glowing and stubborn. God in heaven, what she would give to hear from them again. Just a few scrawled lines to carry about in her pocket, to read over and over again whenever the homesickness bit too deep.

But it was impossible to wish for such a treasure. As impossible as looking upon their beloved faces one more time. Lord, how she'd taken them for granted the past years, even felt a little burdened by their dependence on her. But now . . .

"Nothing is forever, sir," she said. "The day may come when no more letters arrive. When there is no one left to send a reply to, no matter how desperately you want to. Then, I promise you, you will wish you'd taken some of your precious time to write them."

"My time is my own, Miss Graystone. I hired you to write music, not meddle in my private affairs." Yet he turned away, shrugged. "However, if you are so worried about what my letters contain, you may read them to me. I'm afraid my eyes are strained from the late nights of composing."

Thanking God that she'd at least succeeded in turning his attention away from her past, Hannah crossed to the desk and took up a handful of the most recent letters.

Breaking the seal, she went to hold the paper to the light. Then she began to read a rose-scented missive written in a delicate, feminine hand.

> *Dearest Austen,*
> *You unspeakable rogue! You must come home for my wedding. My happiness cannot be complete without my dearest, most wonderful brother there to tease me. I am so deliriously happy, and Mama is in her glory planning the most beautiful wedding there ever was. She does not say anything, but I know she misses you even more dreadfully than I do. Sometimes I catch her crying. Perhaps I should not have told you that, but I vow I will stoop to the most shameless coercion in order to see you again. Please, Austen, for me?*

There was such innocent hope in the lines, such bright splashes of humor tempered with intelligence and the unmistakable tang of loneliness. Hannah's chest tightened. She finished, glancing up at the man. He had slouched his long, lean frame into a chair angled a little way from his desk. He'd settled his crossed legs atop that surface, his boot heels crushing a mound of papers.

He leaned his head back, regarding a painting of a pack of hunting hounds, his features so neutral Hannah wanted to kick the chair legs out from under him. How could he be so unfeeling?

"Ah, one can always count on Letty for a bout of dramatics. If things don't work out with this Fitzherbert fellow, she might have a career on the stage. Now that you've begun, you might as well read the next one. That way I can feed them to the fire and clean off my desk."

Hannah ground her teeth, but she plowed through the other letters as well. A family sprang to life in the words, so vividly she could almost see them, felt as if she knew them. A sister named Madeline who seemed to be about fourteen years old grieved over the death of an old dog named Puggsly, confiding that she'd buried him in the churchyard after everyone was asleep. And if she went to hell for it, she didn't care as long as Puggsly went to heaven. Though everyone was trying to be kind, Madeline was certain they didn't understand. No one would until Austen came home.

The girl's longing seemed so at odds with everything Hannah knew of Austen Dante it astonished her. Of course, she'd seen more than one little sister shamelessly adore a tyrannical, unworthy elder brother.

But it was the writings of Dante's mother that cut straight to Hannah's heart. Simple letters filled with the daily workings of the household, bright bits of gossip, charming insights, words that did little to conceal a mother's sorrow. Not once did she join her daughters' pleas begging her son to come home. Somehow that made it hurt all the more.

She merely asked if he was eating well enough—he always dashed out without dinner unless someone dragged him back by his collar. She hoped he was getting enough rest, and not riding his horses too wild. She told him she was using the pen wiper he'd made her for Christmas the year he was twelve. And she sent him her love, but not just in her words.

It was as if she had layered it over her letters with

every pen stroke, pressed it into the page with fingers Hannah sensed ached with the need to stroke Austen Dante's dark mane of hair the way she had when he was a child.

Determinedly cheerful, amusing, this was not the kind of mother who would take to her bed for a month with a megrim, bellowing out orders in a voice stentorian enough to give her daughters headaches.

She was the kind of mother who would soothe her children's hurts instead of demand they comfort her. The kind of mother with the courage to let her children fly free, no matter how much she wanted to tug them back into her arms for just a little while.

The woman who had penned these letters would never make use of that staple of motherly armaments—guilt. She would never demand that Austen Dante return to her, no matter how much she might wish to.

God in heaven, if Hannah had only had a mother like this, someone she could turn to when trouble had consumed her, she wouldn't be in this predicament.

No, such thoughts would do her no good. They would only make her bitter. Far more wise to remember the good facets of her own mother. The mother she loved though she couldn't lean on. The mother who had once been laughing and lovely and gay, before they'd brought the love of her life home crushed and broken, in the back of a farmer's cart.

Even so, Hannah still wanted to shake Austen Dante until his teeth rattled for his thoughtlessness in causing such a courageous lady pain.

She finished the last of the missive, a farewell so full of tenderness Hannah's eyes filled with tears.

The chamber was quiet, deathly quiet as the words faded away. He hadn't moved at all, merely sat, turned into the shadows, tapping a bright polished rock in his fingers against the desk in a rhythm that was slowly driving Hannah insane. Where had the stone come from, anyway? It was so incongruous in comparison to the rest of the chamber's elegant trappings. Somehow it made her even more angry.

"I don't suppose you can be troubled to write your mother back—just to let her know you haven't broken your fool neck by now," Hannah snapped.

Dante shoved himself to his feet and gestured to the chair. "By all means, if it will make you happy, Miss Graystone. I'll dictate a letter and you can write it down. There are writing supplies in the middle drawer."

She wanted to tell him to go to the devil, but the memory of his mother, wistful, waiting for a letter that never came, made Hannah swallow her irritation for once. She rummaged in the desk getting out what she needed, preparing to write.

Austen strode to the window and stood with his back to the room, staring out at the sweep of lawn that led to the untamed expanse of moors.

> *Dear Mother,*
>
> *Congratulations on your latest achievement! Astonished to hear you have managed to get Letty betrothed at last. Unfortunately, I do not dare come to the ceremony myself. You know what a muck I always make of things.*
>
> *Doubtless, I would tell Fitzherbert how bad her temper is or how much she spends at the dressmaker's and the man would flee for his life. Besides, I already promised Fredrick Walstone that I would come hunting with some of the fellows from Cambridge up in Scotland.*
>
> *Draw on my banker for whatever you need to get the midget a present. You know what she likes.*
>
> *Yours in a tearing hurry,*

Dante turned toward the woman sitting at the desk. He didn't know what he expected to see—but it wasn't the fiery rage that shimmered about her like some unholy aura. She looked wounded, furious. And in that instant, all he wanted was to escape the accusation in her gaze.

"You may go now. Leave the letter on the desk," he said with a wave of his hand. "I can sign it myself."

"I wouldn't want you to strain yourself from the exertion." Hannah rose, holding the page as if it might turn into a snake at any moment. She turned, walked to where a fire blazed on the grate. In a heartbeat she crumpled the missive into a ball and hurled it into the flames.

Dante made an involuntary lunge toward the flame-licked page. "What the devil did you do that for?" he roared.

"You hired me to write music," she said in accents filled with loathing. "Not to break your mother's heart."

Dante turned away. "Breaking my mother's heart would be redundant, Miss Graystone," he said. "I've already seen to it myself."

Chapter

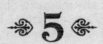

Blast the woman, Austen Dante berated himself grimly. He should have known better than to give Hannah Graystone a carving knife and let her slice away at wounds no one else knew existed.

Every day since he'd left Austen Park, he'd faced the stack of letters from his family. They had trailed him across the continent, to Rome and Venice, Switzerland and Spain. Wherever he tried to drown out the clambering of his own guilt.

For years, the pain had been so great he'd taken them, unopened, and flung them into the fire, watching as the wax seals bubbled and burned, the delicate script of his mother and sisters consumed by hungry flames. It had been like flinging his own heart into the grate, but he'd had no choice except to do it. For it had been worse, far worse, to face those missives day after day, silent crushing accusations, testimonies of how badly he had hurt them, was hurting them still.

There had been times he'd almost opened the letters, just to run his fingers across the inked lines, to feel closer to the people he'd loved and yet disappointed. He'd wondered what the letters contained, felt a ravenous hunger just to hear tiny snippets of life he knew they'd carry—things he'd taken for granted for so long. Things he never would again.

But he'd known in his soul that hearing the letters would be both joy and torture, that the words would test his resolve, plumb the depths of his guilt. That they would bring everything flooding back—that horrendous day when he'd left them—he'd vowed forever.

He paced to his desk, scooping up the polished stone that lay there, glimmering with the luster of a thousand summer days. A soft, lovely rose color, it glowed like crystal, smooth and cool as a rose blossom encased in ice. A fool's gift it had been. But he'd been so damned delighted with it—the perfect gift for his mother on her birthday.

She'd smiled in gratitude at the lovely laces and pearls his father had given her, and she'd praised the bits of stitchery his sisters had offered. But none of them had understood what delighted her soul more than Austen had. Odd butterflies captured in bottles, rare, lovely plants pressed, roots and all, beneath a stack of books, stones to be examined and studied, to research in the scientific journals she spent so many hours poring over.

But he'd never gotten a chance to give it to her. It had still been tucked in his pocket, wrapped in a handkerchief, when he'd bolted away from Austen Park that grim morning. He turned the smooth stone in his fingers, a symbol of all he'd lost that day. Everything bright and beautiful, innocent and new. A youth's wonder, a boy's delight, sacrificed for a man's bitter choices.

Choices that seemed even more grim now, with Letty's excited prattle about her marriage to a man Austen had never met, Madeline's grief over the death of the dog she'd adored. Austen should have been there to rake this Fitzherbert over the coals, to make bloody sure the oaf was worthy of his little sister's hand. He should have been there to comfort Maddy. He should have been the one sneaking into the churchyard to bury her beloved pet. The pup that had been his gift to her the last Christmas they had spent together as a family.

And his mother—God, her courage, and her sorrow . . . he could feel it, sense it—and how much she missed him.

Damn Hannah Graystone to hell! He'd summoned her down here to answer questions he'd had every right to ask, what with her living beneath his roof. But she'd evaded him neatly as a practiced swordsman, turning his own words against him, dragging out memories, emotions, guilt. Why had he let her goad him into listening to those letters? Why had he allowed her to conjure up voices from his boyhood, Letty's mischief, Maddy's headstrong ways and fierce devotion, and his mother's hidden sorrow? Sorrow he'd put in her loving heart.

He'd hoped against all reason, waited with his heart thundering and his gut knotting for the letter he knew wasn't there—a few scrawled lines from the one person who hadn't tried to contact him in all this time.

No, there hadn't been so much as a whisper from his father. But he hadn't expected one. He understood Joseph Dante far too well—the fierce pride bred in his Italian blood—that was the one thing Austen had inherited from his father—that and the dubious gift or curse of his music.

Dante slammed the polished stone back on the desk with a snarl. Damnation, what a fool he was! Who would have imagined he'd still be waiting, hoping for some word from his father after so long? That that was why he hadn't been able to fling the letters into the fire?

That he'd hoped for what? Absolution?

Jamming his fists in his pockets, Austen stalked to the window. Thunderation, this wasn't helping—it would be so much easier if he could dismiss his father as a cruel bastard, the way Hannah had her son's father.

Dante closed his eyes, remembering the boy lying so still and helpless in the big bed. Forgotten. At least that was one thing that had come from his confrontation with Hannah—he'd discovered some of the reason for the child's wariness. It buried itself like a thorn under Austen's skin, disturbing him, needling him.

Blast this strange obsession with discovering the secrets in Hannah Graystone's eyes. Why the devil should it matter to Austen Dante, master of Ravenscar, where the woman had come from? He'd had countless assistants, so many he barely remembered their names. But this woman, with her determined chin, her embattled eyes, and her love for the frightened, pale little boy, stirred up some answering stubbornness in Austen's own chest.

He'd always hated being thwarted once he'd set his mind on something. That was all this was. She piqued his temper, goaded that somewhat spoiled boy he had been. But he'd developed an almost uncanny skill for getting his own way, and this would be no different.

If Hannah Graystone wouldn't give the information he sought, then the boy would. He'd distract her somehow, get her to help Becca with some task. And then he'd have the boy fetched down.

Guilt nudged Austen at the thought of using the child in such a fashion, but he brushed it aside. It was the woman's own fault that he had to resort to such measures. Besides, he'd make damned certain the boy would have some fun in the process.

A resolute smile tipped the corner of his lips as he summoned a footman to carry out his orders. It might take some effort to win Pip's confidence, Austen mused, but he was up to the challenge.

And, as everyone knew, there was one sure way to any red-blooded boy's heart.

Four hours later, Dante leaned against the wall near the front door, watching the stairway from beneath half-lowered lids. He tapped one doeskin-clad thigh with a silver-headed riding crop, trying to stem his impatience.

Granted, he'd never been known for his patience, but that didn't explain the odd kind of excitement thrumming in his chest as he glanced out a window to where a groom led two horses around the carriage circle. One was Dante's own stallion, Fire Eater; the other, a sleek gelding with a coat like liquid sunset and a proud spirit that should delight the boy.

Austen gave a nod of satisfaction. Hell, he would have committed murder to be able to ride such a fine animal when he was Pip's age. The plan would have been perfect if not for the ramrod-straight figure striding toward the house.

Atticus. Blast the man, he was becoming as pesky as a swarm of bees. "Austen, I'm thankful I caught you before you rode out. I delivered all the supplies to their respective sites. But there seems to be a problem at the experimental cistern. Enoch Digweed claims I purchased the wrong weight of copper."

Why the devil did it make him so uncomfortable having Atticus here now? He didn't have to answer to his steward for his behavior. "I'll worry about it later. I'm busy at present."

Atticus stared, taken aback. "Too busy to discuss difficulties with the cistern? Is there some sort of emergency I should be apprised of? I am, of course, at your service."

"No emergency. I'm going riding."

"Riding," Atticus echoed, his gaze flicking to the horse. If Dante had claimed he was about to straddle the sun and take it jumping, Atticus couldn't have looked more unnerved. "Sir—" he began, but stopped as Simmons strode from the house.

Simmons stopped before Dante and bowed. "Pardon me, sir, but you wanted me to report on the business at hand as soon as everything was arranged. I've instructed Miss Graystone to help Becca in the Rose Withdrawing Room. It faces out over the gardens, so she should be able to see nothing from there. Louis has gone to the bedchamber to summon the boy as you ordered."

"Boy?" Atticus echoed, his brow wrinkling in inquiry.

"Miss Graystone has a son I forgot about until early this morning. I intend to take him riding."

"A servant's child?"

"And you don't approve of it, do you, you old curmudgeon?"

"Forgive me, but I must urge caution. It's hardly fitting. . . . I mean, showing any sort of favoritism might be dangerous to the harmony of the estate." Atticus flushed.

"Ah, but that's the beauty of it, Atticus. Maintaining the 'harmony of the estate' is your problem. I can do as I please and be damned."

Atticus stared at him, and Dante sensed the old man was groping for some argument to use against him. "It seems you might have asked permission of the child's mother before—"

"Before taking him out to get his neck broken jumping over fences with me? Give me a little credit for sense. Sunset may look like a demon, but he's gentle as a lamb. The boy will adore him. Besides, Atticus, it's hardly your way to run about preaching propriety. Aren't you always telling me a wealthy landowner should be able to do as he pleases?"

"Yes! But what I meant was that you shouldn't be saddled with mundane tasks of running the estate. That you should leave them to me. That way you'll be free to pursue whatever pleasures you desire."

"Today I desire the pleasure of riding with Pip. Now, if you'll be so good as to take yourself off to do some of these mundane tasks, I will meet with you later."

Atticus stiffened. Evidently Dante had pricked at the old steward's pride.

"As you wish." With a curt bow, he turned and strode away.

Within moments Louis approached, leading the way

down the risers, but the boy wasn't clinging to his hand as Dante had expected. Pip's shoulders were rigid, his face pale, and his eyes were huge with nervousness. He glanced back over his shoulder, as if he expected his mother to come charging to his rescue.

Austen felt the tiniest sting of conscience, but he pushed himself away from the wall and strode toward the boy with a winning smile.

"Thank you for joining me," he said with a bow. "It occurred to me that we haven't been properly introduced. Do you know who I am?"

The child swallowed hard. "You're the Mad Bastard of Raben-Scars." The words were barely out of his mouth when the boy blanched. "Oh, no. Nanna says I'm not s'posed to say it out loud, even though you are one."

Austen chuckled, more amused than he would've believed possible. "It seems blunt tongues run in your family, young Master Pip. But perhaps you shouldn't call me that aloud. After all, we wouldn't want the servants to start using it, now would we?"

"Yes, sir. I–I mean, no, sir. Now that we've been 'troduced, I think I had better get upstairs before Nanna can't find me."

"Nanna? You call your mother Nanna?"

The boy looked even more stricken. After a moment, he stammered. "I'm not berry good getting names right sometimes. I said it when I was berry little and couldn't talk so good, an' I can never remember to change it even though I'm big now."

"I see."

The boy looked ready to bolt.

"Wait. I have a task for you." Dante's hand flashed out and he gently grabbed the boy's arm. He was stunned at how thin it was, and disturbed by the way Pip flinched. Yet the boy stood his ground with a quiet resignation in his features. Bloody hell, it was as if the lad were facing an executioner.

An odd sense of kinship echoed through Austen,

memories of another boy standing just so, as if waiting for a blow—a blow that never came. Not a physical one, but a blow he still feared with a child's gut-clenching terror nonetheless.

Bile rose in Dante's throat at the knowledge that he was the one causing the boy's distress. Best to show Pip the delights to come as quickly as possible to put him at ease. "I was thinking you'd best make yourself useful as long as you are staying at Ravenscar House. After all, everyone here earns his supper."

"I–I'm not berry good at much. Papa always said . . ." The child choked back the words, eyeing Austen with alarm.

"You'll handle this task like a little man," Dante assured him briskly.

The words made Pip square his narrow shoulders, suck in a deep breath. And Dante felt a swift stab of compassion for the child. He lay one hand against the child's narrow back.

"You'll do fine, boy. I'm certain of it. Come with me." The boy trailed reluctantly along in Austen's wake as he exited the house.

"I thought that you could see to Sunset. I have been quite busy of late and haven't had the proper time to exercise him."

Pip turned his small face skyward, the breeze wisping his soft curls about his cheeks. "Nanna told me a myth once 'bout a man who dragged the sun 'round in his chariot."

"My powers are not quite that far-reaching. Sunset is a horse."

"A . . . a horse?"

Dante had expected a reaction from the boy, but this passed beyond reason. Pip's eyes all but consumed his pinched face.

Most boys were stuck atop horses before they could walk. Hadn't the poor little wretch ever ridden before? Well, he'd learn quickly enough. Unexpected pleasure stirred in Austen at the thought of teaching this boy about the sport he loved so well.

Best to get him astride the beast before he had too much time to judge the length of a fall from the horse's back to the turf. If Austen knew anything about boys, Pip would be crowing with glee before ten minutes were out.

Dante signaled with his riding crop, and the groom led the beasts forward. He grasped his own animal's reins. "Withers, help young Pip mount up at once."

"P—please," Pip stammered, "I . . ."

"You'll do fine, boy. Underneath all that fire, Sunset is gentle as a lamb. Do as you're told, lad."

Dante swung up, then turned to see Withers lifting the boy into the saddle. Pip looked as if he were mounting a Hydra. His face washed gray, his eyes pools of terror.

Dante frowned. Was it possible he'd made a mistake pushing the boy? But he had no time to ponder his decision. At that instant, a terrible rasping sound erupted from the child's chest. Sick horror jolted through Dante.

"What the devil?" Austen exclaimed in alarm. "Withers, take him down—damnation—something's wrong!"

The groom tried to comply, but the boy's fingers were twined in the horse's mane like grappling hooks, even the gentle Sunset was spooked by the terror pulsing through his rider's small body. The gelding danced sideways, tossing its head, tugging against the reins the groom still held.

Dante swung down off Fire Eater, the stallion prancing away in alarm. "Hold Sunset, damn it," Dante ordered the groom. "Steady!"

Dante grasped Pip's hands. They were icy knots of pure terror. It took all of Dante's strength to peel his fingers open. Twice the gelding's hoof slammed down on the toe of Dante's boot, the horse's tossing head banging into the side of his face, making him see stars, but after a struggle, Austen managed to drag the child down into his arms.

He stumbled back away from the animal. Dante could feel Pip battling to breathe, his chest tight, his body rigid. And as Austen peered into that small, pinched face, churning horror rocketed through him.

Damnation, the child's lips were turning a dusky blue. God in heaven, what was the matter?

"Get Miss Graystone," Dante snapped. "And Withers, take Fire Eater—summon a doctor. Hurry, man!" Dante cradled the boy against his chest and raced into the house, servants spilling wildly to do his bidding.

Dante lay the child on the settee and fumbled to loosen the boy's shirtfront. Within moments Hannah ran in, her face tight with dread but not surprise as she grasped Pip's hands.

"Damn it, something's the matter with him!" Dante exclaimed. "What the devil—"

"He has these spells when he's sick or frightened."

"He's done this before?"

"Countless times. So many . . . but Pip, you've been doing so well, angel! Whatever could have triggered . . ."

"H–horse . . ." the child rasped, his fist clenching against his chest. "I . . ."

"The nightmare again? No one will ever make you get near a horse again. Didn't I promise you?"

"*I* just put him on an infernal horse!" Dante said, a sick sinking feeling in the pit of his stomach.

She turned on him furious, disbelieving, as if he'd sat the boy astride a ravenous lion. "You put him on a horse? Without even asking me? How could you?"

Austen's cheeks burned. *I could hardly ask your permission when my intention was to weasel information out of the boy. You might have said no.* The truth ground guilt into every fiber of his being.

"I was just trying to get him out in the blasted sunshine!" Dante defended. "For God's sake, he's like a damned ghost hiding in that chamber! How was I supposed to know—"

Outrage flooded Hannah's eyes, and Austen saw tears

sparkling on her lashes. "Didn't he tell you he was afraid?"

He'd tried to. Austen knew it with sudden certainty. But Dante had been so intent on his purpose, he'd brushed the signs aside.

"Sorry . . . Nanna . . . wanted to be little man . . . Afraid . . ."

Dante reeled with guilt as Pip rasped his own words back to him. God's blood, how had he forgotten how poisonous that thoughtless command could be? Words that taunted and dared, nudging a boy forward into disaster as certainly as a knife pricking at his back.

"'Fraid he would . . . would hit you." The words shattered on a rasp.

"Mother of God," Dante gasped. "Hit her? I'd never—"

Hannah's words reverberated through him—*Pip's father was the cruellest man I ever knew* . . . Had the child mounted the horse in abject terror? Afraid if he didn't do Dante's bidding Dante would beat his mother?

He hadn't known—hadn't suspected . . . but it didn't matter. Austen was responsible for this disaster, all of it. If anything happened to the child, it would be his fault.

"Never you mind, sweetheart," Hannah crooned. "Just try not to fight it."

"Fight it? The blasted boy's fighting for every breath! He can't breathe! Can't you see—"

But she barely seemed to hear him, cradling the child against her, stroking his hair. "I know your chest hurts, angel. Hold on to me. I'll sing your favorite song. Will that help?"

"It won't do a damned bit of good and you know it!" Dante hated the red tide of panic surging through him at the boy's distress. "Do something worthwhile, for bloody sakes!"

She cast him a glare filled with loathing and fear. "There's nothing I *can* do! If there was, don't you think I'd be doing it? God in heaven, I've never seen him so—

so bad. And your shouting is only making it worse. Haven't you already done enough damage?"

Dante felt more helpless than he ever had in his life. "My groom went for the doctor, but it could be hours before the man gets here," he ground out. "There has to be something we can do!"

He clawed through his mind, trying desperately to think of something, anything that might ease the child's suffering. Some medicine, some herbal remedy the crofters used.

The crofters. Suddenly he remembered the dim-lit confines of a crofter's house, a mother's face half wild with fear as her child's racking coughs echoed in the night.

"Becca, get me some boiling water and a blanket," Dante ordered the little maid hovering near the door.

"Aye, sir." The maid raced out.

"What for? What are you doing?" Hannah demanded.

"I'll be damned if I'm going to stand here like an idiot until the doctor arrives! I know something that might help him."

It seemed forever, but it was mere moments before one of the footmen came charging in, a big tub of steaming water splashing his immaculate livery, Becca a step behind with a blanket clutched against her chest.

Dante dragged Pip out of Hannah's grasp, setting the struggling boy on a chair in front of the steaming pot of water.

"Pip, I'm going to make a tent over your head with the blanket—"

"Nanna!" the boy rasped, trying to reach for her hand. "It hurts. I'm 'fraid . . ."

"You're going to suffocate him!" Hannah cried. "He already can't breathe!"

"The blanket will keep the steam underneath. It will help him—" Dante dragged the length of cloth over the child.

"Breathe in, boy," the footman urged.

"It doesn't make any sense!" Hannah cried. "What if the steam burns him?"

"It won't!" Dante assured her. "Don't get too close, Pip. Just lean over. Trust me!"

"Trust you?" Hannah demanded in a broken, brittle voice. "Why should we? You take Pip without my permission—put him on a horse. This is your fault!"

She was only echoing Austen's own raging guilt. Nothing she could say could be worse than his own self-loathing.

"Come on, Pip," Dante urged. "Breathe . . ."

The rasping emanating from beneath the blanket tore at Austen, and he wished he could pump his own breath into the child. Yet more than anything, he feared a terrible silence. Pip was so small, so undernourished. The sickness that held him in its grip was so strong. What if the child's laboring lungs surrendered their fight?

And all because Dante had been a stubborn fool.

Blast, could there be any punishment worse than watching this boy fight for air?

He glanced at Hannah. How had he ever thought her hard? Cold? Her eyes were soft as the centers of pansies now, hollow with grief and love—so much love. Her capable hands were quivering where she touched the child, and she suddenly seemed small and frightened and terribly alone. Yet she was fighting back with a courage that humbled him, a valiant defiance as if she and Pip were pitted against the world, yet the love between them was enough.

How many times had Hannah suffered through this endless torment of helplessness, fear for the boy she so obviously adored?

He remembered the night she had begged him for shelter. Pip had been hiding in the shadows, coughing. . . .

When he'd discovered Hannah sleeping at her writing table hours before, Dante had wondered what could drive a woman with such fierce pride to beg help from a stranger. Now he knew. At this moment, Dante would strike any bargain the devil might name just to let the child breathe easily again.

Please, God, Dante prayed silently. Don't let him . . . Die?

Dante didn't even dare think the word. Hell, he'd thought he'd changed, worked so hard to change. But it was all for nothing. He was the same Austen Dante he'd always been, charging in heedless of consequences to anyone else, stubbornly set on getting his own way, the devil take the cost.

He raked his fingers through his dark hair and paced around the table, his eyes never leaving the child half-hidden beneath the blanket.

It seemed as if they balanced forever on a knife blade of remorse and terror and the tiniest thread of hope. Three times, Dante added more hot water to the tub while Hannah rubbed the child's back, crooning to him a broken lullaby in Irish.

The melody was wistful and aching, beautiful and humbling, as if every mother's terror and love was pressed within the notes that had been handed down through generations. It was almost as if in that soft song she was not only comforting the child but begging him to stay with her, to live, suffusing him with her own strength.

Austen strained, trying to hear the child's breathing half concealed by the song, trying to decide if his own desperation was altering the rasping sounds, making them less harsh, less frequent.

He wasn't certain until Hannah's gaze faltered up to meet his. He saw her swallow hard, a silent plea in her eyes. "I think . . . I think he might be . . ."

Better. Dante could see she was terrified to say the word aloud, as if some evil fairy might be lurking nearby waiting to cast another malevolent spell on the boy. Dante reached out to lay his hand on Pip's back. Some of the awful tension had melted out of the child. The rhythm of his breathing was easier, gentler.

"Thank God." Dante closed his eyes, a huge lump of gratitude swelling in his throat.

"Pip, angel, how are you feeling?"

"Tired. I'm so tired. Want to sleep."

Hannah drew the blanket back from Pip's tousled curls, and Dante saw tears of relief dampen her lashes. Huge, dark circles still rimmed Pip's eyes, but his lips were a soft rose color again instead of that alarming shade of blue.

Dante felt an uncharacteristic urge to lift the child into his arms, to carry the boy up to the bedchamber and tuck him in. But he'd already terrorized the child enough. God forbid he might send Pip into another spell. He locked his hands behind his back.

Hannah gathered the boy into her arms and Pip nuzzled against her, looping his arms around her neck.

"That scared me," he murmured. "Don't like the dark . . ." And Dante could see countless shadows in that face, so young, so innocent. Shadows of other terrors—shadows of someone cruel enough to strike a woman with his fists, and strike a child?

Hannah started to carry the boy to his room, but Dante reached out, caught her arm. She stopped and glared up at him over Pip's curly head, accusation still shadowing her features.

But Austen looked down into the boy's face. "I didn't understand how afraid you were, Pip," Dante said, his voice roughened with emotion. "If I had, I never would have put you on that horse."

The child gazed up at him with eyes far too old for one of such tender years. "Want to know a secret? I'm afraid all the time." Pip's face crumpled under the weight of that deep, dark confession. "I bet you aren't ever afraid of anything, Mr. Bastard, sir." Pip whimpered, envy in his eyes.

Austen wanted to touch him to let Pip know he

understood fear far better than the child could imagine. But he stood silent.

"There's nothing wrong with being afraid sometimes, Pip," Hannah broke in. "Everyone is. Even the great and powerful Mr. Dante. Though I doubt he'd have the courage to admit it."

Dante's cheekbones stained dark. Damn the woman for cutting again, swift and sure and clean to the bone. How much did she see with those fiercely intelligent eyes? How much did she guess?

He turned away, shoving his hands deep into his pockets as she swept from the room with all the maternal fury of a lioness protecting her cub.

Do you want to know a secret? Pip's words echoed in his mind.

No. Dante pressed his fingertips to his brow, burning, aching. He didn't have room for any more secrets. He had far too many of his own.

Chapter

Hannah paced the confines of the bedchamber, restlessness and outrage, relief and dread warring in her breast. It infuriated her that sometime during the endless day and night since Pip's ordeal, dread seemed to have won the battle.

A sick dread that tumbled like moss-slicked stone in her stomach, taunting her with the memories she recalled far too vividly.

Relentless rain running cold down her back, the pinched white of Pip's mouth as he trudged along beside her, so hungry she could sense it in every fiber of her being. The only taste on her tongue were the stories she told him—stories of refuge and safe haven and a cozy cottage where the thatch would be like a fairy king's shield, shutting out the danger that stalked them. She glanced back to where Pip curled up in bed, the nearby table littered with the doctor's remedies. He was smiling at Becca as the bright-eyed maid created shadow pictures on the wall by the light of a candle, entertaining the child with delightful energy that Hannah could not muster.

Waiting for Austen Dante's summons was like waiting to be taken to the gallows. Excruciating suspense and crushing inevitability. He would summon her. Question her about Pip's fear. And when he did . . .

Hannah hugged her arms tight around her middle, remembering the tempestuous expression she'd seen so many times, a wildness, a recklessness, and an iron-honed will few would dare to challenge. He'd been shaken by Pip's illness, more affected than Hannah would have believed possible. And Austen Dante wasn't the kind of man who would shrug the happenings of the night before aside with an "all's well that ends well." He'd expect an explanation, and there would be no more evasions. He would demand the truth—a truth she dared not give him. And when she refused? Was it possible that he would decide that housing an ill boy and a secretive woman was too wearing on his temper? Would he cast her and Pip into the street?

Hannah shuddered. When she'd stolen Pip away from Ireland, she'd been so innocent, so determined, so certain of her own resourcefulness. She'd been afraid—yes. Only a fool would not fear the wrath of Mason Booth.

But somewhere along the endless path of her flight, those fears had taken on new shapes and textures and tastes. Hunger had become a familiar gnawing in her stomach; cold had penetrated deep into her bones as she'd struggled to sleep, huddled with Pip against the trunk of a tree, trying to block the chill fingers of the wind that tugged at the meager shield of her cloak.

And somewhere she had lost her confidence that she was strong enough, clever enough to protect the child she loved more than her own life.

What would she do if Mr. Dante sent her packing? A knock on the door drew a squeak of surprise from her throat, and she wheeled to see Pip and Becca staring at her in astonishment.

"That startled me," she said, forcing a smile. "I must

have been woolgathering." Hannah crossed to the door. Simmons stood outside.

"Mr. Dante will see you at once in the Music Room, miss."

Hannah swallowed hard. Better to get it over with, she supposed. At least if he did fire her, she'd damned well remember to pick up her salary. How long could they eat on what she'd earned?

She followed Simmons, her head held high, her shoulders squared. Dante stood at the window, his hands clasped behind his back. Beyond, she could see the tangles of rose vines and bright azaleas tumbling in exuberant abandon along paths of crushed stone, framed by the purple sweep of moor beyond. Every sinew of Dante's lean body seemed to strain toward the wind and the sun and the heather-spangled moors, as if the exquisite room held him in chains.

He looked like a stranger. His jacket and waistcoat had been stripped away, cast on a gilt chair, his limp cravat puddled atop it where it had been obviously torn away by impatient hands. A diamond stickpin glinted in its folds, abandoned with the same carelessness—a trinket that could have fed and clothed and given shelter to Pip for several years, cast aside as if it were a piece of broken glass.

His shirt was crumpled, the sleeves rolled up over muscular forearms. Smudges of dirt marked the white fabric.

There was such intensity in him it almost frightened her, as if that barely leashed energy she'd sensed so many times before had escaped its dam, and the confines of the Music Room could no longer hold him.

Somehow, he looked more *real,* with his hair wind-tossed and his eyes turned out to the moors.

"Sir?" the footman announced, "Miss Graystone has come."

Dante turned, and Hannah had to struggle not to take a step back. Suddenly, she felt an unaccountable need to tame the lightning-flash brilliance, the hard, masculine beauty of features that might have graced those of a fallen angel.

Dante dismissed the servant with the wave of a hand and stood there in silence until long after the footman fled. Hannah's chin jutted up with a belligerence she did not feel. She'd be damned if she broke the infernal silence. If he wanted to stand there like a statue, let him.

Yet as the minutes ticked past, tension cinched tighter about her throat until it was so excruciating she couldn't bear it another moment.

"I hardly think you summoned me to discuss the window glass," she snapped. "However if you want to stand here all day, I suppose it's your prerogative."

He turned and scowled darkly. "You know damned well why you are here, madam. It's time for some answers. That boy almost died yesterday because of what you did!"

"What I did?" Hannah gasped in outrage. "It was your fault he got sick!"

"Is that so? Exactly what did I do that was so terrible? You have been keeping the boy locked upstairs in that chamber as if he were some sort of prisoner ever since you arrived here. And before that—God knows how the poor little wretch didn't perish from being dragged around in the rain. It's no wonder the boy is so sickly and pale."

Hannah flinched as if he'd jabbed a dagger into an open wound. She wanted to rage at him, tell him how hard she'd fought to find shelter for Pip. She wanted to smash her fist into that arrogant face that had never known hunger or want, never been homeless and afraid. But she clenched her teeth so hard it was a wonder they didn't shatter. She wouldn't give him the satisfaction of knowing how bad things had been.

"How dare you pass judgment on me," she said.

"Oh, I'd dare one hell of a lot with you, Miss Graystone. That child nearly died because you refused to answer a few simple questions. Questions I was justified in asking."

"Shillings might buy my time. They do not buy my soul."

He swore under his breath. "You want to blame me for what happened to Pip. So, tell me, just what was my heinous sin? Taking the child out into the sunshine for a little while? Offering him a ride on an infernal horse?"

"Without my permission! You didn't even ask me!"

His eyes narrowed, glinting and dangerous as thin ice upon a rushing river. "I've asked you plenty, madam. I just haven't gotten any answers. What was I supposed to do? Trail after you as you helped the maid and say, 'Pardon me, Miss Graystone, will your son half kill himself with terror if I put him on a horse?'"

"You could have written me a note or sent one of the servants to ask me. Any one of a dozen things."

"I am hardly accustomed to ask permission of my servants for anything, Miss Graystone."

"Well, perhaps you *should* become accustomed to it. No, that would be impossible for *the great and powerful master of Ravenscar.*" The words dripped with venom. "Servants might get the idea that they are people allowed feelings, joy and pain and sorrow. It would interfere with the smooth running of your household, and God forbid you should suffer any inconvenience. Besides, this whole matter with Pip and the horse makes no sense. Why should you bother to take Pip riding? You hardly seem like the kind of man given to entertaining a servant's child."

A muscle tightened in Dante's jaw, the storm in his eyes more turbulent. "Occasionally I'm struck with inexplicable urges to do something decent. I suppose this was one of them."

His cheekbones stained dark, that gaze that had always been so piercingly direct flashing away from her. "Every boy in England rides, for Hades's sake," he bit out defensively. "I would've committed murder to ride a horse like Sunset when I was Pip's age. What boy wouldn't?"

"A boy whose father forced him onto a mount five times too spirited, then vowed Pip would ride that horse even if it killed them both. And when his mother tried to interfere after he'd been thrown a dozen times—" A fist of agony crushed Hannah's heart. "The monster turned on her and beat her until she lay unconscious . . ." Tears of outrage and helplessness and fury stung her eyes. Through the hot blur, Dante's face swam, white and drawn.

"But even that wasn't punishment enough," Hannah plunged on, wanting to hurt him as she hurt. "He told Pip he couldn't have it known that his son couldn't ride the animal. Oh, no. Heaven forbid he should be humiliated in front of his friends. So do you know what he did, *sir?*"

"No," Dante ground out, braced as if for a blow.

"He shot the horse right in front of Pip's eyes." She swiped the tears away with the back of her hand. "Better that the animal was dead. That way the bastard could tell his friends that it had broken its leg while Pip was jumping a fence."

Dante looked sick. She was glad. Her own stomach was roiling.

"Pip would have ridden the hounds of Satan himself if his father had commanded it. Anything to keep him from getting angry."

"Who the hell is this *man?*" Dante demanded in a voice deadly quiet. "Tell me."

Hannah flushed, suddenly aware of her recklessness in spilling out the story. What had she been thinking? If Dante mentioned it to anyone, it would be just the kind of clue Booth would need to find them. "I've already said too much," she said, suddenly, fiercely frightened.

Dante grabbed her arm, and she could feel the force of

his will pulse through the hard plane of his palm. "Damn it, you can't tell me such horrors and just expect me to walk away. You owe me answers. You're living under my roof. When I think of what almost happened yesterday because you wouldn't answer a simple question, my blood runs cold. Think of the boy, for God's sake. Think what this is doing to him!"

"Don't you think I *know* what this is doing to him?" Hannah's voice cracked on the hard-edged sob she fought to stifle. "It's all I think about!" Pride stung. She stiffened. "But Pip is *mine* to love and worry over. He's nothing to you."

"Damn it, I won't be ignorant in my own house, not knowing what the devil is going on. You'll tell me, or else—"

"Or else what? I'd sooner be on the road than suffer you meddling in affairs that are none of your concern. We'll be leaving now, if you would give me my pay." She thrust out her hand.

"The devil I will!"

Fury and sick helplessness set her stomach churning. He was refusing to pay her salary? A chilling thought lanced through her. Had he realized she was duping him all along? Playing him for a fool? No. There was no triumph, no grim satisfaction in his voice. But did it really matter *why* he was refusing to pay her? The results were the same. She was helpless.

What possible recourse could she have? She could hardly go to the authorities. Dante must know that. He had suspected she was running away from something from the first.

Hannah shuddered at the thought of taking Pip back onto the road. Without coin it would be worse than ever.

Before, there had been an unreality to it, as if it were a nightmare she'd soon wake from. Now she knew in harsh detail how it felt to look into Pip's eyes and know he was suffering silently.

"You owe me that money," she insisted.

"And you owe me an explanation, but it looks like neither of us is going to get what we want. Blast it, this is a dangerous game you're playing. From what you've said, Pip's father is a son of a bitch capable of violence. You can't pretend that kind of evil away."

"So what am I supposed to do?"

"Stop being so infernally stubborn. Let me help you." It was a command, fierce yet careless. He could have no idea what dragon he was volunteering to battle. If he did, he'd take back his rash words. He was offering only because he didn't understand. When all was said and done, he'd be loyal to his social class and to the law of the land. Or would he?

For a heartbeat, Hannah stared into those vivid eyes, drowned in their blue-fire depths. For a heartbeat, she was tempted to take the risk, to trust him.

She turned away, haunted by gray-green eyes filled with torment. Wasted hands already cold with encroaching death, clinging to her with their last bit of strength. You've never broken a promise to me . . . swear you'll never tell . . . it's the only way he can be safe.

Rivers of terror iced through Hannah at the knowledge that she'd considered for even an instant betraying that vow. She dammed them up the only way she knew how. "I'm supposed to let you help me?" she forced scorn deep into her voice. "Considering the letters I read to you yesterday, I'd say you can't even help yourself."

She saw emotions flash like quicksilver over those handsome features—anger and surprise, a sudden pain so deep it stunned her. And she knew she was looking at the real Austen Dante, perhaps for the very first time. Like a wounded beast struggling to hide any weakness, he spun on his heel and stalked from the room.

Hannah trembled all over, confused and furious, ashamed and glad, sick and full of dread.

Damn him! Damn him for his arrogance. Damn him

for refusing to pay her, in an attempt to force her hand like a common bully. She swept the pile of clothing from the settee in frustration.

Something bounced off the toe of her worn half boot, and she looked down to see the diamond half buried in the pile of the Axminster carpet.

Her heart leapt as the jewel winked at her like an eye with its own magic, enticing her, tempting her, daring her . . .

To what? Become a thief? Steal it?

It wouldn't be stealing. Not exactly, she reasoned. He owed her money he refused to pay, and she could hardly chip off a few shillings worth of diamond. Besides, it was his own fault he'd driven her to such desperation, wasn't it?

She moved closer, peering down at the glinting jewel. Austen Dante had so much, he could cast the diamond about as if it were no more than a bit of ice.

Would it be so terrible to take this? So Pip could have shelter? Food?

But if she were caught— She shuddered, imagining a cold cell, Pip taken away from her, then the journey to the gallows and death.

Her fingers clenched so hard her fingernails cut into her palm. But wasn't a hangman's noose already threatening her because of what she'd done in Ireland? And what good would it do to save Pip from the brutality of his father, only to let the child starve in the street?

Hannah closed her eyes, remembering the cold late at night, the sharp stabbing of hunger, the sickly pallor of Pip's face wet with rain. The image twisted in her breast. Before she could change her mind, she swept the diamond into her hand. The pin gouged deep and she felt the hot trickle of blood, but she ignored the pain.

Heart in her throat, she turned and raced up the stairs.

Hannah stuffed the last of their clothes into the portmanteau, the diamond hidden in the toe of one of her stockings. But the jewel seemed to have a power of its own like the treasure of some sorcerer king, as if at any time it might start glowing so fiercely the rays of light would pierce the worn sides of the bag and betray her.

Guilt and desperation thudded in her chest with each beat of her heart, and she found it astonishing the courts had ever had to execute thieves. If every criminal's first experience was as traumatic as her own, most of them should perish of panic long before they reached Old Bailey.

She fastened the portmanteau closed with fingers that trembled, then she shuddered as she caught a glimpse of herself in the looking glass. Her face was a taut white mask except for two hot spots of color in each cheek; her eyes were clouded with dread. Her bottom lip was chafed from the countless times she'd worried it with her teeth.

Thank goodness she'd sent Pip and Becca out into the garden. If they'd remained behind to watch her bumble around they would have known something was wrong.

She supposed she should at least be grateful to Mr. Dante for that much—the accusations that had cut her so deeply had provided her with the reason to shoo them out of the chamber into the sun. Their absence had given her time to make the necessary preparations, pack the few belongings brought from Ireland, raid the kitchen for enough food to get by for a few days.

She bundled the loaves of bread and mound of apples in a blanket stripped from the bed in hopes that the length of wool would provide enough shelter until she and Pip were far enough from Ravenscar to pawn the stickpin. She didn't dare chance it before they were out of the area. She couldn't risk someone recognizing the bit of jewelry and reporting her to the authorities.

She'd expected to feel nervous about making good their escape. What she hadn't expected was to feel a kind of sadness about leaving this room, the first place she and Pip had been truly warm, felt at least a little safe.

However careless Austen Dante might have been with

his bounty, it was possible he had saved Pip's life—first, the night he'd given them shelter from the rain, and then again yesterday, when he'd bathed Pip's face in steam. And how had she repaid him? With one lie after another.

Even her outrage over the fact he hadn't paid her was based on deception. The hours she'd spent while he labored over the piano were wasted, the lines she'd scribbled nothing but gibberish. And now she was stealing from him.

But he had so much—more than he'd ever need . . . or did he? There was something beneath that arrogant exterior, something in the curve of his mouth, something beneath his lashes when he thought no one was looking. Something that unsettled her, whispered to her.

She closed her eyes, the threads of his music twining through her memory, the vision of him bent low over the keys with a kind of desperation, frustration, yet even more, a sadness that echoed in her soul.

For heaven's sake, she barely knew the man—and what she *did* know she didn't like overmuch. Why was it that the thought of him alone in that elegant music room troubled her so deeply? Why did she feel as if she were betraying him, not only by stealing the diamond, but by leaving Ravenscar at all?

She was being ridiculous. Austen Dante would be well rid of her. She was only making a muddle of things. If she wanted to drown in guilt, there would be plenty of time to indulge in that later, once she and Pip were safely away from this place with its disturbing master.

Gathering the portmanteau and bundle of blanket, she crossed to the door and peeked through the crack, relief stealing through her as the corridor stretched out, blessedly empty. If she could just dodge the maids and footmen, sweep Pip out of the garden, they could be gone before anyone suspected a thing. But if one of the servants saw her . . . She shoved the thought away and stepped into the hallway.

It seemed as if she wandered for an eternity, hideously

exposed. Twice she had to duck into empty rooms to evade the ever-vigilant Simmons.

Her heart was thundering in her head when she finally reached the door leading to the outside. She stepped into the sunshine, the glare blinding her for a few moments. Stuffing her burden beneath the thick foliage of a nearby rhododendron bush, Hannah scanned the perfectly groomed garden, searching for Pip. But she only saw Becca, blushing and breathless as the gardener's boy stole a kiss.

"Becca what are you doing?"

The girl sprang away from her beau. A guilty flush stole into her cheeks.

"Beggin' pardon, ma'am," the youth stammered, "but Becca had somethin' in her eye, she did. I was just tryin' to get it out. And I did. Get it out, I mean. I'll just be goin'." With a languishing look, the lad scooped up his spade and darted through a break in the yew hedge.

"Hannah. I just—I didn't mean to be . . . dawdling," Becca started to apologize.

"I thought you were watching Pip."

"The master said I didn't have to anymore. He took him off awhile ago."

"And you just let him?" Hannah's stomach sank. "After everything that happened yesterday?"

"Wasn't for me to tell the master no!" Becca gasped, astonished. "I'd lose my place certain-sure, and then how would my brother be gettin' away from the mines?"

The girl was right, Hannah knew it. That didn't stem the panic thrumming through her veins. "What would the man want with Pip? It doesn't make any sense!" She was sick at the knowledge she'd have to face Dante again. It was one thing to resort to thievery and slip away. It was another proposition altogether to steal a pin, then confront those eyes that were so piercingly intelligent, that seemed to have an almost uncanny ability to peel back the layers of deception to see what lay beneath.

What an absurd image, she brought herself up sharply. She'd concocted lie after lie and he hadn't discovered her deception yet, had he?

Despite her rationalizing, for an instant she was tempted to return to the bedchamber and wait there until Pip returned. It would be safer, to her peace of mind anyway. But it was vital that they get as far from Ravenscar as possible. Tonight. Any delay might be disastrous. Besides, she didn't dare leave Pip with Austen Dante after what had happened the last time.

She struggled to compose features far too expressive into a mask of calm.

"Where did they go?" she inquired.

"Toward the stables, I think." Becca twisted her hands in her apron. "The master had something he wanted to show Pip."

"Stables? Horses again! After the disaster he caused yesterday?" She all but ran down the path. But when she reached the stable it was empty.

"Have you seen Mr. Dante?" she asked a groom with straw yellow hair and gap teeth.

"He's out back, I thinks."

Hannah hurried in the direction the groom pointed. But as she neared the second door at rear of the stable, she heard something—a sound so rare she barely recognized it. Pip's voice, high and filled with excitement.

"She won't stop!" Pip squealed. "Why won't she—"

"Don't be afraid. She's just getting to know you."

Surely the man couldn't be doing something with horses again, could he? If he was, Hannah vowed she'd strangle him with his own cravat.

Hannah rounded the corner, saw the two figures outside a pen of some sort. Pip sat cross-legged on the grass, while Austen Dante hunkered down behind him. Broad shoulders sheltering the boy from the gentle buffeting of the breeze, the man's dark head bent protectively over Pip's fair curls. The man's sensual mouth was softened with pleasure as a tiny bundle of brown and white fur wriggled in Pip's arms, eagerly licking the boy's face.

"What on earth?" Hannah gasped out loud.

Dante looked up, startled. Hastily, he straightened his tall frame, an almost sheepish expression buffing the hard edges from his face. The man looked as chagrined as if she'd caught him sobbing over a French novel in a fit of sentimentality.

Pip spotted her at that moment. "Nanna! Oh, Nanna! I'm the luckiest boy in the whole world! Look!"

It was a puppy, a spaniel, impossibly tiny, with gleaming black button eyes. In the pen beyond lay a mother dog, serene in the midst of a batch of gamboling offspring who were far larger than the one Pip was cuddling with such delight.

"The man who takes care of the dogs said I should take one of the biggest, most 'citable happy ones. But then I saw this one. She wanted to be friendly, but the others were pushing her away and not even letting her eat, just 'cause she was the littlest one of all. She looked so sad 'cause they were all bigger and braver than her."

"She looks happy now," Hannah said, ruffling the creature's silky ears.

"Mr. Dante said I could name her anything I wanted. I want to name her Lizzy."

Oh, God. Hannah's heart twisted. No. She couldn't think. Dared not . . . she had to keep it bottled up the way she had the past weeks, locked away in some dark raw cavern in her heart where it couldn't tear her apart.

"Elizabeth, is it?" Dante asked. "Named after the Virgin Queen?"

"No. After an angel." Pip's eyes grew large and soft and pleading. "Do you think she would mind, Nanna?"

Mind? Was there any more loving tribute a five-year-old boy could bestow? It made Hannah's heart hurt. "No, Pip. I think she would like it very much."

She felt Dante's gaze on her, intense, probing. "Who is this angel?"

The words splashed ice through Hannah's veins, taunting her with a new danger. One she hadn't recognized until this moment. What if in this new closeness between the man and the boy, Pip should stumble, betray something about the Lizzy they'd left behind? Pip was so little . . . and there was something about Austen Dante that drew out secrets one never intended to tell.

Hannah stiffened. She'd have to be careful. She'd have to warn Pip again. But they'd soon be far from Austen Dante's probing gaze.

"Don't you have guardian angels in England?" she gave a shaky laugh. "Pip, it's time you put Mr. Dante's puppy down. You know that being around animals can make you sick."

"I'm not feeling sick—not at all. And 'sides, Lizzy's *not* his puppy. At least not anymore." Pip's eyes shone with a light she'd never seen before—pure pleasure. It wrenched at her heart. "Mr. Dante said he was sorry 'bout the horse and all. He wanted to make up for the mistake, so he said I could keep any puppy I wanted for my very own."

"He *what?*" Hannah choked out, but the child who had once been so sensitive to every shift in her mood was oblivious.

"Lots and lots of people want this mama's puppies—the groom said they're fighting over 'em. But I got first pick and I picked Lizzy."

Hannah glared at Austen Dante. The man grimaced, that dangerously handsome face suddenly, devastatingly boyish as he shrugged one broad shoulder. "Miss Graystone, I can explain."

"Explain?" Hannah sputtered under her breath as Pip went off in another gale of laughter. "You most certainly can explain—exactly why it's impossible for Pip to keep that puppy."

"Why?" Damn the man for looking genuinely confused.

Why? Because we're running away. Because I don't

even know if I can feed Pip, let alone a puppy—especially one that will grow as large as that hunting spaniel.

"Surely you can understand why I want to make amends to the boy," he said. "Don't worry. This time I talked to Pip *before* I brought him out here, so there wouldn't be any misunderstandings. He says he loves dogs."

"That has nothing to do with anything!" Hannah blustered. "He likes cows, too, but that doesn't mean he can keep one for a pet!"

Pip looked up, and she could see from his expression that he'd caught the gist of their argument. "Please, oh, please. Let me keep her." His arms tightened about the wriggling puppy as if he were afraid she'd wrench it from his arms. Hannah ached at the knowledge of just how much had already been torn away from this little boy. "Lizzy isn't so *very* big," he pleaded. "She won't eat hardly anything at all. I'll share my food with her so no one'll even notice she's there."

How those green-gray eyes tugged at the raw places inside her. This child, who had been so hungry offering to surrender his plateful of food. After all, what was mere food when he was hungry for something warm and full of love?

It ripped her heart out to refuse him. "Pip, I don't think—" She started to explain, but Dante cut her off.

"That's a brave sacrifice you've offered to make, boy—feeding the spaniel from your own plate. But it's hardly necessary." He flashed the child a smile so dazzling it could have melted stone. "I think the pantries at Ravenscar are deep enough to feed one small boy and his pup."

"Maybe so," Hannah snapped, "but we won't be h—" She choked off the words, heat flooding her cheeks beneath Dante's puzzled gaze. Horrified with what had almost fallen from her mouth, she chose a different tack. "Exactly what happened to your ultimatum, sir?"

One dark brow arched. "Ultimatum?"

"In our previous interview, you made it clear that I either had to tell you what you wanted to know, or Pip and I would have to leave Ravenscar."

Pip gave a little gasp, peering up at his new hero in disbelief. "Did you . . . did you say that?"

"Of course not!" Dante exclaimed. He gaped at her, taken aback. "For God's sake, do you think I'd throw this child out of the house, no matter how much you infuriated me? What kind of monster do you think I am?"

The words reverberated between them, resonating with a moment of complete understanding. That sensual mouth tightened in repressed anger. His eyes flashed, and for an instant Hannah enjoyed the image of Mason Booth being speared by the loathing, the power in those eyes.

But the thought was obliterated as she glimpsed Pip, his laughter stilled, his eyes wide with pleading as he clung to the puppy nestled in his arms. It had been forever since she'd seen Pip's eyes lit with sparks of pleasure. He'd been quiet and still and afraid for so long, she'd begun to fear that he would never be able to shed the somberness that shrouded him, be just a child again.

Perhaps it was unreasonable to hope that every last shadow would ever be sponged from his face. Yet somehow, when Austen Dante had placed the puppy in his arms, it had given Pip hope. Something to hold, to protect. Something Hannah could not give Pip, no matter how desperately she wanted to, because all her energies were consumed with keeping him out of his father's brutal grasp.

Did Dante really mean it? That they could stay? Hannah wondered, amazed. But she'd already packed their belongings, taken the food, stolen the diamond pin. If he knew the truth about what she'd done, Austen Dante would be hurling them out the gates himself. Or would he?

She peered up into those features that were soulshatteringly handsome, all planes and angles, a patrician nose, full lips that could have seduced the wings off an angel. And eyes filled with quicksilver emotions raging like a white-foamed river, so swift she wondered if it was possible no one had ever seen what truly lay in their depths.

She was stunned to see Dante lay one hand gently atop Pip's curls, as if he sensed the child's turmoil and her own.

Blue eyes gazed so deep into hers, it seemed as if they touched her soul. "Hannah, don't go." The words were soft, a request instead of a command. Hannah came undone. She couldn't stifle the relief that surged through her at Austen Dante's plea, or her dismay.

She'd been running for so very long. Running from Mason Booth, from a thousand regrets, and grief so crushing she was afraid she'd shatter if ever she surrendered to it. Grief Pip had touched with the name of an angel.

But to stay here at Ravenscar—with this man who disturbed her to the core of her soul, who taunted her with his sensual smile, disarmed her with the shadows in his eyes, tempted her with flashes of gentleness that stunned her, touched her heart. The possibility was too terrifying, too dangerous.

She had everything prepared for their flight, everything planned and ready. Merciful heavens, what was she going to do?

Slowly, she knelt on the ground before Pip, and stroked the puppy's silky ears. "Hello, Lizzy," she murmured peering into black button eyes that suddenly seemed windows to a soul old as time. "I've missed . . ."

God above, what was she saying, doing? What if Dante saw—what? The ragged edges of her heart?

She glanced up at him, seeing a rare solemnity in those incredible blue eyes. "Stay," he said. One word. So simple. Infinitely complicated.

She blinked back tears she dared not shed. "Lizzy,"

she whispered that beloved name aloud, as the puppy licked her hand. "You're very lucky to have chosen such a wonderful boy."

She could feel the walls around her grief crumbling, could feel it breaking free. "I have to—to go," Hannah stood amid protests, Pip's sweet voice, Dante's whiskey-warm, masculine one. But she turned and fled, feeling the tears prick at her eyes.

She never knew how she got through the Ravenscar garden, remembered nothing of rushing up the sweep of stairs inside the grand house. She found herself in her bedchamber, her back against the closed door.

She closed her eyes. For countless miles the memories had chased her, followed her, tormented her with their blinding flashes, but she'd managed to shove them away. She'd never reckoned on the power of one heartsore little boy, a puppy clutched in his arms.

Her name is Lizzy . . . after an angel . . .

Lizzy. She'd always reminded Hannah of a butterfly cradled for a moment in her hands.

For years Hannah had watched her sister's wings grow, gauzy, painted with the delicate hues of girlish dreams, until Elisabeth had seemed forever turning her face to the breeze, waiting for the wind to lift her up, carry her away.

If only they had known she was flying into the flame. . . .

"Lizzy," Hannah whispered. "I miss you so much. I'm sorry—so sorry for everything . . ."

Hannah sagged down onto the bed, allowing the tears to come at last, the windswept moor beyond the window dancing before her eyes until it shifted, changed, the panes of glass framed in gray stone, the lands beyond the wild, sweet green of Ireland.

Chapter

7

Hannah stared down at her sister, lost in the huge state bed, the bloom gone from her cheeks, her sunshine-bright hair faded and lank. All the sparkle dashed from eyes that had once danced with merriment and the delight of a young woman certain of her feminine powers.

"You've come," Lizzy whispered, weak tears of relief pearling her lashes. "I was afraid you wouldn't come."

"How could you ever doubt it? Of course I came, the moment I got your letter saying you were sick." Hannah took up a hand so fragile she feared it might crumble beneath her touch. Her heart wrenched as she remembered the last time she had seen it, dimpled and rosy, a gleaming wedding ring clasping Elisabeth's finger as her new bridegroom handed her up into his elegant traveling coach. Was it only six years ago?

It had seemed an eternity to Hannah, an eternity of loneliness and disillusionment, and a hollow ache of loss. Yet nothing prepared her for what those same years had done to Elisabeth. They had transformed a glowing bride into a mere shade teetering on the brink between the mortal world and the hereafter.

"Oh, Lizzy, why didn't you send for me sooner?"

"Because I was afraid. So many letters from you in the years past, begging to come visit. And every time I turned you away."

Hannah winced at the memory of how much those rejections had hurt her—house parties to be attended, time at court, a social whirl that had engulfed Elisabeth from the moment she'd become a baronet's wife.

In the years after their father's death, it had been painful to see Elisabeth languishing in the tiny dower house on the edge of their uncle's property, making do with faded ribbons and twice-turned gowns. Hannah had tried to be glad of the change in her sister's fortunes— yet from the day Elisabeth had first voiced it, Hannah had feared the resolute vow the girl had made.

One of us must marry well enough to save the family fortunes. Since you will never bend to the will of any man, it will be up to me . . .

"I know your ways, Hannah," Elisabeth whispered. "Know how much it cost your . . . pride to keep writing, keep asking. And then, then after Pip was born the letters came less and less often, until only at Christmas and on my birthday."

Hannah swallowed hard, remembering how devastated she'd been—never being allowed so much as a glimpse of her tiny nephew. A child she'd instinctively loved as much as she had her sister. Nothing—not even the death of her father—had shattered her so completely. But that was past. Over. The only thing of importance was Elisabeth's suffering. "That was all a long time ago," she said. "It doesn't matter, Lizzy. I'm here now."

"It does matter." Elisabeth's face contorted with regret. "I hurt you, Hannah. I know. But I was so . . ." Her voice broke. "So ashamed."

The words turned like a knife in Hannah's heart—her

most beloved sister—the one who had once delighted in Hannah's unconventional ways, probed past Hannah's steadiness and practicality to the soft heart beyond, had become embarrassed by the very sister she'd once adored.

"Ashamed," Hannah echoed, contrasting the drab dower house to Mason Booth's elegant estate, her blunt verbal blunderings with the artful deceit of society prattle. "That is what Harriet and Fanny said, but I didn't want to believe that you were." Heat stung Hannah's cheeks.

Realization dawned in Elisabeth's gray-green eyes, and her voice caught on a laugh that might have been a sob. "All this time Harriet and Fanny thought I was ashamed of them? Of Mama and you and our poor dead papa? How could I be ashamed of you when I love you all so, so much?"

Hannah reeled. "But you said . . ."

"I was ashamed of myself, Hannah." Bitterness darkened the voice that had always been so bright and full of joy. "Ashamed of the disaster I'd gotten myself into. Of my own weakness. Helplessness."

"Lizzy, I don't understand." Hannah shook her head in confusion, tightening her hold on Elisabeth's hand. "But none of this matters now. We'll find some way to make you well. There must be some medicine . . . something to fight this sickness."

"There is no sickness to fight. I'm not ill, Hannah. There are injuries, deep inside me where no surgeon can reach." Elisabeth brushed her hand across her midsection. "There is nothing anyone can do."

"Injuries?" Hannah groped for the hem of her sister's nightgown, lifting it out of the way, as if by force of will she could stop whatever power was draining Elisabeth's life away. "But how—"

The words tore into silence on a horrified gasp. Hideous purple markings stained Elisabeth's delicate skin, bruises bleeding together in a rainbow of hues.

Most disturbing of all, Hannah could see other bruises half healed, yellowing at their edges.

"Dear God, what happened? A carriage accident? A fall from a horse?"

Elisabeth turned her face aside, burrowing deeper into the pillow as if to hide there. A hot spot of color stained the paper white cheek that was still exposed. Her hands clenched on the coverlets. "You never liked Mason. Do you remember, Hannah?"

Remember? From the first time she'd set eyes on the dashing Englishman, a baronet with silver-gilt hair and perfect features, she'd loathed him . . . an instinctive, visceral emotion. His face like an exquisite mask, as if he were somehow acting a part, and no one but Hannah saw beneath his facade.

How many times had her mother or sisters berated her, telling her that no man would have been good enough, in her opinion, for her precious Lizzy? There had been enough truth in the statement to give Hannah pause. Mason Booth had been the master of vast estates in both Ireland and England. He was rich, titled. A far better match than a dowerless girl like Elisabeth Gray should have been able to make, the neighboring gentry had whispered.

Most of all, he had loved Lizzy after his own fashion. He'd been besotted by her. Even Hannah had been forced to admit that much. But it hadn't quelled her apprehensions about the match. Power and wealth did not buy happiness, though there were those who would disagree. And even from the beginning, there had been a possessiveness about Booth, as if he couldn't even bear to share Lizzy with her own sisters.

"Do you remember on my wedding day? You tried to talk me out of . . . of going through with the ceremony? You pleaded with me to reconsider."

Hannah had cursed her outspokenness a hundred times—fearing it had cost her her sister's love. Mother had always insisted Hannah's tongue was the reason she had never been welcome in Elisabeth's new home. "What does this have to do with anything?"

"Everything," Elisabeth admitted, wearily. "Hannah, you were right about Mason. He has a . . . rather unfortunate temper."

A suspicion too terrible to grasp took root in Hannah's chest. "Lizzy, what . . ."

"He beats his dogs when they displease him, and his horses. And . . ." Elisabeth's voice dropped to a whisper, "his wife."

"No." Murderous fury poured through Hannah's veins, hatred so virulent her breath was fire in her lungs. "Your husband did this to you? As God is my witness, I vow I'll kill him."

"No." Lizzy clutched at her convulsively. "That won't bring me back, Hannah. Won't change anything, only ruin your life. If that was all that could be done, I would have taken my secret with me to the grave."

Tears seared Hannah's eyes, blurring everything but the horrific vision of what Mason Booth's fists had done to Elisabeth—an image Hannah knew would haunt her nightmares forever. "You can't expect me to do nothing to that sadistic monster!"

"I'm his wife, one more piece of his property under law. And I . . . I fear I provoked him."

"Provoked him?" Hannah cried in disbelief. "Of all of us, you were the sunniest-tempered! You've never offended anyone in your whole life!"

"I knew when he was getting angry. But I just couldn't stop."

"Stop *what?* Damnation, Lizzy, don't even try to convince me this was your fault!"

"I always tried to make certain my baby was safe, tucked away with his nurse when Mason was in one of his . . . moods. When Pip was first born, Mason was so proud—a son, an heir—he acted as if he were the first man ever to produce one."

Wistfulness touched Elisabeth's features, as if that

man were some dream that had faded. "But when it became obvious Pip wasn't strong, he got angry. He'd try to force Pip to—to do things that terrified him. Said he was trying to make a man out of Pip. The day I got hurt, he had summoned Pip from the nursery. There was a horse, a great, hulking horse he wanted Pip to ride."

Elisabeth sucked in a shuddering breath. "It was half-wild. He couldn't breathe, he was so afraid. Pip's lungs have always been weak. He was gasping, trying not to cry. Time after time, Mason forced him back onto that horse. And it threw Pip off. I couldn't . . . couldn't bear it anymore." A thread of steel wound through that faint, pain-filled voice. "I *wanted* him to beat me, Hannah, instead of torturing my baby."

Horror, rage, fierce regret rended Hannah with their talons; the picture Lizzy painted was so vivid, so terrible, Hannah feared she would be sick. Lizzy baiting a madman, trying to turn his wrath away from her child.

"Dear God, why didn't I just ignore your letters and come to Booth Hall no matter what you said about inconvenience? I spent my whole life defying Mother and looking after you! But no, my pride had been wounded. I couldn't risk . . . and all that time, you were helpless in the hands of a beast! I'll never forgive myself."

"It wasn't your fault, Hannah. No time for regrets, now, for either of us. There is something . . . I need to ask you. Hannah, my Hannah." Slow tears oozed from the corners of Elisabeth's eyes. "I'm dying, Hannah. Terrified to leave my baby to be . . . hurt."

"Mason Booth will never hurt either of you again," Hannah vowed, clenching her teeth.

"Before Mason beat me this last time, I was going to run away. Take Pip somewhere safe. I sewed my jewels in the lining of a portmanteau. Packed it with his little clothes. But I can't run now. You have to do it for me. Take Pip far away. Hannah, keep him safe. My little boy . . . my poor, poor baby."

"I'll take care of him. I swear it. I'll take you both home with me, where you can have peace."

"Mason would follow, drag us back. The law is on his side. We can't risk that. Our whole family would be in danger. I wish I didn't have to ask you to sacrifice—"

"I'd do anything for you, Lizzy. You know that."

"Mason is gone. Hunting. He left the morning after—"

"He left you dying?"

"He didn't know. He always leaves after. Just disappears for a while. That way, he doesn't have to see the bruises. No time to lose. You have to take Pip now."

"Oh, God, Lizzy, but I've just found you again! How can I leave?"

"Not afraid to die alone."

"Lizzy, no!" Hannah struggled to deny her. "Don't ask this."

"Don't you see, it's the only way? Hannah, you've always been the one to stare reality square in the face. You can't look away now."

It was the most painful truth Hannah had ever been forced to face. But Lizzy was right. Always, Hannah had been the strong one. But now, as she gazed into her sister's eyes, Lizzy seemed to hold all the strength in her fragile, wasted hands.

"You'll be carrying everything I love away with you," Lizzy said gently. "I'm already . . . gone."

And Hannah ached with the knowledge that this was the last thing she would ever be able to do for her beloved sister.

Elisabeth reached over, giving a weak tug at the bellpull beside her. In moments, a servant appeared, very real grief in the girl's plump face.

"My lady?" The girl's eyes were red and puffy from weeping. There was a strange comfort knowing that someone at Booth Hall would grieve when Lizzy was gone. "Can I bring you a sleeping draught? The doctor left plenty."

"No, thank you, Ann. Bring down Master Pip. I wish my sister to . . . meet him."

"O' course! The sight of him always heartens you up. Dear little master." The maid bobbed a curtsey and left.

Hannah had dreamed of this meeting, imagined it for years. But never under such grim circumstances. To surrender Lizzy to death . . . to take her son into her keeping.

Both prospects were terrifying—she had no delusions about how dangerous this mission was. If Elisabeth had taken her son, she would have faced dreadful consequences. But if Hannah did—a woman not even the child's mother taking the heir to a peer of the realm . . . Worse still, she'd never even met the child. How would this little boy who had suffered so much, seen so much, lost so much, ever learn to trust her?

Hannah was stunned to find herself shaking, her knees trembling, her hands knotting together. She crossed to the shadowy corner of the room, trying to put herself to rights. She didn't want to frighten the child. Pip had suffered enough trauma. She owed it to both Elisabeth and her son to have some command of herself.

After a few minutes, she heard a timid creak at the door, saw a slice of thin little face peeping in. Sleep-tousled and frightened, Pip crept through the door, his golden curls shining, his eyes huge and afraid and filled with guilty anguish.

It struck Hannah to the heart to see he was the image of Elisabeth, the sweet curve of his lips, the broad brow, a gentleness of spirit that glowed like the wreath of light from a candle. He didn't even notice Hannah, only had eyes for his mother.

"Mama?" He edged over to the bed as the maid exited and quietly shut the door.

"Pip." For the first time since she'd arrived at Booth Hall, Hannah saw Elisabeth smile—the angel's smile that had made countless men her slaves, the smile so painfully familiar, melting with love.

"Mama, I knew you'd still be here! Nurse said you were going away! That you'd never come back. But I knew you wouldn't leave me alone."

Hannah couldn't breathe. Pip's confidence in his mother clamped the vise of pain even tighter about her ribs.

"Nurse is right. I have to make a journey, sweeting," Elisabeth held her hand out to her son.

Pip crawled ever so carefully up onto her bed. "Can't I come, too?"

"Not for a long while, I hope. You see, I'm traveling up to heaven."

"But that's where—where dead—" Pip clutched at her hand, the horror too great to hold. "No, Mama! I'll be a good boy! I'll ride Papa's horse forever and ever! Just don't go away."

Hannah could feel how much it was costing Elisabeth to keep from crying. "I don't want to go, Pip. But I have to. I can't . . . can't stay."

"But I don't want to be alone! Mama, please!"

It was tearing Hannah's heart from her breast.

"That's the very best thing of all," Elisabeth said, with forced brightness. "You won't be alone. Pip, do you remember all the stories I told you about your Aunt Hannah?"

"She taked care of you when you were a little girl. And you read her letters to me, over and over and over. You love her best of anybody in the whole wide world except for me."

"Now, she's going to take care of *you*. Take you far away where you won't ever have to be afraid. And every time you hold each other tight, you'll both know that I'm still with you. Here." Elisabeth pressed Pip's tiny hand to her heart. "Loving you."

"But I want *you* to hug me! I want *you!*"

"Hannah!" Elisabeth cried in a raw, broken voice. "Help me!"

Help her? How did one explain death, brutality to a

child? Were there any words? But this was Lizzy, her
Elisabeth, so tired, so sad, trying to be brave.

Hannah stepped from the shadows, knelt down, and
touched Pip's babe-soft cheek. "I want her to stay, too.
More than anything in the world. But your mama is—is
broken inside."

Gray-green eyes flashed up to hers, a child's eyes, yet
unutterably old. "It's because of Papa, isn't it?"

"Yes, Pip."

Slowly he reached out his hand and Hannah took it,
feeling Lizzy's love, her hopes and dreams all pressed in
the warm clasp of her son's tiny fingers. The little boy
gazed up at her, raw understanding in his eyes.

"We have to go away before I get broken, too."

The yipping of a puppy shattered memories too sharp,
too clear. Hannah swiped the tears from her face and
turned just in time to see Pip enter the room, the spaniel
in his arms.

"Nanna, the mad Bastard says puppies sleep in the
kennel, but do you think it would be all right if she
snuggled up under the covers with me?"

"I'm not sure, Pip. Your breathing . . . I don't want
you to get sick."

"When I was little and 'fraid and had bad dreams,
sometimes I sneaked out of the nursery, and Mama
would take me into her big bed. It was warm and soft,
and she smelled like flowers. We pretended it was magic,
like Morgause's invisible wall in the Arthur stories.
Nothing bad could come inside. I want to show Lizzy
nobody will bite her or shove her away ever again."

"I know you'll take good care of her, angel."

"Like my mama tried really hard to take care of me.
Nanna, I think Lizzy is lonely," Pip stroked the pup's
furry little muzzle. "It hurts real bad to leave your
mama."

She stroked the curls back from his brow, wishing she
could take away his pain, his loss, knowing she never

could. "Pip," she hesitated, trying to think of how to put her warning in words. "Remember when we first left Ireland, and we talked about—about things we'd have to do to keep ourselves safe?"

"Like making people think you were my mama?"

"Yes. You've done so well, sweetheart. I just . . . just need you to remember that you must never slip and say anything about your real mama to anyone but me. No matter how kind they are to you. Not even Mr. Dante."

"Mr. Dante would never tell Papa where we are. There are angels in his eyes, even when he tries to act mad. But don't worry. I'll be good."

Hannah couldn't help but smile despite her worries. She wondered what Austen Dante would say if he heard Pip's description.

Somewhat reassured, Hannah reached over, turning back the covers. Pip flashed her a smile and clambered up on the bed. As Hannah helped him undress and pull his little nightshirt over his head, Lizzy tugged at sleeves and hems, nosing around under the pillows making Pip laugh.

Hannah glanced out the window at the stars sparkling in far-off heaven, and she prayed that wherever she was, another Lizzy heard the sound, Pip's first new taste of joy.

Who would have guessed it would come as a gift from a reckless, dangerous man, a myriad of secrets hidden in his eyes.

In that frozen instant she decided and was stunned to feel her heart flood with gladness and dismay. She would stay here, at Ravenscar a little longer. Stay with Austen Dante in his elegant prison with its pianoforte and its letters he'd never opened.

But first there was something she must do. Carry the hidden bundles back up to her room. And then, most important of all, return the diamond that ground into her conscience like broken glass beneath the sole of a satin slipper.

There had to be a way to undo everything she'd done. To make everything all right. She could smuggle the food back to where it belonged, then creep back into the Music Room tonight after everyone had gone to bed, slip the bit of jewelry onto the settee where she'd found it. That way, Dante would never know what she had done.

Chapter

The ormolu clock on the mantel struck two in the morning when Hannah slipped from her bed. Lizzy, snuggled next to Pip on his pillow, raised her silky head to peer up at Hannah, then with a contented sigh, nuzzled into the warm cove of Pip's neck.

Hannah's heart ached a little as Pip's arm tightened around the ball of fur even in his sleep. He'd been elated by Dante's promises for the morrow that he would show Pip how to care for the dog himself, brushing out its coat, feeding it from his hand.

And as Pip had prattled on and on about Austen Dante, something hard that had encased Hannah's heart for so long split like a spring-kissed bud, straining toward a warmth she'd almost forgotten.

Crossing to the table, Hannah groped for the stocking she'd set on the top of the portmanteau. Withdrawing the pin, she hid it in the curl of her fingers, then ventured once again into the corridors.

The door to Austen's bedchamber was closed. She'd seen it thus a dozen times, yet never before had she wondered what lay beyond that door, in Austen Dante's most private domain. Memory stirred—those incredible eyes, the almost vulnerable curve of that mouth as he'd watched Pip delight in the puppy.

Who would have thought the mad master of Ravenscar would have understood the secret loneliness inside a little boy's heart? Who would have believed him capable of the tenderness that had been in his touch as he curved his hand over Pip's curls?

Who was he? An enigma like the ancient Celtic shape changers her nurse had told her about as a child—never what they first seemed to be, forever altering before one's eyes.

Hadn't there been a tale of a fairy king trapped by a sorcerer's spell? Freed when the lady of his heart had gazed into his eyes and seen what he truly was—all the pain and uncertainty, courage and fear? All the beauty and blemishes on his soul?

Hannah grasped the diamond pin so tightly it pricked her, and she was glad of the stinging pain, bringing her back to her senses. She needed her wits about her to accomplish this task, and here she was wandering around, as moonstruck as a fairy-kissed maid. There was always a chance someone might be wandering about.

She shivered as a draft penetrated the thin cloth of her nightgown, the carpet crushed beneath her bare feet as she neared the top of the stairway leading down.

But in the middle of the risers, she stopped, her pulse leaping as something soft drifted toward her. The lullaby she had sung for Pip as he'd battled for breath. The melody rippled from the pianoforte in invisible fingers to pluck at the chords of her heart.

She trembled, seeing in her mind's eye Austen Dante lost within the room that seemed to hold him under some dark and painful enchantment. Alone. Always alone, in this house full of people. Alone until he'd knelt beside a wistful little boy with a puppy in his hands.

She caught her lower lip between her teeth. Saints

above, what was she going to do? She should turn around, hasten back to her own bed. Listen until he came upstairs to his bedchamber. She could steal down to replace the pin later. No one had even missed it yet.

She hesitated there for a moment, teetering on the edge of a decision that seemed an insane risk—that or the first honest thing she'd done since Austen Dante had taken her in out of the rain.

Sucking in a steadying breath, she glided down the remaining stairs like a ghost in her nightgown, and entered the Music Room.

A branch of candles glowed atop the pianoforte, its shimmering surface littered with the letters she'd read to him what seemed an eternity ago. Candle shine cast Dante's features into a montage of light and shadow, accenting the lean planes of his face, the arrestingly handsome curve of jaw and slash of cheekbone.

A dressing robe of rich blue and cream stripes gilded his shoulders, his dark hair tousled as if he'd run his fingers through it a dozen times in frustration.

Only rarely had Hannah felt the flutterings her sisters had over a primally attractive male. But it was as if in this moment all those instincts saved up from the time she should have been a giddy girl spilled into her blood—heat and uncertainty, inexpressible longing.

Her heart thudded as he drifted out the final chords of the melody, then buried his face in his hand. In that instant, she wanted to reach out, to touch the dark silk of his hair in comfort, and for the fire of need she sensed it would unleash in her most secret places.

But she didn't dare. She purposely jarred a table, making noise so he would hear her.

He turned, his eyes naked for a heartbeat, with a vulnerability she'd never suspected, before he shuttered it away.

"Hannah. Did you hear me hammering away on this rot?" He forced his lips into a rueful smile. "You didn't have to come down here. I thought I'd let you get a full night's sleep for once. God knows, you looked tired and pale when you came to the kennels this afternoon."

"I didn't come down to write music, unless . . . unless you'd like me to."

"No. I've stolen your song, you see. It sounds far better than anything I've bludgeoned out of the instrument these past months."

"I suppose it's only fair that you did." Hannah swallowed hard, not wanting to upset the strange new sense of understanding between them.

Ridiculous notion—what could she have in common with Austen Dante? A practical woman with a sharp tongue and independent ideas that irritated every man she'd ever known, and a wealthy landowner with a reckless male beauty that would make an angel weep, and a birthright of power bred into his bones that she could never match.

"I don't understand," he said, his eyes narrowing in question.

"Today, when I came to find Pip, I was . . . I'd already decided to leave Ravenscar. My bags were packed, under the azaleas."

He paled visibly. "But I hadn't given you a shilling! What would you have done for food? Shelter?"

"I would have . . . I mean, I'd made some provision—" It was harder than she had imagined, looking into those mesmerizing eyes and confessing what she had done. "Mr. Dante, I stole this from you." She thrust out her hand, opening it to reveal the diamond pin. It winked up like a condemning eye.

Dante's gaze traveled ever so slowly to her upturned palm. He was silent for a long moment. She couldn't breathe, waiting for him to speak. They'd been locked in a battle of wills from the instant they met. Argued, baited each other. She was stunned to realize just how much she dreaded the disillusionment, the betrayal that would darken his eyes.

"You'd taken off your cravat and just left this lying

atop it, so I took it. When you said you wouldn't give me the salary I'd earned . . ." she faltered. Earned? Her cheeks burned with shame, the lie rough on her tongue. She had earned nothing but Austen Dante's contempt. Had lied to him from the first.

What was she trying to do, babbling here like an idiot? Explain away the fact that she would steal from the man who had taken her and Pip in out of the rain? She could rationalize all she wished, but the truth was still simple, ugly, laid bare in the stolen pin upon her outstretched palm.

"It doesn't matter *why* I did it," she admitted, swallowing hard. "I did. If you want me to leave Ravenscar now, I understand."

God in heaven, how long was he going to stare down at her hand with that strange expression on his face? As though searching for the answer to some age-old riddle collapsed down into that single shining jewel? She'd never seen him so still.

After what seemed an eternity he reached out, curving his long fingers about her own. Hard, astonishingly calloused were his hands, so strong they amazed her, so warm that they set her soul trembling. He curled her fingers back around the jewel, his voice low, rough.

"Keep it."

"Wh—what?"

"That way, if you're ever fool enough to run away again, I won't have to wonder if you and Pip have had enough to eat or if you have a roof over your head."

Hannah gaped at him, stunned. This man with his power and his wealth worry about the two of them on the road? The possibility had never occurred to her. But no one could doubt the stark sincerity that transformed those dauntingly masculine features.

"But—But sir, you don't understand. I . . . I *stole* this from you."

"Consider it a gift."

"I couldn't possibly accept," she stammered.

His lips curved in a smile unlike any she'd ever seen, ironic, yet warm as brandy over a flame. "You were ready enough to accept it when you stole it, weren't you?" he asked gently.

"That—that was different! It must be worth a fortune!"

"If it will make you feel better, we can pretend this conversation never happened, and you can steal it all over again. My valet will grouse over my carelessness, and I'll shrug, and buy another one. Or, perhaps . . ." He paused, his gaze intensifying. "Perhaps it would be simpler if I merely asked for something in return."

"Yes. I mean, no . . . I . . ." Hannah stiffened, certain he'd push again for the information he wanted, things she could not tell him.

"It's not such a very great request, but it would give me much pleasure." He only looked down at her hand and she was suddenly, fiercely aware it was still cradled in the sinewy heat of his own. "Call me Austen."

"A—Austen?"

"It's been a very long time since anyone called me by that name."

"Austen." Her cheeks burned. Her hand trembled. It wasn't at all proper how right his name sounded on her tongue. Rich and sweet as melted chocolate, velvety and intoxicating. "But I don't think . . . I mean, it's hardly appropriate—"

"Please, Hannah." Vulnerability was etched into the arrogant lines of his face. He was bone-meltingly beautiful, bewitching as he gazed down at her. And suddenly, incredibly accessible, as if he'd stepped down off of some unseen stage and cast away his disguise just for her.

Now was the time to tell him that she couldn't write music. Confess that much at least. But would his anger at her betrayal overrule his astonishingly generous nature? The music lost—music he had labored over so painfully. Music that was both his curse and, she sensed, vitally important in some way she didn't yet understand.

She swallowed hard. The Music Room had been a prison to both of them. Yet, suddenly, the hours spent there seemed precious—hours she could watch his changeable face, the quicksilver emotions, the blinding-bright intelligence, the passion and the pain. Hours in which she could try to understand the man, Austen Dante—instead of the notorious mad master of Ravenscar.

A man who could take strangers in from the storm, yet ignore the letters his family had written. A man desperately alone, despite the fact that every line from his mother and sisters had been layered with such poignancy and longing they had wrenched at Hannah's heart. Was it possible that longing was echoed somewhere hidden in Austen Dante's face?

She peered up at him as if for the very first time, a man so devastatingly handsome he stole her breath away. Eyes so intense they seemed to probe to the very center of her soul. A man. An enigma. One she desperately wanted to understand. But how? Where to begin to unravel the tempting mystery that was Austen Dante?

A fragment of candlelight caught her eye, its flame captured in glimmering reflection atop the pianoforte.

The music . . . Hannah thought suddenly. Perhaps that held the key. But did she dare probe something that was so obviously painful to him? Yet if she lacked the courage to do so, she might never be able to know him—really know him. Something she wanted with astonishing passion.

"Austen," she began before she could change her mind. "May I ask you a question?"

"I've asked you more than enough of them. Not that my inquiries have done me any good." He flashed her a wry grimace. "So what is this mysterious question, madam?"

Hannah's lips didn't so much as flicker into a smile at his attempted jest. She drew in a steadying breath. "Why is the music so important?"

Whatever he'd expected her to ask about, it was not his music.

Dark brows drew together. "Pardon me?"

"Why are you so obsessed with the music?" She was going to bungle this, but there was nothing to do but plunge on. "I could understand suffering so much out of love for it. But that's not the reason you spend so much time chained to the pianoforte. I've watched you for days, fighting so hard—hour after hour. Sometimes I think you hate it. So why put yourself through the misery—unless there is some very compelling reason?"

"Ah, so my lack of talent has finally driven you to beg mercy, has it? You don't need so elaborate an excuse to convince me to—"

"Don't."

"Don't what?"

"Don't make a jest out of this, dismiss it. I only want to be your friend." It sounded absurd even to her own ears, but the words were out. There was no way to take them back.

"My friend." He rolled the phrase over his tongue as if tasting it for the first time. His mouth curled into a slow, wistful smile.

"It's been a very long time since I've had a friend. Not since Chuffy—" He stopped, warm color darkening his cheeks. How could this man be so alone? A man of wealth and breeding, wit and intelligence. *And kindness,* a voice inside her added. Surely she and Pip couldn't be the first less fortunate he'd been generous to. No, kindness like Austen Dante's on the night of the storm was rarely a single act.

Yet now as she stared up into the stark planes of his fallen-angel face she sensed she had gone too far, cut too deeply, touched something inside him so raw no one had ever done so before.

The knowledge frightened her, entranced her. "Please, Austen," she asked. "Tell me about the music."

She expected him to close her out—eyes shuttered,

mouth hard, reprimanding her for her impudence. But he only regarded her for a long moment, as if he were trying to decide to step off of a precipice. Intensity burned her through his thick lashes. She could feel the breaking away deep inside him, and the dread as he decided to leap.

"Hannah, have you ever failed someone—completely? Someone you loved?"

A giant fist squeezed Hannah's heart. She was flooded with regrets all shaded in the once-vibrant hues of Elisabeth's face. Images weighted her soul like chains—each link an insight into what her sister's life must have been like before Lizzy had died, terrifying, hopeless, helpless. "I—"

"No," Dante cut her off. "You would never let anything defeat you. My intrepid Hannah." His voice softened with tenderness as he stroked the curve of her cheek with one long finger. The touch seemed to melt into her very soul.

"You're wrong about me," she confided, vowing to meet his courage with her own, astonished at how good it felt to say the words to another human being. "I've failed the one person I loved most in the world besides Pip."

His gaze met hers and held. "Then you know you'd do anything to make it up to them. To tell them you're sorry. No—telling isn't good enough. You have to show them."

There had been so little time with Lizzy. So many words they couldn't say. "Sometimes, all it takes is a touch," Hannah said softly. "It can say everything. At least I pray it can."

Dante's face tightened with pain. "Words. Infernal words. Worthless things. I've always been damnably clumsy with them. God, who could suspect they could wound so deeply."

"I've always been clumsy myself. Words falling out of my mouth, abominably blunt."

Dante gave her a smile so sad her breath caught. "I

haven't that excuse. That it was an accident, I mean. I wounded on purpose. Used the words like a sword to drive him away so he couldn't see . . ." His voice broke, and Hannah couldn't bear it. She reached up, stroking back a lock of dark hair that tumbled over his brow, offering comfort as if he were no bigger than Pip. What could this man have done that was so terrible? Or was he hiding something? Something so painful he couldn't bear it? Did the particulars really matter? He was hurting. And she wanted to ease the pain.

"Sometimes we're all afraid to let anyone see who we really are. To trust them with that."

"To allow them to see all our flaws? All our petty deceits? The ugly places of the spirit everyone tries so damned hard to hide?" His voice stung with bitterness.

"It seems to me that love makes one overlook such things—see only the beauty."

"Providing there is any beauty to be found. However, if a man is— What was it you said? Useless as a polished rock?"

"It was very wrong of me to say that. You've proven your generosity to Pip and me over and over again. You've asked for nothing in return." Her throat tightened with what it cost her to reveal emotions she'd always kept so guarded. "How can I ever hope to repay you? I have nothing of value to give."

Something flickered in his eyes, an awakening that made her breath catch. "You're wrong. So wrong to underestimate yourself, Hannah," he said tenderly. "You have more to offer a man than you could ever imagine."

Fire burned up her cheeks, and she lowered her gaze from his face, then wished she hadn't as it fell on a deep V of satin dressing gown that framed a hard wall of masculine chest. Sun-bronzed muscles rippled in the gilt liquid of the candle shine, a dusting of dark hair tempting her to touch.

What would it feel like to press her palm against the beat of his aching heart? To feel his mouth on her's, banishing a little of their aloneness for just a while?

The thought frightened her, made her feel stripped to the soul, shaken. Hannah Gray, with her iron will, her fierce control, stuffed with fantasies of strong arms around her, a man's hunger consuming her. Her heart was fluttering like the silliest flirt ever born.

Lord, why had her sisters ever enjoyed this sensation? It was like tumbling off a cliff into the depths of this man's eyes.

Eyes suddenly hot, hungry swirled with dark mysteries. His gaze flicked to her lips, lingered there, his thick, dark lashes falling to half-mast. He didn't have to touch her mouth with his. She felt his intensity down to her very toes.

"Hannah . . . I . . ." He reached behind her nape, catching the thick rope of her braid with his hand, winding the shining plait around his palm as if to make himself prisoner to the wild enchantment even now whirling up between them.

She stared into his eyes, wanting . . . wanting . . . yet so very afraid. Afraid of the vulnerable places he could see in her candlelit face, places she couldn't hide when he was touching her. But there was no triumph, no scorn, only astonishment in his handsome features, as if he were as surprised as she was.

Ever so slowly Austen tipped her face up to his. Hannah couldn't breathe; time froze as his sensual mouth hovered over hers for an instant. She was terrified he would pull away.

But he did not. With indescribable tenderness, the warmth of his mouth sought hers. Hot velvet—sweet supplication coaxing her very soul from her body—his lips mated with hers in a kiss at once melting and avid, hungry and filled with awe.

Never before had Hannah tasted a man's mouth, yet

she knew in that instant that if she'd sampled kisses freely as her mother did bonbons, Austen Dante would have wiped away all memory of any other man.

A low groan tore from his throat and he gathered her against him, branding her soft nightgown-gilded form with the hot, hard contours of his own body. Her breasts were crushed against his chest, her legs brushing his hard thighs.

She was stunned to feel a tremor work through him. Desire? For her? It seemed incredible that this man, so perfect he might have been coaxed by Michelangelo from living marble should want practical, plain Hannah Gray.

His tongue traced the crease of her lips. "Open your mouth, Hannah," he murmured. "Let me taste you inside." The plea was intoxicating, wicked, wonderful.

She opened to him, and he made a foray to her slick hidden center. And Hannah sampled male desire in its most potent form.

With exquisite care, he explored her mouth, the ridges of her teeth, the tip of her tongue, coaxing her, making her want ever more. And her senses filled with the taste of him, the feel of him, the scent of him—recklessness and secrets, vulnerability and desire, loneliness and bay rum.

Her fingers tightened over the diamond until the pin bit into her hand, but she barely noticed the pain. Never had she allowed herself to melt into a man's arms, to feel his strength surrounding her, protecting her.

Spreading the fingers of her other hand, she glided them over his collarbone, up the corded power of his neck, to thread them through the rough satin of his hair. The silky lengths sifted between her fingers, a sweet seduction that made her heart ache.

A raw groan reverberated through Dante's chest, and she felt it like a caress in the burning tips of her breasts.

"Hannah," he breathed, skimming his palms over her body. "Hannah . . . Hannah . . . Hannah . . ."

Cloth gathered beneath the heat of his hands as he

explored every curve and dip and hollow. The worn cotton rubbed with sensual abrasion over skin that felt aflame from his touch, the cloth bunching then rippling back into place.

Hannah whimpered, her tongue daring to touch the tip of his, her nipples tingling and burning with a need that set her cheeks afire and her mind reeling.

She wanted him to fill his hands with the bounty of her breasts, wanted so much more. . . .

Unable to stop herself, she glided her fingertips down his throat, flattening her palm on the V of naked chest framed in the satin of his dressing gown. Dark hair prickled at her skin, teased it, the muscles beneath rippling and hot, the skin surprisingly satiny.

She shivered as he glided the edge of his thumb along the plump side of her breast, sensation spearing through her as he brushed the sensitive point of her nipple for the first time.

"Oh . . . Oh, please . . ." she whimpered, but she wasn't sure if she were begging for him to stop this sensual torture or to go further, faster, unleashing the blaze he had started between them. "I can't . . . can't bear it."

"Don't pull away from me, Hannah." The rough throb in his voice rocked her to her core. Frightened her. Thrilled her. The idea that Austen Dante needed her. But what could he possibly need? "I won't hurt you like he did," Austen promised.

He? Who in the world was he talking about? Hannah wondered, befuddled. Then it struck her. Dante believed Pip was her son, that she'd lain with another man, let him do everything Dante had done to her, and so much more. Everything he wanted, needed from her. To take her to his bed. To strip away her nightgown until there was nothing between them but the lies she had told.

Lord, whatever had she been thinking to allow him to touch her this way? Wasn't her situation precarious enough already? A pulse of panic jarred her.

"Please, stop!"

The words seemed to jolt through him and he broke the kiss, holding her away from him. His eyes burned, blue-hot coals in a stricken face, the pulse beat at his throat pounding erratically, his dark hair tousled from the loving of her hands.

He looked surprised, disoriented, as if he'd suddenly awakened from some enchanted sleep still hungry for the taste of his dreams.

God above, what must he think of her? The notion that he believed, even falsely, that she held her body so cheaply made Hannah sick to her stomach. But she could hardly blurt out the truth, could she?

I've never come to a man's bed . . . never even been kissed, until you—

"This should never have happened." Hannah pressed her fingers to lips still trembling from his tender onslaught.

Those blue-fire eyes stripped her to her soul. "Perhaps it shouldn't have, but I can't be sorry I kissed you, Hannah." The rough confession stirred her to her core. "I needed to touch you. And I think you needed me, too."

Dante watched the emotions clash in her face, saw the truth in those expressive eyes. And the fear. It must have felt horrendous—Hannah, his independent, gallant Hannah, reaching out to someone for comfort. What had it cost her? Especially after her experience with the brute who had fathered her son.

She said nothing. She didn't have to. He had peered into her soul.

He stood mesmerized as she walked away, her dark-fire hair spilling in a thick braid down her back, her shoulders squared. Yet for the second time since she'd come to Ravenscar, he'd glimpsed a softening in her, an uncertainty that made his knees weak and his pulse throb.

His gaze clung to the rippling white of her nightgown

as she moved toward the door, golden fingers of candle-light illuminating her long, shapely legs, silhouetting the delicate curve of hip, the feminine dip of her waist.

Who would have thought that beneath her drab gowns his prickly, sharp-tongued Hannah would hide the kind of body that made a man's mouth water? Yet there was some indefinable quality deeper than mere beauty of face or form that yanked at Dante's heart, demanding some answer he wasn't certain he was capable of giving.

"Hannah," he called out, unable to let her merely slip from the room, leaving him alone. "I'd never hurt you. Do you believe that?"

She paused, one slender hand on the door, turning just enough that he caught a breath-stealing glimpse of the breast that had felt so full, so warm, so right in his hand. The slightly darker circle of her nipple tempted like the sweet center of some exotic confection gilded with the thinnest rim of sugar.

"I know you would never mean to hurt me," she said. "But sometimes things happen. Things no one can help."

"Like the kiss we just shared?" Dante asked. He'd only meant to drink in her courage, taste whatever it was inside her that made her so strong, so certain.

But then he had taken her breast in his hand, pressed her supple body against his until he was wild with the craving to feel her beneath him, naked, needing.

Hellfire, what a monster he was, taking such things from her when she was so vulnerable, so alone. Did she have any idea that he could still feel the worn-smooth cotton of her nightgown crushed in his hands? That he longed to hear the soft rustle as he drew it over her head?

She'd be horrified if she suspected it. She'd have every right to be. But there was something about this indomitable lady that challenged him, infuriated him, seeped into the dark corners of his soul like some shimmering enchantment.

"Hannah, do *you* regret what we just shared?" The possibility wounded deeply.

God, how did she seem to know that? Sense that? Her eyes flooded with such understanding and pain it took his breath away.

"It was wrong. I never should have—" she faltered. Then her voice gentled so slightly no one else might have known. But he did. Heaven help him, he did. "It wasn't your fault," she absolved him. "I mean, I shouldn't have been wandering about in my—my nightgown."

"Someone should have warned you the night you arrived at Ravenscar not to trundle about in such garb." He grimaced. "It's my custom to kiss every one of my servants I find in their sleeping attire. Why, just three weeks ago, I caught the housekeeper—"

"Don't! I know you didn't mean for it to happen any more than I did. I don't want you to think that I—I blame you for everything. I just . . ." She hesitated, her cheeks flushed with color, rounded and sweet, worlds away from the sunken pallor that had stolen their bloom when he'd first found her outside his door. When had she grown so beautiful in his eyes?

"What happened here doesn't change the way I feel." She was a damned rotten liar. Everything had changed the instant he'd taken her in his arms. "I want to thank you, sir. For all your kindnesses. I—I don't deserve them." Guilt shredded the edge of her voice, leaving it ragged.

"Austen." He rasped his name, stunned at how hungry he was to hear it from her lips.

"What?"

"Not *sir*. Austen."

She hesitated, her lashes dipping down. "Austen," she echoed, the gentle Irish lilt in her voice turning his name into something lyrical, a poetry of the heart.

He didn't dare to look at her, terrified that his emotions would be exposed in his eyes. He heard the soft padding of her bare feet on the carpet, knew the instant he was alone, the sweet, soapy clean scent of her fading away, the whisper of cloth around her legs silenced.

He wanted to chase after her, imagined his hand closing about that fragile wrist, Hannah turning, her eyes wide with yearning.

He could scoop her into his arms, carry her back into the Music Room, or up to his bedroom where he had always slept alone. And he could finish what they'd begun.

And what was that? a voice inside him demanded.

Reality plunged a spike of ugliness in the center of such sweet dreamings. What could he do? Take this woman who had been so abused by some other man, enjoy her body and sate his own carnal need? Make her his mistress for a little while? Until time or circumstances brought an end to their liaison?

The thought of Hannah surrendering herself to such a base position made his gorge rise. She had been fashioned to sail through life head high, pride gleaming in those intelligent eyes. Not to be whispered about by servants, secretly scorned, lowered to a mere trifle necessary to most highborn men, a dalliance common, yet vaguely unclean.

God's wounds, pawing her in the Music Room tonight he'd been little better than the bastard who had defiled her. Dante had all but laid her back onto the hearth rug, taken from her everything a woman could give in an effort to fill the empty places inside himself with her courage, her secret softness, her fire.

Desperately as he wanted Hannah, he could never be selfish enough to succumb to those needs. She had already suffered too much. He'd cut off his own hand before he hurt her even more.

Had Pip's father ever considered what he'd condemned her to when he'd bedded her? A child born out of wedlock. Ruin that could never be sponged away. What other alternative except the position of mistress was left for Hannah, if she ever wanted to feel a man's arms around her? A suitable marriage was impossible for her now.

Why did the thought open up a hollow place inside him, somewhere he hadn't known he was aching? He closed his eyes, picturing her as she must have been six years ago—no frivolous luxuries and giggling behind fans for Hannah, yet painfully young, thinking she was so very worldly-wise, invincible to seductions other girls might fall prey to. Yet somehow she had been lured into succumbing to a cruel and brutal man—or been forced to. The mere thought was enough to make his fists clench. That seduction had stolen all chance of a proper home from her, a husband who loved her, who would show her passion in the night, and fill her womb with brothers and sisters for little Pip.

Blood and thunder, why should that stark reality rake through him so cruelly? It wasn't as if he'd been pining for the blissful state of matrimony himself. He'd always seen it as excruciating intimacy where one's soul lay in peril, where a woman might discover the ugliest blemishes within . . .

He'd always known eventually he'd be forced into some kind of union to fill the family cradle with an appropriate heir. But such was more a business transaction—like breeding a particularly fine stallion to a mare's exalted bloodline. Something cool and impersonal, incapable of causing any but the most dispassionate pain.

But Hannah—Hannah unleashed so many things inside him, fears and hopes, pain and dreams, an opening of the tight fist where all his secrets were hid.

It was true she deserved a man to love her—but she deserved a whole man. One who could match her intelligence, her courage, her honesty. A man worlds different from Austen Dante.

He'd been selfish most of his life, so wrapped up in protecting himself, shielding himself, guarding his secrets, that there had been little energy left for anything else. Yet now he found himself hungering for something far different. A giving that had nothing to do with what he might receive in return.

He crossed to the pianoforte, took up the branch of candles. Dante slipped through his house that had been so empty only a week ago, his memory echoing with Pip's laughter, and visions of a puppy's pink tongue kissing roses into the boy's thin cheeks.

He felt the wild lurch of his heart turning over again as it had the moment he'd turned to see Hannah hovering near him, her nightgown flowing about her like an angel's wings, her eyes soft and vulnerable and filled with a gnawing sense of guilt and sadness.

Guilt because of the diamond stickpin? Or had there been more? Even after he'd told her to keep the bauble, the shadows hadn't gone away.

He wanted so desperately to heal her. But Austen had never had the power to heal anyone, had he? What was it Hannah had said in her anger? From the looks of the letters she'd read to him the day before, he couldn't even help himself.

Perhaps not, but he could help her in a dozen little ways, if he could only get past that stiff-necked pride of hers.

Quietly, he stole from the room and mounted the curving sweep of stairs. He'd climbed it so many times before, seeking escape in the darkness of sleep which wouldn't come.

When he reached the door of the bedchamber across from his own, he hesitated, heard the soft swish of Hannah in the room beyond. No, she hadn't yet gone to sleep. She was pacing, troubled, unsettled . . . just as he was.

Was she reliving the taste of his mouth on hers? Experiencing the flashes of desire that had shot between them as he'd gathered her against his body? Did she still feel his hand seeking out her breast, his thumb whispering caresses across her taut nipple?

Or was she afraid, shaken that he'd beckoned her so close to—to what? Disaster? A disaster she'd experienced once before, one that had left her battered, alone, with a child to care for. One that had left her afraid.

No. No matter how his body clamored to delve into Hannah's own, he wouldn't hurt her as that other bastard had. He wanted to help her, didn't he? That was all.

God above, what secrets did she hold locked so tightly in those steady eyes of hers? And why did he fear that they might hold the power to send her running away again into the night where he might lose her forever?

The thought raked through him with razor-sharp claws. Lose her? Hannah Graystone wasn't his to lose. She was a valiant, intelligent, passionate woman who had found shelter in the most unlikely hands. Yet the thought of anything happening to her or to the boy was anathema to him.

If only she would trust him . . .

Trust. Such a fragile thing. Why should she extend it to him? Up until an hour ago, she'd believed him capable of throwing her and Pip out into the street to starve because she dared defy him.

But sometime during their exchange over the glittering diamond, they'd traded something far more precious—bridged misunderstanding, probed past pretense and half-truths and masks they'd both worn. He'd glimpsed beneath Hannah's brave facade a yearning that had transformed that resolute face, a longing buried so deep Dante doubted Hannah even knew it was there.

If only there were enough time to wait until she opened up to him, confided her secret. But he didn't dare. If he did, it might be too late to shield her from whatever dark storm was threatening to overtake her.

Still, what choice did he have? He'd tried bullying her, cajoling her. Hannah had made up her mind not to tell him, and the woman was damnably stubborn. As for any other course, he dared not probe for an answer with Pip again. The child had suffered enough.

No, Dante reasoned, if he wanted to help Hannah, he'd have to find another way. But how?

Suddenly his brows crashed together. Of course. Business affairs had been piling up abominably in the past year. It was long past time he made a trip to his solicitor's in London. Once there, he could make inquiries, find someone reliable to get the information he needed.

Employ some spy to ferret out Hannah's secret? Unmask her past? He'd never been overly scrupulous. Why did this make him recoil?

It would be a betrayal of the worst kind, striking at the fierce independence in Hannah's eyes. And yet . . . he only wanted to protect her. That was the reason he felt this burning desire to know everything about her, wasn't it? Or was there another reason, something hidden, something he couldn't even put into words?

He suppressed a sting of doubt. Blast, it didn't matter. The result would be the same whatever his motives.

Dante raised one hand, flattened it against the door to her bedchamber. But instead of the wooden panel, he imagined the supple warmth of Hannah's hand, felt her soft pulse beating beneath his fingertips, the indescribable sweetness of her mouth opening beneath his own.

She would be safe here. He vowed it. Safe from whatever dark secret stalked her. The devil take the cost.

But after all was done, one last question would remain.

Would Hannah ever forgive him?

Chapter

The day he'd arrived at Booth Hall to find his wife dead, his son stolen away, Mason Booth had vowed there was nowhere in the bowels of hell that Hannah Gray could hide. He would run the interfering witch to the ground, and when he did he'd make certain she paid for what she had done.

Every day since, he had renewed that vow.

He would flay her to the bone, subject her to the same torture she'd put him through these last six years. Hannah—the bitch who had cost him the affection of his wife. The shadow that had forever lain between him and Elisabeth . . .

Hatred seethed through Mason Booth's veins like poison as he guided his horse through the Wicklow hills, his silver-gilt hair wind-lashed from sharply honed features, his green eyes cold as bottle glass.

It had been vile enough that Hannah had attempted to dissuade Elisabeth from marrying him a mere hour before their wedding—the church already packed with illustrious guests, the bridal party waiting. A sin for which he'd never forgiven her.

He'd heard Elisabeth's stammer as she repeated her vows, saw the clouding of doubt in her beautiful eyes, and he'd been sick with rage, fearful that someone else would be cunning enough to see that his bride was suddenly less than eager.

And in the years that followed, Hannah had always stood between them no matter how ruthlessly Mason had struggled to tear her out, refusing all but the most cursory contact, forbidding his wife ever to allow the woman to darken the doorway of Booth Hall.

But even from a distance, Hannah Gray had still infested his wife with her venom, until his lovely, sweet, malleable Elisabeth had defied him—pushed him, angered him—so much that he'd had no choice but to lash out as any red-blooded man would have, to force her into obedience.

Grief welled up inside him, a hot, thorny thing. Yes, Elisabeth's death was on Hannah's head, not his own. But even that sin was not enough for the hell-born woman. No, she'd committed the unforgivable— Hannah Gray had stolen his son.

Rage shimmered, a red haze before Mason's eyes, and his hands tightened on the reins of his hunter as it hurtled over a piled-stone fence. It was damned embarrassing for a man to misplace his heir, no matter how weak and sickly the boy might be. And half of Ireland knew that Pip was missing.

Hannah had made him look a fool. And she'd threatened to do far worse. To expose his darkest secret. She'd left him helpless as he dashed about the countryside in search of them. Every lead he'd managed to dredge up had led nowhere. Every effort he'd made futile, as if he were trying to capture the wind.

But now there was a chance—just a chance that the die was cast in his favor.

The note he'd found on his desk at Booth Hall a month ago seemed to burn in Mason's waistcoat pocket with a life of its own. *If you dare to follow us, I will tell everything I know. I will expose you for what you are—*

Did Hannah—witty, clever Hannah, reeking of superiority—realize that with those words she had signed her own death warrant? Made certain he would never stop searching for her until he felt her slender throat between his hands, his fingers crushing the life from her?

Did she guess his one pleasure, thick and potent, in the past months as he'd searched had been anticipating that glorious moment, just before death claimed her, when she would know he had triumphed?

Yet that fantasy had seemed farther and farther beyond his reach as each day passed, until a bedraggled manservant had shown up at Booth Hall six hours ago.

He guided his hunter around a copse of trees, his gaze fixing on a smear of gray stone just visible upon the hill—a house as practical and dowdy and run down at the heels as Hannah herself was.

Perhaps it was perfect irony that he'd been summoned to this house where he'd courted Elisabeth and first loathed Hannah for her interfering ways. That the women left behind there had offered their aid . . .

Dearest Mason,
Make haste to come to Dove Cottage. A disreputable tinker who claims to have helped Hannah abduct Pip is even now in the kitchen. We are doing all in our power to detain him until your arrival. Pray God he can help you find your son.

Pray God, indeed. Or to the devil. Mason did not care which. He would barter his soul to either in exchange for Hannah Gray. He had to stop her before she made good her threat. Before she told—

No. He would find her. He would silence her. He would take back his son and make a man of him, if it killed them both.

Mason hadn't even reined his horse to a halt before the door to Dove Cottage flew open, Mrs. Gray stumbling out in a cloud of fussy lace and anxiety, her daughters in her wake.

"Mason, my dear boy!" his mother-in-law gasped. "Thank God you are here! I think that tinker *must* be the despicable person who convinced Hannah to be so wicked. He said he wanted to make certain I knew she was well, that his own daughter had run away, once, and he recalled how distraught he was until he heard she was safe. As if such a person could compare his feelings to my own!"

"It must have been horribly upsetting to you, being harassed by such a lowling," Mason commiserated. "I'll make certain he never accosts you again."

"You *will* find Hannah, won't you?" Mrs. Gray pleaded, her fingers plucking at Mason's cloak. "Horrified as I am at what Hannah has done, I'm still her mama. I'm frightened that in her grief for Elisabeth she's lost her reason, snatching Pip off like this. Someone must help her."

"Oh, I promise you I'll help poor, misguided Hannah," Mason vowed.

Tears tracked down Mrs. Gray's face, a face so like an overindulged child's. "You are always so good to us, Mason. Even though Hannah never had the wit to appreciate it, the rest of us are exceedingly grateful for your kindness. I cannot thank you enough for attempting to save Hannah from herself."

Mason felt a surge of triumph. "Where is this tinker your messenger informed me about?"

"The tinker?" Mrs. Gray echoed. "Oh. Yes. The tinker. We did everything we could, but were unable to detain him any longer! He left nearly half an hour ago."

"Why didn't you—" Mason bit off his sentence, finishing it in his mind. —*tell me the instant I got here instead of wasting time with your prattle? Because you're a gaggle of accursed idiots! That's why!* Mason swore under his breath, barely keeping himself from grabbing the babbling woman and shaking the information he needed out of her. "Which way did he go?" he asked with admirable restraint.

"To the west," nineteen-year-old Harriet piped up, waving her bonnet toward a ribbon of road. "I told Mama not to worry! You're such a superb rider I was certain you would catch him, Mason."

It was a damn good thing he was, or Hannah would have slipped through his fingers again. "I must go."

"Do you need a fresh horse?" Theophania asked, grabbing his reins. "You could borrow one of Uncle's from the big house."

As if he'd ride one of Gray's insufferable nags! There wasn't one in the stable that could catch a lumbering oxen, let alone a tinker trying to melt into the mist. "Thank you for your offer. Brutus will be fine."

"The girls and I would do anything in our power to help you find Hannah and poor little Pip." Mrs. Gray's hand fluttered to her ample breasts. "Hurry, dear boy. Our prayers go with you!"

Mason touched one hand to the brim of his hat, then dug his spurs into his horse's barrel, running hell-for-leather in the direction Harriet had pointed.

God, what a worthless bunch of females! He'd heard that old Sir Lucius Gray had leapt to his death from the roof of a building. It was little wonder he was driven to extremes, but he should have heaved his wife off instead. It seemed like a damned good notion! He shoved the pleasant image away.

He leaned low over the neck of his horse, urging it faster, harder.

Nothing from the ineptitude of a gaggle of bungling women to the cunning of a rat of a tinker would keep him from his goal. Every man had a price, and this tinker should be easier to buy than most. He would hunt down this lowborn scum and offer whatever coin was necessary to get the information he needed to find Hannah Gray.

And if the tinker was fool enough to refuse coin . . . there were other ways of getting what he needed. Mason's lip curled in distaste.

He would do what he had to to work his will, no matter how unpleasant. Just as he had with Elisabeth. After all, a man could do no less.

Mason's riding crop dripped blood, his gloves spattered crimson as he towered over the old man huddled in the dust of the road. The eyes that had been so shrewd, so contemptuous when he'd flung the offer of money back in Booth's face were hollow now with pain.

"I warned you not to make me angry!" Booth snarled, drawing back his aching arm to strike the tinker again. "Damn you, don't make me keep hitting you. Where did Hannah Gray go with my son?"

The tinker tried to force himself up on his elbows, spitting hatred. "Go to hell, ye devil! She tol' me enough about ye, I know yer kind. An' the rest I saw in the eyes o' the boy! I'll never tell ye what ye want! Been beaten by far more imposin' men than you, and never did they get the truth out'a Padraic Hussey. The lady and the boy be out'a yer reach, for certain-sure. An' there's nothin' ye can do to me that'll make me betray 'em."

Mason glared down into that weathered gnomelike face. His whole torso burned with the strain of beating the man, and in that instant he knew the tinker was right. He could flay the skin off Hussey's body one knife blade at a time and the old Irishman would never tell. Damnable breed—defiance bred into their very bones. Still, there had to be some weakness in the man . . . some way to force the old dog's hand.

The drab gray horse hitched to the gaudily painted tinker's cart snorted and side stepped in its traces, worried equine eyes finding the old man. And at that instant the tinker betrayed himself, his gaze falling on the horse with love.

Of course.

Mason's lips split in a smile over bared teeth. "Perhaps you're right, old man," he sneered, knowing the triumph of a wolf with its teeth poised just above the jugular vein of its prey. "There is nothing I can do to you. But I wonder . . ."

He crossed to the horse, catching hold of its rein. "I'd imagine it gets lonely on the road. No one to talk to."

"Considerin' the conversation I been treated to since ye rode up behind me, I'm not missin' much."

"I'd imagine your horse would become your family after years on the road. Like your children, friends—"

"What the divil does it have to do with anything? A horse is a horse," the old man scoffed. But the glimmer of fear in his eye betrayed him.

Casting aside the riding crop, Mason drew a knife blade from his boot top, turning it until the sunlight glinted along the razor-sharp edge. "I wonder how much agony a horse is capable of suffering? As much as a man, do you think?"

"Wh—What are ye doin'? Stay away from Finn!"

Mason poised the blade against the taut tendon at the back of the horse's front leg. "One little slice—"

The tinker tried to struggle to his feet, failed. "No! Ye leave the horse alone!"

"It would be a shame to lame the horse forever," Mason observed. "You'd have to put the animal down. There'd be no way to heal it." He arched one brow. "I don't suppose you could afford another?"

"Damn you! You're Satan's own! No wonder the poor lady was so fearful o' ye—monster that ye are!"

"You know my price. What's it to be, old man? Tell me what I want to know, or you'll force me to slash this knife deep. I don't have all day to waste here, discussing this with you while the woman buries herself deeper and deeper God knows where. I'll give you to the count of three to decide."

The old man's face crumpled in an agony of indecision. "Curse ye! Ye cannot—"

"I can. And I will. One. Two—"

The horse neighed, tossed its head as Mason pressed the knife deep enough to draw blood.

"Nay! Stop!" the old man shrieked. "I'll tell ye. Lucifer take ye! I'll . . . tell." The tinker sucked in a breath, his mouth pulled into a sickly grimace. "America. She's goin' to—"

"Liar!" Mason bit out savagely. "I tracked her all the way to Cork Harbor. She never sailed." The knife bit deeper.

"Fine, damn you! She didn't sail! I put her on a fishin' boat, all secret like. So it could carry her an' the boy away."

"Where? Where was this ship going?"

Those old eyes flickered, and Mason could sense that for a heartbeat Padraic Hussey was thinking of lying again. "Don't make another mistake, old man. My patience is gone. Don't make me cut your horse."

The Irishman cast one last glance at the animal, then closed his eyes, all the life seeming to drain from his body. "T' England. May God damn yer black soul t' hell along wi' mine! The girl went off to England."

"Where in England? Tell me—"

"I don't know! Told her to go as far away as she could, somewhere you'd never think to find her!"

"Where were they landing?"

"Plymouth."

"It should be easy enough to find her trail there."

"I hope ye never find her! I hope ye sink into the sea!"

"Did she tell you she stole my son, old man?"

"Aye—an' I say may Jaysus, Mary, an' Joseph bless her for it! I saw in the boy's eyes what ye've done!"

The old man crawled toward his horse, tears streaking his face. "They'll damn me t' hell if I've helped ye t' find her."

"Oh, I'll find her."

"What're ye goin' t' do?"

"Take my son back."

"And the girl? What 'bout her?"

"There's only one thing to do with poor, misguided Hannah," Booth purred, and a smile of anticipation curled his lips.

Kill her.

Chapter

❦ 10 ❦

If last night was the tiniest sample of what a bride experienced on her wedding night, it was a miracle any woman had ever survived the morning after without dying of embarrassment, Hannah thought, casting one last glance at her face in the looking glass.

Eyes that had always been piercingly direct shone bashful and uncertain, stripped to the soul where all her vulnerabilities could be found. Austen Dante had painted into the landscape of her face emotions she'd always managed to hide.

Lord, she must have been mad, letting him kiss her like that, touch her like that. She should have shoved him away, hot with righteous indignation, not dissolved with the liquid fire of passion.

She should have turned brisk and prickly, freezing him out with that aloof glare so icy it put frost on the noses of those who dared offend her.

At the very least, she should have appealed to reason—his and her own—insisting that they were playing with emotions dangerous as any powder keg.

If it had only been a fire of the body that had been lit

between them it would have been much simpler. But so much more had beckoned her from Austen Dante's blue-flame eyes. So much more had whispered to her heart in the awed brush of his hands. Loneliness, isolation, and something shared—the weight of secrets pressing on the soul, the grinding of self-blame, and grief hidden deep.

But regardless of what they shared, it didn't matter. She couldn't let it matter. Even long before she'd stolen Pip away from Mason Booth, Austen Dante was far beyond her touch, a man of great wealth and social position.

But is it possible to climb back onto the safety of the shore once you've launched yourself over a waterfall of sensations? Hannah wondered, her stomach knotting. Had she taken some irrevocable step last night when she had melted into Austen Dante's arms?

Was it possible that Austen was as off balance as she was? As bewitched and bewildered? Or was he merely tempted in a way he'd been tempted many times before? By a carnal need?

Hannah chewed at her lower lip. What must he think of her? And how on earth were they going to return to working together in the Music Room hour after hour?

She winced. She would just have to make it clear to him that last night had been a mistake. They'd both been tired, on edge. She'd been so touched by his gift of the diamond that she had forgotten herself.

For the first time in her life, she had abandoned her practicality and had gone where her heart bid her.

She hugged her arms tight against her breast as if to subdue such traitorous feelings. She had to march downstairs and confront Dante immediately. Get this hideously awkward first meeting behind them. Set rational rules and boundaries to keep such reckless idiocy from happening again.

She would go to Austen, tell him what she felt, why she'd allowed him such liberties last night, but must never, *never* do so again.

And exactly *what* reasons might those be? The man had to know she was attracted to him. And he believed that she'd been another man's mistress, bore him an illegitimate child. He was providing food and shelter for her and for Pip, supposedly in exchange for Hannah transcribing his music. Yet that was one more lie, one more deception, one more obligation she wasn't able to fulfill.

Shouldn't Austen Dante receive *something* real for his generosity to them?

Her cheeks burned. What was she thinking? Was she actually considering surrendering her body to this man as some sort of payment?

Or more despicable still, was she rationalizing the decision, drawing it in a manner she could accept, because deep inside the core of her soul, she *wanted* to cross that hallway, enter Austen Dante's bedchamber?

She wanted to shed her inhibitions, slip the satin robe from his shoulders and allow him to lay her back into the downy softness of his bed. Allow him to make love to her, brand every line of his body, every kiss, every sigh into her memory so that when she had to leave Ravenscar she could carry it with her like a treasure.

It was true. She had lost her wits. But the only thing to do was to march down to the Music Room and make it crystal clear to Austen that there would be no more such encounters. They were far too dangerous in light of the man hunting for Hannah and his son.

Even more, they were dangerous to Hannah's heart. Doubtless Austen Dante, with his breath-stealing male beauty, social rank, wealth, and quick intelligence, had had many such encounters with women and would be able to shove any tryst with her from his mind as soon as the novelty of it paled. But she would not have that luxury. And she had already carried far too many regrets away with her from Ireland to add any more.

Smoothing her hands over her faded gown, she strode resolutely from the door, down the stairs to the Music

Room. But for the first time, not so much as a sound drifted from the doorway—no music, good or bad, tormented or joyous, issued from the chamber.

Silence. It closed about her throat like a strong hand, squeezing off breath, stifling the words of greeting she'd practiced so hard. She entered the room, fully expecting to see Austen somewhere, restless, as unsettled by the night's events as she was.

But the Music Room yawned empty and silent, not even the smallest fire glowing on the hearth.

Footsteps in the corridor behind her made Hannah start, and she spun around to find a man who would have made a perfect Roman senator in the days of Julius Caesar. Garbed in a riding coat, an ornate silver crop tucked under one arm, he glared at her as if she were some sort of adversary. She'd never even seen the man before!

"Pardon me," she said. "I was just looking for Mr. Dante."

"He rode out before dawn, bound for London."

"London? But he didn't mention . . . I mean, he said nothing to me about . . ." She faltered, squirming a little under the man's challenging gaze. God above, had Austen been so appalled over what had happened between them, he'd raced off to escape her?

"If Mr. Dante feels no need to discuss leaving with the steward who takes care of his lands, he'd hardly clear his schedule with a mere servant the likes of you, madam."

"You are . . . I don't believe we've met, sir."

"I am William Atticus, Mr. Dante's cousin and his steward. I am in complete charge of this estate and everything on it, from a five-shilling gatepost to the thousands of pounds it costs to run this household. Don't bother to introduce yourself. I know who you are, Miss Graystone." He sneered at her. "I'd recommend you not mistake my position in this household. Just because Mr. Dante has been rash enough to hire you without my knowing, I do not think it wise to take in beggars from the street and make servants of them. And the instant you give me a reason, I will be most pleased to hurl you back onto the open road from whence you came."

Hannah raised her chin. "I don't think my position is quite as precarious as you would have me believe. Just last night, Mr. Dante specifically asked me to stay. Do you know when he will return to Ravenscar?"

The steward's mouth thinned in censure. "Whenever he wishes. It could be days. Weeks. Months. Each year Mr. Dante gives a festival for all of his tenants at the end of July, and he often is present. *If* it amuses him to be so."

Hannah stared. He'd be back whenever it amused him to be so? It seemed last-minute reprieves were highly overrated. She'd mustered all of her courage, marched down here as if going to her own execution. It was dashed irritating to find that the headsman had found something more entertaining to do.

Worse still, she'd have no idea when the ax would fall.

Hannah tried to cling to aggravation. Tried to summon up relief. But all she could find was confusion and a stark disappointment. Why had he said nothing to her?

Absurd. She had no claim on Austen Dante. She barely knew the man. It wasn't as if . . . as if he belonged to her.

But where had he gone? What was he doing? And why was it she suddenly felt bereft and left behind?

Almost as if she loved him.

The thought lanced through her.

Hannah turned away from Atticus and fled out to the gardens in an effort to hide her sudden fear from his too-keen eyes.

Beside a bank of azaleas she sank onto a stone bench, her heartbeat racing, terror pulsing through her.

Thunder in heaven, what had she done?

Austen watched the door close behind his solicitor, leaving no one behind save the man lounging in a nearby chair. A man the faithful family retainer had insisted he would trust with his last drop of heart's blood. Austen could only pray the solicitor's faith was well deserved.

Rangy and ungainly, with legs too long for his body, Tolliver Hockley's face was so lean it seemed shaved to the bone. But his eyes fairly burned with intelligence.

"I understand that you are a Bow Street runner?" Dante asked, pouring himself a glass of the solicitor's unpalatable brandy. "And that you've solved some remarkable cases."

"I've been with Bow Street for the past eight years and have been hired privately during that time as well."

"Is that so?"

"The Duchess of Tetbury employed me to catch the thieving scoundrels who stole her jewels. Discovered the footman who poisoned the Earl of Clare. And I've been often employed by Mills Bank. Ugly thing, embezzlement."

"And that has never bothered you? Dealing with . . . *ugly* things? It's obvious you don't mind boasting about it."

"You asked. I answered. I assume you want to employ someone with expertise in such an area; otherwise I would not have been summoned here."

There was something insufferable in the man—an arrogance, a cunning that set Dante's nerves on edge. But then, Hockley had looked into the eyes of the vilest criminals and bested them. If Hockley was to be any good at his job, Dante could hardly expect the man to have the countenance of an altar boy. Still, best to set boundaries at once.

"Mr. Hockley, in my experience there is nothing more dangerous than a loose tongue. Can I trust you to hold yours? I've summoned you here to discuss a matter of some delicacy. I expect the strictest secrecy. And I'm willing to pay well for your trouble."

"That goes without saying." Hockley's smile bordered on a smirk as he rolled one slightly uneven shoulder.

"I'm in such great demand that I only take the highest fees. If you pay it, I'm sure there's no reason to be taking an advertisement out in the *Times* about your business. Just exactly what situation did you wish me to look into, sir?"

Dante shot the man a hard look. "This has to do with a woman."

One aesthetic brow arched. "I see. Your mistress?"

"Of course not!" Dante was stunned at the indignation that shot through him, made far hotter by the fleeting, all too vivid image of Hannah in his bed.

"Your wife, then?"

"She's not my wife!" he ground out. Why did the words cause him a pang? Blood and thunder, it was as he'd suspected all along. Hannah *was* finally driving him insane.

"I see." The infernal man sounded as if he saw all too clearly. Dante felt his temper rise.

"She is a woman in my employ. I suspect she is in some kind of trouble. I want you to find out exactly what or whom she is afraid of."

"Perhaps you should ask her what is amiss?"

"Mr. Hockley, do you think me merely hopelessly inept or do you think me stupid?" Dante asked so quietly anyone at Ravenscar would have been praying for last rites.

"She wouldn't tell you, then?" Hockley's eyes sparked with interest, and Dante could almost feel the man fingering his impressions, trying to gauge what this was about—the things left unsaid. "That itself is worth remarking on. The woman is desperate, yet refuses your help? A powerful, wealthy and—I might guess—romantically unattached man like yourself? I'd like to meet this lady."

The notion appalled Dante. "That's out of the question! She has no idea I'm making this inquiry. Nor will she. Ever. Do you understand?" He was furious to feel his cheeks heat with guilt, shame.

"Whatever you wish. Then the question is where to begin. If you have a copy of the letters of recommendation you received from this woman's former employers, it would give me a place to start."

Dante shook his head. "I don't have any such records."

"Then I'll take whatever you used to make your decision to hire her. Anything that might provide a link to her former life. Come, sir. There must be something. No one would be reckless enough to take a servant, a stranger in off the streets without some sort of reassurance that they weren't a thief or a cutthroat or God knows what other kind of scum. It would border on insanity."

Dante raised one brow with the hauteur of generations of aristocrats. "You forget yourself, sir."

Hockley tugged at his rather wilted cravat. "Forgive me, sir. I only want to be of service to you. If you could—ah—tell me anything you know about the lady in question."

It seemed sordid, somehow. Ugly. Dragging out what he knew of Hannah, those bits of her former life she'd entrusted to him. Telling them to this man he'd just met. Dante hesitated a long moment.

"Sir," Hockley said quietly. "I know it's difficult. But you cannot expect me to discover anything of value without some information to go on. If you want to help the lady, you will tell me everything you know of her. The smallest bit of information, something you think is totally irrelevant could easily hold the key to what you want to know."

The man was right, damn him. Dante had two choices. Turn and walk away, ride back to Ravenscar and endure the feeling that some evil, inexorable tide was drawing ever closer to Hannah and the boy. Or he could take the risk and tell Hockley everything he knew.

But how did one begin to explain a woman like Hannah in mere words?

"All right. I'll tell you. But if you betray any of this to anyone, I swear hell won't be dark enough to hide you."

Hockley nodded, settling at the solicitor's desk, drawing out paper and pen.

"Her name is Hannah Graystone," Dante began, to the scratching of Hockley making notes. "And there is a child—" It disturbed Dante to realize just how little he knew of her—concrete things, her past. Why was it then that he felt he knew her more deeply than any other woman he'd ever known? That he understood her. That she had some odd kind of hold on his heart?

By the time he'd finished relating everything he could think might be of value, Hockley was ink-spattered and bemused.

"Mr. Hockley, do you think you can find out what I need to know?"

The detective rose, sifting his fingers through his thinning hair. "I should be able to find something. But sir, I want to warn you—I've discovered that whenever there is an investigation, people tend to find out things they *don't* want to know far more often than those they *do.*"

"What are you saying?"

"This woman stumbled in from the streets, half-starved, with an illegitimate child and stories of some kind of abuse. You know next to nothing about her."

"I know everything that matters," Dante said fiercely. "Except why she is afraid."

"I know that you believe you do, sir. It's just that some women are consummate actresses, and—"

"Not another damn word about such rot," Dante bit out.

Hockley watched him, closely. "Just one thing we need to get clear before I begin. I don't believe in killing the messenger."

"What the devil is that supposed to mean?"

"If I bring you information you don't like—find she's

involved in something immoral or illegal—I still get paid."

"Of course I'll pay you, man. But don't be absurd. You won't find anything like that about Hannah." Dante gave the man a distasteful glare. "This woman is the most relentlessly honest person I've ever met."

Hockley gave a nod far too knowing and world-weary. "Aren't they all, sir. I'll be in touch. Send you a report with my findings as soon as I find anything."

"No. Don't send it to me." Dante objected far too quickly, then in the throbbing pause tugged his neck-cloth with one finger to loosen it. "My steward is a Mr. William Atticus. Send the information to him and he will relay the message."

"Whatever you wish, sir." The Bow Street runner stood and sketched an awkward bow. "You won't regret hiring me."

Dante watched the man shuffle out with his odd gait. A cold stone sank in his stomach. *Regret hiring the man?* Some part of him already did.

If Hannah ever discovered what he had done . . .

The image of her disillusioned, irate, betrayed, burned in Dante's stomach, firing the edginess that was so much a part of his nature. Blast, he was worrying for nothing.

Hockley was greedy. He would never tell a soul—as long as the price Dante paid was high enough.

And he would pay whatever it took to drive the haunted, hunted expression from Hannah Graystone's eyes.

But what had put that pallor in her face, that darkness in her eyes? Something far too horrible, too painful to bear. Was it possible that she . . . what? Was involved in something illegal?

She'd stolen his diamond stickpin, hadn't she?

She'd been desperate, he excused her. He'd refused to pay her. She'd tried to return the jewel in the end. But wasn't it possible there might have been other endings to such misadventures at other times in other places she'd never told him about?

He winced, remembering all too clearly the hint of guilt in her eyes. The fear that had marred her face, that desperate look that had made him take a bedraggled, rainsoaked stranger and her waifish son beneath his roof.

God in heaven, what if something lay beneath that remorse? Dante wondered. Something dark and deadly as a swift river beneath black ice? What if Hannah were guilty of something?

He tried to shove the thought away. But still he couldn't shake free of it.

Was it possible that instead of helping Hannah, he was drawing danger down upon her head?

Chapter

❧ 11 ❧

Eight days Austen Dante had been gone. An eternity without so much as a word from the man who had kissed her to madness that night in the Music Room.

Hannah had envisioned a hundred different meetings, all agonizing, embarrassing. Prepared a score of different speeches in her head to diffuse the unbearable tension unleashed when he'd taken her in his arms.

In the end, she'd only wanted that first meeting to be over with. But Austen Dante had found ways to discomfit her from the moment he'd charged into her life, and it seemed this instance would be no different.

How dare the man ride off God knew where without so much as a word, leaving her . . . to what? To remember his kisses time and again. To recall her own weakness as she melted against his body. To feel again the terrible thrill of having those fingers that rippled with such sensitivity over the pianoforte's keys skim over her body.

How could she have been so foolish? She'd made matters infinitely worse when she'd gone so willingly into Austen Dante's arms. Her life was already far too complicated. She didn't need her own heart to turn traitor as well. Didn't need to be dreaming of impossibilities—emotions and fantasies meant for angelic beauties like Elisabeth, not a fiercely opinionated woman like Hannah.

She would have killed for any occupation to distract her, but even Pip had deserted her. The boy had become fast friends with Ruggles the kennel master, and vanished each dawn with Lizzy in his arms.

And the notoriously capable Hannah seemed only to make a muck of trying to help the maids. Her concentration was every bit as shattered as the bits of porcelain she'd knocked from mantel and table in her efforts to help clean, and the housekeeper had begun to fear such clumsiness might infect the rest of the staff.

She sighed, girding herself for yet another day of aggravation as she walked into the kitchen for breakfast. But the reception she was given was far grimmer than the mere destruction of porcelain should have warranted.

The heated conversation around the table died the instant she breached the door, a battery of eyes turning upon her like enemy cannon. Only Becca and her gardener's lad failed to look at her. Flushed and uncertain, the little maid kept her gaze fixed on her plate.

Hannah's stomach clenched. Instinctively, her chin tipped up. "Good morning," she said. "Who am I to help this morning?"

"Yerself, I'll be bound, an' doin' a fine job o' it, too," a dour scullery maid sniped with a knowing smirk that stung like nettles under the skin.

"You hush yourself, Sadie Mills." The housekeeper quelled the other woman with a hard look.

Hannah frowned. "Is there some kind of problem?"

"Of course not," Mrs. Clay said. "It's just that there are more pressing matters for you to attend to than dusting and such today. On Mr. Dante's orders."

"He's back?" Hannah gripped the edge of the table to

steady herself, her knees suddenly feeling like blanc-mange. "Did he arrive late last night?"

"Pah! *She's* asking *us?*" the boot boy grumbled to one of the undergardeners, casting her a sly glance.

"That's enough!" The housekeeper's order sent the lot of them scurrying back to their plates and eating with almost alarming intent.

"Miss Graystone, Mr. Atticus, the steward, has requested a meeting with you in the Green Drawing Room."

"Mr. Atticus?" Hannah echoed, the tension inside her wrenching even tighter in instinctive dislike. She had not seen the man since that first morning outside the Music Room. "Why would he wish to see me?"

"Mr. Dante has some most specific tasks he wishes you to attend to before he returns to Ravenscar, and he has no tolerance for bumbling. Mr. Dante always sends us word of his wishes through Mr. Atticus. That way there can be no chance of mistaking his intent. Gemma, show Miss Graystone to the chamber where she is wanted."

The parlor maid swept up, icily polite. But Hannah noticed the woman took great care not to let her skirts brush against Hannah's own. What on earth could be responsible for this shift in their behavior? She hadn't a clue. Bewildered, oddly stinging at the rejection of the servants who had begun to be so kind to her, Hannah trailed after Gemma.

The woman swept open the door to a lovely chamber with soft green walls iced in gilt. It was obviously a room designed for entertaining the most esteemed of guests, but its confines had been invaded by objects Hannah was certain had never dared cross its exalted threshold before.

A spectacular wooden lion big enough to ride, its paws mounted on rockers, brigades of toy soldiers making war upon several tabletops. A barrel hoop and the stick to bat it and send it rolling leaned up against the fire screen.

"What on earth?" Hannah gaped at the treasures, disbelieving.

"They are toys, Miss Graystone. Very expensive ones, I might add."

She stiffened as the masculine voice slipped beneath her skin. Squaring her shoulders, she turned to where William Atticus stood in sartorial splendor, his hand curved about a glass of Madiera, a surprisingly large emerald winking on one finger. Clothing as finely tailored as Austen Dante's own yet made of even richer fabrics molded his towering frame. However could he afford it? Hannah wondered, nonplussed. Yet hadn't she seen constant evidences of Austen Dante's generosity? Even so, despite the blandness of the steward's features, there was something in the man's eyes that put Hannah on guard.

"I can see that they are expensive," she said. "But I still don't understand what they are doing here."

"I think you do, madam. Mr. Dante has sent them from London as gifts for the boy. Cloth as well. Buff cotton, linens, some wool. The maids are to help you make them up."

Even her irritation with Atticus couldn't dull the tugging at Hannah's heart. Such incredible kindness from Austen Dante, and yet a dangerous generosity. For with each gift he was weaving invisible chains binding her and Pip ever more tightly to this place and to him.

What would happen when they had to face the inevitable? When they had to leave Ravenscar and Austen Dante behind?

"Mr. Atticus, surely you can't begrudge Pip a few clothes?"

"It isn't my place to begrudge anyone anything." Was it possible for the steward's voice to get any colder? "But I suppose no one can fault Mr. Dante for aiding a starveling child, no matter how ill advised. It is the other gift that raises questions."

"I can't imagine there could be more!"

"This is for you." The steward shoved the stack of cloth for Pip away, revealing yet another square of folded cloth beneath it.

Numb with astonishment, Hannah crossed to the settee.

A length of soft blue muslin the most exquisite color Hannah had ever seen spilled across the upholstery.

The feminine core of Hannah, so long denied, ached with the need to touch the beautiful stuff.

She tried to be resolute, but she couldn't help running her fingertips over a wisp of heavenly blue.

She was stunned by the depth of feminine longing the tempting hues stirred inside her. At Dove Cottage, she'd made certain Elisabeth had such flower-garden hues, and Harriet, and Fanny. To make up for the extravagance, Hannah had bought for herself cloth no one else wanted.

She'd told herself she didn't care. After all, no one would ever mistake her for a beauty, and she hadn't an artistic bone in her body. A gown painted by angels in heaven wouldn't have the power to change her into something lovely and graceful and wonderfully feminine. She would still be sensible Hannah. And yet . . . sometime during the magic and madness when she'd touched Austen Dante, some part of herself she'd thought long buried had begun to long for transformation.

"But what . . . who . . ."

"There is no need to insult my intelligence with such dramatics. It is for you, Miss Graystone. Obviously."

The truth was sweet and terrifying, painful yet wonderful. Impossible, no matter how much she wanted to scoop the beautiful stuff into her arms and hold it forever.

"I can't accept this." She clenched her hands behind her back, not certain she could trust herself. "Of course, I appreciate Mr. Dante's generosity to Pip. He does need the clothing, and badly. But this dress length—it is too much. There must be some mistake."

"Mr. Dante does not make mistakes." Atticus cut her off with a brisk wave. "He even sent along a page of *La Belle Assemblée,* with a picture of how he wishes the gown to be made up."

The steward thrust a paper into Hannah's hands. She glanced down at it, bewildered. Her breath caught in her chest.

She'd seen her sisters poring over the publication a lifetime ago in Ireland, sighing over exquisite pictures of the most recent fashions. Elegant ladies in flowing gowns, their hair done up in flower-bedecked bonnets. Skirts falling like the petals of lilies from beneath darker-hued spencers and pelisses, languid hands clasping fans or reticules. But this gown was simple, lovely beyond imagining.

"This is hardly proper for a servant to wear," Hannah faltered.

"That may be. But the master of Ravenscar determines what we are all to wear, according to our *position* in his household." Atticus's gaze met hers, and in that frozen instant it was as if a curtain had been torn away, exposing what every snide remark, every furtive glance, every cool reception she'd received this morning had meant. "Mr. Dante is somewhat discriminating in what he prefers on his ladies."

Her position . . . his ladies . . . Dear God!

She flung the page onto the settee as if it had suddenly caught fire, humiliation burning hot spots into her cheeks. "I am not his lady. There's been some mistake."

"Has there? I must admit I was somewhat bemused when I was first informed of the master's philanthropy where you were concerned. But now it makes perfect sense. By the time he returns to Ravenscar house, Mr. Dante expects the boy installed in the bedroom adjoining yours, the antechamber turned into a playroom, complete with the toys you see here. Your bedchamber is to be yours alone, and this gown is to be completed to his specifications."

"Mr. Atticus, I have been hired to be *the master's* assistant. To help him with his music. That is all."

"Come, Miss Graystone. It's rather too late for you to play the innocent, is it not? It's obvious you are acquainted with the ways of the world. You have borne one man a bastard child. Why should Mr. Dante think you adverse to joining him in his bed?"

Hannah felt raw, stripped naked beneath this man's condemning gaze. "I don't understand how Mr. Dante could think . . ." No, she couldn't even finish the sentence aloud. It was too humiliating.

How could he think she would consent to be his mistress?

How indeed? She'd only been in his arms with a mere wisp of nightgown and his dressing robe layered between their nakedness. She'd only kissed him, allowed him to touch her breast . . .

He'd said he wasn't sorry he'd kissed her. That he'd needed to touch her. Perhaps there were other needs he expected her to satisfy as well. Austen Dante was a man, young and strong and virile, with a potent masculine beauty and a restlessness of spirit that reflected the wildest passions.

Doubtless he was used to taking any woman he wanted. And he believed her to be no virgin, thought her experienced in the ways of desire. She winced inwardly, hurt so deeply it surprised her. Did he believe she held herself so cheaply? That she would trade her body for one lovely gown and a batch of playthings for Pip? That she would strike a bargain based on the kisses she'd shared with him in the night?

"Miss Graystone, I have been with Mr. Dante since he was a child, and I accompanied him on his travels after the break with his father. I understand him better than anyone on this earth. One of the benefits to being a cousin dependent on family charity. Therefore, let me take the liberty of explaining this to you. It is clear what Mr. Dante wants with you. His time in the country must have become more tedious than I imagined. He's not the first gentleman to seek diversion in the bed of a servant woman."

She felt sick, horrified. "You're wrong! He couldn't—"

"It is none of my business what transpires in my employer's bed, madam. However, let me give you fair warning. I do take exception to anyone who would dare attempt to take advantage of his generous nature. I would advise you not to become grasping and greedy."

"I don't want any of this! This dress, these toys for Pip!"

"You may discuss your . . . *desires* with Mr. Dante when he returns. However, the rest of us will not be party to your temper tantrums. Our employment depends upon following Mr. Dante's orders to the letter, madam. And when he returns to Ravenscar, everything will be done to his specifications. Surely you don't want to be responsible for the maids losing their employment?"

She was well and truly trapped. She couldn't allow Becca and the other maids to play in the unpleasant scene that was to come. A scene she was loathe to admit she'd brought down upon herself with her lies and her rash surrendering to his caresses. What else was the man to think of her?

And yet—he should have known, should have sensed she was made of something finer. He should have . . . damn, she wouldn't let him hurt her so badly. She'd confront this disaster as she had every other one that had barreled into her life—with her head high, her pride blazing.

"Fine," she said, meeting Atticus's gaze with a level glare. "We'll make the gown exactly to *the master's* specifications."

That way it would be ready when she threw it in Austen Dante's face.

Chapter

❦ 12 ❧

Dante reined Fire Eater down the road toward Ravenscar House, unable to shake the strange uneasiness that had settled in his very bones. Every length of the stallion's stride on the long road from London had echoed a fearsome restlessness deep inside Dante, filling him with something disturbingly like anticipation.

He remembered the feeling from when he was a boy—fingers ink-stained from hopelessly illegible copybooks, his backside still tender from his most recent caning, his belly leaden with the last of the school fare he'd choked down before he left the hallowed halls of Eton behind.

Drunk with boyish glee, he'd hung his head out the window of the traveling coach his grandfather had sent for him, the wind whipping his hair and buffing his cheeks as he watched the unfamiliar landscape sift through the sunbeams and change into the hills and vales of Derbyshire he loved so well.

The closer he got to home, the slower the horses seemed, until he'd been tempted to jump out the window and run across the heath himself to get to his destination faster.

The coach was supposed to go straight to the big house where his grandfather would be chafing at the bit to give him a new horse or a new hound or a new gun, whatever the old man thought might delight a boy's heart. But the equipage was always waylaid by a band of miniature highwaymen in petticoats. His sisters, Letty and little Madeline, would be dancing with impatience outside the smaller brick house near the gate where the Dantes lived. Mama's whole face would light up as she sailed over from her favorite bench under an oak tree, and he'd be glad she hugged him, though he'd growl out a boyish gruff denial. He'd show them the treasures he'd managed to collect while he was gone, delicate images from ages past pressed into stone, bird's eggs, and the glossy feather of a raven.

A jolt of pure shock went through him. *That* was what these emotions reminded him of. *It was almost like coming home . . .*

And *why* was he suddenly feeling this way? Because he'd had a few toys delivered for Pip? Because he'd seen to it that the boy would have something decent to wear? Perhaps in part. But if he dared to be honest with himself, something else had piqued his imagination far more.

A length of blue muslin delicate as the cup of a bluebell, soft and feminine enough to tempt any woman who ever breathed.

He'd been purchasing stuff for Pip's little breeches when he'd first seen the muslin, a gift so perfect for Hannah he hadn't been able to resist.

On impulse, he'd ordered the linen draper to add it to his order. Why? He still wasn't certain. Perhaps it was no more than an effort to ease his guilty conscience for hiring Hockley to make inquiries into Hannah's private affairs.

If so, his ploy had worked admirably well. In the days that followed, he'd shoved the Bow Street runner to the back of his mind, almost stifled that sting of dread deep inside when he wondered what Hockley might discover.

What he hadn't suspected was that purchasing the surprise would give him more pleasure than he'd experienced for a very long time. Pleasure and apprehension.

He'd chosen the design as well, leafing through the pages of *La Belle Assemblée,* past fashionable dresses trimmed with frills and ruffles, muslin prints and rosettes, until he found a gown softly flowing, simple, the perfect foil for Hannah's quiet beauty.

The corner of his mouth turned up as he imagined her reaction when Atticus bestowed his gifts. Doubtless Hannah would be stunned—and prickly as a babe in a nettle patch at the idea of "charity."

From the instant he'd conceived of buying things for Pip, he'd reckoned he'd have the devil of a tussle with Hannah's infernal pride. But he was beginning to find that particular trait of hers vastly entertaining. A challenge worthy of his formidable powers of persuasion.

From the time he'd been a sticky-fingered boy pilfering pieces of sugarloaf from the cook, he'd been a master at charming people into getting his own way. But when it came to Hannah, nothing so subtle as charm would do.

Orders—that was the only way to circumvent Hannah's pride, especially from the distance of London. Send specific commands as to what was to be done under the seal of the master of Ravenscar Estate.

He'd wager such high-handedness had put her in a foul temper, all right. But no doubt she'd be over the worst of it by now—even Hannah couldn't maintain a fit of high dudgeon for three weeks. It would be too exhausting.

And even if his stubborn Hannah still balked when he arrived home, he was certain to get his way in the end. It was always easier to convince someone to accept something they truly wanted. And Hannah wanted, needed something pretty.

He had glimpsed that almost buried yearning in her eyes, sensed a quiet hunger he doubted she'd allowed anyone else to see as she labeled herself as plain, as practical, logical. Pragmatic and sensible she might be, but she was still a woman with a woman's inborn hunger for something pretty.

Would she like the cloth he'd bought her? He could scarce believe such a small matter would make him so blasted edgy. It shouldn't be so important. After all, the gown was a mere trifle. And yet this was the first time in his life Austen had ever experienced this fierce desire to please a lady. The first time he had ever risked . . .

He shoved the thought away. One thing was certain, he would discover Hannah's reaction to the gown soon enough. Knowing Hannah, there would be no maidenly sighing and stammering. No being confined by propriety or reserve. She would tell him exactly what she thought about his present. Whether he wanted to know or not.

He grimaced. The problem was that he *did* want to know, with an urgency that alarmed him.

He couldn't wait to see her in the gown. He'd pictured it far too often in the past weeks as he dispatched his business, imagining so clearly how the soft muslin would cling to her slender form, cup her breasts, accent the glowing ivory of her throat. No frills and laces and other female fussiness for Hannah. A gown as simple in its beauty as any wildflower from the moor.

Why was it that the thought of Hannah dressing in it, just for him, filled him with such secret hunger?

Dante guided Fire Eater around a corner, the stallion lengthening his stride as he scented the stables ahead. Ravenscar House loomed up against a gray-cast sky, the pillars gleaming white in the twilight, the first bits of candlelight glimmering in the windows.

Dante's heart leapt and he leaned lower over the horse's neck, as eager as the beast to reach their destination.

Soon. Soon he would watch the emotions play across Hannah's animated face—and she wouldn't be able to hide anything from him, no matter how hard she tried.

But first he'd shed clothes layered with travel dust, rid his jaw of bristly stubble. Turn himself over to his valet for a bath and a shave. Once that was done, he would summon Hannah in great state to the Rose Drawing Room.

He grinned in anticipation.

What would she say? Do? A spark of delight warmed his chest. The only thing anyone could be certain of where Hannah was concerned was this.

She would do the unexpected.

Dante could hardly wait.

Hannah had been waiting three weeks for this moment. Time that only hardened her resentment, steeled her resolve.

Her stomach knotted tight with outrage as she clutched the newly sewn gown against the front of her frayed gray dress.

Mr. Dante desires the pleasure of your company in the Rose Room. The smirking footman's message still stung Hannah's pride. *You will don the blue gown as Mr. Dante instructed.*

It had been all she could do not to say, "Tell Mr. Dante to go to the devil." But passing such a message by servant would be far less satisfactory than delivering it to the high and mighty master herself.

She marched down the stairs burning for a fight. What she didn't expect was the betraying lurch of her heart when she saw Austen framed in the doorway of the Rose Room. Black breeches clung to sinewy thighs. A sapphire stickpin flashed from the pristine cravat knotted beneath his clean-shaven jaw. Black hair glinted like a sunstruck raven's wing, waving back from his high brow.

But it was his eyes that pierced to the core of her— blindingly bright, filled with a smugness that bordered on arrogance. His sensual mouth curved in a smile that all but shouted how infernally pleased with himself he was feeling, no doubt because he was certain to get his way.

No, Austen Dante wouldn't doubt for a minute that poor, plain Hannah Graystone would be grateful to be taken to his bed and used like a common trollop. Doubtless this was a game he'd played many times before.

The instant he saw her, his face lit up with pleasure, but that elation was erased from his features in a heartbeat as his gaze fell on the crumpled mass of cloth that she carried.

His brows crashed together in confusion. "Isn't the gown finished yet? I thought I gave orders . . ."

Damn him for looking so bewildered. The sight only fed her fury even more.

"You needn't fear. It's finished, sir. Exactly to your specifications." She thrust the gown at him. With lightning quick instincts, he caught it in his arms.

Blue eyes flicked to the waves of sky-shaded muslin. "Uh . . . am I to take it that you didn't like the color?" Was that a shadow of disappointment bruising his eyes? "If you prefer something different, I'm certain we can arrange to have it sent from London."

"Thank you so very much, sir! But you needn't put yourself to so much trouble on my account," she said, brisk as winter wind.

"It was no trouble." He hesitated, then his eyes widened as the realization struck him. He shot her a rueful grin. "Hannah, if I've managed to chafe at your pride, I'm sorry. Please accept the gown out of mercy to me. All those drab browns and grays were dampening my creative processes. Intruding on my music."

His lips curled into that slow smile so warm and persuasive it should've melted the ice around any woman's heart. "After all, we don't want everything I write to be funeral dirges."

"Only if the funeral in question could be *yours,* sir!"

"It's been at least a month since you've contemplated my murder. What the devil is this all about?"

Damn him for acting so bewildered! But he'd not slide out of this with his smiles and his teasing. He'd run her through a gauntlet of humiliation, one that had stung and burned all the worse because for a moment, just a moment in the Music Room, she'd been fool enough to think he understood her.

Hannah raised her chin, glaring into his face. "It's been a most enlightening few weeks since you've been gone. The servants all whispering behind my back, half of them barely speaking to me, the others trying to curry my favor, hoping . . . hoping to gain God knows what through my influence!"

"I can't imagine kitchen gossip would daunt you. Especially after you've faced me down when I was in a temper. I'm certain I can get to the bottom of it."

"Oh, it's no great mystery, I assure you. Everyone at Ravenscar knows how vastly I am in your debt. But you've made a fatal mistake regarding my character!"

All traces of his smile vanished. He'd always been so restless, as if any chamber was too small to hold him. But now he was still, suddenly terribly still except for the muscle that ticked in his jaw. "The gown is a gift, Hannah," he said quietly, "not some kind of charity."

"Don't you mean payment for services rendered? Or should I say, services *anticipated?* I must say, the toys for Pip were a masterful touch. I doubt most men would bother to go to such lengths. But there is just one problem. Consider how he'll feel when he has to leave them behind."

"They're his to keep."

"How comforting!" She was furious to feel tears pricking at the backs of her eyes. "I'll just strap the rocking lion atop my head when we set out on foot again!"

His eyes narrowed. "You're not going anywhere. I thought we had agreed on that."

"That was before I realized how cheaply you hold me."

"Cheaply? These things were damned expensive, if you want to know the truth. Hannah, you're being irrational."

"You'll have to forgive me. This is all new to me, kind sir. Perhaps you are accustomed to showering fripperies upon women to bend them to your will, but I live by a far higher code."

"You're wrong. I'm not used to this. I've never bought so much as a fan for any female except my mother and sisters."

"Oh, I see. Your *other* ladies demanded coin instead of goods, did they? Cash on demand."

"I meant what I said, Hannah. This was the first time I ever bought a gift for a lady." He was staring at her intensely, a spot of color darkening his cheekbones at his confession. "What is this all about?"

She faltered for a moment, caught off balance by the astonishment still evident in his face. An expression that might almost have made her feel guilty were it not for the brutal truth William Atticus had dragged out before her. But the truth was ugly and painful. Why shouldn't Austen Dante be forced to face it, as she had?

"Perhaps it was foolish and reckless of me to allow you to touch me, to kiss me that night in the Music Room," she said. "But I would have preferred you to be honest, tell me face-to-face what you expected, rather than concocting this idiotic bargain of yours." Her voice caught and she hated herself for it. "I might even have agreed to do as you wished in an effort to repay you for food and shelter and such like."

"Hannah, you're not making any sense."

"Then let me state it clearly. You want me in your bed? Say so! I'll trade my body for food and shelter for Pip. But I'll be *damned* if I'd become your mistress for the price of a new gown! I wouldn't sell myself so cheaply!"

Every muscle in his face was so tight it seemed likely to snap, his face white as a winter storm. Strong hands clenched in the dress as he turned and put it very deliberately upon the escritoire in the corner.

"Miss Graystone, you are mistaken. I have no intention of making you—or any other woman—my mistress. Now or ever." A world of barrenness was captive in those words, a sweep of desert, an eternal exile she'd never expected to find.

"You—you what?"

"We shared a few ill-advised kisses, true. But have I ever done anything to give you the impression I'm the kind of beast who would demand you to become my mistress in exchange for a full stomach for your child?"

Hannah flinched, remembering his face the first time she'd seen him charging down the steps of Ravenscar House. Most men would have swept a starveling woman and child off their property like so much rubbish. Most "gentlemen" wouldn't even have seen them, let alone taken them in, made certain they were fed, warmed by a fire.

Austen Dante was fiery tempered, impatient, arrogant, and stubborn. But he'd let Hannah see a facet of himself he fought hard to keep hidden. He'd trusted her with a heart far more vulnerable than anyone else could have guessed. "I . . . No. You've never been anything but kind."

"Then where did you get such a crazed idea?"

"Mr. Atticus—he made it clear that—that you expected me to become your mistress in return for . . . The servants, they all believed it, too." It should have made her feel better to spill out the truth. Instead, she felt smaller, ensnared in gossip of the ugliest kind.

Quiet. His voice was deathly quiet, deafening in its censure. "So that is what this is all about. Kitchen rumors. I had no idea that Atticus and the servants would misconstrue the gift of a single gown in such a way. That they would imagine an affair between the two of us. Most of them have been in my service long enough to know that I don't indulge in such dalliances."

It was a confession that would have cost most men dear. Amorous exploits were the staple diet of the young and handsome, wealthy and powerful landlord. Few would have the courage to admit a lack of such adventures to anyone—most especially a lady. But there could be no doubt of the truth in Austen's gaze.

"But you . . . the gown . . . all the toys . . . Why would you send such things unless—" She faltered. But Austen finished for her, the words tinged with bitterness.

"Unless I wanted something in return?"

She looked away, but couldn't deny the truth. She'd always been a terrible liar. "Yes," she admitted.

Candle shine carved lines and hollows about his face, casting the planes into shadow. His fingers strayed up to the sapphire buried in the folds of his cravat. He looked away. "I did want something, Hannah. I wanted to give you a taste of happiness. God knows, you and the boy look as if you've had little enough of it in your lives. I wanted him to have toys to play with, to help drive back the shadows of whatever is haunting his eyes. And I wanted you to have something pretty. You're always worrying about Pip, what he feels, what he needs. For once, I wanted you to have something for yourself."

Hannah pressed her hand to her breast, the worn cloth abrading her palm like a schoolmaster's willow switch, sending shame crashing through her in a suffocating tide.

All her life she'd been waiting for someone to say just those words to her—years of pushing her own needs aside so her mother, her sisters, her father all could have what they needed, what they wanted. Years in which her quiet sacrifices went unnoticed. Even Elisabeth, who had understood her better than any living soul, had been convinced Hannah was satisfied with her lot.

How strange that it was Austen Dante who had seen

through her protestations, her clinging to the practical, the logical. How had he known about the secret part of her that had longed for something pretty?

And how had she repaid him? She had flung his gift in his face, hurling out hurtful accusations until the pleasure that had made his eyes gleam died, that careful mask descending.

The Austen who had given Pip the little spaniel and closed her fingers around the diamond stickpin had vanished. Only the master of Ravenscar remained. And Hannah felt the loss down to her very toes.

Blast, she was ten times a fool! They'd shared a few kisses. That was all! How had she ever allowed Atticus to convince her that Austen Dante desired her in *that* way—wanted to make love to her so badly he would be willing to bribe her into his bed? Why did the knowledge it was laughable hurt so much?

Her cheeks stung, her voice unsteady. "Forgive me. I thought—"

His gaze met hers. "Rest assured you've left me in no doubt of what you think of me, Miss Graystone. Although I must say I preferred being worthless as a rock to being the kind of monster who would coerce a woman into his bed."

"It was a mistake! I am sorry I misjudged you. But what else was I to think?"

Blue eyes stripped her to her soul, and she knew she had wounded him in some tender place no one else had ever been allowed to enter.

"I thought you were beginning to know me, Hannah," he said quietly.

Her pride, her damnable pride wouldn't let her look away. If she did, she was afraid her tears would break free. And even now, she couldn't afford such a show of weakness.

"I am grateful for your gifts to Pip." She hated the trembling in her voice. "And I will—will accept them in the spirit they were given. But what should I do with the dress?"

He raked his hand through his hair, and suddenly she was aware of how very tired he looked. Hollows dug beneath his eyes. His broad shoulders slumped. "Do whatever you damn well want with the thing. It doesn't matter to me."

He sketched her a stiff bow, then turned on the heel of his polished Hessian and strode out of the room.

Hannah stood there stricken, her stomach roiling with regret. Damn her temper. Her abominable temper.

Dear God, how could she have been so thoughtless, so cruel? *But I didn't understand* . . . a voice inside her cried. *I didn't know* . . .

Know what? That Austen Dante was kind? He'd shown that to her in a hundred different ways since she'd arrived at Ravenscar. Hadn't known that he would be so generous, so selfless? Or that he'd understand secrets and dreams all but forgotten? She'd witnessed his unique ability to do so when she'd found him behind the stables, Pip holding the wriggling puppy in his arms.

Austen Dante had filled Pip's arms with a bundle of love tied up with a wagging tail and floppy silken ears. He'd given the child something Hannah never could have, realized intuitively so many things Pip had never confided.

Every day she'd seen new evidence of Austen Dante's generosity, actions that shattered all the rumors she'd heard about the mad master of Ravenscar when she and Pip had wandered through Nodding Cross. But she'd let servants' gossip and her own stiff-necked pride over-shadow all of that. And she'd wounded the man. Deeply.

Ever so slowly she crossed to the escritoire, her fingers stealing out to touch a puff of blue sleeve. Mercy, how she had loathed every fiber and thread, every button and seam. How she'd wanted Austen Dante to pay for what he'd done.

She'd just never realized that his capital offense had been generosity once again. He'd been selfless and kind. He'd concocted this surprise for her only so he could see her smile.

And how had she repaid him? By making the vilest of accusations. And by flinging the gown in his face, vowing she would sooner die than wear it.

But the other servants had believed he intended to make her his mistress, too. Everyone from Atticus to Becca to the housekeeper, Mrs. Clay—

Was that supposed to be an excuse for her behavior?

I thought you were beginning to know me . . . Dante's words echoed through her, heavy with disappointment.

He'd offered up pieces of himself that night she'd meant to return the diamond, given her rare glimpses of the man who lay hidden behind the estate of Ravenscar.

A man of incredible sensitivity, capable of great tenderness, with an astonishing ability to see straight into a wounded heart. That was the man who had plotted and planned every seam of her gown, every gleaming uniform painted onto a toy soldier. And all he asked in return was to see her garbed in blue muslin.

Hannah swallowed hard, remembering the expression on his face when she'd first descended the stairs. Arrogance? Smugness? Had she been so sure she'd find those emotions that she didn't see what was really there? An almost boyish, painfully endearing desire to please? A gruff, shy thoughtfulness from this man who hid his gentler side so fiercely?

She'd hurt him. And there was no way to take the damning words back. Hannah gathered up the blue muslin gown as if seeing it for the very first time. Austen had selected it himself. Planned it in an effort to bring her pleasure. And truth to tell, the gown was more beautiful than anything she'd ever owned.

Who would have guessed a man like Austen Dante would know exactly what would suit her—something deceptively simple, subtly elegant.

It was a gift given with such pure understanding it terrified her, awed her. But it was too late to embrace his offering now. Too late to say how very beautiful the gown was.

With exquisite gentleness, she folded the gown and took it up to her bedchamber. She tucked the heavenly blue muslin away with the lock she'd kept of Elisabeth's hair and the twice-mended miniature of her laughing, loving, careless papa, leaving it in the place where her deepest regrets lay waiting.

Chapter

❧ 13 ❧

Branches of candles set the study alight as Dante drained another glass of brandy. He had no idea how much time had passed since the miserable scene with Hannah. He only knew that no one in the household had dared to disturb him.

The master of Ravenscar in a temper was common enough, a predictable inconvenience to be weathered like the force of a hurricane. But Dante quiet, silent, still . . . that was enough to make everyone on Ravenscar land cower in fear.

He was glad of it. Glad that no one dared disturb him. Perhaps if he were very lucky, some footman would be brave enough to slip a fresh decanter of brandy just inside the door, so the monster within could snatch it without snapping off anyone's fingers.

Damnation. How had this happened? How had everything grown so muddled? Worse still, how had those secret desires, those wishes and needs he'd barely even acknowledged inside himself been dragged out for the whole blasted household to gossip over?

He closed his eyes, remembering the roughness shredding the edges of his voice as he demanded Hannah tell him where she'd gotten the idea he would make her his mistress. Her reply had been unsteady, yet unswervingly honest.

Mr. Atticus—he made it clear that you expected me to become your mistress in return for . . .

In return for the gifts Austen had sent. A few trinkets in cold exchange for a woman's body. *Hannah's* body. The mere thought of any man inhuman enough to strike such a bargain was monstrous.

But even that wasn't most disturbing of all. What rocked him to the very core was the knowledge that she *would* have come to his bed if he'd asked it of her. He'd never forget the fierceness in those silver-gray eyes, the willingness to surrender herself to demands he'd never made.

Most painful was the certainty that he wanted her with a power that astonished him, sent cold fear trickling through the hot surge of desire she loosed in his veins. But he didn't want her in his bed because she was desperate. No. The truth was, he wanted Hannah to want *him,* to be tempted to lie with him because she too felt the pull of attraction spinning ever tighter between them in some gossamer enchanted thread.

He wanted to see fire in her eyes, a flush of passion in her cheeks, a ripeness in her lips daring him to taste because she wanted him as a woman wanted a man, in a way that was primal, too powerful to cling to her precious reason.

God's blood, it had been so long since he'd felt the secret velvet of a woman's skin beneath his hands, made that wondrous voyage of discovery in a lover's arms. He'd made damned certain he was too busy to care, managed to quell such needs entirely except during the dark hours just before sunrise, when even the night seemed to be wooing its lover, the dawn.

But he sensed that no matter how hard he worked to distract himself it wouldn't matter where Hannah Graystone was concerned. The woman had crept beneath his defenses when he wasn't looking, seeped into his soul with her courage and the tenderness she kept so well hidden from the rest of the world. She'd touched that part of Austen Dante that was raw and aching from the moment she'd confronted him on the rain-soaked carriage circle, her sick little boy cowering behind a pillar.

How had he come to care for Hannah Graystone? Want things from her he could never hope to earn? And how was he ever going to bury these dangerous emotions now that servants' gossip had raised images in his head, and in hers?

Images of tumbled coverlets and kisses so fiery they could melt a man's very soul. Visions of wringing sighs of pleasure from her throat, surprising laughter from her lips, and maybe, in the shelter of his bed, making her feel so safe she would dare to trust him with whatever had put the lurking fear in those intrepid gray eyes.

The very thought wrenched at Austen's heart. Blast, what was he thinking? Had he lost his infernal mind? He had nothing to offer Hannah Graystone except his protection. He'd decided long ago not to drag some innocent woman into his life, risk that she would be ashamed . . . that he would have to face the horror of seeing pity in her eyes.

No. Better to quell these mad imaginings at once. And there was no better way to do so than to confront the damned fool who had dredged such deep-buried emotions out before the entire bloody household. There was only one thing to do.

Austen rang for a footman. Matthew Simmons peeked in a moment later, his Adam's apple bobbing wildly in his throat.

"Sir?"

"Summon Atticus here immediately."

"Aye, sir." The footman scrambled away as if the hounds of hell were snapping at the seat of his breeches.

It seemed forever, but was only a brief time before a knock sounded on the door, making the throbbing behind Dante's eyeballs fiercer. "Come in," he enunciated with exquisite care.

William Atticus strode into the room, flashing him a broad smile. "Welcome back, sir. You'll be happy to know I've handled everything exactly to your specifications in your absence. The drums for the cisterns are coming along well, though we had to try several different materials before we got it right and——"

"I don't give a damn about the cisterns at the moment."

"Sir?" Atticus froze. "Is something wrong? Surely you're not still blaming yourself for that accident involving Digweed. It was a minor mistake——"

"The man almost lost his leg. And worst of all, I still can't figure out how the machine malfunctioned. I've gone over my design a hundred times, made the calculations. They've always come out the same . . . Bloody hell. There's time to dredge this all out later. Now I have something more pressing to discuss with you."

"More pressing?" Atticus echoed, stunned. "I don't understand——"

"You don't need to understand anything but this. My personal affairs are none of your concern."

The steward's lips pursed in offense. "I would never presume that they were."

"I'm glad to hear it." Dante pinned him with a glare. "For future reference, if I ever decide to take a mistress, I will inform her of her *good fortune* myself."

Realization dawned on Atticus's face, accompanied by excruciating discomfort. "Miss Graystone told you . . .?" Atticus stopped and cleared his throat, spreading his hands out in chagrin. "I'm sorry, sir, if I overstepped my place. But I followed your message to the letter, moved the boy into his own bedchamber so there would be no disturbances. Had the maids construct the dress as you commanded. The fabric was uncommonly fine. What else was I to think except that you were planning to have an—er—intimate liaison with Miss Graystone?"

"I don't pay you to think, Atticus. I pay you to follow my orders. Only my orders. No more. No less."

Atticus stiffened. "It's obvious I've made a mistake, and I regret it. But surely you can't be overly concerned about a misunderstanding between your steward and a mere servant. Obviously, Miss Graystone has been beset by a bout of hysterics, has blown the incident far out of proportion."

"I've never met a *less* hysterical woman in my life," Austen bit out. "In fact, I'd wager my best hunter that Miss Graystone is far more capable of provoking hysteria in others than experiencing it herself."

Atticus stared as if Dante had thrust a knife between his ribs. "Sir, I cannot believe you would take the word of that woman over mine. Haven't I served you well all these years? Tried, to the best of my ability, to be a friend to you?" His voice dropped low on a note of hurt. "I even attempted to be something of a father when your own had cast you aside. Surely such a paltry misunderstanding with a servant shouldn't stir up such a tempest between us."

It shouldn't, Dante thought, staring into the face of the one man who had never betrayed him. But somehow, it did.

"Sir . . . Austen. The best thing that could happen would be for Hannah Graystone to leave this house. There is something about her that is disturbing. Something I do not trust. A woman with so much intelligence is unnatural. A revolution against the natural order of things."

"Now I understand why you and my mother never got along. I would've loved to hear you debate that issue."

"Your mother was laboring under the misguided notion that I was distressed over the fact that you were made heir to Ravenscar in my place. I suppose it was only natural that she mistrusted me. But I've proven myself loyal to you a hundred times over, have I not? Managed your estates, your financial affairs, freeing you to work on your inventions. And even in more personal matters I've sought to give you my unfailing support. Why, I've begged you a dozen times to reconcile with your family—if you would care to discuss it—"

"No!" Bloody hell, he had enough of a headache without raking all that up.

"Concerning Miss Graystone, then, I assure you, she is just the kind of woman to stir up turmoil in a household. I'm certain it's just a matter of time before she goes prying in affairs that are none of her concern. She is distressingly independent and challenges authority whenever it pleases her."

"Perhaps that is why she and Pip are still alive."

"Have you ever stopped to wonder, sir, what disaster turned them out onto the road in the first place?"

Dante's gut clenched, and he turned away to keep Atticus from seeing his unease. "I will deal with Miss Graystone as I see fit. I will not have you meddling with things again, Atticus. Do you understand?"

"Yes, sir. Is there anything else?"

For an instant Austen hesitated. But Atticus handled every bit of his correspondence from the moment he'd left Austen Park. And he had no one else to confide in. "As a matter of fact, there is something more. A message will be coming from a Mr. Hockley. It is of the utmost importance. The instant it arrives, you will inform me, no matter what time of the day or night."

"Whatever you wish, sir."

Whatever I wish? Dante thought, his gaze turning out the window to where the heather blushed the distant moors with lavender. *I wish I could turn the clock back to the night I first took Hannah in my arms. I wish I could wipe away the ugly thoughts your babbling put into her head. I wish I could make her understand . . .*

Understand what? Why he had given her the dress?

What he had meant for it to say? Bloody hell, he wasn't even certain himself anymore.

"I still don't understand why you are so angry with me, sir. It was a mistake, that was all. Doubtless you've put the lady's mind at rest."

Maybe so, but what about my mind? Dante wondered. *Already I've been tasting her kisses in my dreams, imagining what it would be like to lay her back on my bed. To spread her hair across my pillow and drape her legs about my hips.*

Dangerous—God, yes, it was too dangerous to contemplate. But the words had lit a blaze in the darkest corners of his mind.

Hannah . . . his mistress . . .

"Leave me, Atticus," he said, so quietly the other man went pale.

"Sir . . . Austen, lad, listen to me. . . . You'll feel much better once you start work on the reaping machine again. I'd never presume to guess what went wrong, but you're a genius about inventing such things. Perhaps if you wrote a paper to one of the scientific societies, presenting your findings, they might be able to help you . . ."

Dante turned away, his fists knotted, his face still. "That is the least of my concerns at the moment. There is only one matter I want to make clear. Stay out of my relationship with Hannah Graystone. Do you understand?"

"Yes, sir. I understand very well indeed."

What was it in Atticus's voice that set his nerves on edge?

"Leave me," Austen commanded.

The steward turned and strode from the room, his shoulders square beneath his expertly tailored coat. Every line of the man's body seemed to radiate the question: What had he done that had so offended his employer?

God in heaven, why *was* he so furious with the man? Atticus's greatest sin was giving form and shape and substance to longings Austen had fought so hard to deny. Longings that, if Austen were honest, had already burrowed deep into his being.

He wanted to take Hannah to his bed, feel her beneath him. He wanted her more fiercely than he'd ever wanted any woman. But he couldn't have her. Didn't deserve her.

He closed his eyes. Damn, was that the real reason he'd given Hannah the blue muslin gown? So that the fabric could caress her as his hands never could? Touch the fragile places inside her she fought so hard to hide?

God's wounds, what had he done? He could only thank the fates that she would never, ever suspect the truth. He'd make damned certain Hannah would never know what a fool he'd been.

William Atticus spurred his horse into the wind, his jaw knotted with frustration. Blast, he'd suspected from the beginning that the Irishwoman would be trouble, but had never guessed that it had gone this far. Far enough to shake his cousin's loyalty to him. Deep enough to shatter Dante's fierce concentration on the brilliant inventions that had been the man's passion from the day he'd left Austen Park.

This was a peril Atticus hadn't foreseen. One that must be dealt with at once. No. He couldn't afford for Dante to be distracted from his purpose. Nor did he intend to tolerate that Irishwoman's meddling. She was already currying Dante's favor. There was no telling where it might lead.

There was only one thing to do. He had to find a way to get Hannah Graystone and that boy away from Ravenscar as soon as possible.

Atticus cursed, barely evading a sheep wandering beside the road. Damnation. He'd gone to great lengths to make certain Dante would not be influenced by outside forces. He'd even managed to keep a wedge driven between Austen Dante and his family. Surely if he'd contrived to keep such a rift still raw after so many years, it should be simple enough to get rid of one inconvenient Irish servant. The woman was not even that attractive, for pity's sake.

But something was brewing between his master and Hannah Graystone. Something that must be stopped at once, for Dante's sake and for Atticus's own.

The steward's lips split in a grim smile. If anyone had the skill to untangle them, it was he. And in many ways he had his cousin Austen to thank for it.

There was a certain freedom in living by one's wits, and it was a skill William had cultivated from the day his parents had died without leaving a penny for their only son. Atticus had been eighteen the day he'd realized he couldn't afford the luxury of thumbing his nose at his wealthy grandfather as his parents had. And he'd been more than successful making atonement for his mother's mesalliance until Anne Austen Dante and her family had arrived at the park . . .

Atticus shoved the memory away, and the bitterness. It had all been for the best, in a way. He'd discovered early that everyone had an Achilles' heel. And in the years that followed, he became a master at ferreting such weaknesses out. He'd used them to his advantage and to Austen Dante's own. Of course, he'd never let his cousin know it—God forbid. Despite his self-centered facade, underneath the man was as tediously honorable as his blasted foreigner of a father.

But that didn't matter. Atticus would use his skill for his master's benefit again. It should be easy enough to rid Dante of this unfortunate problem. After all, it was more than likely that a beggar woman with an illegitimate child had more than her share of dangerous secrets.

Atticus just needed to find the right weapon. Then he could dash Hannah Graystone out of Dante's life once and for all. And things could go on just as they had before.

Dante woke feeling as if he'd been run over by Enoch Digweed's wagon, his pride stripped raw as a flogged sailor's back. So much for his foolish sense of anticipation.

Hannah had done the unexpected once again, taken him completely by surprise.

He ground his fingertips against his gritty eyes, trying to blot out scenes from the day before—the gown shoved at him, Hannah quivering with righteous indignation, the sick feeling twisting in his gut when he'd realized that instead of creating a lovely surprise for her he'd managed to set her up to be whispered about and ridiculed by his servants. Proud, defiant Hannah, thought to be the master of Ravenscar's whore.

The master of Ravenscar's whore—what a jest that was. What the devil would everyone say if they knew the truth? That in all his twenty-eight years Austen Dante had never taken a mistress, only rarely bedded a woman. That he'd kept himself as separate and isolated as any man could, venturing out only when the needs of the flesh grew too hot to bear.

He had never had the courage to let a lady be close to his heart, until a sharp-tongued Irish woman with fine eyes and lush auburn hair had charged into his insulated world and dared him to give a damn about her, about himself.

But he'd made a disaster of things just as he always had. Trust Austen Dante to batter up the heart of anyone he cared about, or who was foolish enough to care about him even a little.

Most surprising of all was how deeply Hannah's mistrust of him had cut. He should have been used to failing people by now, disappointing them. He thought he'd grown inured to it, especially since the scenes with his father.

It was disconcerting to realize he could still be hurt. He could still wish—what? To be anything, anyone except himself?

He rolled out of bed wishing to hell he could don his riding clothes, mount Fire Eater, and spur him to the sun. That he could never look back. But there were some things that had to be faced. This morning was one of them.

Always before he'd been impatient while his valet prepared him for the day. The infernal man seeming to move at the pace of a frozen stream. But today the valet swept through his duties like a whirlwind, and far too soon Dante was ready to descend the stairs.

He strode down the corridor trying to look as if he hadn't spent the night restless with regrets. He full intended to go to his study, barricade himself there for a little while. Anything to keep Hannah Graystone from realizing the truth. That she had managed to slip past his armor and wound him in a way no one but his father ever had before. That he had been fool enough to— what? Let her into his heart?

Blast, he needed to get out of here. Call him a coward, but he didn't want to face her this morning. Perhaps he should visit some of his tenants' farms. Yet even that would present far too much time alone riding the fields. Too much time to think.

Unless . . . He glimpsed a ball of brown and white fur dashing through the hall, a golden-curled boy in hot pursuit. Of course! Pip was the perfect solution! The boy could babble on about his pup. The glow in the child's eyes would be enough to distract him.

"Pip?" Dante called out. The boy poked his head sheepishly around the corner, Lizzy clutched in his arms.

"I'm sorry, sir. I'll try to be quieter. It used to be easy, but now it's ever so much harder."

At least *that* was something to be glad about—the child's shedding of his unnatural silence.

"I don't want you to be quiet, boy. In fact, I have an

aversion to quiet today myself. That was why I was wondering if you might like to join me for a ride about Ravenscar lands this morning."

"You would take me . . ." The bright light in Pip's face suddenly dimmed. "I can't, sir. I'm sorry. I'm too 'fraid to ride."

"We could take my phaeton. Would that be better?"

"A phaeton?" Pip crowed in delight.

Dante winced at the sound from the stairway above, sensing who it was before Pip gave a cry.

"Nanna! His lordship is taking me for a ride in his phaeton! It'll be just like you said when I was so tired from walking." Pip grasped Dante's hand, and Austen knew how precious the boy's impulsive touch was. "When I was ever so tired, a man in a phaeton passed by, and Nanna said to 'magine it was a magic phaeton, drawn by horses made of clouds. She said to 'magine it could take us anywhere we wanted to go. Somewhere pretty and bright and safe. She said she hadn't ridden in one since her papa died, but she told me 'zactly what it was like, 'cept even better."

The boy turned the full light of his gray-green eyes upon Dante. "Couldn't she come, too?"

"Pip, no! I don't think . . ." Color flooded into her cheeks. "I'm certain Mr. Dante doesn't want me . . . a-along."

"'Course he wants you!" The boy crinkled up his nose as if she'd lost her mind. "Mr. Dante likes you ever so much, don't you, sir?" Gray-green eyes lanced through Austen, so bright, so sure.

Dante swallowed hard, glancing from Pip to Hannah. He should fight this insane notion of Pip's however he could. Come up with some logical excuse. The phaeton's seat was too small to hold all three of them. There was some pressing work Hannah had to do—recopy one of his compositions or count the strings inside the pianoforte to make certain they were all accounted for.

It should have been easy enough to side step this disaster. So why was he sketching Hannah a bow?

"I would be honored if you would join us, Miss Graystone. Although, I can't boast horses made of clouds, the pair of them drive smoothly enough."

She looked as if she wanted to crawl behind one of the draperies. "Sir, I . . ."

Come on, Hannah, Austen pleaded silently. *You're always so damned smart—think of a way to get us out of this mess.*

But she didn't have a chance. Pip squared his narrow shoulders, bumped up his chin. "I won't go unless you do, too," the boy asserted.

Austen wasn't sure who of the three of them was more stunned at the boy's show of stubborness, or more secretly proud. Pip had damned inconvenient timing, and yet, even if it meant the rest of the day would be miserable, Austen couldn't help but be pleased by Pip's progress. It had to be rewarded.

"There you have it, Miss Graystone," Austen said, flicking an imaginary speck of lint off his biscuit-colored riding jacket. "It's your motherly duty to accompany us. We have to get Pip away from the kennels for a while, or I'm afraid he'll start to bark for his supper instead of asking Cook to pass the pudding."

He could see Hannah teetering on the blade of the decision. Knew that the last place she wanted to spend her day was in a phaeton with him. But in the end it seemed there was no graceful way she could wriggle out of it without hurting Pip's feelings or spoiling his pleasure. Something Hannah would never do.

"I suppose I could go," she surrendered after a long pause. "But before we—we go, there is something I need to say to you. Please let me apologize for the way I acted last night. I was unforgiveably rude. . . ."

Hannah? Apologizing? What must that have cost her? But it only made him even more uncomfortable. The last thing he wanted was to drag the whole dress affair out again, especially with Pip's questioning eyes upon them. "Never mind about that," Austen insisted gruffly. "It's all right."

But it wasn't all right. Atticus's meddling had acted like an evil fairy, conjuring up the word *mistress*. Possibilities that even now charged the air between Austen and Hannah. Like the contents of Pandora's mythical box, they couldn't be recaptured and hidden away.

"Just let me fetch my bonnet," Hannah said.

Dante watched her scurry up the stairs, felt her discomfort mingling with his own.

Damn. So much for his plan to distract himself from his thoughts of Hannah, he mused with a wry grimace.

He had a feeling this was going to be a hell of a long day.

Chapter

14

The phaeton had been designed to fly across the countryside, the exquisite grays in its traces bred to drink the wind. But even if they dashed to the very sky, they couldn't outdistance the tempestuous feelings roiling in Hannah's chest.

She would have done anything to escape Austen Dante's presence, unsettled as she was, still raw from the scene between them the night before. She'd spent the whole night tossing and turning in her bed, its expanse suddenly large and empty and cold without Pip's slumbering form beside her.

There was no doubt Austen had been right, offering Pip a room of his own. Heaven knew Hannah wanted Pip to put the fears of the past behind him, to become independent. And having his own bed was the first step toward healing.

But she hadn't realized how much *she* had needed the little boy's presence beside her, how much she'd come to depend on Pip to keep her own demons at bay in the dark of the night. Loneliness and a vague sense of hopelessness. And the knowledge that her solitary life with Pip could never change as long as Mason Booth was hunting her down.

She shivered, despite the warmth of the sun and the prickling of a fine sheen of sweat between her shoulder blades. Mason . . . how long had it been since she'd thought of the man? Wondered where he was? Surely, he must have run through all the false trails she'd left for him by now. There could be little doubt he'd pushed beyond anger to killing fury.

"Nanna, is something wrong?"

She looked down to see Pip's eyes wide and troubled, as if he were trying to peel away her forced smile, to see what lay beneath. She could never let him know.

"I'm just enjoying the moors. They're beautiful, aren't they? Much prettier without the rain in our faces!"

"But we're not flying like you said we would." Pip looked chagrined. "Because I'm too 'fraid."

"Fear has nothing to do with it, boy," Austen interjected with a wink. "It's a question of using good sense. You can see Ravenscar much better when the horses take their sweet time."

Hannah's heart swelled with something akin to pain at the sight of Austen's big hands on the reins, keeping the team at a gentle walk. Time and again during their ride, those lightning-flash eyes had sought out Pip, making certain no fear darkened the boy's small face.

But nothing Austen could say would protect the child from the echo of Mason Booth's voice in his head, an echo so loud it still brought a haunted expression to those green-gray eyes. "But I am too 'fraid. I wouldn't even take the ribbons behind your hands like you wanted, so I could drive."

"We'll try it another day," Austen ruffled the boy's curls. "When I have a chance to find that magic horse made of clouds Hannah told you about."

Hannah's heart wrenched as Dante deftly changed the subject to the new litter of pups expected any day, dispelling the gloom that had fallen over the child like a shadow.

Pip chattered on in delight as the phaeton rolled along, but despite every effort Austen made to be cheerful, he couldn't fool Hannah. Nothing could completely banish the tension that spun across the carriage seat, twining like a Gordian knot between her and Austen Dante.

She was excruciatingly aware of him—every ripple of his biceps beneath the sleeve of his riding jacket, every finger of wind that sifted through the dark richness of his hair. His hands on the reins, so supple and strong—she remembered exactly how they had felt when they had ghosted up to cup her breast.

Even the wind over the moors couldn't steal away the scent of him, recklessness and danger, sandalwood and leather, a passion for life that sizzled across his skin. He was a storm waiting to break, a tumult ready to whirl across the sea. Most disturbing of all, Hannah realized, some part of her, the woman part she'd kept buried for so long, wanted the tempest that was Austen Dante to consume her.

She shoved the thought away, the images far too vivid. Austen's handsome face looming above her, his arms encircling her, his mouth possessing hers.

She'd never survive this phaeton ride if she didn't master her accursed imagination. Far better to concentrate on Ravenscar land, to try to better understand the enigma of its master instead of conjuring visions of the two of them in the throes of a passion that could never be.

But no matter how hard she battled to focus on the estate spreading all around her, every mile they traveled only confused her even more. Every hour they wandered made her more perplexed, more fascinated, more compelled by Austen Dante.

Nothing about this place was what she had expected it to be.

The people of Nodding Cross might think the master

of Ravenscar had lost his mind, but the simple country folk who dwelt on his lands radiated a respect so genuine it astonished her.

True, they had gaped up at her and Pip, amazed as if their landlord had brought a mermaid and her child touring Ravenscar's fields. But once they'd managed to leash their surprise, they had chattered about crops and livestock, children and rainfall.

Perhaps their landlord had indeed leveled the cottages of his crofters so he could get a clear view of the lake from his study window, and yet the newly constructed buildings glistened fresh and white and lovely against their backdrop of hills and vales, pristine thatch gleaming like spun gold in the sun.

Barns separated from the main cottages held fat cows and geese. Flowers clambered up walls and arched over doorways where plump children frolicked about their daily chores. And everyone from the smallest child to the busiest housewife paused to greet their master and chatter about the celebration that was to come.

Their finest clothes fluttered drying in the breeze, countless homemade presents whisked away at the sight of the tall man driving the phaeton. And Austen Dante looked as uncomfortable beneath their obvious adoration as a rowdy boy trapped in pinching new boots.

Hannah winced at the memory of her own father's estate, staggering under the burden of debts as he gambled away everything but the small pittance that was kept safe by entail.

She had loved every stone and every field of green, but even as a girl it had bothered her to see the weather-beaten ramshackle dwellings where gaunt families shared space with cows and pigs, and mothers didn't keep the cradle near the fire, but rather positioned it so that the leaking of the roof wouldn't douse their newest babe with rain.

She'd realized something was wrong, sensed it. And when Papa had been between bouts of gaming, he'd listened to her childish concerns, his chest rumbling with indulgent laughter. *It's been this way forever, Somberpuss, in your grandfather's time and his grandfather's before him. Who am I to argue? Remember when we found the baby rabbits in their nest? These people are like those babies—they delight in being crowded all together. They're not like you and me.*

She'd loved her papa so much. Laughing, merry, handsome Papa. She'd wanted so much to believe him.

"Hannah?"

The sound of Austen's voice startled her, dispelling images shrouded in the mist of memory.

"Is something wrong?" Not once since he'd helped her into the phaeton had he looked directly at her. Now those lightning-blue eyes probed her own.

"Nothing," Hannah choked out, tipping her head so the brim of her bonnet shielded her face from his view. "I just . . . was woolgathering."

He drove on in silence, but it was as if in that single glance they had both revealed more than either intended. Was it just her imagination, or did more strain seem to be gathering in Austen's shoulders, darker shadows crowding his eyes? After what seemed an eternity, he spoke.

"I need to stop at this next cottage for a little while. But if you'd like me to take you back to the house, I'd be happy to do so."

There was nothing she wanted more than to climb out of this phaeton, away from this man whose whole being seemed to pulse with an energy that seeped into her soul. But that would be revealing a vulnerability she dared not show.

"No. You needn't trouble yourself. I—I mean, I'm enjoying being outside."

Did the man have the gall to look just a shade disappointed? As if he were as anxious to get rid of her as she was to escape his company?

"All right then." He squared his shoulders. "This is

the place I was telling you about. Enoch Digweed's. A master farmer, one of the finest tenants any landlord ever had the privilege to know. Enoch helped me to lay out the new sites for the cottages, and his wife Flossie designed the living quarters."

Hannah turned a questioning gaze on Austen. Despite his obvious discomfort, a warmth, a depth of respect resonated in the deep tones of his voice as he spoke of his tenant. But there was no time for puzzling out an explanation. At that instant a miniature army of children burst from the cottage door that stood open to the fragrant breezes.

"Mr. Dante is here! Quick! Hide the surprises!" a moppet of about four hollered, stumbling over the hem of her fawn-colored petticoat in her excitement.

Overwhelmed, Pip hung back, huddled in the corner of the phaeton, peering down at the mass of children as if he half expected they might start to nip at his ankles. Hannah wondered if he'd ever been allowed to play with another child.

The little girl reached the phaeton and bobbed curtseys as if she were a cork floating down a bubbling stream. But Dante seemed as unsettled by such an enthusiastic reception as Pip was.

The man stiffened even more. His gaze darkened with something that might be guilt as he turned toward a sunny corner draped in rose vines.

Hannah glimpsed a figure sitting in an invalid's chair mounted on wheels. A broad, ruddy, honest face was capped by graying hair. Burly shoulders that seemed capable of balancing the weight of the entire cottage were garbed in a clean, carefully mended jerkin. Hannah watched the man attempt to stand with the help of two sturdy sons.

"For God's sake, Enoch, sit down!" Austen snapped. "The bone setter will have my hide!"

Hannah noticed the sturdy wooden splints bound about the farmer's right leg.

"Good morrow, sir," the crofter said brightly. "Be makin' ice chips in Hades the day Enoch Digweed fails to show you proper respect." There was something akin to worship in the man's eyes. Hannah was stunned to see dull red creeping up above Austen's snowy cravat.

"Don't be absurd, Enoch. Sit down before I make you."

The farmer eased his massive frame back into his chair, a grimace of pain tightening his lips for an instant before he shuttered it away. Hannah heard a slight hiss of breath through Austen's teeth, as if he felt it in his own body.

Digweed peered up at Hannah and Pip with inquisitive brown eyes, and she could see he was torn between astonishment and delight.

"Madam, young sir," Enoch said with an awkward bob of his leonine head. "Welcome to my cottage."

Austen fidgeted with one of the buttons on his riding coat. "This is Miss Graystone and her son Pip. They are staying at Ravenscar House."

"Are they now?" A bushy brow swept upward. "It's that glad I am you've got some company, sir. Flossie'll be pure delighted. She worries over you up in that big place alone."

"Alone?" Austen sputtered. "The infernal place is swarming with servants! I never get a moment's peace!"

"Whatever you say, sir." Digweed grinned, displaying a charming gap in his smile.

"I—I'm helping Austen—I mean, Mr. Dante, with his music," Hannah burst out, not wanting Enoch to get the wrong idea. "He hired me to—" To what? Write music when she didn't have the slightest idea how? Somehow, staring into Digweed's honest face brought hot shame spilling to the surface.

As if he sensed her discomfort, Enoch brushed it away. "Flossie's made up a batch of cherry pies, sir, and she'd be right proud for you to take one."

"Thank you, but I couldn't . . ."

"Sir, don't you be insultin' my baking!" A plump woman with flyaway hair and button bright eyes burst from the doorway, her capable hands curled about the most delicious-looking pastry Hannah had ever seen. "I know it's not as fine as what you get at the big house, but it's cherry, an' it's still nice and warm."

Hannah's mouth watered, and she realized in all the upset over the dress, she'd forgotten to eat so much as a crumb of breakfast.

She wanted to leap down Austen's throat when he waved one hand. "I'm afraid I don't care much for cherries."

The goodwife peered up at him through narrowed lids with the expression mamas have used to unearth the fibs of unruly boys since the beginning of time. "Don't like cherries, do you? You all but licked my pie plate clean the night you helped cure Mazie of the whooping cough." She turned to Hannah with a wide smile. "Most astonishing thing I ever saw—the master putting my baby's head over some steam, making her breathe it in. Thought we were sure to lose her, Enoch and me, but the master wouldn't give up."

Hannah glanced at Austen, his face bright red. "Don't be overly dramatic, Flossie. I just happened to be passing by when my horse came up lame. It was nothing."

"Don't be tellin' a mother who almost had to bury her child it was nothing when you saved her. I've lived places enough to know most landlords would've ridden the opposite way fast as their horse could carry 'em if they'd discovered sickness in a cottage. You cannot imagine, miss, what it meant to me to hear her calming, to see her sleeping peaceful because of what Mr. Dante had done."

Hannah's chest tingled deep inside, warmed by the memory of Pip the night he'd been so ill, drowsing peacefully at last in his bed. But she had not felt gratitude for Austen—her outrage had still been too hot, her fear crowding too close, her secrets suffocating her.

Her heart hadn't been able to admit that she owed anyone a debt of gratitude. Especially not him.

But now, staring down at Flossie Digweed's pie, Hannah remembered exactly how hungry she'd been, how miserable and alone, before Austen Dante had barged into her life.

"There, you see how the lady is looking at the pie! I vow, she all but has tears in her eyes! She must be half-starved!" Flossie cried out triumphantly. "And this dear little boy—doubtless he is hungry as well!"

"Not anymore," Pip piped up, daring to defend his hero. "Mr. Dante doesn't 'llow it."

Flossie's knowing eyes deepened a shade in compassion. "Now, sir, did you hear the little mite? The two of 'em can nibble on the pie as you drive them about. Otherwise, it might be a week before you remember to feed them! Yes, I know your ways, sir. Once you have a mission to accomplish, you'd forget your own nose if it wasn't stitched to your face!"

Was it possible for the master of Ravenscar to look more uncomfortable? There was something heartwarming in the way this mighty, powerful landlord allowed Flossie Digweed to bully him just a little.

"Madam, I'm not usually one to brag," Flossie said. "But our master here is the cleverest man in all England, inventing things no one else ever dreamed of."

Hannah stared, stunned at this new facet of the most complex man she'd ever met. "You're an . . . inventor?" That was where he went late at night, where he unleashed whatever pain had haunted him in the Music Room. Why was it that Flossie's claim suddenly seemed to make perfect sense?

"Flossie's exaggerating. I tinker with a few things, but—"

"Tinker? I'll be blessed! Why Mr. Dante swears that before he's done he'll have hot water—that's right, *hot water,* running to every floor of the big house."

"Hot water? Impossible!" Hannah shook her head. "It can't be done."

"If anyone can do it, Mr. Dante can. Why, he—"

"Enough, Flossie! I surrender!" Austen seemed about to choke on his neckcloth. "I'll take the blasted pie!"

"You do that, sir," Enoch piped up. "You'll be needing all the energy you can get. I'll be bringing my fiddle to play you a birthday tune. And my oldest boy, he'll bring his tin whistle."

"Birthday?" Hannah echoed.

"I'd think the whole estate would be babbling about it, what with it being scarcely three days away," Flossie said. "Surely you've heard?"

Hannah glanced from Flossie's face to Austen's. "I've heard there was to be a celebration, but no one mentioned it was for Mr. Dante's birthday."

"That's what all the celebratin' is about!" A boy of about eight chirruped. "Mr. Dante gives the most wondrous feasts in all of Yorkshire! An' there's dancin' an' games, an' prizes you can win! An' everyone gets somethin' they need. That's how Thomas got his tin whistle."

The lad made a face. " 'Course, I think the master sets things up so the little ones get a chance to win, too."

"It's time we were going," Dante cut off the boy's raptures. "I was wondering if we could borrow your Christopher one day this week, Flossie. As a playmate for Pip. The boys could run in the gardens and play at the kennels."

Flossie turned her motherly gaze upon Pip and smiled ever so gently. "Christopher's out mindin' the sheep right now. But he would be delighted to come. I'm sure of it. An' you needn't be afraid he'll raise too much of a fuss, Master Pip. He knows when to be quiet-like, does Christopher."

Pip managed a quavery smile. "I like to be quiet sometimes, too."

"Now, Miss Graystone, if you've any influence with

Mr. Dante at all, you make certain he takes you to Potter's Lake. It's a pond tucked back in the loveliest little spot where hardly anyone goes. Peaceful and sweet-smelling and pure choked up with flowers. Perfect place to nibble a bit of pie."

Why was it that Hannah wanted nothing more than to sit by this woman's hearth, drink in her simple wisdom and her warmth? She was a mother whose children might run to her with their troubles, certain of a cakie pressed into their hand and a brisk kiss upon their cheek. Certain that she would listen . . .

"Thank you, Mrs. Digweed."

"Flossie. Just plain Flossie." The woman pressed Hannah's hand with her own work-roughened fingers. "It was a rare pleasure meeting you, miss." She thrust the pie into Hannah's hand, the warmth of the pan seeming to seep through Hannah's fingers and into her heart. "Take good care of the master for me." She cast Dante a critical glance. "He does a rare poor job of takin' care o' himself."

Something in the goodwife's chatter made Austen dashed uncomfortable, because in an instant he was beside her, taking up the reins. But instead of gigging the phaeton into action, he hesitated. And Hannah sensed he was finally getting around to the question he'd been waiting to ask the whole time.

"Enoch, the leg . . . how is it mending?"

"Bone setter says it's doing well enough. We'll be putting the finishing touches on that new reaping machine of yours before you know it."

"Reaping machine?" Hannah echoed. "I've never heard of such a thing."

"You will someday, miss. And every farmer in England will be praising the name of Mr. Austen Dante."

"Enoch, don't. The last time we experimented with it you nearly lost a leg. I still don't know how the devil that accident happened. Can't figure out what went wrong."

"We'll get it right the next time," the farmer insisted.

"As for the leg, don't be worryin', sir. Enoch Digweed's tough as the most stubborn oak that ever put forth leaves." He rapped on the wood of the splint.

Hannah saw Dante wince, knew that Digweed glimpsed it as well.

"I never would have risked testing it if I hadn't been sure the design was safe," Austen insisted, regret threading through his voice.

"It wasn't your fault, sir." The farmer said, suddenly sober. "No one blames you at all."

But as the phaeton pulled away from the cottage amid cries of farewell and waving hands, Hannah knew Enoch was wrong. Whatever accident had happened to the farmer's leg, there was one person who blamed the master of Ravenscar entirely.

That was Austen Dante himself.

Chapter

❧ 15 ❧

Any sane man would have driven the lot of them back to Ravenscar House, retreating to his study where he could drown himself in the finest brandy his wine cellar could provide. But it seemed that the heartless master of Ravenscar who struck terror in the breast of every villager in Nodding Cross wasn't immune to a pair of pleading gray-green eyes shaded by a boy's blond curls.

He'd never been one to offer excuses. Along with hunting and drinking, riding and shooting, one of the lessons his grandfather had drummed into his head was that a man of property was not accountable to anyone.

Yet Austen was certain he could have come up with some reason to return to Ravenscar House if he tried hard enough. It would have been simple to say the horses were tired. He had work to do. Or just plain *no* would have sufficed. But Pip's tentative query about seeing "the pretty lake the pie lady told about" obliterated any thought of beating a hasty retreat.

Blast. When had the notoriously self-centered Austen Dante come to care so much about another person's feelings? Austen Dante, who could tread on his servants' bleached bones and not even hear them crunch, couldn't bear the tiniest wince of disappointment in the little boy's face. What the devil was happening to him?

Yet, as he peered down at Pip dozing beneath a gnarled oak tree, he was damned if he could regret his weakness.

Pie crumbs and cherry juice had been washed away with delighted splashing, and droplets of water still clung bright as diamonds in Pip's hair. The boy's pond-wet clothes were spread to dry across a stone, his small body swallowed by Dante's own dry shirt. And the long crescents of his lashes lay pillowed on sun-kissed cheeks.

Dante lay back in the sparkling cool water, and despite the troubles crowding his mind he couldn't stifle a smile.

It seemed that learning to swim was exhausting work. Fortunately, the venture had turned out to be far more successful than Dante's own ulterior motive—cooling the fire Hannah Graystone's nearness had started in his blood.

Carrying Pip in his arms in the water, feeling the child clinging to him with such trust, had been an experience that defied description, there was such beauty in it.

But even stripped down to nothing but his breeches, splashing and floating, teasing and dunking the boy, there hadn't been a moment when Dante wasn't aware of the woman who had taken up a perch on a massive stone jutting just above the water.

The unusual warmth of the day made tendrils of auburn hair cling to the column of her slender throat, just begging a man's fingers to pull the strands gently away. Her stockings were stuffed into her cracked, worn shoes, tucked in the shade where she'd drawn them off. The water lapped at her bare feet, the delicate bones of her ankles visible where she'd caught up her skirt.

Though Dante knew she'd made a mighty effort to keep her gaze turned modestly away while he'd frolicked with Pip, time after time, Austen felt her eyes watching him.

He'd wondered what she was thinking, what she was feeling. She'd looked so beautiful there, so quiet, he'd wished he could keep her far away from the brutal man who had hurt her, keep her from finding out about the Bow Street runners he'd paid to unearth her secrets.

Unforgivable, that breach of trust. And yet, Austen knew he would risk far more to keep her safe.

Even after Pip had tired so much he'd crawled out to take a rest, Dante had remained in the water, trying with each stroke across the silver surface of the pond to outdistance guilt and regret, and the quickening in his loins every time he felt Hannah Graystone's gaze touch him.

Damn William Atticus to hell. Because of his interference, every glance, every sigh, every brush of hands as he helped her into the phaeton seemed laden with undercurrents that taunted, tempted.

Better to end this torture and leave the water, gather up Pip and Hannah and head home. There could be no self-recriminations now that he'd granted the boy's wish. No regrets.

Except one. Now that Pip lay sleeping, he wanted to draw Hannah into the pond, wanted to tumble her into a cascade of diamond-bright droplets and heat her water-spangled lips with his kiss.

He imagined bringing her back here when night had blossomed, a thousand stars swimming overhead, the moon trailing a ribbon of silver across the pond's surface. He would strip away her garments until her skin glowed pale ivory beneath his caress.

He would take down the glorious mass of her hair, then he would carry her into the water. Make love to her as if they were the only man and woman on earth and Eden had opened its gates for their delight.

Damnation, he was a fool, torturing himself with such imaginings. And yet, it was as if he'd been destined to come here with Hannah since the beginning of time.

Dante should have kept his distance from the fairy

maid upon the stone. But she had woven some sweet enchantment that lured him closer to the white flash of ankle, the stirring of delicate toes rippling the water. The blisters and bruises he'd found the night he slipped her shoes from her feet were healed. He wished he could wash away her other wounds as well, the wounds in her heart, in her spirit, the sadness that lay hidden in the silvery depths of her eyes.

He ducked beneath the shimmering surface until it hid him completely, then slowly, deliberately stroked toward her underneath the water. When he saw the blurry shape of her rock an arm's length away, he dug his feet into the pebbly bottom launching himself upward. She started, drawing her feet back toward the rim of the stone as he burst through the pond's surface.

And in that instant he wondered what she would do if he grabbed her by her leg and pulled her down into the water. If he kissed her the way he wanted to—hard and hot and needing.

Blast, this was no way to settle down the pulsing she'd stirred in his veins. He fought to shove the emotions back, seeking some meager shelter in teasing her.

"Wouldn't you like a swimming lesson as well?" he asked, arching one brow. "I'd wager you could float almost as well as Pip with a little help."

"No thank you," she said, so quickly he knew he'd shaken her. "I mean, I can't imagine when I'd ever need to—to swim."

You'd need to swim when I make love to you here, so I can chase you in the water, catch you, tickle you until you laugh and all the shadows that haunt you fade away.

God, he was being absurd. Dante leaned back half floating, letting the water lap at his bare back. He was excruciatingly aware of Hannah's gaze skimming across his gleaming bare shoulders. A tremor racked him as he remembered the feel of her hand when she'd pressed it against his naked chest, the leap of his heart beneath her soft palm.

"My grandfather insisted everyone should know how to swim," he tried to distract himself. "One never knew when he might be tossed off his finest hunter into some plaguey stream." Austen grimaced. "My grandfather had a habit of taking a few too many stirrup cups before a foxhunt."

"Did he teach you?" She peered determinedly over his left shoulder. "To swim, I mean."

"No. My father did." The words were out before he could stop them, bringing with them their usual sting of pain. His answer should have been enough. He should have deftly changed the subject or maybe made a grab for her ankle, obliterating that questioning gaze, replacing it with the wild fluttering he was certain any touch between them would bring.

He stunned himself by drawing a pattern in the water with his hand, continuing his tale. "We were still living in Italy at the time, at my father's family home. He took me into the most exquisite lake I've ever seen. I kept wanting to go in deeper and deeper. Wouldn't listen to his warnings. Finally, in desperation he swam underwater when I was venturing too far. He sneaked up on me, grabbed my leg, and pulled me under."

Her gaze found his, a crease of concern between her brows. "It must have frightened you terribly."

"Actually, his strategy turned against him." Dante couldn't stifle a wistful grin at the memory. "I loved being dunked. Wanted him to do it all the time. He spent the rest of the day swimming underwater and pulling me beneath the surface. It was a game to me."

"It sounds wonderful. I'm certain Pip's father never took the time to . . ." She stopped, a wary light flashing into her eyes. "What I mean to say is—" She was trying to change the subject. He could see it in her eyes as they flicked down to where beads of water were running down the contours of his chest. But it was a grave tactical error. Her eyes widened, and she swallowed hard. God above, was her mouth as dry from wanting as his was? She moistened her lips.

"Your—your father was from Italy, then," she plunged on, determined. "How did you come to be master of an English estate?"

Was he out of his mind, talking of this to anyone? He never had before. But somehow he found himself continuing. "My mother was the favorite daughter of a country squire with vast holdings throughout England. She was as headstrong as the old man, and three times as brave. She disgraced him by falling in love with her music master, then made it a hundred times worse by actually marrying the man. The squire swore he'd never see her again. I know it hurt my mother, but I'd never seen a more determined woman." He glanced at Hannah and smiled. "Until I met you."

"So what happened?"

"We lived in Italy, and Father did well enough. Then, one day a message came from the vicar of the Austen Park parish. He warned that my grandfather was deathly ill. We made the journey to England so my mother could make peace with him."

"Thank heavens there was time for your mother to do so. There's nothing worse than regrets, not being able to tell someone you love him, that you didn't mean to hurt him." What sorrow was darkening her sunstruck face? "It must have been a sad homecoming for a little boy, though."

Austen laughed. "For me, it was a grand adventure. My grandfather was a stranger to me, so no one really expected me to mourn. I remember being so excited at the end of the journey I was nearly wild, especially when I discovered the kennels."

Dante closed his eyes, remembering. Derbyshire, green and wild and lovely, stables bursting with the finest horseflesh, kennels filled with the county's most exceptional foxhounds.

"With death hovering about the house, no one was paying much attention to one small boy. I let the dogs out and brought the whole pack of them racing into the house to show my mother. Grandfather was lying on his bed, Atticus holding his hand. I don't think Atticus had left his side from the moment he got sick. The solicitor was dripping sealing wax on some document in the corner. Everyone was already sobbing as if Grandfather had died."

The corner of Austen's mouth ticked up. "I burst into the room half-buried in that pack of dogs, clambered up on Grandfather's bed, and told him that if I had such capital dogs I'd try a lot harder to stay alive."

Was that a smile he'd surprised from her? One that was soft and uncertain. "He must have been astonished."

"To say the least. In the years afterward, he often said that it was such good advice he decided to take it. Sent the vicar away, ripped up the solicitor's paper, and told my mother to cancel the order for his coffin. Sat up and ordered beefsteak and a bottle of claret for breakfast. Sometimes I think the whole illness was a ruse to get his daughter across the ocean without having to beg."

"It's a wonderful story."

"Not exactly. Grandfather was so taken with me, within weeks of our arrival in England he offered to adopt me and make me his heir. He would give my parents a house just outside the gates, while I learned to be an English gentleman. I remember Father and Mother talking all night—hearing their voices, the sound of my father's pacing. I don't know what they said, but in the end my parents agreed to Grandfather's proposition. Once they had, there could be no returning to Italy."

"Your grandfather must have loved you very much."

"Too much, I think. I stayed at the big house instead of with my parents. I was able to visit whenever I wished, but Grandfather's attitudes about what made a fine man were far different from my father's views. Riding hell-for-leather behind the hounds, being the best shot in the country and able to hold three bottles of spirits without slurring your words—those were triumphs for Grandfather. My father was a studious man, devoted to his music and his books."

Austen hesitated, a whisper of the confusion he'd felt, a sense of detachment stealing into his voice. "It was odd being part of the family and yet not belonging anymore. I suppose if I'd protested loudly enough, the old man would have let me return to my parents. But I chose to stay with Grandfather. Truth to tell, I was damned relieved. The old man was crusty as the barnacles of hell, but he understood me. Didn't demand things of me I could never give."

"I can't imagine there is anything you'd set your mind to that you couldn't accomplish. I'm certain the Digweeds don't think so."

"I wouldn't give much creedence to what Enoch and Flossie say." Austen gave a wry laugh. "They're daft, the Digweeds are. Sixteen children. That's enough to shatter anyone's reason." He ducked his shoulders down in the water for a moment, smoothing his hands across the surface. He should have changed the subject, but he found himself lapsing into silence.

"Forgive me for asking," Hannah ventured after a moment. "But . . . I still don't understand. If your grandfather adopted you, wouldn't your last name have changed?"

"Officially it has. But after he died, I . . ." Defiance and sheepishness warred within him. "I decided to go back to using the name I was christened with in everything but official business. As you might have guessed, I'm not overly concerned with other peoples' rules."

She peered at him, the tiniest crease of confusion forming between her brows. "But I thought you were . . . I mean, considering the letters from your family you hadn't opened, I assumed you were estranged."

"We are. Make no mistake about it." Dante closed his

eyes, splashing water onto his drying face, wishing the clear drops could rinse away a thousand regrets.

Had his pain shown in his features? He wasn't certain. He only knew that it was Hannah who switched the subject, a new gentleness threading through her voice.

"Austen, I want to thank you for today. For being so patient with Pip. He'll remember this day always."

Why did she sound as if she were hoarding memories somehow, stringing them like pearls in a hidden corner of her heart? It was damned disturbing, almost as if she were already looking into the future to the time she would leave. Dante stood in the waist-deep water and slicked back his wet hair in an effort to hide his uneasiness.

Despite the clinging of memories, the regrets and the pull of attraction, he might have come up with some amusing quip to distract them both. Might have thought of something brilliant. But in that unguarded instant, the side of Hannah's bare foot brushed his naked chest. Then he couldn't think at all.

The contact sizzled through him, wet flesh to wet skin, the barest hint of what it might feel like to touch as lovers. Instinctively he curved his hand over the delicate arch of her foot, trapping it against him.

Her breath caught and he saw her eyes widen as if the most dreadful of calamities had struck. Hannah had felt it, too, he realized with a jolt. That swift surge of something elemental, something dazzling, something dangerous. Lust? Or an emotion he dared not name?

Hell, why did she look so surprised by the sensation? She'd known the taste of passion before, hadn't she? The night she'd conceived her son? Not that he could ever allow that experience to matter, use it as some kind of an excuse to take what he desired.

He pulled away, but it was too late. He knew as long as he lived, he'd never forget the precious weight of her foot against his bare skin, the fragile warmth of her skin trapped between his chest and his palm.

"I think we should be getting back now," Dante ground out. But it didn't matter. There was no going back from that moment's touch. It had changed everything.

He bit back a curse, then splashed out of the water, bundling Pip into the phaeton, heading home. But even the wind cooling his wet skin couldn't banish the heat she'd branded into his chest or ease the fearsome tightening in that part which made him a man.

Perhaps Atticus's blunderings had forced him to confront the fact that he wanted Hannah in his bed. But this unguarded moment in the pond had made matters far worse.

It had made Dante realize that somewhere inside, no matter how hard she was fighting it, Hannah Graystone desired him, too.

It didn't matter. He couldn't let it matter. He had far too many ghosts of his own to battle to invite an innocent woman into his own personal corner of hell.

Who would ever have guessed that a man's naked skin would feel so silky, so delectably hot? And who would have guessed that the slightest touch for just a moment could sear itself forever into a woman's soul?

Hannah cradled Pip against her as Austen guided the phaeton along the winding country road, his face drawn in a fierce mask of concentration, every muscle in his body rigid. He'd yanked on his riding jacket oblivious to the fact that Pip still wore his shirt. But glimpses of that powerful masculine chest still taunted Hannah beyond the flapping edges of cloth.

Every line of Austen's body screamed with tension, with an almost savage need to drive the horses to their limits of speed, of endurance, as if to outrace some demon nipping at the master of Ravenscar's heels.

But still he held the team ruthlessly to a walk, ever mindful of the little boy still drowsing in Hannah's arms.

Not another word had Dante spoken. He didn't have

to. Without Pip seated between them, every bump of the phaeton made Hannah's thigh brush against Austen's breech-clad leg, the dampness from the cloth seeping past skirt and petticoat to her own skin.

Her muscles ached with the effort to keep distance between them, but it was as if some mischievous kelpie were delighting in tormenting her, jarring her toward Austen again and again.

As if she needed any other touch to remind her of the suppleness of his skin, the texture of his muscles, the taste of his mouth.

This was madness—this craving that tingled and burned in her most secret places. She was courting disaster every time she managed to see past Austen Dante's careless mask into the vulnerable man who lay beneath. The boy who had gained a fortune but lost his family. The man who did not read his mother's letters, and yet spoke of her with a yearning and a sadness few would ever discern.

Who was this man who raked himself with guilt over a crofter's broken leg? Who fought like a fury to save a sick child? Who took a half-starved woman and boy off the street and made them feel warm enough to hope, safe enough to picnic beside a glistening pond?

But they weren't safe, Hannah reminded herself. This life at Ravenscar House was all an illusion.

When had it happened? When had she been lulled into a sense of security that had stilled the desperation that had driven her from Ireland? She'd spent so long fleeing the specter of Mason Booth, looking behind her, tallying how much time they had before he'd blunder through all the false trails she had left behind.

She'd tallied up the time it would take for her and Pip to disappear into some obscure little village in the middle of nowhere. To assume different names and build a secret life in a tiny cottage where Booth would never find them.

But somehow in the weeks she'd spent under Ravenscar's exalted roof, those plans she'd made for the future had faded away like some half-forgotten dream. She'd come to adore the battle of wills she and Austen engaged in, delighting in the flashes of humor and sensitivity and understanding—yes, and even anger when it flared.

And as the days bled into nights, hours spent watching the shifting expressions in Austen Dante's handsome face, she hadn't *wanted* to remember any life but this.

How had she allowed this to happen? She'd been a fool, a reckless fool, pretending—what? That she and Pip could remain here forever? God in heaven, what had she done?

Somewhere between the time she'd cradled the blue gown against her, seen the hurt in Austen's eyes, and the moment he'd granted the wish of a little boy's heart, Hannah had done the unthinkable.

Fallen in love.

The knowledge tore through her, jagged edged, agonizing. She loved this enigmatic, reckless man with his fiery temper, his fierce intelligence, his secret pain. Love was the only thing that could hurt this badly. But it was futile. Impossible. It had come too late.

She glanced up at Austen's face, the harsh planes and angles as far beyond her touch as the stars. He was fashioned of lightning, bold and wild and beautiful, illuminating everything around him with flashes of brilliance. She was a prisoner of the shadows.

If she loved him, how could she keep putting him in danger? Condemn him to Mason Booth's vengeance, chain him to her own desperate flight with Pip?

She should run, scoop Pip up and race away from this place, this wonderful, generous man, before she entangled him in this disastrous web. And the longer she waited the more agonizing their parting would be. But she couldn't leave. Not yet.

Her memory conjured up one of the most precious scenes of her life. Austen's hand curling her fingers back around the diamond stickpin, his voice roughened with emotion, his eyes dark with concern. *Keep this . . . that way I won't have to wonder if you've had enough to eat, a roof over your head . . .*

No. She would stay a while longer, at least until his birthday. The little Digweed girl and all of Dante's other tenants had fairly shivered with delight as they spoke of the celebration to come—their one chance a year to honor their magnificent landlord.

Austen had fairly chafed with discomfort at such adulation, and yet Hannah sensed that he needed this show of affection. He valued the opinion of these simple, good people who dwelt on his land. It filled an empty place inside him, soothed a raw wound he desperately needed to heal.

She would stay through his birthday celebration. Store up every moment, every smile, every brush of hands to remember during the long years that were to come. She would take comfort in the fact that only her own heart was in danger.

The morning the celebration was over, she would leave this man, this place, this wisp of a dream.

It was long past time she disappeared into the night.

Chapter

❧ 16 ❧

Ravenscar fairly buzzed with preparations. The kitchen burst with pies and cakes and puddings, the garden's finest blossoms were woven with ribbons and draped about the makeshift tables that filled the sweep of lawn.

Pip had already wandered off with little Christopher Digweed, the two boys delighting in each other's quiet company. And Atticus had made his excuses, doubtless still stinging from the argument he and Austen had had. Austen hadn't made even a token protest, suspecting that Hannah would enjoy the festivities all the more without Atticus to dampen her pleasure. He was sure of it when he saw the relief in her eyes the night before.

Even so, Austen felt uncommonly restless. It was as if he were waiting for something—what? Gifts from his sisters? Or from his mother? Or, more laughable still, a loving message from the father who had seemed determined to forget his very existence?

Damnation, but he loathed this day nearly as much as Christmas. Everyone on Ravenscar land would be singing his praises just now—their generous lord and master. What would these good people think if they knew the entire celebration had been designed to keep him so damned busy on this day that he could forget his family, forget his failings, forget everything?

Worse still, what would Hannah think?

Hannah. She had been acting so strangely the past few days, one moment glowing as if she'd discovered some wondrous secret, the next, her eyes alive with a grief so great it hurt him to look at it.

He'd tried everything to coax her to speak to him, to tell him what was wrong. But she'd only shuttered away her wistfulness and looked so fragile he didn't dare press her. Hannah fragile was more unsettling than he ever could have imagined.

He'd be bloody relieved when the celebration was over, when things would get back to normal. Even the time he and Hannah had spent in the Music Room since his return from London had been tense, filled with distractions. Though blast if his music wasn't a trifle better than it had been before he left.

Still, he'd had the devil of a time concentrating, wanting to use their time together to gently pry about, to discover what was troubling her. But she had seemed so delicate, and he hadn't dared try to persuade her to tell him what was haunting her so.

There would be time enough for that after the celebration. But for now, there was nothing to do but go outside where the crofters were waiting, break the ceremonial oatcake so that the festivities could begin.

When he reached the landing he heard something soft, almost wistful. Music. A simple melody played with one finger.

Hannah. He knew it instinctively, felt her presence like a fist in the gut. What in the blazes was she doing in there? Hadn't she spent enough time imprisoned in that room? And yet, this time something was different; he could feel it, sense it captured in her plaintive tune.

She was there waiting for him. Not as the master of Ravenscar, not as her employer, but as a man.

The realization stunned him, flooded him with emotion. He crossed to the door, pushed it open.

At the sound, Hannah jumped up from her seat at the pianoforte. She wheeled toward him, and he stared.

Late afternoon sunlight filtered through the window, casting a halo of gold about her, illuminating a gown so breathtakingly lovely Dante could scarcely think.

Blue muslin cupped her breasts as tenderly as his hands had longed to, skirts rippling like the waves of a river of enchantment. Even her hair had been labored over, curled and twisted, plaited and pinned into something feminine and lovely and soft. *For him,* Austen realized with a swift stab to the heart. She had done it for him.

Her eyes were large and soft and filled with regret—a stark vulnerability and a sweet sadness that tugged at his heart.

"Hannah," he rasped, unsteady.

"Happy birthday, sir." She plucked at the gown with nervous fingers. "Although I think I'm the one who has gotten the most lovely gift."

"I thought you'd—you'd gotten rid of it. The dress, I mean."

"You told me to do whatever I wished with it. I wished to wear it tonight. It is beautiful, don't you think?"

Austen was awed by the soft glow in her eyes, her willingness to dare the whisperings of servants, of his whole estate, to give him the pleasure of seeing her in the gown he'd given her. "You didn't have to do this," he said. "I should have realized from the beginning that buying the cloth was a mistake."

"Was it?" Her fingers caressed the folds with an awe the greatest actress in Drury Lane could not have forged. "How could any mistake be so perfect?"

"I don't understand."

"Neither do I. How did you know, Austen? Exactly what I would think beautiful?"

The raw places in his heart warmed, his infernal throat

aching. "I saw it shining in your eyes, when you didn't think anyone could see." He turned away, hating the unsteadiness in his voice. "The servants—you were right. God knows, how they gossip. Hannah, I—"

"I don't care what the servants say. I don't care what anyone says. I know you, Austen Dante. And this gown—it's the most beautiful gift anyone has ever given me."

He knew how much courage it took for her to close the space between them, lay one hand upon his sleeve. He felt her touch to his inmost core. *Courage should be matched by courage, shouldn't it?* a voice inside him demanded. But it was difficult. So damn difficult to follow through.

He sucked in a steadying breath. "Will you think me a fool if I tell you I imagined you wearing it, more times than I could count?" He hesitated, his cheeks burning. "But none of my imaginings could equal you, now. You look like an angel, Hannah Graystone."

Her rueful smile pierced his heart. "Considering my behavior of late, I doubt I'd gain entry into heaven's gates. Unless they needed a patron saint of stubborn pride. Then I might do well enough."

Dante was stunned to feel her take his hands, her fingers so warm, so delicate, supplicant in his. "Austen, I'm so sorry. Please allow me to thank you for everything you've done. Your gifts to Pip and to me."

God, why did her eyes seem to pierce to his heart?

"They were nothing. Mere trifles."

"You're wrong. They were the most generous things anyone has ever given me."

He stared down into her eyes, drowning in them, wanting her with a fierceness that terrified him. "Give me a chance, Hannah, and I will give you so much more."

Pain tightened her lips, joy sparkling in half-hidden tears beneath her lashes. "You've already done too much. Because there's something else you've given me far more valuable than anything coin can buy."

"What could that be, Hannah?"

Her eyes shone up at him, brave yet shy, honest yet suddenly so very young. "You've given me faith in someone again. You've shown me that—that the world isn't all darkness and selfishness, carelessness and cruelty. You've given me hope. Forgive me for not recognizing the gifts you offered. It's been a very long time since . . . since anyone . . . anything . . ." Her voice broke, and Dante felt the painful battlements around his own heart crack. "Since I let myself believe."

What had it cost her to humble herself thus, to admit she was mistaken? How painful had it been for her to delve so deeply into emotions she strove so hard to deny? Hannah—independent, needing no one. Hannah, who saw the world as it was—stark and real, without fairy dust or magic or dreams.

Not because she was meant to see it that way, but because life had forced her to surrender such things to survive.

He held on to her hands tightly, fighting the need to draw her into his arms.

He wanted to kiss her, hold her, tell her all the things he was feeling. But he didn't dare.

She'd given him something more precious than her kisses.

Hannah had given him her trust.

Dante felt the weight of it close around him, recalling Hockley's shrewd gaze, the detective's grim warning.

You won't regret trusting me, Hannah, he vowed. *No matter what the man finds. I'll never let anyone hurt you or Pip again.*

But how could he tell her? Merely say, *Don't worry about the detective I've hired to unearth your secrets. It won't matter what he finds?* Guilt surged through him, and resolve that he would keep her safe.

He tried to ease his conscience and her unease the only way he could.

"Hannah . . . I want you to feel a part of things tonight. I want you to know . . ." He reached up, running one finger down the petal-soft curve of her cheek, his voice dropping low. "Ravenscar is your home now, for as long as you wish it."

"Home." She flinched as if the word hurt her. And he wondered if she'd ever been warm and safe, if she was remembering another place swimming in the mist of Ireland. Where had she come from, his lost, wandering Hannah? What had she left behind?

"Austen, Pip and I have a present for you, too. Something we made. It's not much, but we wanted to try to tell you how much your friendship has meant to both of us."

She drew out a tissue-wrapped package, small and square. "It's a book we made of writing paper and string."

Austen's fingers clenched on the parcel. He swallowed hard.

"Pip drew the pictures and together we wrote special messages to you on every page. I wish we could have given you something wonderful, but—"

"This is . . . wonderful."

"Why don't you open it?" She smiled at him, a tender, shy smile.

Austen's fingers smoothed over the wrapping. "Do you mind if I save it? Draw out the anticipation?"

A rap on the door made them leap apart as Simmons entered the room, his face split by a wide grin. "Sir, everything is in readiness. If you don't break the oatcake soon, there will be nothing but a few crumbs left. Caught Freddy Digweed taking a pinch of it just a moment ago, and the rest of the babes seemed to think it was a capital idea."

Austen tucked the gift into his pocket, relief stealing

through him. He was already feeling unsettled enough. Then his eyes narrowed. It struck him suddenly *why* he'd hated celebrations like this for so long—because he was the only one truly alone.

But he wasn't alone today. Hannah was here. And Pip. His heart warmed with an excitement he hadn't felt since he'd been a lad—a sense of peace. A sense of purpose. He smiled.

"We'd best not keep the children waiting any longer." Dante grasped Hannah's hand and drew it through the crook of his arm. His birthday . . . a time of new beginnings.

Why did he suddenly feel as if he had a chance to be born anew because of the light in Hannah Graystone's eyes?

Hannah would always remember this night. Tables groaning with food decimated by hordes of the hungry, homemade birthday offerings opened and admired by Austen, only the gift she and Pip had offered still tucked away in his pocket.

Each farmer and his wife marveled over some little gift from the landlord himself—a length of cloth for a new apron, a sewing box or a pair of shears in the shape of a crane. Men delighted in pouches of tobacco and bottles of brandy far finer than anything they could afford. Fresh hats or bonnets decorated heads, while new fobs dangled from cherished watches.

Scores of children raced about with trinkets in their hands—penny tops and little rag dolls, brightly painted drums with wooden sticks. Paper cones held sparkling drops of horehound and flat sticks of peppermint, chocolaty nonpareils sprinkled with tiny white balls of sugar. Anise candy and licorice stained small mouths, and a mountain of juicy round oranges from Ravenscar's orangery had been thrust into small hands.

Tin whistles blew and dogs romped. For once, mothers

and fathers didn't need to chase after their offspring. Everyone merely chided the little one nearest him, as if they were one big family in which everyone belonged.

Everyone, Hannah thought sadly, except for her and Pip. She'd never known that affection and acceptance could hurt instead of heal. Now she understood the shadow in Austen's eyes when these good people lavished him with adoration.

Every goodwife and her man, every child, from little Bella Digweed with her thumb tucked in her mouth to strapping Thomas, made every effort to see that their master's lady guest was made welcome.

"Miss Graystone?" Flossie Digweed stole up looking sweet as a fresh-picked apple in the rosy bonnet Austen had given her. "I just wanted to say how glad we all are that you've come to Ravenscar House."

Hannah flushed and looked away. But it was a huge tactical error, for she could see the children's games being played on the lawn—ninepins in one corner, paper boats sailing upon the lake, and footraces being run.

"See my Christopher, there?" Flossie said, following the direction of Hannah's gaze with a smile. "He has to pair up with our eldest, Thomas, this year, what with poor Enoch being laid up with his leg. Near broke both their hearts, it did. But young Thomas is a good deal more spry than Enoch is, especially since he's been spending every spare moment chasing after his sweetheart over there." She nodded toward a charming lass with a smile bright as starshine. "Who knows, maybe my boys will win the prize this year."

"Enoch, race? I don't understand."

"Mr. Dante makes it the high point of the day—matching up children and their fathers for the games. He's responsible for the lads and their papas spending ever so much time together. They have to practice, don't you know, if they're to have a hope of winning. And winning the master's birthday race is a matter of some pride hereabouts."

Hannah's heart swelled, and she found Austen among them, his hair wind-tousled, his cravat cast aside. His fine jacket had been shed somewhere—perhaps to lay someone's sleeping baby upon.

"Looks like the master is joinin' in the games today," Flossie said. "Seems as if he's got *himself* a boy this year."

At that instant, Hannah saw Pip bobbing at Austen's side, strips of cloth binding his short leg to Austen's far longer one. Even from the distance, she could see a grin lighting up the child's whole face.

Oh, God. Her heart hurt. Her eyes burned as a different batch of children and their fathers hopped awkwardly toward the finishing line. They stumbled and tumbled in tangled balls of arms and legs and laughter. And Hannah ached with the knowledge of the gift Austen had given to all of them.

Time. Precious time and sweet memories, given by the little boy who had lost his family but gained wealth and a great estate. She wondered if Austen thought the trade had been worth it.

The next set of children and their fathers came up to the line where a plump carrot-haired crofter prepared to start them. Dante's dark head towered above the rest. "Forgive me, Flossie," Hannah said. "I want to—to get closer."

"Of course you do, dearie. Go cheer your men on to victory."

Hannah scooped up her skirts and ran herself. Breathless, she reached the edge of the crowd just as the farmer dropped his red signal handkerchief and shouted "Go."

"Nanna!" Pip cried, waving instead of running. But in a heartbeat Austen swept the child along, the two of them dashing madly, stumbling, laughing.

Twice Pip nearly fell, and Hannah's heart stopped. But each time Austen managed to keep them upright. When they finally tumbled across the finish line, falling to the grass, Pip gave a little cry of pain. Hannah knew she'd never seen anything so beautiful as Austen untying the bindings, then bending solemnly to examine the scrape on Pip's knee.

Hannah had to be near them both, wanted to touch them, to make certain this was real, not some dream. Austen glanced up as he heard her coming.

"Only a minor casualty, General, sir." Austen gave her a mock salute.

"Oh, bother about the scrape," Pip said, looking chagrined. "We lost."

"How about this, Colonel?" Austen tweaked the boy's pug nose. "The two of us will practice all this year so that next time, we'll give the leaders a race for their money." The promise struck Hannah like a knife, burying deep.

Pip positively glowed. "We could practice every day. And I'll probably grow some, too, so my legs'll be longer."

"The way you've been eating, boy, you'll grow a dozen inches by next year. Don't you think so, Hannah?"

She couldn't bear those blue eyes upon her, that smile that was so tender. God in heaven, things were worse than she'd thought. She had only meant to rest a little while at Ravenscar. She'd never intended to stay. But with every day it had grown harder to do what she knew she must—to walk away from this place, this man. So she'd waited, made excuses. And now?

There was one thing of which she was certain. It was wrong to let Pip and Austen get even more attached to each other, then tear them apart. Both of them already had too many gaping holes in their hearts.

Pip had lost his mother, Austen his entire family. They were trying to fill the empty places with each other. It was too cruel, knowing such a healing could never be.

She turned away. "I'm thirsty, suddenly. I'm going to get some punch."

She stumbled away blindly, wanting only to escape the press of gazes upon her before she shamed herself by breaking into tears. By the time she reached shelter in the garden, she'd managed to stem the tide of moisture in her eyes. She blessed the shade of hedges, the veil of rose vines, the sanctuary of being alone for a moment or two to compose herself.

Still, she wasn't surprised when a few minutes later a warm, strong hand closed about her arm with infinite gentleness.

She angled her face up to see Austen hovering near her, his handsome features drawn with concern. "Hannah. What's wrong?"

Her throat swelled, her hands trembled, and she feared she was going to humiliate herself by allowing hot tears to fall free. "Do you have any idea what a fine man you are, Austen Dante?" The words spilled out, her voice shaking. "You are the finest man I've ever known."

He grimaced. "You must not know many men, Miss Graystone." The most endearing thing of all was that he was totally sincere. He had no idea what a wonder he was, how special, how astonishing in a world of greedy, selfish men grasping only for the riches and power they might gain.

"These people are so lucky to have you," Hannah insisted.

"Oh, yes." Austen raked one hand through his hair. "They were ever so fortunate that my ancestors snatched up all this land like greedy children. Then, out of the goodness of their hearts, allowed these people to do all the *hard* work for them while my powerful family bled their meager purses dry."

His lips twisted cynically. "By God, when I inherited this place, the cottages along the lake weren't fit to house pigs in. And the night air down there was full of sickness. So damp. It was a wonder any of the people were still alive."

Realization struck Hannah. "So that's why you knocked the cottages down. I'd heard it was so that you'd have a clear view of the lake from your window. I wonder where people got that idea."

Austen became endearingly absorbed in uprooting a stray weed with the toe of his boot. "It's astonishing how such rumors can get started." Yet there was a twinkle in his eye that made Hannah certain that the rumor had originated with him. God forbid the mad master of Ravenscar reveal his generous heart. Far better to start some crazed rumor to conceal his motives.

He shrugged. "The cottages were in such abysmal condition, there was nothing to do but tumble them down and try to do better."

"And you have. If only my father's vision had been half as generous as yours, so much pain could have been spared." Hannah stopped, fidgeting with the sleeve of her gown.

But Austen prodded her gently. "Your father? What kind of vision did he have?"

It was madness to give Austen Dante even a fragment of her past, and yet she wanted—no needed—to share it with him. "Papa's vision was centered on making his next wager, I'm afraid. It didn't matter what—faro, hazard, horse races. Why, I think he once won thirty pounds because he guessed how long it would take a bug to crawl across a taproom table."

She was trying hard to keep her voice light. But Austen wasn't fooled. His face was still, his mouth tinged with compassion.

"And was your father successful in his wagers?"

"If you asked Papa, he was brilliant. Always a whisper away from regaining every shilling he lost. When things didn't go well, he would promise never to turn a card again, but even on the day he died—"

Don't, Hannah, the voice of the child she had been echoed inside her, ten years old, heartbroken, terrified. *Don't tell. Never tell anyone it was your fault. Even Lizzy won't love you anymore.*

"What happened the day he died?" Austen took her hand.

"It was my little sister's birthday. Lizzy had seen a doll

she wanted. I'd saved a bit of money—shillings I'd earned sewing buttons for the vicar's wife. I had just enough for Lizzy's doll. Papa knew how ... disappointed I'd been in him. He was going to town, cajoled me into giving him the money. I made him promise he wouldn't come home without the doll. He said ... said *I swear I'll bring home the pretty for Lizzy, else may God strike me dead."*

Austen had led her to a stone bench, but she didn't remember walking there. She was only grateful to sit down. His fingers were stroking her hair, gently, so gently, drawing her closer into the haven of his arms.

"I hated him that night. Hour after hour passed and he never came home. Lizzy's birthday was ruined. She'd cried herself to sleep by the time I heard the cart rattle up. Papa was dead. He'd lost everything dicing and had been drinking more than he should."

"God, Hannah. I'm sorry, love. So sorry." He pressed a kiss to her temple.

"That wasn't the worst of it. Papa's friend told me that Papa had been desperate to win back three pounds. Had an errand to run, he said, and he'd made a promise." A heartbroken smile tugged at the corner of her mouth. "Papa was a man of his word."

Austen waited in silence while she gathered strength inside herself to continue, his patience a comforting thing. Hannah swallowed hard. "Papa bet Squire Warbler that he could leap from the roof of the Dancing Bear pub to the roof of the shop across the street. No one could stop him. He tried it and fell."

Austen's hand tightened around hers, fiercely, silently, lovingly.

She sucked in a shuddery breath, remembering how many times she had seen her papa in her dreams falling, falling. "He did it because of me, Austen. Died trying to win back the money for that ridiculous doll."

Tears fell and she didn't care. For the first time in her life, Hannah Gray was weeping in front of someone else instead of burying her tears and her grief in the silence of her pillow.

"It wasn't your fault, sweetheart." Austen drew her into his arms. "Your father chose to gamble the money. Chose to make that last wager. Don't you understand, Hannah? If it hadn't happened because of the doll, it would have been over something else. It was just a matter of time."

Hannah clung to him, feeling his strength, his goodness. "Do you—do you really think so? I always felt so badly, I'd hated him, Austen, while Lizzy was crying that night. I'd wished—for just a moment, I wished . . ."

"You didn't wish your father dead, Hannah. Didn't your mother tell you that?"

"Mama never knew. My mother isn't like yours, Austen. She—she does the best she can. She loves us in her way. But she was never very strong. After Papa died, she barely came out of her bedchamber."

"And everyone leaned on you, didn't they?"

"There was no one else. My sisters, they needed someone. We lost everything. Had to move into a little house with barely enough to scrape by on."

"How old were you?"

"Ten."

"My God, how did you survive?"

"I'm not sure. We managed. Eventually one of my sisters married a wealthy Englishman. Her . . . *husband,*" bile filled her throat at the word, "wasn't adverse to casting charity to her poor relations. At the time, it seemed the only way we could keep going, keep our home, but I would rather have starved."

Austen buried his lips against her hair, and she wanted to stay where she was, safe and warm and cared for, in his arms forever. "You'll never have to be afraid again," he promised. "I'll take care of you, Hannah. I swear it."

But that was impossible no matter how she might want him to. Still, to know that there had been someplace, someone who had offered her shelter . . . that gave her the strength to go on. If there was only something she could give him in return. She closed her eyes, remembering the pile of unopened letters, remembering Austen's face turned away, half-hidden by his hand as she had read them. She'd thought him heartless, cold, that day. Now she knew him so much better.

She dared to gaze up into that handsome, beloved face. "Austen, please. There is only one thing I ask of you. In the end, I lost them all—all my family. I can't explain how. But every day I ache for them, for just a word, just a smile. I think I'd be crazed with joy if Lizzy were able to thrust a bonnet at me, begging me to change the ribbons."

"Hannah—"

She laid her fingers against the fullness of his lips to stop him. "No, let me finish. Please. I've never told anyone the truth about Papa, but I told you because . . . it was too late by the time I realized how much I loved him. Too late to say I was sorry. It's not too late for you."

She felt him stiffen as if she'd dealt him a blow, but she was already feeling battered inside herself. She grasped Austen's hands, held on tightly. "I read those letters from your mothers and sisters. I know your heart, Austen, how much you miss them, no matter how hard you try to pretend not to. Everything at this celebration revolves around family. I think that's because you've lost your own. I'm begging you. Mend your relationship with your family."

His voice was low, rough with pain and yearning. "Some things can't be mended, Hannah. You don't know—"

"Then tell me. I've torn the darkest secret from my heart for you. Trust me, Austen." *Before it's too late. Before I have to leave you here in this great house, alone with letters you never open and music that torments your soul.*

"My father wants to forget I ever existed. It's only fair that I let him."

Could the father who had taught Austen to swim in that distant Italian lake, who had surrendered his homeland for his son, truly be so cold? No. She'd seen the warmth of memories softening Austen's face, the quiet longing. A sadness over all he'd lost. "I don't believe that."

"It's true. You know he surrendered me to my grandfather. And, God knew, Father didn't approve of my upbringing, my running wild and careless about the estate. But he had nothing to say about it anymore. Whenever I saw him, he looked so worried, he'd try to caution me, tell me he was afraid that someday I would get into a scrape even Grandfather couldn't haul me out of. Father was right."

"What happened?"

"I brought my closest friend—hell, my *only* friend—home for holiday from Eton. Charles Edwin Wallace. We called him Chuffy. He was plump, with hair that stuck out all over, and eyes squinty from reading too much. I teased him unmercifully but would thrash anyone else who dared to try it."

Why was it so easy to see Austen championing someone weaker than himself? Hiding his own goodness by seeming to torment the boy he was actually protecting? Doubtless little Chuffy Wallace had discovered the truth about Austen as she had.

"I was doing my damnedest to impress Chuffy, all the insane games boys will play, the risks they'll take. The best apple tree in the county was in the center of a pasture. We weren't allowed in there, but I didn't care. I was determined to steal one. Chuffy didn't think it was my brightest idea."

She could see how much the tale was costing him, and she held his hand tightly, trying to give him the strength to continue, as he had given it to her minutes ago.

"I'd left Chuffy far behind as usual. His legs were so short he couldn't run very fast. I vaulted over the fence, ran nearly to the tree, when I heard Chuffy screaming.

The farmer had a bull—mean as hell. They called him Madman. Even the bravest boy near Austen Park had the sense to be afraid of it."

"The bull . . . was it . . . ?"

"I saw it out of the corner of my eye. It was charging toward me. I was caught halfway between the tree and the fence."

"Dear God, Austen!"

"It was hopeless, but I started running for the fence knowing, just knowing, the bull was behind me, hearing him thundering . . . but then he changed directions, and I saw Chuffy standing inside the pasture, flapping his coat at the bull, trying his best to distract it from me."

She reached up, stroked his face, wishing she could wipe away the pain in his eyes, the ruthless self-blame.

"I yelled at Chuffy, told him to get out of the fence. I ran like blue blazes. But Chuffy panicked. He tripped and the bull—" Austen paused, the muscles in his throat iron-taut, and Hannah could feel the crushing grief he still suffered. "Chuffy died at Austen Park before his parents could arrive from Sussex. I still remember him crying for his papa."

"It was a mistake, Austen. A costly one, but just a mistake. Any loving father would have to forgive his son for that."

"Father thought I was being reckless as usual, thought I'd gone into the pasture on a dare, knowing the bull was in there. But I hadn't."

"Why didn't you tell him? Surely he would've understood."

Austen looked away. "I couldn't. It doesn't matter anymore. There were other fights—plenty of them—before I left Austen Park for good. But that was the day that changed things between us forever. I was a disappointment to him in every way imaginable. In ways he didn't even know."

"So change things again for the better. All that matters is healing the breach between you and your family."

He peered down at her, his eyes bright with tears he hadn't shed. She cupped his cheek in her hand. "Do it, Austen. Now. Before it's too late."

"I think I might have the courage to do it, Hannah, with you to help me. My sister is getting married soon. If I were to go, would you—" He hesitated, sucked in a steadying breath. "Would you and Pip consider coming with me?"

Hannah reeled at the trust in those words, the chance he was offering her to help him, be his strength, stand by his side while such old wounds healed. For they would heal. She needed to believe that. And yet she had to refuse his request. She groped for some reason he would believe.

"No. I—I couldn't . . . they'd be horrified at the intrusion. Think, Austen."

"I am thinking clearly for the first time in a long time. But I don't want any secrets between us. There's something I need to tell you—"

Fear flared in Hannah's breast, fired by the knowledge that she would be leaving this man tomorrow, hurting him. She couldn't bear to do so, to carry any more secrets away with her. Secrets that couldn't change the fact that she had to leave him.

"Don't," she breathed. "I can't—can't . . ." . . . *listen anymore to your passion and your pain, or how will I ever leave you?*

"Mr. Dante, sir?" A call from somewhere in the garden made them spring apart. Hannah swiped at her cheeks, dashing away the last traces of tears.

"Here. On the bench," Austen answered, rising to his feet. She was touched to see him angle his broad shoulders to shelter her from view so she could compose herself.

"Sorry to disturb you, sir," Simmons said. "But Enoch refuses to strike up the dance until you're there. Don't want to disappoint the ladies."

For a moment, Austen looked as if he wanted to tell

the lot of them to dance off the nearest roof. But the caring landlord took precedence over the man with his private needs. Hannah loved him all the more for it.

He turned to her, apologetic. "Hannah, they wait all year for this. I have to go."

"Of course you do."

"I'm expected to dance the first with the lady of my choice," he started to explain, then paused, his eyes suddenly intense. "But this year perhaps Flossie Digweed will have to dance with her boy Christopher instead. Hannah." He hesitated, an almost boyish shyness stealing into his face. "Would you consider honoring me with the first dance?"

He'd entered the race with Pip and now was offering her a chance to dance beneath a canopy of stars. Almost as if . . . as if the three of them belonged to each other. It was all a beautiful illusion. A dream. But it was *her* dream for tonight.

She smiled up at him, her heart breaking with the knowledge that this would be the only time she would ever dance in Austen Dante's arms.

"I'm not very good at dancing." She managed to say. "But, yes, Austen. I'll dance with you." She'd take this one dance because it was all she'd ever have. She'd never even have the chance to tell him good-bye.

He took her hand, cradling it in his own large, strong one, and led her from the fragrant bower where they'd shared their most painful secrets, into the shadowy expanse of lawn dotted now with scores of colored lanterns. Blue and gold, red and green, they flickered against the swirling pools of the encroaching darkness.

There was a murmur from the crowd, a ripple of applause. "Trust the master to choose the prettiest girl here," Flossie teased.

But Enoch only snorted as he resined up his bow. "Took his time in askin' her, though."

"Stop your grumbling, old man, and play." Austen said, and music rippled out at his command. Lilting, lovely, the fiddle sang to the darkness. A fist seemed to squeeze Hannah's chest. How had Enoch known? He'd chosen an Irish dance, one that seemed born of fairy dreams and mist and tempted feet to flight. She'd heard it on her father's lands, sweet melodies from tumble-down cottages, beauty spun from the hands of people with barely enough to eat. Singing in the face of unspeakable poverty. It took a special kind of courage. She hoped to God their new landlord was like the man who now whirled her in his arms.

They went through the patterns of the dance, hands clasping then releasing, arms curving and turning her around. The blue muslin swirled around her legs, and her senses were filled with Austen—the feeling of hands calloused from working on ideas so new, so brilliant no other man had dreamed them before. The flash of his smile, the lithe grace of his muscular body. His hair gleamed with sparkles of color reflected from the lanterns, while the night caressed his face like the fingers of a lover.

Hannah felt a stab of jealousy as the image reverberated through her. How strange to be envious of shadows and wind, rippling soft cotton, anything that was allowed to touch Austen's skin. His gaze clung to hers, heated until his eyes burned in the night, his mouth that of a man desperate to taste her lips.

Time and again as the hours passed, he drew her among the dancers, his hands lingering a whisper too long about her waist, his body brushing just a little too close to her breasts, until even the thin veil of night breeze between them seemed a space far too vast.

She wanted the night to last forever. But no matter how long she wove in the familiar patterns, no matter how Austen teased and taunted and dared his crofters to dance up the sun, the children nodded off and were carried to their beds one by one. Pip surrendered and was borne away by Simmons. The little Digweeds were swept together like unruly chicks by young Thomas and his sweetheart. And at last, all the other dancers drifted away.

The silence when Enoch tucked his fiddle back in its battered case was the sweetest sorrow Hannah had ever known. Austen drew her into the shade of a towering oak and looked down at her, and the regret in his shadow-cast features made her eyes burn.

"Hannah, do you know I always hated celebrations like this. I always felt detached somehow, as if I were watching it all from a distance, and no one would ever notice if I disappeared. I never knew why before tonight. You see, I was always alone, watching everyone else with people they loved, people who cared for them in return." His lips curled in a soul-stealing smile. "But tonight I had Pip to run races with, and you in my arms."

His hand curved upon her cheek and he tipped her face up into the moonlight. His lips drifted down ever so gently, taking hers in a kiss so exquisite it brought tears to Hannah's eyes. Heat flared, passion throbbed, her head whirled in its own primal dance. She wanted to melt into Austen's embrace, taste the rare, sweet fire his lips promised.

She whimpered, craving so much more, but Austen pulled away, flushed and breathless. She could see how much his noble sacrifice cost him, the price etched in every line of his face.

"Sleep late tomorrow," he said. "There's no need to come to the Music Room. I promised I'd help Thomas Digweed draw up plans for a new cottage today. Seems he made use of the festivities tonight to get himself a bride."

She should be grateful. That would give her even more time to get away before he would know they were gone. Yet, Hannah couldn't help but envy young Tom and his beloved, with wedding vows and all the days of their lives to enjoy together.

"Until tomorrow," he breathed, skimming his thumb across the moist curve of her lower lip.

But there wouldn't be a tomorrow, Hannah thought with a raw pulse of pain. Tomorrow she'd be gone.

Hannah swallowed hard, her heart breaking into a thousand tiny pieces as she pulled away from his touch.

She could feel his gaze upon her, feel the tears choking her throat. "Goodbye, Austen," she said, then turned and fled, leaving him alone with the guttering lanterns and the darkness.

Chapter

❧ 17 ❧

Hannah stood at the open window, the night breeze riffling her nightgown. The sweet smell of roses drifting up from the garden whispered to her of touches and trust, unburdening secrets and surrendering the wariest of hearts.

Three times she'd opened her door a crack, listened to the soft shushing sound of Austen pacing in the chamber beyond. Just a few steps away, the turn of a door handle, and she would feel his gaze upon her again, might even tempt him to touch her.

God in heaven, had she lost her mind? What kind of madness was this, that painted countless pictures of what *might* be if she dared. The touch of a man who cared about her. The taste of his passion. A night in his bed. Hadn't she surrendered all hope of those things the day she'd done what Elisabeth had begged her to do, taken Pip and fled toward an uncertain future?

With Mason Booth on their trail there would be no way to have the sort of life with Austen she wanted, needed. She'd known even then there were things she must surrender. The rest of her family. Her own future.

But before she'd left Ireland she'd not believed she would ever fall in love. She had never guessed that she would tumble headlong into the spell of a dark-haired man. That she would let herself be vulnerable to him, want so badly to trust him.

Austen. She wrapped her arms tightly across her breasts remembering every smile and touch, the haunted, somber light that sometimes eclipsed his eyes. Austen—everything she could never have.

Except for tonight. She caught her lip between her teeth, hovering on the brink of an abyss she wanted desperately to embrace. Would it be so terrible for her to cross the slight barrier between them? Tell him . . . what? That she loved him? That she wanted to lie with him in his bed, to seize this one, this only chance she'd ever have to taste the passion of a man, to be made a woman when he joined his body with hers?

What would Austen think of her? And yet, she had so very many regrets. Papa and Elisabeth. The things she hadn't said. The visits she'd never made. If only she'd been able to swallow her pride, she might have visited Booth House before Mason struck his final blows. Lizzy might be alive.

Yet, it wasn't the same. Austen would never know how close she'd come to asking him to make love to her. Only she would see the path forever, another path not taken. Only she would wonder what might have been if she'd had the courage to take this one night the fates had cast into her hands.

Did he love her? She didn't know. But she'd seen the desire flaring in his eyes, felt the hunger in his touch. Austen, who hadn't taken mistresses like other men. Who hadn't showered other women with meaningless baubles. Austen, who had given her a gown lovely as spring's first bluebell.

God above, did she have the courage to offer him not just her body, but some irreplaceable part of her soul?

The wind whispered through the window as if in warning. Dawn would come no matter how much she dreaded it. Austen would ride away to work on the plans for Thomas Digweed's cottage, and she and Pip would vanish into the moors.

Unless she decided soon, opened that door to a night filled with possibilities, it would be too late.

Heart thundering, hands curled tight, Hannah crossed to the portal, opened it, revealing the subtle candlelight that still burned in the corridor beyond. A strip of brighter light gleamed from the crack under Austen's door. And the sound of his pacing murmured to her of a restlessness they'd stirred in each other's blood.

Mustering all her courage, Hannah padded across the hallway in her bare feet. Then quietly opened the door.

Austen was bent over the book she and Pip had made him, his fingers running over her penned lines with a wistfulness that broke her heart, his features reflecting both joy and pain as he looked at the pictures Pip had labored over. A puppy with ears longer than its legs. A pond with two figures splashing in it. A phaeton with a horse made of fluffy clouds.

Austen turned at the sound of the door creaking as she opened it wider, his brows lowering in surprise. "Hannah." He thrust the book away almost guiltily, shoving it under his cast-off cravat. "Is something amiss?"

"No. I mean, yes. I . . ." She couldn't think, couldn't form a coherent thought. His shirt hung open down the front, revealing a slice of his chest, rippling and golden brown from the sun. Droplets of candle shine caught in the fine webbing of dark hair that arrowed down his flat stomach to disappear in a dark ribbon beneath the waistband of his breeches.

Merciful heavens, he was even more beautiful than she remembered. Tall and powerful, devastatingly handsome.

"Is Pip sick?" he asked, starting for the door. "Damn, I was worried the racing might be too much for him!"

"No." Hannah caught his arm to stop him. Her fingers trembled.

Relief dawned in Austen's eyes. "Then why . . ."

"I'm here because . . . I couldn't sleep. I thought—" she trailed off, feeling abominably foolish, her cheeks fire hot. *Thought I would ask you to make love to me.* Her fingertips strayed to the faded ribbon that gathered her nightgown in a crescent above her breasts. Oh, heaven, this was harder than she'd ever imagined.

She caught her lip between her teeth, turned away. "It's absurd. Ridiculous. I should just leave."

Footsteps echoed until he stood behind her and strong, gentle hands curved about her upper arms. The contact sizzled through her, liquid fire. "Hannah, don't you know by now—you can tell me anything."

Warm, moist, his breath stirred the fragile hairs at her nape, coasted across the tender skin of her neck, his voice low and rough with some emotion she dared not name. Slowly he turned her around until they stood mere inches apart, the tips of her nightgown-veiled breasts nearly brushing his naked chest.

Her senses filled with the heat of him, the power of him, the sensitivity, all the more precious because he kept it hidden beneath his careless facade. He smelled of wood smoke from the bonfires and spices from the cakes, his eyes so blue she could drown in them.

Silent. Damn him for being silent, so patient—this man with his quicksilver emotions, his restlessness, his fire.

"I . . . there's something I need to tell you," she said, desperately needing to fill the silence. "About—about the dress."

"Not another word. I—"

She reached up, laying her fingers on his lips, feeling the heat in those warm curves, the promise of passion. "Please, listen. There is a reason I got so angry about— about kitchen gossip. It was because . . ." she swallowed hard. "Because some part of me actually wanted to . . . When you kissed me, touched me, I'd never felt anything like . . ."

"Hannah," he rasped. "What are you saying?"

She tipped her chin up, her gaze capturing his for what seemed an eternity. "I want to feel that way again, and more, Austen. I want . . . *this.*"

She tugged at the ribbon gathering the neckline of her nightgown until the satin loops slid free, the delicate cloth drooping open to show the curves of her breasts. Austen's gaze dipped down, his breath like a dying man's, his eyes shimmering with fierce passion, tempestuous with dark, primal need. Hannah started to tremble.

"Hannah, we can't. I don't want to hurt you."

"I'm hurting right now." A quavery smile tipped her lips. "Do you know, this is the first time I've ever admitted such a thing to anyone. I need you to touch me, Austen. And I think that maybe . . . maybe you need me, too."

Anguish contorted his face. "Blast it, don't you know I've thought about it a hundred times? You in my bed, my hands on your body, my mouth . . . Bloody hell, the whole time we were dancing . . . I've never wanted any woman the way I want you. But it doesn't matter what I want, what I need. You're so fine, Hannah Graystone. So rare. I can't give you what you deserve."

"I'm not asking for promises or happily ever afters. I'm not some moonstruck girl filled with romantic dreams."

"But you deserve dreams, Hannah." His eyes went dark with intensity and despair. "I'd cast my soul to the devil for just one chance to give them to you."

"I don't want a dream. I want . . ." Words failed her and she reached up, sliding her hands beneath his open shirt. His skin was rough satin beneath her palms, his heart thundering against his ribs.

Was this how passion tasted? Heady-sweet, hot with spices, a surging, roiling, pounding need? A melting of the soul?

"Damn it, Hannah! We can't do this."

A low groan tore from his throat as her thumbs skimmed his nipples, her hands sliding the fabric over his shoulders, down the knotted muscles of his arms.

A shudder of pleasure went through him, his breath hissing between his teeth. "Hannah, are you sure? Be damn sure, because once I let myself touch you I'm not certain I'll be able to stop."

She took his hand, that sensitive, supple hand, and brushed her lips across his knuckles. Then, her cheeks afire with embarrassment, her body aching with need, she molded his fingers around the soft globe of her breast.

Hannah could see a lifetime full of defenses tumbling down in Austen's eyes.

Need—almost savage in its intensity. Passion—too long restrained. The reflection of all his fantasies was there for her to see. Nights of seeing their shadows melding together, their hands touching, mouths clinging . . .

She knew the instant his control snapped. He scooped up handfuls of her nightgown and dragged the garment up over her head. Heat flooded her cheeks as the cool air swirled against her skin, and she couldn't keep herself from instinctively crossing her arms over her breasts.

She'd never felt beautiful, blessed with that feminine grace so many other women took for granted. And she was suddenly terrified that this man—breath-stealingly handsome, with his powerful body and his artist's soul—would find her lacking.

She closed her eyes; her breath caught in her throat. Silence. Not a touch. Not a word.

She opened her eyes, and what she saw brought hot tears stinging beneath her lashes. Awe. Wonder. There was a reverence glowing in his features as he lifted two fingers and touched the hollow of her throat.

"Yes," he whispered, running his fingertips across the arch of her collarbone, down the inside of her arm. "I knew you would look like this. Every time I closed my eyes, I could see you as you were that night in the Music Room, your nightgown barely veiling you from my eyes. Candlelight shone through the cloth, gave me the sweetest glimpses of how beautiful you are. Roses and cream, soft and yet so very, very strong. Hannah, do you have any idea how badly I want you?"

He slid his hand around her nape, burrowing his fingers into her hair as he drew her mouth to his. Soft, melting heat sluiced through her as bare breasts touched his chest, naked skin to naked skin, with nothing but his breeches between them.

She slipped her arms about his narrow waist, flattening her hands on the rippling muscles of his back, drowning in the texture of him, the scent of him, the heat that permeated her very being.

His tongue traced the crease between her lips as if seeking some mystical honey, and she let her mouth open, inviting him inside. He explored her as if she were some new creation, something marvelous, conjured from the reaches of his brilliant mind. He glided his tongue across the ridges of her teeth, stroking in a heated rhythm that left her burning. But even that didn't seem enough.

His arms banded around her, crushing her against him as if he wanted to meld their two bodies into one forever. Eager, hungry, his hands glided over her skin and he kissed her until her head spun and her knees melted.

Through the frustrating layer of his breeches, she could feel a hard ridge pressing against her belly. She should have been embarrassed, should have been afraid from the few tales she'd heard of the act she was about to commit with this man.

Instead a wild curiosity swept through her, a primal need to learn everything, know everything about him, touch this wonderful, beautifully flawed man every-where—on his body, in his soul.

He swept her up into his arms, carried her to the huge bed that dominated the chamber. "I'll make it good for you, Hannah." She silenced him with her mouth, kissing him with all the passion hidden in her soul, with all the hunger she'd never allowed herself to feel. He laid her on his bed, the softness tinged with the scent that was Austen's own, her head upon the pillow where he'd spent so many nights dreaming of this very moment.

Then he stood, his gaze locked with hers as his fingers worked the fastenings of his breeches. The tiniest flare of panic jolted through her, the knowledge that she didn't have any idea what to do next. Only that she was burning, burning, burning, and Austen was the flame.

He hooked his thumbs in the waistband of his breeches and slid them down his lean hips, his powerful thighs, until the cloth rustled against the carpet beneath his feet.

She couldn't believe her own daring, her own bold-ness, but they had only tonight, one night, and she wasn't going to waste it by surrendering to the shyness that stole through her.

Swallowing hard, she looked at his beloved face so familiar, then her gaze slid down the breadth of his shoulders, tracing the path where the droplets of water had sparkled that day at the pond. She let her gaze stray lower to narrow hips, long, muscular legs, and to the ridge of flesh that had taunted her when he'd crushed her against him.

Her heart skipped a beat, she became mesmerized by the sight of him, all of him, so beautiful, so strong, so powerful. And she couldn't believe that this man was going to be her first lover, her only lover. That by dawn, he would know every mystery of her woman's body.

And she wanted him to. Wanted to give him every-thing she was, everything she would ever be.

He laid down beside her stroking her, his hands

measuring the weight, the roundness of her breasts, his mouth trailing devastatingly intimate kisses across her skin.

God in heaven, what was he doing to her? She clenched her thighs together against the unbearable heat his caresses built in her most secret places. Her nipples tightened into hard little buds, craving something she didn't understand. But Austen did. His lips grazed the stinging point, once, twice, then he drew her nipple into the liquid heat of his mouth.

"Austen . . ." His name broke on a half sob. She'd never known—never guessed that a man would want to suckle like a babe. Or that the feel of his mouth there, drinking in her very essence, would shatter her to her soul. Sensation lanced from her breasts, through every fiber of her being, until it tightened an unbearable knot of need in the very heart of her femininity, pulsing there, taunting her.

"I've wanted to taste you for so long, Hannah," he murmured against her skin. She threaded her fingers through his hair, whimpering as he trailed kisses across the valley between her breasts, seeking her other nipple and wetting it with his tongue.

One large hand splayed on the soft swell of her belly, edging lower, ever lower, until the edge of his little finger brushed the border of her feminine curls. He hesitated one heart-stopping moment, then gently delved through the silky ringlets to the damp petals sheltered beneath.

Hannah stiffened, gasped as his fingers learned the texture of delicate folds, the melting heat that pulsed there.

"It's all right, Hannah. I swear I won't hurt you like he did."

His words penetrated the passion-hazed fog of her brain. He thought she'd done this before. Ridiculous man. As if she could ever have surrendered herself to anyone but him.

Secrets . . . more secrets . . . but they didn't matter. She wouldn't let them matter. Not here. Not now.

"Austen . . . Austen, I—"

"Hush, love. Part your legs for me. Let me touch you, inside, so deep."

She edged her legs apart but it wasn't enough. Austen's hands curved around the sensitive flesh of her thighs, opening her to his gaze. His eyes darkened, his breath snagged, and he glided his finger into her untried opening.

His lashes drooped shut, as if to savor the sensation and a groan of satisfaction reverberated through him. "Hannah, you feel so good. So right."

He pressed a hot kiss to her belly, the cool silk of his hair drifting across the fragile skin, teasing her, tempting her to yet another level of passion.

She didn't know what to do. Didn't know how to touch him, where to touch him. She only knew she wanted her hands all over him, wanted to taste him everywhere. Wanted him to cover her body with his until she could feel every beat of his heart, every breath he took, every ripple of sinew beneath the dark satin of his skin.

He strung a chain of kisses down her thigh, the inside of her knee, and her legs trembled. But suddenly he journeyed upward yet again. She stilled, disbelieving. Surely, he couldn't possibly intend to . . .

The thought splintered as his mouth found her very center. She jerked at the contact, cried out, feelings so intense shooting through her she thought she might come apart. The tip of his tongue swept out, toying with her in a way that made her whole body shake, desperate, questing gasps and moans tearing from deep inside her.

Hannah, who never allowed her vulnerabilities to show, was melting, entirely entrusting herself to this man who held her in thrall with his hands, his mouth, his body.

She drove her fingers back through his hair, holding him against her as he hurled her into a realm she'd never believed in, casting her toward the heavens like a handful of stars.

She burst, wept, cried out his name as hot, dark pleasure split her very soul. And then he was rising above her like some pagan god of the night, and she could feel his shaft, hot and hard and hungering for her, brushing the quivering flesh he'd just abandoned.

"I can't—can't wait any longer. Have to be inside you." A grimace of ecstasy contorted his features as he braced his arms on either side of her, and then drove his shaft deep with a powerful thrust.

Pain tore through Hannah, surprising a cry from her, a tearing sensation dulling her pleasure.

"What the hell?" She heard a low curse, saw Austen's face swimming above her, his eyes seething with confusion and desire. "Damn it, Hannah, you've never . . ."

She clung to him, terrified he'd pull away from her. "It doesn't matter, Austen. I wanted this." She didn't care about the pain. She wanted him, all of him, wanted to gift him with the mind-shattering pleasure he'd given her.

She hid her embarrassment by burying her face against his chest. Tried to outstrip her web of lies by kissing him, nipping at him. He tasted of the slightest tang of salt, and as she instinctively glided her lips to the flat disk of his nipple, then took it into her mouth as he had done to her, a guttural cry reverberated through him.

His jaw knotted, every muscle in his body tensed as he moved in a cadence as old as time. Gentle, he was so gentle now that he knew she'd been a virgin. He guided himself into her body with a tenderness that brought tears to her eyes, leashed his passion with a ruthless determination that broke her heart.

But the emotions between them had never been easily chained, and as she ran her hands over his back, the clenching muscles of his buttocks, as she lifted her own hips to receive his thrusts, urging him deeper, his control slipped a notch, and then another.

"Damn it, Hannah, I don't want to hurt you!"

"Please, Austen. Closer . . . I want you closer, deeper inside me."

With a roar of surrender, he took her harder, faster. His passion broke over her with the furious beauty of a storm-swept sea, until he started a new fire inside her.

But this time she knew, knew what that burning promised, felt that glorious release dangling just beyond her reach. And she wanted it. Wanted to feel it burst over her again with Austen joined to her.

"Hannah . . ." He murmured her name, his powerful body burying itself inside her again and again. "Feel it, Hannah. Reach for it. Come with me."

She writhed against him, reaching for that unchained beauty with every fiber of her will, every sinew of her body, every fragment of her soul.

Then his hand stole between their bodies, his fingers finding the tiny bud where all her pleasure was centered. He skimmed tiny, light circles around it, over it, his body keeping up its dizzying, pounding rhythm until she was sobbing with need. Then she came apart.

She shuddered and writhed, her head tossing on the pillow, her legs clinging tight around his narrow hips. And as the contractions tightened the secret passage that held him prisoner, she felt Dante stiffen and bury himself inside her deeper still. A low roar of triumph, of pleasure, of pain ripped as if from the center of his heart as he spilled his seed inside her.

He collapsed against her, his weight wonderful, right, so very right. And Hannah fought back the burning of tears at the knowledge that she would never know the magic of Austen's touch again. Never experience the wonder of his lovemaking.

He'd claimed he'd had no mistresses, few lovers. And she knew it was true. Austen had guarded his heart as

closely as she had. That knowledge made this joining of
their bodies even more beautiful. Yet even that beauty
carried a sting of shame, for now he knew she'd deceived
him even when she'd come to his bed. There had been no
other man. No one but him. Austen. Uncertainty racked
her. Would he be glad he was her first lover? Or would
the lie overshadow everything? She dreaded seeing disillusionment in his eyes, yet another untruth between
them.

I love you. She ached to say it, to tell him. But she
didn't dare. She mouthed the words against the sweat-
sheened curve of his shoulder, knowing she could never
say them aloud, never see them echo through him, never
see the expression they would make blossom in those
intense blue eyes, that exquisite moment when she
might—just *might*—discover the most wondrous miracle of all . . . that he loved her, too.

But it wouldn't matter. It wouldn't change anything. It
would only make leaving harder. And if she loved Austen
Dante, she could never drag him into the morass Mason
Booth had created, throw him into such danger.

Austen raised his face from her hair, levered himself
up above her, one arm braced beside her breast. Regret
wove its shadows across his features. "Why? Why didn't
you tell me that you'd never lain with a man. I would
have been gentler, I would have—"

"You couldn't have been more gentle, Austen. Making
love with you was beautiful. It was what I wanted. So
very much. I've never known anything so deep, so pure.
So right."

"Oh, Hannah." He closed his eyes, his face tight, but
his fingers were gentle as they stroked her cheek. "You
must've been so damned afraid to be forced into a lie.
You're the most honest person I've ever known."

His understanding broke her heart. What would happen when all the lies were laid bare? Shame stole through
her, her cheeks stinging. "You're wrong about me,
Austen."

"I don't think so. Hannah, my sweet, brave Hannah, can't you trust me even now?" His plea squeezed her chest.

"I want to. I do." She nibbled at her lip.

"Then let me help you. Pip is not your son."

"No."

"I never would have guessed it. You love the boy as if he's your own heart's blood."

"He is."

"But who is he, Hannah? How did you come to have him?"

God, if only she could tell him everything. Cry out her fear of Booth, her grief over Lizzy, her terror that she would fail her sister once again. But she only shook her head. "I still can't tell you anything except that I'm the only person he has on earth."

Austen smoothed back a tendril of her hair, his face serious, so beautiful it broke her heart. "You're wrong," he said softly. "You both have me."

The words pierced her. Oh, God. She'd watched her father waste away a fortune with a boy's carelessness. She'd struggled under the crushing weight of her mother's dependence, and even her sisters' needs.

Never in her whole life had anyone offered her such a precious gift. Someone to hold on to when the storm was too brutal, a shoulder to lean against when she grew too weary. Someone to count on even when things were dark and frightening, ugly or sad.

"Austen, you can't—can't know—"

He cradled her face in his big hands, the beauty of their lovemaking still shimmering in his eyes. She felt as if he were peering into the depths of her soul. "I know this," he said. "I would move heaven and earth to protect you. Hannah, I'm in love with you."

"No. You—you can't . . ." He was devastating her with his tenderness, with his passion.

"I didn't want to love anyone. I didn't mean to. But I

saw your courage out on that road, the night you all but bludgeoned me into letting you come inside. I watched you with Pip, and there was something inside you that wouldn't give me any rest. Blast it, Hannah, you were so damned stubborn, I couldn't help myself. There were times I thought you'd bewitched me out of spite."

"Austen, please . . ."

"Hannah, I know you. You love me. You would never have come to my bed unless you did."

Was there any use in denying it? He would never believe her. She tried painful honesty instead. "Austen, I can't stay here. I'm no fit match for you."

"You think my love is so shallow I'd surrender you because society might not approve? I don't care where you come from. Don't care who your family is. I don't give a damn what anyone thinks. I'll make you my wife, Hannah, the instant I can get a special license to wed you. No one will ever dare to hurt you again."

His wife. To spend the rest of her life in his arms, in his bed. To laugh with him, help him tend these lands, lay babes born of their love in his arms. Heaven could not be any more perfect, nor further beyond her reach.

"Austen, you don't even know me. What would you say if I told you that all your work, those hours you spent in the Music Room with me writing were for nothing. If I told you they were wasted."

He flashed her a chagrined smile. "Hannah, this is a damned inconvenient time to bring up what's lacking in my music."

"It's not wasted because of you," she said hastily. "It's because of me. I lied to you. The closest I'd ever been to a sheet of music was when I lifted it off the music rack to dust my sister's pianoforte."

Austen frowned, his brows lowered over eyes washed with confusion. "But you—I watched you—saw . . ." As if suddenly realizing how he'd betrayed himself, his jaw clenched, hot color flooding his cheeks.

"I just wanted shelter for a night. I figured you could throw us out the next day. We were so hungry. Pip was so cold."

"Damn it, I'm not asking *why* you did it. Remember, I was the one who found you that night."

It was agony to wound him, but it couldn't be helped. "When you didn't discover what I'd done, I just thought Pip would be so much better if he had a little while to rest, good food, a warm fire. I didn't mean to hurt you."

"You must've thought I was a damned fool," he growled, looking painfully abashed.

"No. Never that." She caught his hand, held it tightly. "There are scores of people who can't read music. It's a wonder to me that you can play the instrument at all, compose without reading a note."

Why did he suddenly flinch, as if she'd dug too deep, hit something too raw. "Damn it, Hannah, I don't care about any of that." He took her hands, held them tight. "Do you have any idea what it was like for me, making love with you? You've charged through my defenses, burrowed your way into my heart."

Oh, God, she should stop him. Shouldn't let him pour out his very soul into her hands. She was leaving when the sun rose. It was torture to know what she would lose when she walked away. But his words were too beautiful, too precious. All she could carry away with her from this magical night.

"Damn it, I wanted you so bad it was driving me to madness. Needed to be with you—inside you—a part of you. But I fought it, Hannah, told myself it was because I was trying to save your honor. But that wasn't the reason. It was to save myself."

"Oh, Austen." She reached up. Framed his face with her hands, memorizing the full curve of his lips, the tiny lines that starred outward from the corner of his eyes, the straight black brows, thick dark lashes. The arrogant slash of cheekbones, the tiny cleft in his chin.

"I knew from the first moment there would be no holding back with you. Your courage, your intelligence, your goodness demanded that any man who dared to love you had to surrender no less than that to you. Everything he was, everything he'd ever dreamed he could be."

His gaze lowered overbright, his voice roughened with awe. "But then you came to my bedchamber—my brave, independent Hannah. You offered yourself to me even though I wasn't worthy to touch the sole of your slipper. You stormed into my house, barged into the empty places in my life, challenged me, dared me, loathed me, and then by some miracle, you gave me your heart."

"No. You took it," she admitted. "Against my will." And he would keep it for all time.

"I'll never forget tonight, Hannah. The scent of your hair, the shimmering of discovery in your eyes. You stripped away the pain of the boy I had been, lit up the darkness inside me, just like the fingers of night awaken the moon."

A poet's soul, a knight errant's heart, they lay hidden within this wonderful enigmatic man. What would it do to him when she disappeared?

"Hannah, I want to be husband to you. A father to Pip." He raised her hands to his lips, kissed her knuckles, then looked up into her eyes. "I'd give my life for you," Austen vowed.

And he would. She could see it in his eyes, feel it in his touch. Austen, who had fought so hard for his tenants would battle to the death for anyone he loved. And he loved her. It was a miracle. More than she'd ever hoped for, believed she could have.

"Hannah, trust me. If you love me, it's my right."

She stared up into those eyes, wanting so desperately to take what he offered. Dreaming of a forever in this house, in Austen's bed. A husband who loved her and maybe, someday, babes of her own. She closed her eyes, imagining the indescribable sweetness of giving Austen a child, Pip stealing in through the door to touch the baby's petal-soft cheek with wonder.

"Impossible."

"Damn it, Hannah—"

The sudden sound of a knock made them start. Alarm jolted through Hannah as she clutched the coverlets to her breasts.

"Who the blazes . . ." With a low curse, Austen leapt out of bed. He threw Hannah her nightgown and she caught it with trembling fingers. She had tugged it over her head by the time he had dragged on his breeches.

"Damn it, I'm not to be disturbed," he ordered whoever cowered on the other side of the closed door.

"Forgive me, sir," Simmons apologized. "I never would have awakened you if it wasn't vital."

Hannah thrust her arms through the sleeves, but the nightgown might as well have been nothing but mist. Good God, if anyone found her here . . .

"Whatever it is, it can damn well wait until tomorrow," Austen growled, grabbing up his shirt, pulling it on with angry movements.

"Yes, sir. I mean, I'm afraid it can't, sir. Mr. Atticus assured me you gave strict orders that he should report to you the instant he received this communication."

"Simmons, enough blathering," an impatient voice echoed from the hallway. "I *will* see my cousin."

"No, damn it!" White faced, Austen lunged for the door, but it was too late.

Hannah clutched the coverlets against her in horror as William Atticus swung the portal wide.

Dante dodged in front of Hannah's nightgown-clad frame, blocking her as much as possible from view, and she sensed he intended to shove his steward out the door. But he never had the chance.

"Sir, I—" Atticus's shrewd gaze flashed past him, and Hannah felt sick, hideously exposed as it found her tumbled in the coverlets.

Atticus schooled his face into one of righteous indignation, only Hannah was able to see the spark of triumph in his eyes. "Miss Graystone."

"Get out, Atticus. Now," Austen bit out. "I'll see you in my study."

A thin smile twisted the steward's lips, slipping like a knife under Hannah's skin. "I think it might be better if we discuss this here, now, with Miss Graystone present. After all, it does concern her."

Austen went white, every muscle in his body rigid. "Atticus!"

"Sir, I've received word from the Bow Street runner you hired in London."

"B—Bow Street?" Hannah felt as if the floor had just split wide, sending her plunging down into some vast wasteland. "You hired a detective . . ." Her gaze found Austen's, saw the agony in them. It was answer enough.

He reached out, grasped her arm. "Hannah, I can explain—"

"She is the one who has explaining to do," Atticus said ruthlessly. "This woman is the vilest kind of thief. She stole an English baronet's son."

"Pip was my sister's child! She begged me to take him."

"You ripped the child from his dying mother's arms. It was the merest good fortune Mr. Hockley crossed paths with the poor desperate father searching for his child. Hockley was checking through ship logs trying to trace Miss Graystone's path when Sir Mason Booth arrived from Ireland and began similar inquiries."

Hannah's whole body trembled with panic, her stomach churning. "Mason . . . here . . . in England?"

"He's riding to Yorkshire even as we speak," Atticus snarled. "It's our duty to hold you prisoner here until his arrival. And then . . ." Atticus's lip curled with scorn. "If there is any justice in England, madam, *you will hang.*"

Chapter

❧ 18 ❧

"Atticus, get out." Austen's voice was deadly quiet. Hannah shuddered as the lovemaking that had been so magical vanished, obliterated by the ugly haze that consumed everything Mason Booth touched.

"She's broken the law, sir," the steward said with cold logic. "She has to pay. If you interfere, there's no telling what the consequences might be."

"Damn it, I said *go!*"

Atticus sketched him a stiff bow, then he and the footman fled, closing the door behind them, leaving the room in silence. She saw Austen drive his fingers back through the midnight waves of his hair. Then he turned, his face seeming to be conjured from the darkest reaches of hell.

"Hannah, I just wanted to help you, keep you safe. That's the only reason I hired Hockley." He reached out to her, and she could sense his desperate need to touch her. She dashed his hand away.

"Don't come near me!" She climbed from the bed terrified and numb, sick with betrayal. Her fingers clenched into hard fists. "I could almost forgive you for hiring the detective, I could even understand why you did it. But you knew how afraid I was! I'd told you enough so that you knew. How could you—*how could you*—have the information sent to *him?*"

"Atticus always handles my correspondence." How dare he look so battered, so filled with pain? "Blast it, this doesn't matter. I'll find a way to protect—"

"Your correspondence?" Hannah cut him off bitterly. "And couldn't you bother to make an exception just this once?"

Candle fire cast his profile into harsh planes and angles. "Damn it, Hannah, it's not that simple."

"Explain it to me, then!"

"I had no other choice! You wondered how my father could blame me for Chuffy's death?"

"I don't care what happened then! I just want to know why you—"

"I'm trying to tell you!" he bellowed, his eyes hot pits of rage and grief, self-loathing and shame. She glared at him, hating him in his terrible beauty.

"There were signs posted all around that infernal pasture," he said, pacing the floor like a trapped beast. "Warnings about that devil of a bull. Any fool could have read them, Hannah." He wheeled on her, his gaze piercing hers. "Any fool except me."

She tossed back the waves of her tumbled hair, loathing the crushing misery in her chest. "What are you saying?"

"I had the letter sent to Atticus because . . ." his voice dropped to a tortured rasp. *"I can't read."*

She gave a wild little laugh. "Don't be absurd! Of course you can read!"

But something was so still in his features, so wretched, she couldn't breathe.

"There's something broken inside me—no matter how hard I tried, I couldn't. Or maybe I was just too damned stupid. I don't know. I only know I did whatever I had to in order to conceal it. Tormenting my tutors, pretending any learning was a waste of time. Haunted the hills and the hounds my grandfather offered as an escape."

Hannah staggered beneath the weight of it, the secret she had sensed, the source of his pain, the reason he'd fought to keep everyone at a distance so that no one would ever know the truth.

His handsome features burned with shame, those fiercely intelligent eyes blazing with defiance. "For God's sake, Hannah, if I could read, don't you think I would've read the letters from my sisters? From my mother? But I couldn't have Atticus read them to me. I knew they were writing from their hearts, and their pain was too private to be dragged out in front of anyone else's eyes."

"Then why did you let me read them aloud?"

"I don't have the damnedest idea! Do you have any idea how badly I wanted to hear Letty's babbling, Maddy's nonsense? My mother's . . ." He winced, his face contorting with emotion suppressed far too long. "You challenged me, Hannah. Downright dared me. I took that chance."

She remembered the way he'd listened to the letters, pictured him when she was done, his face buried in his hand. She'd thought him so cold, but he was battling to keep his vulnerability from showing. His loneliness, his yearning.

"Dear God. That explains . . ." Everything. So much. The wistfulness on his features when he'd gazed down at the book she and Pip had made for him—a puzzle for which Austen Dante had no key.

"You know me well enough now not to be fooled. Know I'm not a monster. Don't you think if I'd been able to I would have written them? Set their minds at ease?" His voice broke, and he paused for one aching heartbeat to steady it. "So there it is. Every ugly detail. Now are you satisfied? You're the only one in the world I've told the truth, except for Chuffy. Poor, kind little bastard that he was. Spent half the night reading lessons aloud for me at Eton until I could memorize them. It was the only way I could get through school. And how did I repay him?"

Austen gave a bitter laugh. "He ran into that bull's pen because he *knew* I couldn't read. He'd come to try to warn me away from the pasture before I got hurt, but it was too late. And so Chuffy died in my place."

Hannah's heart broke for Austen, the wound he'd exposed so devastating, so raw, hidden away and festering so long. What had it cost this man? This brilliant, inventive, proud man to tell her that he couldn't read? To expose what he thought was a hideous flaw, open himself to the possibility of the scorn he must have feared from the time he was a small boy? How was it possible no one had ever discovered the truth?

Because Austen Dante was brilliant. Brilliant enough to fool them all . . .

Austen crossed to her, grabbed her hands tightly, so very tightly. "Hannah, I know I bungled things hiring Hockley. But I meant everything I said. I love you. I'll do anything to protect you. We'll run away together, you and me and Pip. Somewhere the law will never find you. It doesn't matter where."

He was willing to surrender everything he loved for her. The knowledge humbled her, hurt her. "But your land, your tenants . . . your family."

"Blast it, they'd be better off without me! Let me take you—"

He held on to her, offering her everything she'd never dared to dream of—love and strength, shelter and passion, and understanding. He'd hired Hockley, true. Brought Mason Booth down on her head. And yet he'd done it because he'd wanted so desperately to help her. And she hadn't trusted him enough to let him.

But what would it cost this man if she threw herself into his arms, threw her fate and Pip's into his keeping?

He'd never have the chance to reconcile with his mother, the sisters who so loved him. He'd be exiled forever from this land he'd loved and tended so well.

What might happen to the people here, Enoch Digweed and his family and all the others? Would Ravenscar fall into disrepair? Landlords like Austen Dante were rare as blue diamonds. And his work, his inventions, the passion of his incredible mind—how could he create such marvels if he was forever running with her?

She teetered on a knife blade between what she wanted with the fiercest fervor in her soul, and what she knew was right for Austen . . . for this man she loved.

Loved too much to condemn him to her brutal fate. And yet what could she possibly do to dissuade him? To turn him from this course? His eyes shimmered with resolve, his jaw tight with stubbornness, his hands holding hers, fairly pulsing with love.

For her. Oh, God, for her.

"Austen, I won't let you do this. Sacrifice so much for me. You would be outlawed. Disgraced."

"I don't give a damn."

"You should! You don't know what it's like running, forever looking over your shoulder, no place to call home."

"My arms will be your home, Hannah."

"And while you're running with us, what will happen to Ravenscar? To the other people who depend on you? Who will help take care of the thousands of things you do for your tenants?"

"Atticus will see to it."

"Somehow I can't see him tending a sick child as you did Mazie Digweed. I can't see him helping a lovesick boy plan a cottage for his bride. And what about your own family? Letty and Madeline? Your mother? They've been waiting, hoping, praying to be reunited with you for eight years. Doesn't your mother deserve to see you again? To hold you even for a little while? You're her son. Her firstborn. She's never stopped loving you."

Austen raked one hand back through his hair. "And what about you, Hannah? You and Pip? For Christ's sake, *I love you!* How can I let you both go, knowing the danger you're in?"

"I'll thank God every day that I met you, because you showed me that people could be good and trustworthy and generous. That they can be responsible for the people in their care. Don't you see, Austen? The people of Ravenscar deserve better from you. They depend on you. You can't just turn your back and walk away. Cast them to the devil and damn your responsibilities. I'm leaving now, Austen. And you're staying here where you belong."

It was the hardest thing she'd ever done to turn and start out the door, but Dante caught her, spun her around. She could feel the warmth of his body, the intensity, remembered with anguish the awe that had transformed his face when he'd first made them one.

"You're not going anywhere."

"I have to leave! Booth is coming, and I'll die before I let him touch Pip again!"

"He won't come near you," Austen vowed fiercely. "I swear it. Hannah, there is only one way you and Pip can be free." His voice dropped low, rough. "I'll kill him for you."

Kill him? God, she'd dreamed of Mason's death since the night she'd run from Booth Hall—the freedom it would bring from fear, the chance to build Pip a life in which he wouldn't have to look over his shoulder. There were times she'd hoped to kill Booth herself. But if Austen were to do such a thing, he might go to prison . . . hang . . .

"You'll become a murderer? Destroy not only your own life but the lives of everyone who loves you? That's no solution! Or do you want your mother and your sisters to come to your hanging?"

"Christ, I have to do something!"

"Kill Booth and you will! Run away from Ravenscar

and you will! You'll prove that you're an irresponsible
fool! Is that what you want, Austen? To prove that your
father was right all this time?"

A raw cry tore from Austen's throat, and Hannah felt
his pain lance through her own soul, discovered something awful about loving someone—that you knew just
where to wound them.

Every vulnerability ripped bare, he stared down at
her. She had to leave now, had to go . . . before she
couldn't bear his agony and took him into her arms.

His features hardened like stone, his eyes glittering.
"There's no way in hell I'm letting you and Pip walk out
of here alone."

Her chin jutted up, every fiber of her body spitting
defiance. "And how do you propose to keep me here, sir?
In chains?"

He glared down at her, tempests raging in his eyes.
"Trust you always to come up with a practical solution,"
he snarled. "Unfortunately, the wine cellar will have to
do."

"The what? What are you—"

At that instant she realized his intentions. She swore,
kicked as he scooped her into his sinewy arms, imprison-
ing her against the granite-hard wall of his chest. He
hauled her out of the bedchamber, down the corridor.
Her efforts to escape were hopeless as the thrashings of a
sparrow trying to get loose from the jaws of a wolf.

"Damn you, Dante, let me go!" she raged as he bore
her down the stairway. "Help me! Someone—"

Maids popped their heads from doorways, their eyes
huge with disbelief and alarm beneath their white caps.
Footmen scurried into their path, their livery askew.

"Get the key to the wine cellar," Austen bellowed as
he reached the bottom landing. "We have to lock her in.
And clothes! You, Becca, get whatever she needs."

Simmons cast him a wary glance, his gaze flicking to
Hannah with sympathy and some affection. "But sir, you
can't just—"

Atticus stepped from the study, arms crossed over his chest, and Hannah's blood chilled at the triumph in his features. "I knew you'd see reason, sir. And clothing her is a fine idea. We can't have the lady in dishabille when the magistrates arrive."

"There will be no infernal magistrates." Austen said, hauling her toward the back of the house and the staircase that led down into the cellar. "I'm going to save this woman's neck whether she likes it or not."

"But sir, you can't mean that!" Atticus sputtered.

"You think I'd risk getting my eyes clawed out unless I was in deadly earnest? Now, damn it—ouch!"

Fierce satisfaction streaked through Hannah as her heel narrowly missed his groin.

"Sir, I beg you to pause, to consider the consequences of such a rash action," Atticus pleaded, ashen. "There's no telling what might happen."

"Just open the damn cellar door or find yourself a position somewhere else, old man!"

Dismayed, Atticus grabbed the key from the butler and ran ahead, doing as his master ordered. Still, the steward couldn't keep from arguing. "Austen, have you lost your mind? This is dangerous. It's illegal."

"Simmons . . . the boy," Austen managed while struggling to subdue her on the way down the damp staircase. "Hate it like hell, but we'll have to lock him in, too. Be damned if I let that sadistic bastard anywhere near Pip."

Hannah hit her head on the door frame, raging in fury as Austen plunked her down on a wooden crate. Two footmen dashed in, pinning her down by her arms. An army of servants blocked her only escape. "Damn you, let me go!" she cried, begging aid from each maid and footman. Why would no one help her?

Her heart clenched as she heard Pip's tiny, frightened voice. "Nanna? What's wrong with Nanna?"

"Pip!" Tears seared her eyes as she wrenched at the hold of her captors, but they only tightened their grasp. "Please, Austen! Let us go, for the love of God! You don't know Mason! Don't know what he's capable of! He beat my sister until she was dying! But she was his *wife,* so no one could stop it! No one could prove . . ."

She glimpsed Simmons lifting Pip high, putting the boy into Austen's outstretched arms. The sight of the child cradled so lovingly in Austen's grasp shattered Hannah, fear jolting through her.

God in heaven, why had she let herself love them both so much? She couldn't bear it if she lost either one of them. And the devil himself was coming to call.

"Pip," Austen said, smoothing the boy's hair. "Do you trust me, boy?"

"Y—Yes."

Hannah knew just how hard it had been for Pip to trust any man, knew that Austen was aware of just how astonishingly rare the gift was Pip had given him.

"But Nanna's crying." Pip's voice quavered. "Nanna never cries."

"You have to stay here for a little while. Can you be very brave?" He hesitated for an instant as if weighing what he was about to say. She saw the flash in his eye as he decided to tell Pip the truth. "Your father's coming to Ravenscar."

"P—Papa?"

Hannah's heart wrenched at the terror in Pip's voice. The child started trembling, his gaze seeking her frantically. All the joy, all that tentative, beautiful spark of hope Austen had put in the child's face fled as if some evil demon had blown out the sun. "He's . . . he's found us?"

Tears of fury, of grief, of futility surged into her eyes.

"Oh, God, Pip, I'm sorry!" she choked out. "We shouldn't have stayed here. We should never have stayed."

"Pip, listen to me, boy." Austen said, taking him by the arms. "I'm going to make certain your father can never hurt you or Hannah again. I swear it. Do you believe me?"

"But Papa—Papa breaks people. He hurts them when he gets mad. He made my mama go to heaven." A tiny sob tore through the child. "I don't want you to go to heaven. Don't want Nanna to go there without me."

Hannah's soul tore in two as Austen gathered him tight in his arms. "No one's going to heaven, boy. Hell perhaps . . ." Grim resolve tightened his mouth, then he stopped, casting a glance over his shoulder. "Simmons, get the puppy for Master Pip."

But Lizzy was already snuffling and whining around the servants' feet, searching for her boy. Austen set Pip down and took the squirming puppy, then knelt down before Pip.

"You hold on tightly to Lizzy, Pip, until I can come back to let you out of here," he said, nestling the puppy into the child's arms.

Pip gazed into Austen's eyes with heartbreaking trust. Balancing Lizzy with one arm, he lay his other small hand on Austen's stubborn masculine jaw. "I'm 'fraid again. Like I was on the horse."

Hannah's throat clenched as Austen pressed a fierce kiss to Pip's cheek. "I'm afraid too. Afraid of losing you, losing Hannah. I love you both so much. But I'm even more angry that anyone tried to hurt you. You're strong, boy. Your papa couldn't break you in Ireland. I swear on my life, I won't let him break you here."

Hannah had never loved the man more. "Austen, for the love of God. Let us go! Just let us go!"

He crushed Pip in a fierce embrace, then stood. "See to it they have food, water. Give them some kind of light. And hear this—every one of you." His gaze raked the servants. "No one will say a word about the whereabouts of Pip or Hannah, or I swear I'll make you wish you'd never been born!"

With that he strode out of the room.

Hannah begged, pleaded, and fought while the servants followed Austen's orders, their eyes wide and fearful, their faces brimming with sympathy. *It's for your*

*own good, dear. . . . The master only wants to keep you
safe. . . . Don't be afraid. . . .* The soothing words all but
drove her mad. Enough fragments of her tale spilled
forth to dash any resentment from their gaze, but from
the boot boy to the housekeeper, they supported their
master's decision to imprison her.

And in the end, even Becca wouldn't set her free. Once
Austen's orders had been followed and the things he'd
demanded provided, the footmen released her, Simmons
stopping to murmur, "Be easy, miss. The master never
breaks his vows."

Then the last of them exited, the door slamming shut
in their wake. Hannah stumbled across the room, hammering against the panel with her fists. But her only
answer was the lock scraping as someone turned the key,
and the thundering of her own heart.

"Nanna?" Pip's voice lanced through her, and she
turned to see him, so small, so fragile, trying so hard to
be brave.

"Oh, God, Pip," she cried, dropping to her knees,
holding out her arms to him. "I should never have stayed
here. Should never have . . ."

Pip came into her arms, wiping away the tears she
could no longer stop. "Don't cry, Nanna. Didn't you
hear? Mr. Dante said he loved us. Maybe he isn't mad
anymore."

He loved them. Yes, Austen Dante loved them. He'd
surrendered his wary heart, let crumble the walls that
held the world at a distance.

Hannah could only pray that that love wouldn't cost
him his life.

Chapter

❧ 19 ❧

Her fingers were raw from trying to pry open the latch, her knuckles scraped and riddled with splinters, her voice hoarse from calling out, pleading with someone, anyone, to set them free.

Even the lantern seemed to flicker cold, leaving them with fear and uncertainty as their only companions, a hundred terrifying possibilities clinging to the shadows of the musty room. Pip was sleeping at last, his head pillowed on Hannah's lap.

Dear God, what was happening beyond the cellar door? She felt so helpless, as if her very reason might shatter from not knowing if Austen was safe. Knowing if Booth had hunted them down . . . knowing . . . what? That Austen might die with those ugly, hateful words she'd said ringing in his ears.

Do you want to prove your father was right all these years?

She'd only been trying to convince him to let her go, to save him from becoming entangled in the horror Mason Booth had made her life. But would he know that deep in his heart? Or would he think, even for a moment, that she scorned him for his most painful flaw, that she mocked him because of what he'd had the courage to admit?

Oh, God, what was he planning to do? This man with his secrets, his wary heart, his courage and his secret sorrow? This man who thought he was . . . what had she once said? Worthless as a polished rock? But was truly the finest man she'd ever known.

The least he would suffer for helping them would be the loss of his lands, of his family. The stark possibility of prison. All for assisting her when she'd been hungry, frightened, alone.

God in heaven, if she didn't hear something soon, she would run mad.

As if in answer to her silent cry, she heard the sound of footsteps beyond the door. Her heart hammered against her ribs, her breath quickening.

Carefully laying Pip's head down on a pillow Becca had brought, she climbed awkwardly to half-numbed feet and stumbled to the door in the darkness.

"Austen?" she called softly, pressing her cheek against the rough wood. "Is that you?"

"Quiet!" A muffled voice hissed. "Do you want the whole manor house to hear you?"

She stepped back, staring at the shadowy panel. It wasn't Austen. Who could it be? Simmons? One of the other footmen? She didn't care as long as they brought some kind of news.

The key scraped in the lock, then the door slid open. She stumbled backward in shock. An unearthly glow illuminated the craggy features of William Atticus, his white hair gleaming, his perfectly tailored coat clinging to his shoulders, his powerful hand curving about a brass candleholder.

"You!" Hannah gasped.

"You should be rejoicing at the sight of me. You see, I'm going to give you exactly what you want. Help you escape."

Candlelight flickered across unreadable eyes.

"You're going to let me go?" Hannah choked out in disbelief. "But—But you hate me. I saw it in your face."

Atticus sneered. "You disgust me! Playing the virtuous woman, the wounded damsel, when you were scheming to get into Mr. Dante's bed!"

"Then why would you help me?"

"It should be obvious enough. I've wanted you off of Ravenscar land from the first. Knew you'd be nothing but trouble. And I was right! You've gotten Austen involved in harboring a fugitive from justice. Blast his accursed soft heart!"

"I didn't intend to—"

"You think that matters? The damage is done! I've tried my damndest to talk reason into him, but it's no use. Even now, he won't take the sane course and hand you over to the magistrates. So there is only one thing to do. Help you disappear, then find some way to haul him out of this mess. Everything is in readiness," Atticus said. "I have money, a few of your things packed, and a horse waiting in the barn where Austen builds his inventions. It's safe enough. No one has so much as opened the door there since Digweed was injured."

"Why should I trust you?"

"You shouldn't—but your only other choice is to stay here and let Austen try to defend you. Watch him lose everything—possibly even his life. Is that what you want?"

"Of course not!" Hannah trembled at the thought of trusting William Atticus. Did she dare put her fate into this man's hands? And yet, what choice did she have? The steward was right. He'd wanted her gone from Ravenscar from the beginning. Who better to help her and Pip slip away?

Even so, Hannah staggered under the pain of surrendering her newfound love. But the relief at making certain Austen would be safe was blinding. Her throat ached at the knowledge she'd never have a chance to tell him good-bye.

Atticus cast her a look of acid disgust. "Just fetch the boy, and hurry. There's not much time. Booth could be arriving at any moment."

"But Austen won't know we're gone! He might—"

"I'll tell him you're missing once it's too late for him to do anything about it. Now hurry!"

Hannah hastened to where Pip lay sleeping and scooped the boy into her arms. He lolled against her, oblivious. But his pup was more alert. Her heart lurched when Lizzy raised her groggy little head, silky ears pricking up as she started to pad after them, but Hannah gently closed the animal back in the cellar. They couldn't afford for it to alert anyone.

It was agonizing to leave Austen's first gift behind, and with it the memory of the first time she'd heard Pip laugh. Harder still to imagine telling Pip that Lizzy was gone when the child awoke. But there was no helping it.

Stealthily she followed in Atticus's path, keeping to the shadows, listening for any stirring in the quiet household. She was certain that if anyone from the scullery maid to the housekeeper caught a glimpse of her, they'd shout the house down to summon their master.

After what seemed an eternity, Atticus opened the rear door, guiding her out of the house into the night. Cold slivers of moonbeams filtered through the trees, giving the world a ghostly aura, a layer of mist swirling up beneath the hem of Hannah's gown. Every step was agony as it carried her farther away from Austen.

Even the darkness seemed alive with images of him scowling at her as he tried to scrub the ink spots from her face, laughing as he taught Pip to swim, full of awe as he taught her something new as well. How to be a woman. How to trust. How to surrender to the most gentle of conquerors.

No, Austen had never conquered her, never wanted to. That was why she'd fallen in love with him. The inner strength that had dismayed even her own mother and father, Austen valued. He'd admired the independence that had killed the interest of every other suitor who might have noticed her.

He'd had no wish to change her. And she'd wanted to give him all that she was, all that she hoped to be. Wanted to burrow so deeply into his heart that neither of them would ever be alone again.

I love you, Austen, she whispered to the night, praying that some part of him would hear her and understand. *That's why I have to go.*

Her arms ached beneath Pip's weight, and twice she stumbled upon something in her path, just keeping from tumbling to the ground. Still, she wouldn't let Atticus take the child from her arms, as if afraid Mason Booth would gallop out of the mist, snatch Pip away as he had in countless nightmares.

At last the moonlight spilled silver across the shadowy building Austen had pointed out to her the day he had shown her Ravenscar lands. His hideaway tucked far from the path of anyone who might stray by. Austen's haven, the one place where he'd allowed his creativity, his brilliance free rein. Incredible yearning tightened in her chest as Atticus shoved open the door.

"Lay the boy down on the hay. Then—if you could help load the horse?"

"Of course."

"Just follow the passage to the back." Atticus ordered. "I need to find the bridle." A faint glow of light beckoned from deep in the building.

Hannah turned her back to Atticus as he disappeared down a passageway made of crates that must have held Austen's supplies. She eased Pip down, hating the idea of leaving him even for a moment. But the sooner they were out of Mason Booth's reach, the safer the boy would be.

She smoothed a hand over his silky-smooth brow when he stirred. "Hush, angel. Everything will be all right. I promise. Just sleep . . ." She dragged what looked to be a horse's blanket over the child's small body, then started down the shadowy path the steward had followed. It wound deeper into the belly of the huge barn. She heard a slight shuffle of movement behind the hulking shape of one of Dante's creations.

Her skirts caught on something near the ground, and she paused. "Mr. Atticus," she called softly, stooping down to untangle the fold of cloth. "Whatever our differences in the past, I'm grateful for your help now."

"No, madam. I am the one who is grateful. You've made this far easier than I had hoped." She started to turn, glimpsed a figure lunging out of the shadows behind her. Breath was driven from her lungs as Atticus threw her to the ground, pinning her with one knee upon her ribs. Strips of leather bit into her wrists as he wrestled them together and bound them tightly, then did the same to her ankles.

"Pip!" Hannah screamed. "Pip, run!"

But Atticus only laughed. "I've closed the door behind us. The boy won't be able to hear you."

"What—What are you doing? Why . . . ?"

"You've proven to be a serious inconvenience, Miss Gray. One that must be eliminated," he said, giving the bindings a final, savage tug. "You see, I cannot have you destroying the lucrative position I've carved out for myself here."

He brushed straw from their struggle off his rich coatsleeve, his emerald ring glinting in the lantern light. "Ah, you can't understand how the position of steward can be so very *lucrative,* can you? My cousin is not a man who cares to be troubled with tedious details. Not that he could even if he wanted to." An ugly sneer contorted Atticus's face. "Did he mention while he was bedding you that he can't even read?"

Hannah fought against the bindings, sickened by the scorn in the man's voice.

"I'm in charge of ordering all supplies for his precious inventions. Of course, I tend to exaggerate the cost in my books. And I've become quite adept at making certain key pieces break, so that the *great inventor* will order more."

Horror spilled through Hannah, mingled with killing fear. "Enoch," Hannah breathed, remembering the farmer's injury, remembering Austen's guilt-ridden confession that the man had almost lost his leg. "Enoch Digweed got hurt because of you."

If Atticus were so embroiled in that hideous scheme, what lengths wouldn't he go to to protect himself?

"He wasn't supposed to get hurt," Atticus bristled defensively. "That was quite an accident."

"He could have lost a leg! He could have been killed!"

Atticus cast her a quelling glare. "You think me a wicked man, do you not, Miss Gray? I'm taking only a portion of what should have been my own. When the old squire lay dying, he'd decided—at long last—to leave everything to me. To adopt me. I'd spent years currying the old man's favor. Every spare moment trying to come up with some new way to please him. The document was lying there. All it needed was his signature, when Austen and his family came rushing in for one of those tender deathbed farewells. My esteemed cousin ruined everything. Took what was mine."

Hannah staggered under the loathing in the steward's face, years of bitterness that had shrunken his soul. "Your grandfather probably despised you for a weakling and a coward, as I do!"

"No one who is *weak* can survive—no, *thrive*—as a charity relation," Atticus said. "Despite what you might think, madam, I am not an evil man. My cousin is happy building his contraptions, and I manage to console myself at the loss of becoming a landowner by fattening my purse. He's so rich he'll never miss the money I skim from his coffers. But you are a woman who pays attention to details, Miss Gray. That's why I must get rid of you. To protect my position."

"Your position?" Hannah all but retched. "As head thief?"

"I've already gone to a good deal of trouble protecting my situation with my cousin. Making certain he never questions my loyalty. Ridding myself of anyone who might make unfortunate inquiries into his affairs."

Distaste twisted his features. "Mr. Dante's family, for example. His mother has your unattractive wit—very undesirable in a woman. And his father—he adored his son, even though he didn't understand him. It took a great deal of labor to stir up ill feelings, to sever that bond. It was far easier while the old squire was alive. Though Grandfather never said so, it was obvious he'd decided to use Austen to exact his revenge upon Joseph Dante."

Hannah was sickened, horrified at what Atticus's and Austen's grandfather had done to the father and the son.

"Yes. Joseph had taken the squire's favorite daughter, enticed her into a ridiculous mesalliance. So the old man took Joseph's son, giving the boy everything the Italian never could. Turning the boy against him in a hundred subtle ways and forcing Joseph Dante to watch it, helpless, the boy legally lost to him. It's kept me quite weary, having to make certain they don't reconcile. I even burned the letters that arrived from his father."

"Austen's father wrote to him? My God!"

"No doubt trying to mend the breach between them. I always knew the letters would come. Joseph Dante had a fiery enough temper, and fierce pride. But his love for his son was bound to override it eventually."

Hannah reeled. Austen's father trying to glean his son's forgiveness? To say he regretted the breach between them? It would have meant the world to Austen to discover that unconditional love. Would have healed so many of the wounds in his heart. It might even have given Austen the faith he needed to tell his father the truth, banish the ugly secret between them.

But because of William Atticus, Austen might go on forever believing his father had forgotten him. His father might go to his grave believing Austen had turned his back on him, scorning his outstretched hand.

"You won't be able to keep them apart forever, Atticus," Hannah said fiercely. "They love each other. Austen is planning to go to Letty's wedding. Then your games will be at an end."

Bushy brows lowered. "You'd managed to do more damage than I'd realized, then. But no matter. I'm certain that he'll be far too despondent over his broken affair of the heart to make such a journey now." Atticus smirked. "Especially with me to tell him how happy his father is without him."

"Damn you!" Hannah flung out helplessly, furiously.

"Come, Miss Gray. You pride yourself on being intelligent. I'm certain you see my dilemma. It's unfortunate I have to dispose of you in such a crude manner, but you wouldn't heed my gentler warnings. Now you really have left me no choice."

Hate surged through her. "People have used that excuse since the beginning of time when they were about to do something despicable."

Atticus raised up one hand in protest. "I tried to drive you away with those innuendos about being the master's mistress, but you were most stubborn. So now, I'm afraid I'm going to have to remove you from my cousin's life the only way I can."

"Just let us go!" Hannah tugged at her bindings until they sliced deeply into her wrists. "We'll run far away. Disappear. There's nothing I want more than to get away from Austen! I never wanted him to be ensnared in this disaster."

There was a beat of silence, the tiniest stirring of a sound like a frightened mouse in the corridor of piled boxes. But Hannah glanced past Atticus's shoulders and saw nothing.

"It's too late for that," the steward said. "Mr. Dante would only chase after you, besotted as he is. My cousin can be a most determined man. No, a more permanent solution has been arranged."

Something in his voice sent ice through her veins. "What have you done?"

"Just fulfilled the duty of any loyal subject of the crown. I've sent my most trusted messenger to intercept Sir Mason Booth on the road to Ravenscar and escort him here. That way he can haul you to the authorities in London and reclaim his son."

Hannah's breath caught; her heart threatened to burst. "You can't do that! Pip's only a child! Booth killed his mother . . . might kill him before he's done! You claim you're not evil—*prove it!* Don't cast an innocent boy into the hands of such a monster!"

The man actually looked grieved. "Another regrettable decision I wouldn't have had to make if you'd just been reasonable. Reacted like any other woman, and fled before Dante returned from London."

Hannah started to speak, then stopped, catching a glimpse of a shadowy movement behind Atticus's towering frame. Her heart leapt, the tiniest hope flickering inside her.

Atticus's lips curled over his bared teeth. "With any luck, our Sir Mason should arrive before the morning comes. And then, Miss Gray, I'll turn you over to his oh-so-capable hands."

Horror spilled through her, cold, relentless, giving substance to her most terrifying nightmare. But her horror was magnified a hundredfold as a small figure edged from the shadows. Pip, his face ashen, his eyes haunted and huge with terror.

God in heaven! He was awake! If he could run, escape . . .

Hannah braced her feet against a crate, gauging the

distance between her and where Atticus stood. If she could launch the crate across that space, knock him down, Pip might have a chance to get away.

His only chance.

She shoved hard, catching Atticus in the legs, sending him crashing to the ground the same instant a shriek tore from her lips. "Pip, run! Run away!"

The little boy paused for an instant, and Hannah's heart stopped as she heard the horrible rasping in his chest. Knew he was struggling for breath. Still, Pip spun around, the sounds of his running feet lost in Atticus's savage oaths. Hannah tried to stall him, grabbing his trouser leg with her bound hands, but he kicked free.

The steward scrambled to his feet, bolting through the maze of crates.

"Run, Pip!" she screamed, praying, pleading, making wild bargains with God and the devil.

If only he could reach the road, maybe a tenant would see him, a farmer risen early would happen by. Someone who might give him aid . . .

But would anyone believe the ravings of a distraught five-year-old child over the steward of the lands? Reality struck hard. Yet she could still hope, pray, plead with the heavens. And Pip had his very own angel.

"Elisabeth, for God's sake, help him. He's so little and afraid and alone!"

She struggled to push herself in the direction the two of them had disappeared, straining to hear any sound. A raspy cry made her heart plunge to her toes. Broken, choking sobs—a little boy's sobs.

A deep curse sounded, sharp with pain. "Damn you, boy! Don't try my patience!"

"Nanna . . . he . . . help me . . ." Pip's terror lanced through her.

"You bastard, let him go!" she cried impotently. "Let him go!" Tears streamed down her face, tears of fury and helplessness as Atticus reappeared, Pip clamped beneath one arm. Pip was weakened from his labored breathing;

he couldn't even cry. Still he struggled, and Hannah rejoiced in the small red heel print from the child's shoe that marked his captor's cheekbone.

"Nanna, I'm 'fraid . . ."

"Please!" Hannah couldn't keep from pleading as Atticus grabbed up some rope and tied Pip's hands. "I'm begging you! Listen to Pip—he's sick. We have to help him! You can't just leave him here!"

"Yes, I can." Atticus dumped Pip to the floor beside her with a cynical smirk. "And no one will ever know I have had anything to do with this. That's the beauty of the plan."

Hannah jammed her hands against the splintery plank floor, trying to reach Pip, to touch him. She brushed his cheek with her knuckles. "Slowly, angel. Breathe slowly. Try not to be afraid. It makes it worse, sweetheart."

Try not to be afraid? What was she saying? Bitterness and futility surged up inside her. Pip couldn't breathe. He was terrified. And a monster was coming to carry him away.

A monster she'd sworn on her very life would never touch him again. "Austen will find us!" she said aloud, praying it was so. "He'll search—"

"Doubtless Dante will have servants combing every road leading away from Ravenscar for twenty miles, since everyone will think you were trying to get as far from this place as possible. But I'm afraid you're being overly optimistic hoping for rescue, my dear. Austen doesn't even know you're gone yet. And even when he discovers it, well, he'll hardly think to look here."

Dismay crushed her. Atticus was right. Austen would ride until he was ready to topple from his own saddle, driving everyone else to exhaustion trying to find her. But never would he think to look here, in this building. So close to him. Yet it might as well be a thousand miles away.

She struggled against her bindings, half-mad with fear

for the little boy so helpless beside her. His lips were tinged with blue, his eyes sunken in his taut face.

Atticus drew his watch from his waistcoat pocket and examined it in the light of the lantern dangling from a nail in the wall. "Now you'll have to excuse me. I must make an appearance at Ravenscar House so I can proclaim my dismay at your escape. Perhaps even help with the search. Of course, first I'll have to slip the cellar key into a maid's apron pocket. Make certain she is blamed."

He straightened his cravat, rumpled in his tussle with Pip. "Now let me think, who in the household might have been loyal enough, foolish enough to help you? Perhaps that little maid who befriended you . . . Becca, wasn't that her name?"

"Leave Becca out of this!" she yanked against the leather strips, sickened, her memory filled with a dozen small kindnesses, the girl's bright face, the first overtures of friendship anyone had extended to her since her desperate flight from Ireland.

"Someone will have to be sacrificed to appease Dante's wrath. The girl will be fired at the very least. Perhaps even thrown in jail for aiding a fugitive, but I'm afraid there's no help for it."

"You bastard! You're scaring Pip! Making his breathing worse! Do you think Booth will thank you if he finds his son dead?"

"If the child dies it will be on *your* head, Miss Gray, not mine. I would not want to be the one facing Sir Mason with such news." He started to walk away.

"Wait!" Hannah cried out, groping desperately to find some bargaining tool, something, anything that might move Atticus's greedy soul to release them.

The diamond! Austen's diamond, still tucked away in her room.

"Wait! I have a bargain to make, a ransom I could pay if you'd just free us."

"What could you possibly have that I would want?" A scornful laugh echoed from Atticus's throat. "You hadn't even a decent dress on your back the day you arrived at Ravenscar."

"When I admitted I'd almost run away again, Austen gave me a stickpin—a diamond—worth a small fortune, so Pip and I would have money to eat. It's packed in my portmanteau, in the toe of one of my stockings. Let us go, and it's yours."

"I'm afraid you've made a fatal error in strategy, Miss Gray." His lips curved in a smirk. "The pin is mine for the taking. But I fear your little maid must be blamed again. I wonder what the penalty is for such a grand theft? Hanging?"

Hannah wanted to retch, to scream, Pip's rasping breathing pushing her to the edge of madness.

Oh, God, Austen, where are you?

But Austen didn't even know they were missing yet. How could she have been so foolhardy? To trust a man she knew was her enemy? This was her fault! Even much as she'd loved Austen, she hadn't been willing to trust him with this, share the burden of protecting Pip, risk that Austen would fall into danger as well. He'd wanted to share this burden, to fight Mason, the two of them together. But she had run away, and into the arms of disaster.

"Now I must hasten," Atticus said. "Take care of these trifling details so that I can be here when Sir Mason arrives. After all, I'll have to be here to let him in. The locks on this building are of Dante's own special design. I doubt Saint Peter himself could get into heaven if Austen's locks were on the gate. Besides, Hockley wrote that the baronet has offered a most substantial reward for the two of you."

"Nanna," Pip choked.

"Don't worry, boy," Atticus ran a mocking hand over Pip's fragile curls. "Your Papa will be coming to take you home very soon indeed."

With that, Atticus walked away, leaving Hannah prey to something far more terrifying than nightmares. His footsteps grew fainter. Then there was only the rasping of Pip's breath in his lungs as he huddled in the lantern light, chilled by the merciless onslaught of Hannah's own deepest fears.

Chapter

20

Austen jammed a lead ball down the barrel of one of his German silver pistols and rammed it home, every sinew in his body thirsting for blood.

He wanted Mason Booth dead. To rid the world of a monster. The coward who had murdered Hannah's beloved sister. The sadistic cur who had put the gut-chilling horror in Pip's tiny face. The bastard who had been hunting Hannah, trying to run her to ground.

Even now, Mason Booth was thundering toward Ravenscar.

Dante would be waiting.

"Sir?"

Austen checked the priming of the pistol one last time, then lowered the weapon's hammer carefully before he looked up. Matthew Simmons stood just inside the door frame, shifting from foot to foot, his features anxious above his midnight blue livery. "Cook stirred up some sugar buns and was wondering if someone could take a few down to the cellar right hot from the oven. They're Master Pip's favorite. And that way, we could check to see that Miss Hannah and Pip are all right. It must be driving them both half-mad, this waiting."

Simmons might as well have flung a glass of brandy into Austen's face. "Damn it to hell!"

The footman nearly jumped out of his skin as Dante wheeled on him.

"If the woman had been reasonable, she wouldn't have to be locked in the blasted cellar! But I know her. Give her one chance, and she'd be halfway to Scotland by now and I'd never find her again! I had no other choice!"

Was that empathy clouding Simmon's eyes, or contempt? "I wouldn't presume to question your decision, sir," he said softly.

"Wouldn't you? I saw your face when Atticus read that infernal letter. You were horrified that I'd set that detective dredging out Hannah's secrets. And I saw all of you servants gaping at me when I hauled Hannah down the stairs and locked her away."

"Sir, we—we were surprised," Simmons faltered. "And alarmed. We've come to respect the lady. Have some affection for her. Our concern was only natural . . ."

Austen ground his teeth, wishing like hell he could break something. Preferably Mason Booth's neck. "You think I'm a bloody beast, don't you? But I assure you, Simmons, the beast is the man who is out there." Austen jabbed a finger at the study window. "And he should be arriving at Ravenscar any moment."

The footman cast a glance toward the window, as if he half expected Booth to fly through it like some slavering dragon of old. "What are you going to do, Mr. Dante? When Sir Mason comes?"

Curse Simmons for asking the impossible question. He winced, remembering Hannah's fierce demand. *If you kill Booth, what will happen to the people who depend on you?*

"I don't have the damndest idea." Austen wished he could just blast Booth into hell where he belonged. But this was no time to be blinded by rage. He had to think what would be best for Hannah and Pip. Come up with some way, any way to see them safe. Mustering iron-willed control, he laid the pistol down on the polished surface of the table before him.

Dante picked up the second weapon, began loading it again with the same meticulous motions. He hesitated, aware of the footman still standing there watching him. "Simmons, was there something else?"

"Yes, sir. I suppose. I was just . . ." The man stammered like a blithering idiot, raking Austen's nerves. "I was just thinking. Mr. Atticus said Miss Graystone had broken the law."

Austen rounded on the footman, a muscle ticking in his jaw. "You saw Pip the day we put him on that infernal horse. Saw the terror in him! Christ's blood, the boy could barely breathe. Hannah's crime is snatching Pip out of the clutches of the man who put that fear in his eyes. The man who had murdered the boy's mother."

"I've nothing but admiration for Miss Graystone, sir," Simmons nearly tripped over the words in his haste. "It was a right brave thing for her to do."

Austen closed his eyes, remembering the first night he had seen her, half drowned by the rain, cold and hungry, yet with the flashing eyes and fierce pride of an embattled queen. He wondered if in some part of his blackened soul he'd loved her from that moment. His throat tightened. His hand trembled. "She was magnificent."

"I'm just afraid that this Booth person won't come alone. What if he brings the authorities with him? Runners, or magistrates to take Miss Graystone to prison?"

A feral need to protect, to defend, throbbed through Austen's veins. His eyes opened, his hand steadied. "Then I'll need to load more pistols," he said in deadly quiet. He saw Simmons blink, absolute disbelief on the man's face.

Yet if Austen had a dozen pistols, would it change

anything? He craved Booth's death with a savage passion. But to kill other men—men whose only sin was attempting to do their sworn duty—was another thing entirely. Blast, he could hardly kill them all.

Austen ground his teeth. What the hell *was* he going to do? He'd raked over it a hundred times in the hours since he'd shut the cellar door, Hannah's face, forever frozen against the dim-lit interior. Rage and fear, pain and despair, hopelessness and loathing. He'd seen them all in her beloved features as he imprisoned her below.

He'd wanted to scoop Hannah and Pip out of harm's way, load them in his coach, and bolt like blue blazes for the coast. Fling them onto a ship and sail God knew where, someplace, anyplace they would be safe. He had money enough to take them to any corner of the globe.

But she'd already spent too long fleeing Booth, glancing over her shoulder afraid. Austen knew what it was to be hunted, haunted. Every moment, a special kind of hell, racing over quicksand, never knowing when the ground would shift beneath your feet, drag you under, hurl you to the mercy of your greatest fear.

No matter how far she ran, how well she hid, Hannah could never make a life for herself until this disaster with Booth was settled once and for all. And Austen wanted a life with her. With Pip. Though God knew, after today she might never forgive him.

Austen winced at the stark betrayal that had enveloped her features, his nerves frayed to a jagged edge. He hated the feel of Simmons's gaze upon him. "Damn it, man, leave me in peace!"

"Yes, sir. But—but you never answered my question."

"What infernal question?" No judge handing out a death sentence could have sounded more forbidding.

"The sugar buns the cook made. Could we take some down to the cellar?"

Austen's head threatened to explode. Blast the cook, what did the woman think? Sugar buns could cure the nightmare Pip had suffered through? And yet it drove

Austen half-mad to think of Hannah and the boy down in that chamber alone. It touched him somewhere deep to know that his servants were also worried about Hannah and the child.

"All right," Austen surrendered. "Move the whole blasted pantry down there if you want to. Give them anything they need to be comfortable. And Simmons . . ." He hesitated for a heartbeat. "Tell them . . . tell them not to be afraid. I'll die before I let anyone harm them."

"I believe you would, sir." Simmons's eyes were filled with respect and a very real affection. "If you need another man to handle a pistol, I would be honored to assist you."

Austen stared at the servant, astonished at the loyalty in every line in the footman's frame. "I couldn't ask that of you, Simmons. You might be courting prison. Hanging. Or worse."

Simmons's expression disappeared into the mask that servants had worn since the beginning of time— unreadable as the sphinx. Yet it was too late. Austen had already seen the emotion in the man's eyes.

"You haven't asked me a thing, sir," Simmons reminded him. "I offered." With that the footman bowed, then exited the room.

Austen peered after the man for a long moment, his heart painfully full, his mind still roiling with countless possibilities. A labyrinth of paths he could take—any one that could end in Armageddon for Hannah and the boy. Was there any escape from this at all?

It was a tangle of law and courts, justice and cruelty, where all the rules had shifted and nothing was as it seemed. Brutality against a wife? One was allowed to abhor it in private, but interfere in the workings of a marriage? *Never.* Act as if it were invisible as the beggars coachmen nearly ran over in the London streets.

And a child was nothing more than chattel, property of his father. No court in the land would dispute that.

Anyone involved in the case would be damned furious with Hannah for forcing them to look at something so unpleasant.

Had she known how much danger she was embracing when she'd taken Pip and run? Guessed how dire the consequences might be? Austen's chest hurt, a grim smile filled with love twisting his mouth. Of course Hannah had known. But she hadn't given a damn. She'd just fulfilled her sister's desperate plea, protected the boy she loved.

And now, Austen resolved *he* would find some way to protect both of them. But could he really leave Ravenscar behind? The people he'd come to love? The land he'd poured his heart into? He'd worked so hard to make certain he wasn't irresponsible. To be a man his father would respect, even though Joseph Dante might never know it. He'd tried to be the landlord his grandfather had failed to be. He'd given these simple people hope and security. Could he take it all away?

And could he abandon the hope Hannah had stirred in his heart? She had convinced him to make peace with his family—dangled that almost impossible dream before him—could he face forever knowing he'd never see his sisters again? His mother?

Dante paced to the window, eyes narrowing as he searched the horizon, the ribbon of road that led to Ravenscar House. It was empty, yet with every beat of his heart the invisible coil of tension inside him tightened, his awareness honed like the edge of a master swordsman's blade. Every second he expected to see a rider appear in the distance.

The waiting was hell, but at least he could haunt the windows, pace the rooms, check the loading of his pistols again and again. It was only an illusion of control. But an illusion was better than the abject helplessness that Hannah must be suffering.

Thunderation, he'd do anything to spare her pain or fear, except allow her to disappear back into the moors, into the mist and the rain, where her eyes would grow haunted again and she and Pip would be at Booth's mercy forevermore. God knew he didn't want to, but he'd sacrifice whatever he had to—yes, damn it, even Ravenscar, and the chance to see his sisters, his mother again, if he could only see Hannah safe.

Time. He had to find some way to buy time so he could think of a solution to this mess.

A sound rolled down the hall like thunder, cries erupting from deeper within the house, resonating with alarm. Austen's heart slammed against his ribs, his hands burning for the cool grip of a pistol in his hand. Had Booth arrived?

With an oath, Austen scooped up the weapons and thrust them in the waistband of his breeches, then strode toward the door. Simmons all but bowled him over, the footman clutching the front of his livery, his eyes wide with disbelief and terror. Austen's blood turned to ice.

"What is it? Damnation, man—"

"It's Miss Graystone and—and the boy, sir. I took the buns to them as you said I could. But when I got there—" Simmons sucked in a raspy breath.

Austen grabbed him by the shirtfront, wishing he could shake the man until his teeth rattled. "Tell me!"

"Sir . . . the door was unlocked, and Pip and Miss Hannah—they were gone."

"Gone?" Austen's heart plunged. "Are you out of your mind? Even Hannah couldn't possibly escape from behind that door!"

"Someone must've let them out, sir. It was unlocked, and—"

Austen bolted down the corridor, pelted down the stairs, his heart thundering, his breath rasping as he slammed to a halt just inside the open cellar door.

The lantern still glowed, coverlets and pillows tucked on the floor, food untasted on a table someone had put in one corner. The pup he had given Pip snuffled about, its worried spaniel eyes gazing up at Austen in a silent plea.

"How the devil could this have happened?" Austen snapped.

"I don't know! The key was missing. I had to find the spare one to unlock the door."

God in heaven. Hannah was gone. Austen's blood ran cold. She was lost somewhere in these hills and moors, completely unprotected.

"Get every able-bodied man on Ravenscar land a horse, tell them to search every road and every field leading away from here."

"Yes, sir, but there's so much of it—"

"I don't care how long, how hard we have to search. We have to find Hannah and Pip before Booth does." With that, Austen charged out the door. It seemed forever but was mere moments before he was astride Fire Eater, racing away like the wind.

"Damn you, Hannah!" he swore, the wind lashing him in the face. "Where are you?"

His lands spilled out all around him. She could be anywhere, he thought with a sinking heart. Struggling to travel with a sick child and burdened by her own terror as Mason Booth tried to hunt her down.

God in heaven, Austen thought desperately, he had to find her before Booth did. Had to find a way to shield her before it was too late.

Desperation raced through Hannah's whole being as she stroked her knuckles against Pip's anguished face, trying to comfort him. But her tightly bound hands were ineffectual at best; the rafters of the building seemed to ring with Mason Booth's laughter.

He had won. Won at last. And Pip would pay the most horrifying price of all. A childhood at the mercy of a brutal beast, years of trying to be good, failing, always failing, and then suffering at his father's hands. Perhaps dying as Elisabeth had, his last moments filled with violence and horror.

"Nanna . . ." Pip rasped, his breath ragged, terrifying.

"Don't let Papa t–take me. Don't let him hurt you . . .
like he hurt my mama."

Hannah wanted to scream in fury, in helplessness, the
child's plea flaying her heart. But she couldn't give way
to her own bounding fear. She had promised Lizzy she'd
take care of her little boy! Oh, God, she had to help him!

"I know you're afraid, sweeting." She battled to keep
her voice calm, to ease his crippling terror. "But we can't
think about—about your papa now. What he might do."

Or we might both go mad . . .

"I need your help, angel. You're such a brave, bright
boy. We have to think of a way to get you out of here."

"B–but he tied me up. Made the ropes hurt."

"I know." Her own hands were throbbing with agony,
the leather sawing into her tender flesh, her fingers
swollen and clumsy. "We'll get the ropes off, sweetheart.
Somehow we will. We have to get you out of here, Pip."

Before the monster comes.

Digging with her nails until they pulled back from
their beds, tugging with her teeth until she tasted blood
from her own raw lips, Hannah fought against Pip's
bindings. But the ropes had been knotted with all the
strength in William Atticus's powerful shoulders. She
battled until raw sobs threatened to tear from her throat.
Struggled with the coarse hemp until tears blurred her
eyes, her ears straining to hear the slightest sound of
someone approaching.

She gave a low cry as she managed to dig one finger
beneath a loop in the knot. She grasped the hemp with
her teeth and tugged so hard she thought her temples
would burst. The rope budged, just a whisper, loosened
just enough to give her hope.

She murmured things to Pip as she worked, trying to
sooth him and ease the blind panic in her own breast. At
last the ropes fell free.

Pip cried out in pain as blood pumped into his little
hands.

"I know it hurts, treasure," Hannah said, with a sob of relief. "But we have to get your feet loose now. Can you untie it, love? Tug on this loop here." It seemed to take another eternity before the two of them loosened the knots. But at last the ropes joined the others in a pool on the floor.

Hannah searched the interior of the building, looking for somewhere, anywhere Pip could slip away. Her gaze locked on a place where a metal tube led from some ridiculous-looking contraption to the outer wall. A chimney of some sort? A place for smoke or something to escape? She had no idea.

"Here, Pip. We might be able to squeeze you out here." She maneuvered over to it and dealt it a savage kick with both feet. The metal shuddered and gave, and Hannah glimpsed blessed green, a slice of meadow, a fragment of sky.

Channeling all her fury, all her helplessness, she battered at the thing until it broke away, leaving a jagged opening in the wood. "Thank God," she breathed. "Do you think you can get through it, sweetheart?"

"I think so," Pip said. "But first we have to get your hands untied." He groped for the leather about her wrists.

But Hannah tugged them away. "No, angel," she said ever so quietly. "You have to go without me."

Pip's face whitened as he tried to grasp the inconceivable. "B–but . . ."

"Pip, there is no time. You have to go. Find Austen."

Panic engulfed his small features, and a stubbornness, one that would have brought joy to Hannah's heart any other time. Yet now Pip's resistance could be deadly. "But I don't want to leave you," the boy insisted. "What if . . ."

The knowledge that this little boy would face his father rather than abandon her broke Hannah's heart. But she crushed the tears that sprang to her eyes.

"Nothing is going to happen to me, sweetheart," she said fiercely. "Find someone you can trust, anyone such as the Digweeds or the people you met at the celebration. Make them take you to Austen. Do you understand?"

"Austen."

"Tell Austen I'm in the place where his inventions are. Can you remember that?"

"His benchions." Pip echoed, his whole body shaking.

"Yes. And, Pip . . . I want you to tell him something for me. Tell him I'm sorry. That I trust him with the most precious thing in my life. I know he'll take care of you."

"B—but you promised Mama that *you* would take care of me. I want *you.*" Pip's voice cracked. Hannah felt her heart break.

She remembered Lizzy giving her son away, the agony in her voice. Hannah had been tormented by it, tortured, and yet she hadn't truly understood her sister's suffering until today.

"I don't want to leave you." The little boy clung to her one precious moment, and she took comfort in the strength in him, the throb of his heart, the warmth of his tears.

God help him. He's so little. So afraid.

"You can do this, Pip. I know you can get to Austen. Now hurry. Stay out of sight, in the trees or the fields, until you see someone you can trust."

His arms tightened about her as if he would never let go.

"I love you, Pip. I want you to remember that, do you promise me?" Hannah's throat constricted, knowing this might be the last time she could ever tell him how much he'd meant to her. Praying that those words would be enough to give him strength through what would come.

He nodded fiercely against her breasts, and she would have sold her soul if she could just wrap her arms around him, cradle him one last time.

"Hurry now, angel. Run. Fly."

Doubt clouded Pip's eyes, desperation. "B—but what if I can't—can't breathe, and I . . ."

"You can do this, Pip," Hannah said, trying with all that was in her to believe it. "I know you can. Your mama . . . your mama is an angel, love. She'll give you wings."

With that, Pip scrambled out the small hole. Hannah sagged against a crate, tears streaming down her cheeks.

She strained, listening to his footfalls, terrified that they'd be drowned out by the pounding of William Atticus's horse. But at last she heard nothing but the wind in the meadow grass, the distant calls of birds.

He got away, she told herself. *He got away.* But he was far from out of danger.

Please, Austen . . . find him, she prayed with all the desperation in her heart. *Oh, God, Lizzy, help Pip fly!*

She scrabbled around the structure, searching for something, anything to use as a weapon against the beast who would surely come. Finding an awl with a bent point half hidden beneath a bale of twine, Hannah gripped it in her deadened fingers. Then she leaned against a wall of crates and surrendered to the torment of the damned. Waiting.

The jagged hole through which Pip had escaped grew bright with sunshine, then shadowed with twilight when at last she heard the sound of hoofbeats approaching. She forced herself to her feet, bracing her back against the wall of crates. Then she waited, the awl hidden in the folds of her skirt. Her chin high, her blood roiling with hope and fear.

She heard the barn door creak open, then the footsteps of a lone man. "Austen?" she said the name aloud, as if it were some talisman that could fend off evil. As if her desperation and her love alone could summon him.

Austen, the man who had made love to her with such tender fury, who had shared his most painful secrets, bared the scared places in his soul. The man she'd raged at, fought, when he'd dragged her down the cellar stairs.

To protect her. To keep her safe. While she raked his most painful vulnerabilities . . . *Do you want to prove your father right?*

Dear God, Hannah pleaded with the fates. *Don't let those hateful words be the last I ever say to him.*

But the sound of boot soles wasn't Austen's familiar restless tread. No, it was a swaggering rhythm she knew all too well. She raised her chin, squared her shoulders. She had to buy time. To make certain Pip was safe. That was all that mattered. She'd cling to that through what was to come.

"Help me to be strong, Lizzy," she whispered, picturing her sister's innocent, lovely face when she'd left Dove Cottage a new bride. Picturing her again the last time Hannah had seen her, battered and hopeless, a fragile shell succumbing to death.

But Booth hadn't broken Elisabeth's spirit. She'd been planning to run away from him, escape his brutal grasp.

Hannah's chin jutted up. Mason Booth wouldn't break her, either. She struggled to grip the awl in her numb, awkward hands. If there was a God, this might be the night she could send the beast to hell.

Chapter

❦ 21 ❧

Christ above, don't let it get dark, Austen prayed, pleaded, as if by force of will he could hold back the relentless stain of shadow dying the rim of the horizon. *It will be five times harder to find them in the dark.*

He'd ridden until he was half-mad, his eyes searching every hillock, every copse of bushes, every strip of road, trying to gauge where Hannah and Pip might have gone.

But he hadn't any idea. All he was certain of was this: they'd run away. As far away from Ravenscar as they could get. As fast as they could possibly go.

They had no place to seek haven. No one to run to.

Blast, he should have known Hannah would find a way to escape. Why the devil hadn't he imprisoned her in her room? That way she could at least have taken the diamond stickpin, been able to raise coin enough to take care of them, at least for a little while.

Until he could find them. And he would find them, damn it.

Unless Booth or the magistrates found Hannah and Pip first.

The possibility was unthinkable. His gut clenched, his hand checking one of the pistols jammed in the waistband of his breeches. No. He couldn't even think of Pip in Booth's cruel hands, Hannah at the brutal man's mercy.

He couldn't imagine his proud, brave Hannah in some dank prison cell, with water dripping from the walls and rats scrabbling in the corners. Hannah confronting possible death, Pip torn away from her. Hannah playing over and over in her mind what Booth might be doing to his son, knowing that the child would be sobbing out her name.

Austen reined his horse around, intending to try yet another direction, when he heard the clatter of what seemed a runaway wagon. Enoch Digweed's farm cart bouncing and jarring its way at breakneck pace down the road.

What the devil? Had the horses run away? Cursing any delay, Austen spurred Fire Eater toward the wagon, hoping to cut it off. But as he plunged down the hill toward it, he was stunned to see Enoch's burly frame at the reins, driving the team to even greater lengths. His oldest boy Thomas sat in the back of the cart, a musket in his hands.

What the devil? Austen started, then suddenly glimpsed a tiny figure huddled in the corner of the wagon, his small frame wrapped in one of Flossie Digweed's quilts.

"Pip!"

He could feel the boy's terror pulsing, throbbing, even from this distance. Oh, God—where was Hannah? Panic cut a jagged swath through his belly as he charged down to intercept them.

Enoch glimpsed him at the last possible moment and reined his farm horses in so quickly they all but catapulted the crofter out of the wagon seat.

"Mr. Dante! Thank God we've found you!" Enoch

burst out, his whole body trembling with outrage beneath his jerkin. "'Tis a miracle, I vow it is. When we started out t' search, they couldn't find my Thomas, so we went off without him. And 'twas the angels, I'm thinkin', that kept him in that rye field. 'Twas there Thomas stumbled across the boy, lost an' scarce able t' breathe. Said he had to find you."

"Thank God you're safe, boy." Austen swung down from his stallion and gathered the terrified child in his arms. "Pip, where is Hannah?"

"He . . . he tied it so tight I couldn't get her out. She made me leave."

Austen sat the boy back in the cart, gripping the child's arms, staring levelly into Pip's eyes. "Who tied her? Your father?"

"N–No. The other . . . other big man. He . . ."

Austen struggled desperately for balance, tried not to go mad. It would only terrify the boy further if he bellowed at him. But the thought of Hannah captive somewhere was hell. It didn't matter who had tightened the bindings on her wrists. Time enough to find that out later. All that mattered was getting to her as quickly as possible so he could free her.

"Where is she, boy?" Austen grasped the boy's hands. "Can you remem—" The child winced and Austen looked down, saw the ugly raw marks on his slender wrists. Coarse hemp had torn the tender skin; dark bruises bled away from the marks of the bindings; crescent-shaped cuts marred where Hannah had struggled with her own fingernails to get him loose.

"God in heaven. You're hurt." By all that was holy, he was going to kill whoever did this to the child.

"It's not so *very* bad." Pip tried to tug his hands away, to hide them, but Austen wouldn't let him. Gently he cupped the boy's fingers in his own, wishing he could erase the pain.

"We had to get my hands and feet out of the rope so I

could . . . could run," Pip said. "An' it took forever an' ever. So long. But when we did, Hannah made me crawl out the pipe hole. I didn't want to leave her, but she made me go."

Austen's heart wrenched, his throat crushed with emotion. He could see Hannah fighting to get Pip free, sharing her courage with the boy and her faith in the child's resourcefulness. Believing that Pip would be able to meet this challenge with all the fierceness in her loving soul.

Hannah making sure the child escaped, while she was left alone to face the devil himself.

"Where is she, boy? Do you remember?"

"She—she's where your benchions are."

"Benchions?" Austen echoed. What the devil were those? He was so close, he couldn't fail her now. "Can you tell me what it looked like, Pip?"

"A big barn with giant tubes an' tools an'—"

"Inventions! Where I keep my inventions! That's clear on the other side of the estate." Austen swore low under his breath, then swung up on his horse.

"The man said he was bringing Papa to get us," Pip said as Thomas wrapped the quilt around him again. "An' we tried to get the ropes off for such a long time. I'm scared he'll be there by now."

Austen's jaw set grimly. "Enoch, take Pip back to Ravenscar. Guard him yourself. Shoot anyone who dares come near him, do you hear?"

"With pleasure, sir," Enoch promised, a dangerous curl to his lips.

"No!" Pip cried, even deeper alarm sparking in his gray-green eyes. "You can't go yet! I have to—to tell you something first. Hannah made me promise."

Austen reined in Fire Eater, casting a glance back at the boy. "Tell me what?"

"She said she loves you. That she—" Pip frowned, trying to grope for her words through his fear. "She trusts you. She said you'd take care of me. An' I didn't have to be afraid."

She was facing the possibility of her own arrest, a terrible death before a jeering mob, but she was confronting her fate with valor. No plea for Austen to hurry, to save her. Only her worry about what would happen to Pip. Austen's heart felt afire with love, with pain.

She was giving Austen the child she loved more than her own life. Entrusting him with Pip's safety, with his future, depending on him to banish the little boy's nightmares if she should die.

It was a tribute beyond imagining to her love for Austen, and her faith in him. A faith he wasn't certain he deserved. But he wouldn't fail her. Damn it, he wouldn't fail her.

"You're safe now, boy. Nothing's going to hurt you."

But a childhood in hell clouded the boy's face, and Dante wondered how many times Pip had lived through this particular nightmare. Being swept to safety while his father raged.

A tiny choked sob tore from the child's throat. "She said to run. That she'd be all right. But if Papa comes, if he wants me, an' I'm not there . . ." Pip's eyes grew huge, haunted with terrors no child should ever know.

"Mama used to hide me sometimes when he was real mad at me. I'd hide in the clothespress an' couldn't get out, an' he'd hit her. Hit her an' hit her, an' he'll hit Hannah, too, an' she'll get dead like my mama. I don't want her to get dead."

"I'll bring her back to you safe, boy. I swear it." With that, Austen spun his horse around. Leaning low over the animal's neck, he drove the stallion toward Hannah's prison.

Hannah clutched the awl, hiding the makeshift weapon in her skirts, every muscle in her body thrumming with fear. But she wouldn't give Booth the pleasure of knowing how terrified she was. She'd show him nothing but contempt and scorn.

Perhaps she was going to die, but maybe she could take the sadistic bastard along with her. Still, every measured step coming nearer made her stomach clench, her hands tremble.

For months Mason Booth had haunted Hannah's nightmares, but nothing had prepared her for seeing him again. Silver-gilt hair gleaming like an unholy angel's crown, his features perfectly chiseled, his green eyes filled with loathing.

But it was the smile that curved his mouth that made Hannah sick to her stomach. The fierce smile of a hunter who at last had his knife against the throat of his prey.

"My dearest little sister-in-law," he sneered, raking a contemptuous glance down her body. And Hannah realized that for the first time, all masks of politeness had been stripped away. They had hated each other for so long, been enemies no one else could see. It was almost a relief to stop pretending for Elisabeth's sake, and for her mother and sisters.

"I'd hoped you'd be on a ship to America right now," Hannah baited him. "I was praying you'd fall overboard. Of course, it's given me no end of pleasure knowing you were running around Ireland as if your tail was afire."

Mason's jaw hardened. "You've led me quite a chase. But your tinker friend was happy enough to help me once I . . . persuaded him."

"Tito?" Hannah remembered those few tension-filled nights by the old man's fire, his wisdom, his generosity, his help. "You didn't hurt him?"

"You think I took pleasure in beating an old man? But he wouldn't be reasonable, damn him!"

Oh, God. That the old man should have suffered for his kindness to her wrenched Hannah with regret.

"Your wastrel father obviously died before he could teach you one of the most important lessons in life,"

Booth sneered. "Only one thing matters in a hunt, Hannah. That's how it ends. Whether the fox has barely leapt from its first hiding place when it's brought down, or whether it has run until its footpads are bloody, the animal's fate is the same. Its life is still in the hunter's hands."

"I've never known how you summoned up the courage for such a dangerous sport. One little fox against a whole herd of men and their packs of dogs? But then, you couldn't even find one woman and child without help. If you hadn't stumbled across that Bow Street runner, you'd still be chasing your tail all over England."

"I would have found you. Make no mistake."

"Where is your cohort? Didn't he want to be in on the kill?"

"Mr. Atticus? Why, I requested that he summon the magistrates to take you to jail." Booth smirked. "This is a family matter, my dear. I told him I wanted to greet you in private. You see, he may be a thief and a liar, but I'm not certain he has the stomach for blood on his hands."

"He'd be glad enough to see me hang."

"But that is from a distance. Besides, I couldn't have him near enough to hear you, if you chose to blurt out that unfortunate information you had. I might not have been quite so vigilant in my search if you hadn't been foolish enough to threaten my honor, my good name."

"Your honor!" Hannah all but spat. "Any information I had about you should have been meaningless. What you did to Elisabeth should have been enough to horrify anyone who heard of it."

"I *loved* Elisabeth!" Booth roared. "What could you understand about such a great love? A dried-up spinster with no passion in your veins. As if any man would want you!"

"I know what love is," Hannah asserted, remembering the sweet fire in Austen's eyes, the gentleness of his hands even in the deepest throes of passion. The willingness to sacrifice himself for her. "Love has nothing to do with violence. You don't hurt the one you love, make them suffer, cut them off from the families who love them!"

"Oh, yes. Forever foisting your opinions on the world! You were always there between us—with your meddling and your prying. I could see it in Elisabeth's eyes even before our wedding!"

Hannah glared at him, wanting to enrage him, wanting to lure him closer in his fury. "I begged her not to marry you. I tried to change her mind, even up to the minute she met you at the altar."

Color boiled up his neck and his cheeks, to where his eyes seethed with hatred. "But you failed. She loved me too much to listen to you."

"Or she was too afraid to fly into the face of convention, felt obligated to go through with the marriage so the rest of us could have some few comforts. She succumbed to the pressure from our mother, my sisters. Everyone who said it was a stellar match and she should be grateful for it."

"She loved me!"

Hannah winced inwardly, remembering the soft glow in her sister's eyes the first time she had danced with Mason, the way her cheeks bloomed with roses every time someone mentioned his name. A girl's first romantic flutterings. The most potent of elixirs, and the most dangerous poison.

"Maybe she did love you at first." It hurt Hannah more than she could believe to admit that. "But when I arrived at Booth Hall several months ago, it wasn't love I saw in her eyes then. It was hate. She begged me to take Pip away from you, with her dying breath."

Mason's features contorted in disgust and fury. "The boy! That worthless boy! Why was she always fussing over the damned boy? I gave her everything she'd ever wanted. New gowns, jewels, I even patched up that ramshackle cottage you were living in! We were happy— she was everything I wanted, dreamed of. And she worshiped me. Can you have any idea how proud I was with such a beauty on my arm? And when I heard she was to bear my child? A son. I needed a son and heir, to take my title and my land."

"Lizzy bore you that son!"

"It would have been better if he'd died at birth! But no! The puling little weakling lived. And because of him my Elisabeth changed. She haunted the boy's bedside whenever he had the slightest cough. Made herself sick and pale, and God knows, she couldn't be dragged away from Booth Hall even to attend any of the fetes we'd gone to before."

"She was a good mother taking care of her child!"

"I hired a nurse to do that—hover over the child's bed. Elisabeth's place was with me!"

Dear God, was that how it had begun? This ugliness? This violence that had cost her sister her life? Booth's jealousy of his own son?

Hannah shuddered, revolted by this man vowing his love for Elisabeth, his face contorted in very real grief.

"You *beat* Elisabeth," Hannah accused, hating him. "Is that how you showed your *love?*"

"It was humiliating to have such a weakling for a son! I had to make a man of the boy! But every time I tried, she interfered. Any man would have lost patience! She knew my temper! It was her own fault I hit her!"

She had to find a way to set him off balance. To provoke him. If he lunged at her, she could raise the awl, plunge it deep into his chest. Yet it could prove a deadly gamble. For if she failed, there would be nothing to stop Mason in his rage.

"She was trying to protect her child from you. She knew what you were! A monster terrorizing someone who couldn't fight back!"

"You don't know what you're saying! Elisabeth was too tenderhearted, and yet deep down inside she understood why I had to do what I did."

"Elisabeth told me when I came to Booth Hall, found her dying from the blows you'd dealt her!"

"Elisabeth knew I only did it for her own good! The boy's own good! She loved me as I loved her!"

Hannah braced herself, her chin jutting up, her hands clenching about the awl. "She was leaving you, taking Pip with her and running away, where you could never find either of them! But you battered her before she could go! Threw Pip up on that horse—"

"I don't believe you!" Booth's face twisted.

"Don't you? How did you think I came by the information that might ruin your *honorable* name? Lizzy told me everything. Your groom confirmed it."

"M—my . . . what?"

"While you were off playing the fool with all your worthless friends, the servants came to love Lizzy. They knew what you were doing to her. But they couldn't stop you! Before I left with Pip, while Lizzy lay dying, the groom swore to what you'd done."

"This is preposterous!"

She could see the rage building—fury at Lizzy's betrayal. Good God, he could beat her to death, and yet Lizzy had wronged him by refusing to carry this dirty little secret to her grave!

"You'd won every race in the county for years, built a reputation for never losing. I can only imagine how that swelled your disgusting pride, let you preen about. But you'd met your match, seen that someone else could beat you."

She could see the tightening around his lips, his eyes narrowing like a cruel child caught pulling the wings off sparrows. "You're daft!" Mason flung out.

"No, you were daft! Daft and desperate, and willing to sacrifice anything to save your idiotic reputation, you pompous, cowardly fool! You made Pip ride that colt, knowing it was far too spirited. Made him ride until the boy was half-killed by being thrown, when his breathing was so bad the groom feared the boy might be dying. But he couldn't stop you. Desperate, the man sent someone to get Lizzy. And when Lizzy interfered, you turned on her, beat her instead!"

A vein throbbed at Mason's temple, his fists clenching. "I told her to go back inside. It was no place for a woman!"

"Why? Were you afraid of what Lizzy would see? That she might guess the groom already knew? Well, she did! You wanted to lame that horse, and you were using Pip as an excuse to do it."

"I'd paid a fortune for that animal! It had never lost a race!"

God above, it was hideous, the man more distressed someone would discover he'd tampered with a horse than that he'd beaten his wife to death. More hideous still was the knowledge that a wife beater would be tolerated by society, but a man who cheated in a race? Never! Hannah braced herself to push his rage harder.

"But the horse was going to lose the next day, wasn't it? So you had to find a way to save your ridiculous pride. Easier to say that your son lamed it and you had to put the horse down than to have your record fall."

She saw the flicker in his eyes, knew he wouldn't bother trying to disguise the truth any longer. She wasn't worth bothering with the deception. "You could never prove it," Booth smirked with ugly confidence. "No one would believe you!"

"Wouldn't they?" Hannah demanded. "You shot the horse, didn't you? The day before the race? If you realized another horse could beat you, don't you think someone else might have guessed it as well? Think, Mason. Doesn't this all look a trifle suspicious?"

"You have no proof!"

"I won't need it, and you know it. Just the hint of doubt, and your racing friends will watch your every move, start questioning the most innocent things. And if any of them have a brain, they'll start to figure out—"

"They'll never hear of it. You pretend to be so intelligent, so far above the rest of us with your intellect. What did you think I was going to do when I found you, Hannah? Turn you over to the magistrates so you could blurt this story out to any fool who would listen?"

Hannah's heart sank, and she bade good-bye to all the possibilities Austen had opened to her, all the hope, all the love. "No. You plan to kill me." Hannah grasped the awl hidden between her hands. "Why shouldn't you when you've already murdered your wife."

"Murdered?" Booth recoiled from the word as if it were poison. "I didn't mean for her to die!"

"What did you think was going to happen, you idiot? Elisabeth was always delicate! You beat her, then you left, you rode away and went foxhunting with your friends! You left her alone—"

Booth had the gall to wince. "I couldn't bear to see her that way."

Hannah gave a scathing laugh. "You mean, you didn't even have the courage to look at what you'd done to her! But I did! Pip did! She was slipping away, and there was nothing we could do to help her! Nothing we could do except *hate* you. But you won't get your hands on Pip! He's safe where you can never touch him."

"Oh, he's here somewhere, cowering in a corner. And even if he isn't, he'll be easy enough to track down. Any court in the land will give him to me. Yes, Hannah, you can be certain I intend to find my son!"

"Don't try to pretend any fatherly devotion, or I fear I might retch! If Pip had been a horse, you would have been happy to shoot him, too!"

"If it wasn't for him, Elisabeth would be alive!" Booth roared. "I'll make certain that boy never forgets it!"

Revulsion tore through her at the possibility that the little boy could be hammered with such cruelty worse than mere fists.

"Blame me, blame Pip. Even blame poor Lizzy! *You* were the one who struck her, Mason. The power was in your hand from the beginning!"

Booth's eyes went dark, and Hannah saw the monster Elisabeth must have faced countless times—rage unleashed, an almost bestial savagery.

"Lizzy told me what an animal you were! How she loathed you! She couldn't bear to have you near her—"

He lunged for her, and Hannah whipped the awl from her skirts, tried with all her strength to plunge it deep. But as the point collided with Booth's hard chest, her numbed, throbbing fingers gave way and the weapon sliced a cut toward his shoulder, then skidded off, clattering to the floor.

A howl of rage erupted from Booth's throat and he lashed one fist at her, cracking it into her jaw. Hannah fell backward, her head reeling, her stomach plunging, as she scrabbled to find the weapon, but just as her hands closed on it, Booth kicked her fingers with a savagery that nearly plunged her into unconsciousness.

A cry of pain, of hopelessness, ripped from Hannah's throat as the awl flew God alone knew where.

She struggled to drive the waves of darkness back. Damnation, if she was going to die, let him see the contempt in her face! "Go ahead, Mason! Hit me! Hit me the way you did Elisabeth! Or don't you have the *courage?*"

He grabbed her by the throat, his hands tightening. "You deserve to die for your meddling! All those letters you'd send her, they made her turn against me!"

"No, you did that yourself!"

"It was you! You and the boy! But there's time enough to deal with him, once you're dead."

Hannah let her contempt spill into her eyes. "Won't it be a trifle awkward, trying to explain another woman beaten to death?"

Rage clouded his face, yet still there was a spark of survival instinct. He swore, then his gaze skated up to the monstrous contraptions that had been Austen's passion, and alighted on a scaffolding that stretched its skeleton high above some huge half-finished hulk of metal. Booth gave a spine-chilling laugh.

"You always were a meddling woman, Hannah. What better way to die than prying around in here, where you don't belong? Taking an unfortunate fall."

Hannah realized his intent, kicked out as he grappled with her. Terror shot through her as he dragged her up the scaffolding, higher, higher.

She was going to die. The certainty ripped through her.

"You're going to be dead, Hannah. Then no power on earth can deny me my son."

"You don't love him! You don't even want him!"

"Oh, I want him. I promise you. He made me kill the woman I loved. I'll spend the rest of my life making him pay."

Austen . . . oh, God, Austen . . .

But she didn't know if Pip had reached him, told him where she was. She didn't even know if the boy was safe.

God in heaven, there had to be something she could do to protect Pip. But time was running out. Booth hauled her higher into the labyrinth of scaffolding, higher.

Twice his boots slipped on the scaffolding, nearly sending them both tumbling below. Hannah knew in that instant there was only one thing she could do. One way to make certain Pip was safe from this man forever.

She wouldn't fight anymore to save her own life. She would take Booth to the grave with her. Five more steps until they reached a board forming a bridge between two sections of scaffolding, five more steps until she had her chance. She tensed, ready to overbalance him.

He'd put one foot on the board when suddenly a strident voice rang out. "Let her go, Booth, or I'll blast you into hell." Austen. Dear God, was she dreaming? She cast a glance in the direction the sound had come from, saw him, pistols drawn, his eyes seething with deadly fury, with fierce, impossible love.

Relief shot through her, and hope. She didn't want to die! But Booth reacted in a heartbeat, dragging Hannah in front of him, a human shield. The board beneath his feet wobbled, Hannah's heart plunging.

"What are you going to do, Mr. Dante? Shoot me? No, I think I'll just wait here until the magistrates arrive. They're on their way by now. And they'll be on my side."

"I don't give a damn if you've summoned the whole blasted army! I'll do whatever I have to do to protect Hannah and Pip."

"A most heroic vow. But you won't be able to protect them, no matter how much you want to."

"You murdered your own wife! Surely I can get some infernal judge to listen."

"They won't think it's any of their business, and you know it. Besides, who says that I killed Elisabeth? Hannah? She's mentally unbalanced. Even her own mother and sisters would swear to it. The boy is my son. My blood. And she stole him."

"You bastard! I should—"

"All I'm trying to do here is to get her down," Booth said, his voice cold as death, pleased as a viper swallowing its prey. "When Hannah saw me, she started raving in her misguided grief, tried to stab me—you see the blood? In a fit of madness, she started to climb up here. I thought she might get hurt. I tried to get her down."

Hannah could feel his satisfied purr. "Of course, I'm afraid she'll slip once the magistrates arrive. Very sad. No one will cry more at her funeral than I will."

"Don't you dare hurt her."

Booth edged out onto an arch of metal that rimmed a giant copper drum. "Dare what? Drop her? Can't you see, I'm trying to help her? Get her down?"

"Let her go!"

"Sir!" A roar came from behind him.

Atticus's baritone boomed out. "Mr. Dante, for God's sake, don't!"

Hannah glimpsed a brace of local magistrates shouldering their way into the area, William Atticus behind them.

Mason moved deeper toward the heart of the construction, his gaze flicking to where a gate for loading supplies opened to the outdoors, a pulley and rope dangling from its peak.

"I'm trying to get her down!" Booth cried. "That man with the gun is mad! He thinks I'm trying to harm her! For God's sake, help me before someone gets hurt."

Hannah knew Austen could never shoot Booth now; they'd only crash to their deaths. Even if that weren't so, that single pistol shot would ruin Austen's life, rob him of a future. And Pip . . . Pip would be alone.

"Put the pistols down, Mr. Dante," one of the magistrates said. "The woman's not worth goin' to prison for."

But Hannah knew Austen would sacrifice himself for her. For Pip.

"Stay the devil out of this!" Austen snarled.

"It's too late for that, and you know it," the magistrate said. "We'll let the courts sort this out."

The courts? Mason would win. Austen would be destroyed. Pip would be at that monster's mercy.

The magistrate stilled suddenly, his gaze flicking above Hannah and Booth, his features suddenly fixed and intent.

"They'll get the gun from your lover," Booth murmured in her ear. "And then I'm afraid I'll have to drop you. Such a tragedy, but I've lost a fair amount of blood from the injury you dealt me. You struggled. I couldn't hold on any longer."

Booth was right. His plan was diabolically brilliant. Flawless. No one would believe Austen—her lover. Not when they'd all seen Booth's performance. The man was a master of charm and sincerity, one who had fooled all of Ireland for years.

There was only one way to make certain Booth's cruelty, his brutality, could never touch either Pip or Austen again.

A chill seeped into Hannah's very bones. Grief welled inside her for all that could never be. A life she'd glimpsed in Austen's eyes, felt the promise of in his touch. A future more beautiful than she'd ever dreamed.

Hannah cast one last glance at Austen, remembering the single night they'd spent in each other's arms. She wanted to tell him she loved him, wanted to tell him so many things in that instant, but to do so would be to bind him more tightly in Booth's web. She prayed Austen's heart could hear her own. *I love you . . . I love you . . . I love you . . .*

She'd keep her promise to Lizzy. It was all that mattered except for the tortured love in Austen Dante's eyes.

"Are you ready to die, Hannah?" Booth whispered, a voice from hell. "I feel my hands slipping—"

Hannah braced her feet against the connecting board. With all her strength, she shoved herself backward. Booth struggled for balance and she glimpsed panic in his face, but it was too late.

"Hannah! Hannah, no!" Austen's voice lanced through her.

She saw a glimpse of a spindly magistrate trying to grab at her from his perch on the scaffold above. Saw the man's horror, his revulsion, knew he'd heard Booth's ugly threats. But it was too late.

The board teetered, tipped, the wood splitting with a spine-chilling crack. Booth clawed at her, at the air, a scream tearing from his lips as he tumbled backward.

Hannah hurtled into empty space to where death was waiting.

Chapter

❧ 22 ❧

An animal cry of horror ripped from Austen as he flung down his pistol, diving toward Hannah. But there was no way to reach her, to save her. Nothing to do but watch her hurtle downward what seemed an eternity, toward the blades below.

Booth's scream was cut off, a sickening crunching sound reverberating through the building as he crashed to his death. Austen waited for Hannah's cry, his heart torn from his body. But suddenly there was a thud and the scaffolding shook as Hannah slammed into the joint between two crossbars.

She hung there suspended over the deadly blades, limp as a child's abandoned rag doll.

Austen scrambled up the latticework of wooden bars, nearly slipping in his haste, reaching her in moments. Ever so gently, he disentangled her, carried her downward. Terror pulsed through Austen, his voice rough, pleading. "Hannah! Hannah, damn you, don't die! Not now that you've made me love you."

"Help him! For God's sake!" A portly magistrate, his

face stricken, reached up, trying to take her from Dante's arms, but he held on tightly.

"Summon the surgeon!" Austen bellowed. "Damn you, hurry!"

One of the men darted out.

Austen laid her down on a pile of hay, stroked her face so ashen, so still.

"Hannah! Hannah, talk to me! Don't do this!"

Her eyes fluttered, opening just a little. "Mason?"

"The bastard is dead."

"Then Pip is . . . safe."

The magistrate who had been near them on the scaffold leapt down, ran one hand through his thinning hair. "That cur was going to kill her! Drop her on purpose! I heard him!"

"Why didn't you trust me, Hannah?" Austen demanded, his voice thick, shaken. "Didn't you know that I'd find a way to protect Pip? Why the hell did you have to take things into your own hands?"

"Only way to be certain Mason could never hurt him again. Pip needed . . . one of us. Knew you'd take care of each other for my sake, if I was gone."

"You're not going anywhere, damn it!" Austen bit out savagely. "You're going to live, Hannah. You're going to marry me!"

"Something . . . I need to say. You have to know I love you."

"Well, I'm mad as hell at you, and you'd damn well better live so I can wring your neck myself for jumping off that scaffold!"

"Listen . . . Atticus is the one who let us out of the cellar. Brought us here. Told Booth where to find us."

Austen stared in disbelief. "What the—"

"He's trying to keep you and your family apart. Been stealing from you. Getting supplies . . . cheaper. That's why . . . machine broke. Enoch hurt."

Austen glanced up at his cousin.

The steward's face was ashen. "She doesn't know what she's saying!"

Rage and betrayal, pain, and sudden, stark understanding seared through Austen. So many things suddenly making soul-sickening sense.

But there would be time enough to deal with Atticus later. Austen stroked Hannah's hair. "Atticus doesn't matter now! Save your strength, love."

"Don't you see? You don't have to suffer over music . . . anymore. Your father . . . wrote to you, Austen. Letters."

"What the devil?" She must be delirious. She couldn't possibly mean what she'd said.

"Atticus . . . burned them." She smiled just a little, a smile that broke his heart. "Your father loves you, Austen."

Austen reeled, stunned. Hope and anguish tearing him apart.

"Love Pip like that, Austen. Be . . . father to him. For my sake."

"We'll take care of him together. Make a home for him. Hannah, you've wandered so far to find me." Austen stroked her hair, rocked her against his chest. "You can't die, Hannah. I wasn't even alive until you came into my life."

"Promise me . . . your parents . . . send for them. Tell your father the truth, Austen. About why you stayed with your grandfather and what . . . happened that day in the pasture. Time for you both . . . to heal."

"I promise." He buried his face against her hair, trying to bite back the bitterness of tears. "But I want you there beside me when I do."

"Tell Mama, Harriet, and Fanny I love them. Understand why they believed Mason. Everyone in Wicklow did. Wish I could . . . see them again. Hardest thing about . . . leaving Ireland. Believing they were lost to me forever. Will you tell them that . . . for me?"

"Damn it, tell them yourself! You have to live, Hannah. Let me take care of you. I'll make every dream you ever had come true."

She raised her bound hands, touched his tear-wet cheek. "Austen."

"What is it, my love?"

"I . . . never had . . . any dreams. Until you."

Austen should have been rejoicing. Hannah sat in the sunstruck garden reading aloud, the ashen color that had terrified him banished from her face, her cheeks tinted with pink. Every hope and dream they'd shared should have been blossoming like the tumbled roses upon the stone wall.

He'd barely left her side during the weeks she'd hovered between life and death, ordering, cajoling, daring her to fight. The only time he'd left her bedchamber was the day he'd gone to face down William Atticus, sending the man to prison.

Atticus had begged, had pleaded for mercy. A mercy Austen might have granted had the man stolen only the money Dante had in abundance. But Atticus had robbed him of things far more precious.

In his mind his cousin would pay, not for cold coin or even for Austen's own pain since the breach with his family, but rather for Enoch Digweed's broken leg, for every birthday and Christmas Austen's mother and sisters had worried over him and missed him. For all the terror Hannah suffered the night Booth had died. And for the anguish proud, sensitive Joseph Dante must have suffered writing of his love, his forgiveness, then waiting for a reply to the letters Austen had never received.

Atticus was gone forever. Mason Booth was dead. The pain, the bitterness, the isolation Austen had suffered for so long had been banished by the hand of the magnificent woman who held his heart.

Pip tossed an india rubber ball for Lizzy, gentle-spirited Christopher Digweed following in their wake. Hannah and the boy believed there were no more monsters waiting in the shadows.

Only Austen knew the truth. One last spectre loomed, so forbidding it threatened to steal the joy from every other triumph.

Austen's jaw tightened as he remembered the magistrate's apologetic face mere days after Booth had gone to hell. Michael Ferrars, the man who overheard Mason's death threats to Hannah, had cleared every charge leveled against her, but as swiftly as he eliminated one horror from their lives he introduced another.

Mr. Dante, I've done everything in my power to prevent it, but there's no help for it. We must contact the child's legal guardian. He's heir to his father's baronetcy and Sir Mason left explicit instructions in his will as to the man he wants to raise his son. No one knows better than I how much your lady sacrificed for the boy, but young Pip is not her child by birth. You will have to surrender the boy—

Surrender him to a total stranger—someone who didn't love him, who didn't even know him? A guardian who was some distant cousin, orphaned and raised at Booth Hall until he'd run away to sea? A man chosen by that monster Booth? He might be as bad as the boy's father, for all Austen knew. God forbid, Captain Burke might be worse.

Austen had prayed for even a temporary reprieve from having to surrender Pip, time enough to find a way around Booth's accursed will, but it was not to be.

Even when Ferrars had informed him Captain John Burke was in port, Austen had not been able to do what instinct urged him to—charge off himself, offer to pay any price to keep the boy.

But Hannah had hovered between life and death during those dark days, still fighting Mason Booth in her dreams. The only things that could calm her were Austen's voice, Austen's touch, Austen's promise that he'd let nothing harm Pip.

No, there had been only one person living whom he could trust to plead his case to John Burke. It had cost Austen more than he could say, but he'd swallowed his pride and summoned Matthew Simmons, asking that the footman write a letter to Austen's father.

He'd wanted to fill it with all the emotion bursting in his chest, wanted to tell his father so much, how sorry he was, how very much he'd missed him, how he finally understood the bond of father and son because of the little boy he was trying so desperately to protect.

But such words wouldn't come. Only *I know I have no right to ask this of you, but you are the one man in all Christendom I can trust. Find this Captain Burke, bring him to Ravenscar—so I can save Hannah's son.*

Austen listened to the rise and fall of her voice, so soft, so filled with contentment as she read aloud to him. He might have delighted in the wondrous worlds she opened were it not for the tension clenching ever tighter in his chest, waiting day after day for the final battle he knew must come.

He'd learned how dangerous keeping secrets could be, learned that love was honesty, even painful honesty and trust. Yet how could he tell her his fear that Pip might be taken away? What would happen to the precious light in her eyes, the fragile hope that tinted her lips? The faith she hadn't even known as a child, trying to stem the disaster of her father's gambling, wastrel ways.

Austen would love her with more passion than any man had ever loved a woman, and yet he'd never be able to fill the hole in her heart should Pip be ripped away. He'd never be able to heal the wound such a brutal separation would leave in Pip's battered soul.

"Austen, something's troubling you." Hannah's voice, weighted with concern, intruded on his thoughts. Austen glanced up at her, her cheeks still too thin, her hand too pale, reminding him of how close he'd come to losing her forever.

"I've been massacring poor Odysseus's latest adventure so badly Homer must be turning in his grave. Considering that you didn't bat so much as an eyelash when Circe drove across the waters to meet him in her phaeton and share the latest issue of the *London Times,* I'd wager you haven't been listening. Would you rather I chose another story?"

Austen felt his cheeks heat with guilt. He unfolded his long frame and took hold of her hand. "I'm sorry, love. I just . . ."

"You don't need to hover over me anymore, you know. The surgeon says I'm doing wonderfully well. A miracle, almost." She smiled. "Sometimes I wonder if Lizzy had something to do with it."

God, if it was so, let Lizzy perform one more miracle for Hannah and her little boy.

"Is it about Atticus?"

"No. It's . . . you know I'd move heaven and earth for you, for Pip, don't you?" *Even though that might not be enough.*

"Of course I do." Lines of worry creased her brow. "Austen, what is it?"

"Mr. Dante, sir?" a voice rang out.

Austen was damned grateful for the reprieve. Matthew Simmons approached, his features taut. "Pardon me, sir, but there is someone here to see you. Mr. Joseph Dante."

"Your father!" Hannah's smile blossomed, her eyes so filled with light they wrenched at Austen's heart.

Austen rose, pressing a kiss to her cheek. His gaze caught a glimpse of Pip's little coattails waving in the wind as he dove beneath an azaelea bush to extract his squirming puppy. For a heartbeat he considered leaving Hannah here safe in the garden, with the flowers all around her, Pip frolicking with his puppy, and her pieces of dreams safe for just a little longer.

Yet that couldn't change the contents of the message his father had brought. Whatever the future held, he and Hannah would have to face it together.

"Hannah, there's something I need to tell you. It's about Pip."

"Pip?" He hated the slivers of unease piercing her gaze.

"A few days after you were injured, the magistrate came, informed me that they had begun a search for the boy's legal guardian. The guardian named under Booth's will."

The delicate rose blush bled from Hannah's cheeks leaving them pale, her eyes wide, her lips trembling. "But Lizzy gave him to me. She—" Hannah stopped, and Austen felt her pain lancing through him.

Hannah—far too wise, far too pragmatic to deny the truth. She'd spent a lifetime trying to pilot her little family away from disaster, forseeing every stumbling block, every barricade, every threat to their security. Had love changed her so very much? Transformed her until she hadn't even thought such a calamity might be lurking? "Dear God, Austen. They can't take Pip away. We can't let them do it! We can't . . ."

"I wrote to my father, asked him to contact this Captain Burke, tell him Pip's story, offer him any price."

"Why didn't you tell me?"

"After everything you'd suffered? You even have to ask? Damn it, Hannah, I worried enough for both of us, I promise you. You were so damned pale, so fragile. Besides, it would have changed nothing."

She swallowed hard, and he could see for a heartbeat she wanted to argue. Then she slipped her fingers into his hand. The walk to the house seemed to take forever. Austen heard his father before he saw him—music, a discordant batch of nonsense, echoed from the pianoforte. The gibberish Hannah had written during the days they'd fallen in love?

Austen's fingers tightened on Hannah's hand as he went to face the man he had not seen in so many years. The father who now held Pip's future in his hands.

Austen's heart stopped as he glimpsed his father. The clock spun back, Joseph Dante appearing as he had countless times before, his broad shoulders bent over the pianoforte's keys, his dark eyes intense. A lock of dark hair tumbled over his brow, wings of gray staining temples that had once been as inky black as Austen's own.

Sensitivity, passion, and an artist's exquisite pain had fashioned Joseph Dante's face; that and homesickness for the homeland he'd given up for his wife and his son. But there was also a very real hope that made Austen's heart pound. One finger traced a line of Hannah's inscriptions, confusion creasing his brow.

"Father."

Joseph Dante stiffened then rose, turning ever so slowly. And in that instant years of resentment, bitterness, rejection shattered and fell away, leaving only the love that warmed his father's eyes. Joseph Dante's gaze seemed to devour Austen as if he wanted to take in every detail, every nuance of the man his son had become in the years they'd been apart.

His father stood stiffly as if it cost him every bit of his will not to close the space between them and gather his son in his arms. The fear of rejection—how deeply Austen understood.

"Austen," he said, with a fluid grace born of the Italian sun, the treasured accents of Austen's childhood before the voyage to England and another life. "And you must be—"

"Hannah." Releasing Austen's arm, she moved forward, reaching out to take Joseph Dante's long pianist's fingers into her own. "I've been waiting so very long to meet you."

It was almost more than Austen could endure, his father cradling Hannah's hands in his own, that steady, kind gaze feathering over her face as if she were an angel.

He was so different from what her own father must have been. Strong hands, strong shoulders, a man strong enough to lean on when tempests blew. Pray God, Austen could be that for Hannah.

"I found your Captain Burke, spoke to him aboard his ship. Burke was an orphan raised at Booth Hall until he ran away to sea at fourteen. He christened his ship the *Deliverance,* my dear. Can you guess why?"

"No. I just . . . Pip, is he going to take Pip?"

"Captain Burke has already signed documents transferring guardianship of the child to Austen."

"Oh, thank God!" Hannah's voice broke, and Austen gathered her into his arms. "But why . . . how did you convince him?"

"The Booths were distant cousins of Captain Burke, and were saddled with him after his parents died. As a child, Burke witnessed all the horror your poor boy must have seen. Sir Mason's father beating his mother and the child Mason turning on Burke in fury. The captain christened his ship the *Deliverance,* because the sea gave him a way to escape. As a child, Captain Burke suffered your boy's pain. He and Booth had loathed each other so much, he was stunned he'd been named Pip's guardian at all. And when I told him of your courage, Hannah, how much you loved the boy, the captain said that you deserved the child. He said he'd thank God forever that you were able to end Pip's suffering, my dear."

Tears spilled from Hannah's eyes, and Austen thought she had never looked more beautiful. "How can I ever thank you for all you've done for us, Mr. Dante?"

"My dear girl, I have seen my son for the first time in years. And I must believe you had a great deal to do with that."

"She never gave me a moment's peace, Father. Even while she lay in my arms, when I was terrified she might be dying, she made me promise to contact you, to tell you . . ."

Austen hesitated, and Hannah strained up on tiptoe, pressing a kiss to his cheek as if to give him courage. Then she turned, and left the room. Hannah, who understood how private the healing of the heart must be. After a moment, the door behind them clicked shut. Austen drew in a steadying breath.

"You must have despised me when I didn't answer your letters."

His father smiled a sad, sad smile. "How could I blame you? I hadn't even the courage to let your mother know I'd written them. I just kept hoping that someday you'd forgive me."

"I never received your letters. Atticus burned them. But even if he hadn't, it wouldn't have mattered."

His father looked away, his features ravaged with regret. "I understand your anger. I made so many mistakes with you, my son."

"No. The reason I didn't read the letters wasn't because of anything you'd done or said or failed to do. It wouldn't have mattered because . . ."

The words choked his throat, lodging there, all the more terrible after so many years of silence.

"Austen, what is it? You can tell me anything." It was the father from his childhood beneath the Italian sun, before the English rains had drowned their special kinship, before secrets had thrown them into shadow.

"Do you remember the day my friend Chuffy Wallace died?"

His father's voice still resonated with grief at the tragedy. "I remember."

"You were so angry with me, so disappointed. You kept asking why I'd gone into that pasture knowing the bull was there. You never said it, but I knew you blamed me for what had happened."

"Boys do foolish things—try to prove their bravery in mad ways. It has been so since the beginning of time. I know you cared for your friend. You never meant for him to be hurt."

"Father, I didn't know the bull was in the pasture."

A line of confusion tightened Joseph Dante's brows.

"But there were signs posted all over the fence, warnings."

"I couldn't read them."

"You mean you didn't pay attention—"

"No." Austen cut him off. "Chuffy was the only one who ever knew the truth. We had a kind of arrangement. I protected him from bullies at school. He read me my school lessons at Eton so I could pass my courses. He knew I couldn't read the signs. I was halfway to the tree when he caught up to me, but it was too late. The bull had already seen me. It charged. Chuffy climbed into the pasture flapping his coat to try to draw it away from me."

"But—but how? You were always the brightest of all my children. Everyone knew it. You drove your tutors to madness trying to escape your schoolwork, but that was only because you were restless, you were . . ."

"Father, I couldn't read." Why did it suddenly feel so good to say it aloud? As if just the words could rob the terrible secret of some of its power? "I did everything I could to hide it. I didn't want you to know. To think I was a fool."

"A fool?" his father demanded aghast. "How could you ever think that? I wondered why it was you could make such wondrous things, build them out of nothing—it was because you couldn't read what everyone else had done! There were no limits, no boundaries in your imagination."

"But, Father, I—" The possibility was too astonishing, that his greatest flaw might also be his greatest gift.

"*I* was the fool!" his father bit out in scorn. "How could I not have seen what you were suffering? No. It was my pride—I believed you had forgotten me, cast me aside for your grandfather, who was so much more what a boy could admire—a horseman, a hunter, a rich man and powerful, instead of a quiet musician. You visited us so seldom, though the house was barely down the road. And whenever you did, you avoided me."

"I didn't want you to see . . . to guess the truth. Grandfather didn't care about books and learning. He only cared that I could ride and shoot and down three bottles of wine without so much as my hand trembling. After awhile I couldn't bear looking in your face, knowing all the lies I was living."

"So you pushed at my pride, jabbed at it until . . . until our anger flared so out of control that we turned our backs on each other."

"I thought it would be easier," Austen confessed. "But it wasn't. Still, as long as I stayed away I didn't have to be afraid that you would be ashamed of me. When no word came from you, I assumed you were glad to be rid of me."

"Oh, my dear boy—how can you have thought for a moment—"

"I wanted to find some way to tell you how sorry I was, how much I missed you. But I couldn't write down the words. So I tried the only way I knew how. By writing music. But nothing I wrote was good enough. Nothing said what was in my heart. I wanted it to be perfect."

Joseph Dante closed the space between them, took Austen's face in his hands. "Do you remember the day before we sailed from Italy, when you found that bird's nest. You placed three polished stones in it and claimed it was a paperweight."

"It never left your desk."

"It is still there today. Not because it was perfect, but because you gave it to me. Sometimes I think it was the last time I ever . . ." His father's voice broke. "You gained lands and riches and honor when we arrived in England. And your mother, she regained her home and the love of her father. But I . . . I lost my son."

"Father—"

"I didn't *lose* him. No, I gave him away to a man who hated me. For your own good, I told myself. So you could have a better life than I could ever give you. But I was wrong. If you'd stayed with me, I might have realized what you were suffering. I might have seen you struggle. I might have known what put the pain in your eyes."

"I couldn't let you see, Father. You above anyone, because—" Austen swallowed hard. His father had given generously of the truth, all his doubts and angers, self-blame and regret. He could do no less. "I loved you more than anyone else. Wanted you to love me."

Warm arms closed about him, Joseph Dante's unashamed tears wetting his face. "You are the heart of my heart. I have loved you from the first moment your mother took my hand and I saw the promise of a son— *my son*—sparkling in her eyes. And now . . . now I think you have found that same kind of love, my son."

"Hannah changed my life. She has given me so much. Her courage, her humor, and my family back. I'm going to marry her. Be a husband to her. A father to Pip. When I think of how close I came to losing her forever . . ."

"But she came back to you. And she gave you back to me. A second chance, my son." Austen's father smiled through his tears. "There is nothing in heaven more precious."

Hannah wandered through the garden, marvelling at the wonder of blue sky and fiery blossoms and shadows that held no more secrets, no more fear.

Austen had been with his father for more than an hour, yet from the instant she'd looked into Joseph Dante's eyes, she'd known all would be well. Love and forgiveness. Acceptance. All had shone in those faintly lined features.

What must it be like? Sharing guilt and forgiveness, taking responsibility, instead of trying desperately to make certain not the slightest blame could tarnish one's shoulders? What must it be like to have the gift of time to make things right?

Lizzy.

She turned her gaze to the sky, clouds snagging above

the trees, the wind dancing in the leaves. God above, what she would have given for the chance, just one chance to tell Lizzy she'd kept her promise. Pip was safe. Mason could never hurt anyone again.

And yet she'd spent her whole life racing around trying to make certain tasks were done, the house was fed, everyone was safe, and supper was paid for. Then, all she had worried about was Pip, stealing him away . . .

She'd been running all her life from her own helplessness, the emptiness inside her, the loneliness. Keeping busy with endless tasks so she wouldn't have to see how much she was missing. Things she would never have.

Like love. A man's passion. Dreams that forever clouded other girls' eyes. Fantasies she'd never had time for. All things she didn't think she deserved after her father's death. Until she'd come to Ravenscar and she'd dared to dream.

"Hannah?"

The familiar voice was rough with emotion.

She turned to find Austen standing there, his face shadowed with a joy almost too painful to hold. Sunlight struck his dark hair, blades of light honing the aristocratic planes and angles of his face. A face with years of anguish washed away. Forgiveness. She wondered if she'd ever seen anything more beautiful.

He flushed almost sheepishly, heart-rendingly beloved. "I've been looking for you. Trying to find you. Father is dashing off a letter to Mama and my sisters, telling them to come to Ravenscar as soon as possible. Since I've got the special license in hand, we can be wed the instant they arrive. Unless you want a more elegant wedding?"

"No. I want our wedding to be like the gown you gave me, lovely, simple. I only wish my own family could see how happy I am."

Austen's smile was tender as he took her hands. "Actually, that's already been arranged."

"What?"

"I had Simmons write a message for me, sent them the money for their passage to England. By my calculations, they should reach Ravenscar within the week."

She flung her arms around him, this wonderful, enigmatic man who understood the most secret workings of her heart. "How can I ever thank you?"

"I wanted our wedding to be perfect. And I wanted you to heal. I know it must've been difficult for you, knowing that your own mother helped Booth trace you here."

"Booth was a master at deceiving people with his charm. Mama never had a chance matched against him."

"You're such a wonder, Hannah Gray—forgiving instead of clinging to pain. Understanding instead of being angry. You knew from the beginning how badly I needed to make peace with my family, with myself."

Austen stroked her face as if she were the rarest treasure. "You were right, Hannah. About my father. He doesn't care that I can't read. He even believes that the reason I can invent things is because my mind isn't cluttered with other people's ideas, limited by their rules. Do you think he could be right?"

"Yes! It makes perfect sense!" Hannah's lips curved in a smile. "I love your father already. You're so much like him, you know. In your heart."

"I hope so. The way he's loved my mother . . . I want to love you that way, Hannah. Forever. More than life itself." His gaze darted away full of emotion, almost shy. "In fact, I have something for you to keep, so you'll always remember how much I love you. A gift . . . ."

"Oh, Austen, you've already given me so much!"

"You gave me my family back. My life. You gave me love, Hannah. A future I never thought I could have." He reached into his pocket, drew something out of it. A roll of papers tied up in a silvery ribbon.

Hannah eyed it in confusion, then took it, her fingers trembling as she untied the bow, unrolling the pages.

Astonishment surged through her, and chagrin. "But—but this is the music I made a disaster of! It's nothing but meaningless scribbles."

Austen's gaze pierced to her heart. "You're wrong. I thought I was writing this as a gift to my father. But I realize now, I was trying to find something inside myself. Reach for something . . . I don't know what. I only know I found it during the hours we spent in the Music Room. The beginning of every dream we'll build together."

He touched the crumpled pages, his fingers trembling with awe. "This is the most beautiful music ever written. It's our love song, Hannah." He drew her into his arms, and she felt his lips claim hers, melting her very soul. "Listen, angel," he murmured. "I can hear it in my heart."

POCKET BOOKS
PROUDLY PRESENTS

MAGIC

KIMBERLY CATES

**Coming Soon
in Paperback
from Pocket Books**

**The following is a preview of
Magic. . . .**

Only madness or desperation would drive anyone to roam the wild hills this night. Druid-trees whispered warning, standing stones reached out in long fingers, awakening unquiet spirits that clung to every shadow, every hollow, every glen.

Billows of shimmering mist swirled up past Fallon's knees, branches catching at her skirts as she made her way up the path that ran perilously close to the cliffs.

Closer . . . She could hear the ghosts of drowned sailors calling from the Soul Cages beneath the crashing sea, luring her nearer the crumbling ledge that plunged to the jagged rocks below. *Just one misstep, and you will be ours. . . .*

But she only clutched the folds of her blue velvet cloak tighter about her, her slippered feet flying, retracing steps she'd taken a thousand times in the sixteen years since her mother had died. A lonely child, she'd tried to outrun the sting of her grief, bathe it in an elixir of magic and legends and possibilities. She'd tried so very hard to believe the tales she gathered at peat fires, the myths devoured in countless books. Even when the march of time and her own reason waged war against it. Even when she'd begun to doubt just a little.

No, no doubts now. She didn't dare. Even if the world thought her mad.

Her eyes turned to where the ghostly battlements of the castle pierced through the unearthly haze, straining toward the full moon that sailed forever beyond its grasp. The wind sobbed, tugging at the raw places in her heart, or was it the wail of wandering souls, those who had watered Irish soil with their blood generation after generation?

Fallon's slipper sole skidded off a damp stone, nearly pitching her over the ledge. Her heart lurched. Such treacherous footing in the quest for freedom as well as on this path. Stumbling, groping, countless mistakes, missteps throughout Ireland's history that had hurled the land into disaster. The most recent one barely two months old.

Fallon winced, the scene spilling back into her memory— the salt wind scouring her perch on the cliffs, the shattered fragments of a boat battering itself against the stones below, the weaponry it had carried lost.

From the battlements of the abandoned castle, Fallon had stared down at the cluster of men, and at the shattered boat, a sick certainty lodging in her chest. It would continue this way forever, desperate attempts to challenge British rule, the high fire of patriotism, courage, the bold charge into the teeth of English power, and the inevitable smashing against the rocks. She'd stood there, desolate, helpless, hating that inevitability, wishing to God there was something she could do to stop it, to find the key. . . .

If only someone would rise up and take charge, unite the rebels. *Lead* them . . . someone they all could trust, like the High Kings of old.

Then, the mist had rolled in from the distant islands, slowly obscuring the pain and the futility. . . . Or . . . whispering an answer?

Of course. The answer had been so simple. Inevitable— like the coming of the mist. And so, while the earth trembled with the pagan rhythm of Beltaine, the veil between the other world and the world of mortals thinning for this night of Bright Fire, Fallon had crept past the servants, past the gates guarding Misthaven. She'd drawn her cloak about her and stepped into madness, or reached out for a miracle. Even now, she wasn't certain which.

She knew only one thing.

Ireland needed Ciaran. Desperately.

She shivered. Tonight . . . it must be tonight. . . .

Beltaine.

And what if she bumbled? Made a mistake? So many years had passed since her mother had spun out the instructions for how to summon the hero from the mist. What if Fallon had forgotten something vital? Worse still, what if the tale of Ciaran was nothing but pretty words, a mother's attempt to soothe her grieving child, to make her feel safe?

The thought twisted in Fallon, spilling hurt in its wake, and understanding.

Fallon swallowed hard, the outermost wall of the abandoned castle rising in front of her. She'd never felt alone while at Caislean ag Dahmsa Ceo. But tonight seemed different somehow, the air too thick for her lungs, the floor unstable beneath her feet. She couldn't rid herself of the feeling that she was being watched. By whom? The ancient spirits? The stones themselves? Was the castle waiting for her? Waiting for the summons that had been passed through generations? Were the window spaces all-knowing, all-seeing, eyes fixed upon her? Or was there someone else? Something far more sinister that had dared come out into the night?

No. She was being absurd. She shook away the odd sensations, resolving to do what she'd come here for. She reached out her hand, pressing her palm against the rough stone, following by touch, until she reached the hiding place she'd found so many years ago. With the tips of her fingers, she loosened the stone, drew it out. Heart hammering, she eased her fingers into the dark space revealed.

Her fingers collided with something hard, and she gathered the handkerchief-wrapped bundle into her palm. Her hand trembled. The pin felt heavy. Real. If only the legend had as much substance. Soon, soon she would know for certain. . . . Nothing, no one, could stop her from trying. . . .

She froze at a sound out of synch with the night, the crunch of a boot sole nearby. Did the *sidhe* make such solid sounds when they moved? Her fingers clenched over the pin, and she turned, scarcely able to breathe. She wouldn't have been surprised to see the pagan son of the sun, Lugh himself, or Mannan Mac Lir, god of the sea, rising from the waves. But nothing could have chilled her more certainly than the figure silhouetted against the stone.

Redmayne. She'd seen the man for barely a heartbeat when he'd made his rounds, introducing himself to the neighboring gentry. But she'd never forget how terrifyingly civil the captain had been as he left no doubt what would happen to any of the landlords weak-hearted enough to give aid to those he'd come to destroy.

What in God's name was the man doing *here? Now?*

It was rumored Lionel Redmayne could peel the skin from his enemies' faces, pry out their darkest secrets with no torture weapon but his eyes. Eyes that seemed to suck in every flaw, every sin, every weakness in the human soul, and take a jaded pleasure in them.

Ruthlessness—it rippled from him in thick waves, an odd sort of omniscience all the more terrifying because of the icy, emotionless calm draped about Redmayne like some dark mantle. Satan surveying bumbling mortals with diabolical patience, certain they would sin.

Those inscrutable eyes raked slowly from the top of Fallon's head to the mud-spattered hem of her cloak. "What have we here?" he asked in a voice so low Fallon had to strain to hear it. "Miss Delaney of Misthaven. So we meet again."

Was it possible he *had* come searching for her? The possibility was too terrifying to even consider. Fallon gripped the pin so hard it pierced her skin, but she didn't feel the pain, didn't feel anything except the primal need to escape that probing gaze. She couldn't let him know the effect his presence had on her, longed to slice into that insufferable arrogance. What better way than to pretend she didn't remember him?

"Do I know you, sir?" she asked in her loftiest tone.

A chuckle of disbelief rose from his chest, a kind of admiration curling his smile. "We met at your brother's house a week ago. Captain Lionel Redmayne, your obedient servant." He sketched her a bow that reminded her of sleek panthers lunging ever so gracefully to tear out a victim's throat—elegant, deadly.

"I'm surprised your brother has allowed you such freedom in a time of unrest. Hasn't he warned you that the night is full of dangers?"

"I'm not afraid."

Fearsomely sensual lips widened in a smile that thrust slivers of ice beneath Fallon's skin. She could hardly breathe.

"Would you be afraid if I told you I was searching for dangerous rebels—desperate men who might enjoy having the sister of one of the landowners in their power?"

Pictures flashed across Fallon's memory of the hours she'd spent surrounded by these "dangerous rebels"— they'd treated her almost as if she were their princess, the keeper of Ciaran's power. She belonged to them in a way a man like Redmayne could never understand. And she was pledged to protect them.

God in heaven. Panic jabbed sharp. Was *that* what Redmayne was doing here at the castle? Had the captain traced the rebels so close to their secret lair?

It took all her strength of will not to glance in the direction of the secret entrance to the souterrains. Did the Englishman know where it was? Desperate, Fallon scrambled to remember—was anyone in the tunnels tonight, laboring over broken-down rifles, questionable ammunition? Sharpening rusted swords that had been hidden away in thatch or under beds, in cow byres or hollow trees?

No. It was Beltaine tonight. They were gone. All gone. Safe.

But no one would truly be safe in these glens until Lionel Redmayne was far away.

The best thing to do would be to appear to leave herself, get away from the man so she might come back, try the ritual before it was too late. Dawn would rise, inexorable, taking with it the one chance of summoning Ciaran this year.

"If you'll excuse me, I'll be on my way." She started to stride past, but with a deceptively negligent shift of booted legs, Redmayne blocked her way.

"I must repeat my warning. Even now, I am searching for

a most elusive fellow—not some bumbling crofter thrashing about with his grandfather's rusted musket, but an adversary far more subtle. He is as insubstantial as your precious Irish mist—no one sees his face. And yet he leaves his mark everywhere. Known rebels about to be taken up by the soldiers disappear, never to be seen again. Families whose men have died on the gallows, or who have fled like the base cowards they are, suddenly produce their rent money just before the landlord is about to evict them. From the tip of Dingle to Galway, people whisper of him, but no one, not even under the most persuasive torture, has ever given him a name."

Fallon had heard of the mysterious force that had done so much good the past five years. But the rebels in the souterrains had been as bewildered by his identity as the English.

"I understand this person has kept the garrison chasing its tail for an embarassing length of time."

"Indeed. However, I intend to change that. You, of course, would offer any help you could give? You might have seen something, someone—"

"You are the only person I've met tonight."

"Little wonder, considering the weather. I'm certain you understand my curiosity, Miss Delaney, finding a lady such as yourself out on such an unpleasant evening. Exactly where are you bound for? Are you an angel of mercy braving the coming storm? Have you succumbed to a pressing need to deliver calf's-foot jelly even at this hour?"

"I often walk at night. And the castle is beautiful in the mist. It's quiet here. A place where one can be alone. Think. Or is thinking against the law, now, Captain?"

"That depends." His voice felt like fingers trying to pry into her mind. "During my visits with your neighbors, they've mentioned that you have some rather . . . unsavory acquaintances among the peasantry. Perhaps idle rumors. But a folly that can be very dangerous, Miss Delaney. No telling what indiscretion they might lead you into."

Fallon swallowed hard, images flashing behind her eyes, torchlight bleeding down the secret walls of the souterrains, impassioned faces, angry voices, and a burning thirst for freedom no whip or chain could kill.

Dangerous . . . perhaps. But it was the one place she felt alive.

She shoved the image away, a cold sweat beading her brow, as if Redmayne could truly read her mind. It was obvious the man wasn't going to let her leave until she gave him some reason for her outing tonight. Best to stick as close to the truth as possible to keep from stumbling. "I happen to love storms. The power of them, the wildness. I often go to the cliffs to watch them."

"And your brother allows it? An apalling lack of discipline. A guardian should take better care of his ward."

"My brother has more pressing concerns. Like how many bales of wool can be loaded in one ship."

"A pity. A young woman of your kind has need of guidance. Women are so easily moved by romantic tales and such nonsense, they can easily be led astray."

He shoved himself away from the wall, pacing the stone floors, running his fingertips over the walls as if searching for some weakness in the structure—or for the loosened brick that had hidden Fallon's treasure.

"I was told that torchlight often flickers here, late at night, and that no one has had the courage to discover why." His teeth flashed, white, in a feral smile. "I fear I'm never able to resist solving a puzzle, Miss Delaney. And this place puzzles me exceedingly."

"It's a castle ruin, just like so many others."

"This is no ordinary castle, or so the simple folk say. It's supposed to be the lair of some sort of ghost, spirit—a hero who is doomed to return generation after generation to perform epic feats. Abominable waste of energy, in my opinion. If he fixed things right the first time, he wouldn't have to keep returning to do the job again. But then, you know all about this Ciaran of the Mist person, don't you, Miss Delaney, despite the ignorance you feign? The legend is linked, somehow, with your family."

He was watching her so carefully, for the slightest shift in her features. Fallon swallowed hard. "You don't strike me as the type of man who believes in fairy tales, Captain Redmayne."

She surprised a laugh from him. "No, I am not. I expected a nest of rebels, or thieves or gypsies at the very least—not a wayward young woman, or a mythical hero. But I *do* believe in learning everything I can about my adversary, Miss Delaney."

God in heaven, Redmayne *did* know . . . suspect that the rebels were linked to Caislean ag Dahmsa Ceo. He must. What could she possibly do to distract him, turn him away?

"You aren't likely to learn anything of value here, Captain Redmayne. The castle has been abandoned for almost two hundred years."

"You disappoint me, Miss Delaney. I had begun to hope you were a lady of some intuition and subtlety. Men think revolutions are won with pistols and swords, but that's not true. Bloodshed only crowns more martyrs to feed the fires of rebellion later on. If you want to destroy your enemy once and for all, you must look into his soul. Every man—or woman—every people, has a weakness, some fatal flaw. Apply the right pressure to that vulnerable point and they shatter."

His voice dropped low. "You wonder what I'm doing here tonight, Miss Delaney? Searching for the soul of the Irish. And I think"—his fingers ran over weather-pitted walls—"I have found it."

"I can't imagine what you mean."

"The trouble with Ireland, Miss Delaney, is this absurd clinging to past glories. Tales of High Kings and heroes that have been dead for centuries—every urchin who can lisp can recite three hours of tales about such nonsense. The people behave as if those feats happened yesterday at the site of their own pig byre. It's time they faced the truth. That natural order placed them where they are. They need to stare into the mirror and see what they are. Dirt-scraping, illiterate beggars, the offal on the boot sole of those who now rule. Tolerated only because one cannot find an expedient way of scraping them off."

"You English were still painting your faces blue when the Irish held all the learning of the world in their hands!"

"Ah, yes. That is your overriding flaw, isn't it, Miss Delaney? You are tainted by this savage blood. A high enough crime, in the eyes of many. Of course, according to the local gentry, your unforgiveable sin is that you take pride in it."

Her chin jutted up. "I could care less what that pack of greedy, pompous fools think of me!"

"Perhaps not. But it's obvious you do care about this island, the people here. This . . . place." His gaze swept the castle, as if it held every secret in her heart. "This entire country is littered with standing stones, ancient dolmens, tombs of warriors long dead. Castles, like this one, towering over their meager little cottages, whispering to them of past greatness. A greatness they believe they can achieve again, if they only have the courage to reach out, take it."

He understood them, Fallon knew with a sick clenching in her stomach. Understood these people she loved, this land of mist and magic and dreams no sword could cut down. To be understood so completely by such a dangerous enemy was more terrifying than she had ever imagined.

But the Irish had clung to their past with astonishing tenacity, through the most horrendous trials imaginable. One lone Englishman couldn't destroy what they'd built over a thousand years. "You cannot obliterate a people's history, Captain."

"Perhaps not. But I wonder how many of your precious Irish would recall the ancient stories without constant reminders?"

"Reminders?"

"What would happen, Miss Delaney, if there were not a ring of standing stones in their pasture, or a dolmen halfway up their hill? If fairy rings and castles steeped in legend were no more?"

Fallon tossed her hair and gave a scornful laugh that sounded brittle even to her own ears. "You should send a missive to the king regarding this brilliant plan, Captain Redmayne. Considering the massive debt left from the war in the Americas, I'm certain his majesty would be overjoyed to pay an army while they tumble piles of rock God knows where. I only wish I could be present when you explain your *strategy* to your superior. Is there a military ceremony for being stripped of one's rank?"

He was smiling. Even white teeth flashing in the moonlight. The sick knot tightened in Fallon's stomach.

"It's been most illuminating speaking with you tonight, Miss Delaney. I look forward to furthering our acquaintance. You'll forgive me if I confess that I can't recall when I've been this intrigued by a lady."

The words unnerved her, and she could almost feel him reaching out to her with his razor-sharp intellect, trying to untangle the tightest secrets in her breast. Her hand trembled, the pin she held suddenly seeming like a ridiculous bauble to fend off such a man.

He sketched her a bow, then turned and walked back out into the night. Fallon shifted to peer out the empty eye of a window, watching as he mounted his horse, guided it into the mist. She listened, long after horse and rider disappeared, tracing the fading sound of hoofbeats, straining to hear them over the thundering of her heart and the crash of the sea.

What if he turned the horse around? Doubled back to satisfy his infernal curiosity? What if . . . ?

Did she dare even attempt to summon Ciaran now? The thought of those inscrutable eyes watching from the shadows as she performed the rite made her cheeks burn. If she failed he'd be so amused. . . .

No. She had to do this as quickly as she could. Surely a legend could dispatch one evil mortal.

Fallon hurried to the stone hearth and laid the brooch upon fire-blackened stone. She cast a desperate glance toward the windows. What had Mama said? That the light of the full moon would strike the jewels? But it was so misty, the silvery light a darting, uncertain thing. What if it never touched the jewels at all?

This was madness, like a nightmare. And yet they needed Ciaran more than ever now, to battle an adversary like Redmayne.

Mama had said to call Ciaran with her heart, her soul. She settled for her lungs. "Blast it, Ciaran, wherever you are, we need you! Please, for God's sake—" But they'd been pagan when Ciaran walked Ireland—had she committed some sort of blasphemy?

"Please . . . Mama said you'd come. . . ." Tears stung her eyes, the mist swirling, mocking, darting about in feathery wisps, obscuring the moonlight. She wished she could reach up, bend the rays with her hands.

"I don't know what else to do," she choked out. "Please,

Ciaran, we need . . . *I* need . . . This is hopeless! Hopeless!" She caught up a broken piece of stone and hurled it at the brooch, the pin skittering to one side. At that moment, a piercing ray sizzled down, burying itself in one of the jewels.

Fallon couldn't breathe, stared, half afraid, half hopeful, disbelieving, yet believing with all her heart. She stared at the golden circle until her eyes burned and blurred and her head ached. Was it her imagination, or did light sparkle, fragment, swell within the stone? Was it some trick born of her desperation, or the mist itself?

A gust of wind buffeted Fallon as if to punish her for her lack of faith. She stumbled back, half expecting Ciaran to emerge from the pin like Athena bursting from the head of Zeus.

The fire soared, raged, half blinding her. Then, in a heartbeat it was gone. The wind stilled, the brooch dulled, mere gold and stone, emptied of all its magic.

"Hugh was right. It was only a story, something to drive back the chill, or the hopelessness. I was a fool ever to believe it was true."

She stilled, the sound of a footstep making her cheeks burn, her hands tremble. Oh, God, it must be Redmayne. If he had seen her total humiliation . . . She pushed to her feet, wiping away her tears and squaring her shoulders as she turned.

Damn if she'd let him see her heartbroken.

"Come out," she ordered. "Show yourself."

Silence stretched out for what seemed an eternity, and she felt like a doe facing the barrel of a huntsman's musket. Fingers of unease trailed down her nape. Redmayne would have strode from the shadows wearing that insufferable sneer. If it wasn't the Englishman, then who could it be? She swallowed hard, remembering the captain's warning about smugglers and theives, and the mysterious rebel leader he'd been seeking. What if there *was* someone desperate lurking in the haze?

No. She was being ridiculous. It was probably no more than a lost sheep, or a red deer foraging in the night. Then why did the quiet tighten about her throat like a hangman's noose?

For the first time in Fallon's life, she hated the mist that obscured the castle walls, the cliffs, the trees, and whoever or whatever lay hidden among them. But she'd always masked fear with belligerence. Squaring her shoulders, she called out.

"I dare you to step from the shadows! Or are you too much of a coward?"

Rustling, the stealthy sound of movement, the crunch of stone. Breathless, Fallon wheeled in the direction of the sounds just as a dark shadow tore from its veiling of mist.

A man seemed to take shape, as if sculpted from raw night by the hands of the coming storm. But the figure that stumbled toward her had none of the dangerous elegance or hard polish of Captain Lionel Redmayne.

Dark hair tangled about a face almost terrifying in its savage beauty, a square jaw, high cheekbones all shadows and planes. Moonlight silhouetted thickly muscled arms and a magnificent breadth of masculine chest. Something sharp and lethal glinted in one strong, square hand—a dagger?

Fallon reeled. God above, could it possibly be Ciaran? It had to be! Who else would plunge out of the mist, looking so—so primitive?

By the snakes of St. Patrick, *she'd done it!* The realization sizzled through her.

It was him.

She'd imagined this moment a hundred times as a child, pictured the warrior of the mist—but nothing had prepared her for the reality of the man who stood before her, draped in midnight shadows.

She hadn't expected Ciaran to be quite so surly. This was no gallant warrior, flinging his cloak over puddles so she could cross, battling her enemies like Galahad from the Arthur legends of old. This was a man of raw animal power, fearsome intensity, not some languishing knight ready to surrender his soul to kiss the hem of her gown.

She could sense something feral in those burning eyes—a wild creature balancing on the thinnest sheen of ice, expecting to crash through at any moment.

She should say something! She *would* say something, just as soon as she was able to breathe again. But it was a surprisingly difficult task when confronted with such a daunting specimen of masculinity. Would it be rude to pinch him to make certain he was real flesh and blood?

Her throat squeezed shut as eyes of the most searing green slashed to hers. No. Better not poke him unless she wanted to feel that dagger blade pressed against her throat.

Saint Patrick and the angels, what had she done? She'd called back an Irish Galahad, and gotten Dailraid the Destroyer. What if he decided that bashing and thrashing was such great fun after three hundred years that he refused to go back where he belonged once she was through with him? This whole night was turning into a disaster! She had to take control of this situation somehow.

She shook herself inwardly, remembering the hours she'd spent in the stables, following the head groom about as he trained the wildest of her father's hunters. What was it old Mac Lysaght had always said? *The secret be this, girl. Never let the beast know he could trample ye to dust whenever 'e felt the urge t'.*

She forced words past the knot in her throat. "I can—can hardly believe you're really here! I was so afraid you wouldn't come. But things were getting so desperate, and you'd promised."

He was staring at her so strangely, angry, wary, searching her eyes almost desperately. Something dark darted across his features. Could it be . . . fear? No. Impossible.

"Do you know why you're here? I mean, is that included in the magic? Or do I need to explain—"

"Magic?" he echoed. The first sound of his voice shivered through her as if she were a harp string he'd touched, the richness of his voice tempered with a slight rasp, as if it hadn't been used in a very long time. "You . . ." His mouth hardened in accusation. "You cast a . . . spell on me?"

"No! I mean, yes. But it wasn't malicious. I—I didn't trick you, like the fairies did."

"Fairies?" His face grew even grimmer.

"This is proper magic," she tried to reassure him. "The only way to get you here. But I—I don't know exactly what—what to do with you now that I've—"

She was blathering like an idiot. Blast, she had to keep her wits about her. After all, just because Redmayne hadn't made a second appearance didn't mean he wasn't on his way back up the cliffs. Trouble was, once she'd gotten the infernal warrior of mist *here,* she'd expected *him* to explain the rules to *her.* It seemed hurtling through the centuries, crashing through the gates of Tir Na nOg must be more of a shock than she'd realized. She tried to stem the quiver of panic that worked through her. It was no wonder the man was sensitive about spell-casting, considering his past. The last thing she needed was to anger him.

"About the magic. Naturally, I wouldn't have bothered you if it wasn't truly important. If you'd just let me explain—" She made a move toward him, and he leapt to one side, light as a cat on his feet.

Whatever explanation had been in Fallon's mind vanished as the shadow bathing him evaporated.

Moonlight filtered down, washing him—*all of him*—in a waterfall of silver. She glanced at him only a moment, but the image seared itself into her memory forever.

Shoulders gleamed like freshly cast bronze, droplets of silver light snagging on a hair-roughened chest before they trailed down a flat belly to long, hard-muscled legs. And there, framed by narrow hips, a dark nest clung between his thighs, outlining . . .

A squeak of disbelief erupted from Fallon's chest, fire spilling into her cheeks as the realization struck her.

Ciaran of the Mist loomed before her, naked except for the dagger in his hand.

Look for
Magic
Wherever Paperback Books
Are Sold
Coming Soon
from Pocket Books